Congratulations to Laura van den Berg

Laura van den Berg

Winner of the

2015 Bard Fiction Prize

Laura van den Berg, author of *The Isle of Youth*,
joins previous winners
Nathan Englander, Emily Barton, Monique Truong,
Paul La Farge, Edie Meidav, Peter Orner,
Salvador Plascencia, Fiona Maazel, Samantha Hunt,
Karen Russell, Benjamin Hale, Brian Conn, and
Bennett Sims.

The Bard Fiction Prize is awarded annually to a
promising emerging writer who is an American citizen
aged thirty-nine years or younger at the time
of application. In addition to a monetary award
of $30,000, the winner receives an appointment
as writer in residence at Bard College for one semester
without the expectation that he or she will teach
traditional courses. The recipient will give at least one
public lecture and meet informally with students.

For more information, please contact:

Bard Fiction Prize
Bard College
PO Box 5000
Annandale-on-Hudson, NY 12504-5000

COMING UP IN THE SPRING

Conjunctions:64
NATURAL CAUSES

Edited by Bradford Morrow

As we struggle to understand how our natural environment is swiftly changing—glacial poles beginning to melt, forests and jungles denuded and compromised, fellow creatures increasingly endangered—our fragile, intimate connection to nature is more than ever thrown into focus. Wordsworth's world isn't what it used to be. And yet nature, or Nature, pervades our lives in the most essential and complex ways, and will surely by one means or another outlive any human follies that might threaten it.

Conjunctions:64, Natural Causes, radically reimagines the venerable genre of nature writing, collecting essays on our far-flung habitats, which are thriving as well as suffering; fictional narratives in which landscape is central, sometimes even a character; and eco-poetry, poetic incursions into the seemingly infinite communities of nature's outposts, from coral reefs to tundras, lush alpine meadows to drought-stricken plains, and on from there. These provocative, innovative works from some of our very best writers will explore what nature means to us—and what we mean to it.

Contributors to this special issue include Karen Hays, Joyce Carol Oates, Thomas Bernhard, and many others.

CONJUNCTIONS

Bi-Annual Volumes of New Writing

Edited by
Bradford Morrow

Contributing Editors
John Ashbery
Martine Bellen
Mei-mei Berssenbrugge
Mary Caponegro
Brian Evenson
William H. Gass
Peter Gizzi
Robert Kelly
Ann Lauterbach
Norman Manea
Rick Moody
Howard Norman
Joanna Scott
David Shields
Peter Straub
John Edgar Wideman

published by Bard College

EDITOR: Bradford Morrow
MANAGING EDITOR: Micaela Morrissette
SENIOR EDITORS: Benjamin Hale, J. W. McCormack, Edie Meidav, Nicole Nyhan, Pat Sims
COPY EDITOR: Pat Sims
ASSOCIATE EDITORS: Jedediah Berry, Joss Lake, Wendy Lotterman
PUBLICITY: Darren O'Sullivan, Mark R. Primoff
EDITORIAL ASSISTANTS: Kelsea Bauman, Grayson Gibbs, Linnea Marik, Haley Nikodem, Ariana Perez-Castells, Jackson Rollings, Benjamin Wiley Sernau, Tina Wack, Geneva Zane

CONJUNCTIONS is published in the Spring and Fall of each year by Bard College, Annandale-on-Hudson, NY 12504.

SUBSCRIPTIONS: Use our secure online ordering system at www.conjunctions.com, or send subscription orders to CONJUNCTIONS, Bard College, Annandale-on-Hudson, NY 12504. Single year (two volumes): $18.00 for individuals; $40.00 for institutions and non-US. Two years (four volumes): $32.00 for individuals; $80.00 for institutions and non-US. For information about subscriptions, back issues, and advertising, contact us at (845) 758-7054 or conjunctions@bard.edu. *Conjunctions* is listed and indexed in Humanities International Complete and included in EBSCO*host*.

Editorial communications should be sent to Bradford Morrow, *Conjunctions*, 21 East 10th Street, 3E, New York, NY 10003. Unsolicited manuscripts cannot be returned unless accompanied by a stamped, self-addressed envelope. Electronic and simultaneous submissions will not be considered. If you are submitting from outside the United States, contact conjunctions@bard.edu for instructions.

Cover design by Jerry Kelly, New York. Cover art by Kerry Miller: *Brehm Djurens Liv* (*Animal Life*) *vol. 14*, 2013. Mixed media, 16 x 11.5 x 2.5 in. © Kerry Miller 2014; all rights reserved by the artist. Credit: private collection, USA. Artist represented in USA by Lawrence Cantor Fine Art, Los Angeles.

Conjunctions e-books of current and selected past issues are distributed by Open Road Integrated Media (www.openroadmedia.com/conjunctions) and available for purchase in all e-reader formats from Amazon, Apple, B&N, Google, Indiebound, Kobo, Overdrive, and elsewhere.

Retailers can order print issues via D.A.P./Distributed Art Publishers, Inc., 155 Sixth Avenue, New York, NY 10013. Telephone: (212) 627-1999. Fax: (212) 627-9484.

Printers: Edwards Brothers Malloy, Circle Press

Typesetter: Bill White, Typeworks

ISSN 0278-2324

ISBN 978-0-941964-79-1

Manufactured in the United States of America.

TABLE OF CONTENTS

SPEAKING VOLUMES

Edited by Bradford Morrow

EDITOR'S NOTE

BOOKS ARE, TO THOSE WHO live and breathe them, all but sentient fellow beings. When a book is closed, it is asleep. Perhaps dreaming, inspired by its reposing words and images. But when a book is opened, it awakens, vaults to life, and interacts with the reader, collapsing time and bridging space. Even the most modest book is by far the finest transportation device ever invented and can carry its reader to every corner of the cosmos. Once closed again, however, it never fully returns to sleep but remains in the reader's imagination.

If, as Cormac McCarthy proposed, books come from books, then the volume in your hands comes from writers who have considered the myriad ways in which that process occurs. It is a gathering of essays, poems, stories, and unclassifiable works that examine what books mean to those of us who deeply depend on them. Every book ever written, from classics and epics to personal diaries to, yes, literary journals, is something of a secular tabernacle that houses not only the history of thought but of life itself—and death. And, as readers of *Speaking Volumes* will quickly discover, each writer's voice here explores the book in unexpectedly different ways. Factual memoirs are nestled beside faux histories. Translations of invented lyrics find themselves alongside narratives that investigate the origins of how writing is read and how writers come to write.

If indeed reading is a kind of writing—in that collaborative readers recreate the signifiers and images on the silent printed page as vivid, even vocal, personal imagery and meaning—*Speaking Volumes* might be seen as a notebook that invites meditation on just how that happens. On how daily engagement with the book enlightens daily lives.

—Bradford Morrow
October 2014
New York City

From Eclipse
A Romance
Samuel R. *Delany*

Do you believe that you lived three thousand years ago? No. But for me, I was at the subsiding of the Deluge, and helped swab the ground, and built the first house.

—Melville, *Mardi*

Woe to him who seeks to please rather than to appall!

—Melville, "The Sermon," *Moby-Dick*

JUST . . . CALL ME—Ishmael?

It's not my name. Try Harry, Hank, even Horace, the Egyptian god of writing and Rome's odist, epodist, and satirist, and the classical world's finest critic till sublime Longinus. *Naturam expellas furca, tamen usque recurret, et mala perrumpet furtim fastidia victrix,* as Horace put it in his epistle from the country to city-bound Fuscus. *Drive nature out with a pitchfork; nevertheless she will hurry back and burst through your futile contempt, the victress.* It's something to consider: That was written by a man who died during a Roman November nearly a decade before the birth at Bethlehem. Nor do I think he was speaking only of sumac and saplings, brambles and berry bushes got out of hand, any more than if he had said it today.

Bankruptcy and our flight to Albany notwithstanding, in their gray silk hats and blue and black scarves, the creditors found us anyway. They arrived early to make their circuit through the house. The first thing they did was step inside, past Mother—she'd been up and dressed in the dark by lamplight for more than an hour—and ignored her "Good morning, gentlemen. Won't you be so kind as to—" Then, blinking, she stopped, since they hadn't even looked at her. She drew herself up in her high-necked mourning dress—brown bombazine traded for the black one she wore to funerals—as if dazzled by a dawn so gloriously golden just breaking outside the door frame, between the hemlocks across the street. She may, however, have simply been non-plussed by their rudeness.

Hauled by three black boys who'd probably been drinking already and an Irishman who certainly had, four long carts creaked and rumbled after them through our front hall door, to press their wheels into our carpets. The mick went open shirted and without shoes. Seconds indoors, he smelled worse than any Jew.

Hired by the real creditors, I suppose, but I didn't realize that either. At least the niggers had jackets and shoes.

But through the morning liquor, all four fellows trailed the odor of laborers' sweat unwiped away for days. Following them, watching to see what Mother would do, we got used to it in minutes, if not moments. It was a bit of the urban outdoors coming within.

Mother followed the men into the kitchen and we followed Mother. The shortest of the three turned and said, "Please, Mrs. Melvill, give me all your money—coin and script, whatever you have in the house. All of it. Now."

"Of course," she said, lifting her purse from where it hung on her hip. "I have it right here for you. I've gotten it all together. By the way—I thought you might want to know. I'm changing the name. It's going to be Melville with an *e* at the end. From now on. I always said to Allan, my husband, that's how it *should* be spelled: M-e-l-v-i-l-l-*e*." She paused, then frowned. "Write it down, please. You mustn't think I'm changing the name to . . . well, to elude you."

"Ma'am, that's your business, not ours. And Mr. Abernathey's. You just give us the money, now. Then we'll start."

"Oh, yes . . ." Mother opened her purse and handed the shortest and dumpiest some folded bills. "But I just didn't want you to . . ." Then she went on. "There . . ." A mixing bowl (ceramic, not wooden), in which Gerty used to stir up cake batter and pancakes both, while I used to watch, was a third full of silver and copper. "That's all the . . . all the coins in the house."

"You went through and got all the children's, now, didn't you? Often they'll try to hide some. If we find any when we're going around upstairs, we'll just have to take it."

"Oh, no . . . !" she said. "No. They're good children. They understand." I hadn't understood, actually, though grudgingly I'd given up my pennies and nickels and dimes and the silver dollar Father had given me. Tommy had cried when Mother took his five pennies away, and for moments I'd thought she was going to relent and let him keep them—and, when I thought that, I hated him, and was glad that

9

she'd made him cry. "Really, that's all we have in the house." He'd only cried ten minutes.

Turning to the taller of his well-tailored partners, the short creditor said, "See, she didn't give me no argument." He looked at my mother sternly. "You're a wise widow." Nodding and slipping them into a wallet, he returned it to an inside jacket pocket. "Good, ma'am." He picked up the entire bowl and took it out under his arm.

When we came out of the kitchen, we were already curtainless (I remember the black porters holding the rods, the ivory rings slipping and clicking along them as they came free, and how the black boys stood by the bare windows and clumsily folded them, one summarily taking them away from Paddy's hands, clearly not trusting him), and even while I watched, we became carpetless (another memory from outside the sitting-room's arch, looking in and seeing beneath them, as they come up from the floor; from the horsehair pads beneath them, the ticks and squeaks as tacks tugged loose, another and another. Once a pad and rug were rolled to the side, tacks lay around the boards. The planks had that smoky discoloring they get when they've been covered with rugs for several years. Tacks were scattered like black bugs, till Helen stepped on one—in her shoe: It pierced to her sole, though, so that she cried out—and hopped about and pried it loose with her nails. In exasperation she went to get a broom and a dustpan, from one of the carts. (They were taking those with them as well.) She swept the black things up, realized they'd taken our big wicker refuse basket too, so took the rattling dustpan into the kitchen and pitched them out the window, while the porters inside continued their devastations. Would the roving nighttime Irish get them in their feet? Paddy managed to avoid them, though he cursed the loudest of the three—and the most obscenely—when he saw them). At first, it was just as though we were moving—and had almost the same excitement about it.

Then—the five of us children, with Tommy in Helen's arms—we followed them through the house. The bowl was left in the back bed of one of the carts; the temptation to retrieve a handful of coins was like the temptation to plunge a hand into a cold spring, when you look down and see a mosquito about to feed on the back of it. The porters left the barrow carts downstairs too, one in the hall, one in the kitchen, and two in the sitting room (in one of them the money bowl), then tramped up to collect things and carry them down, singly or in pairs, while—in the hall—we looked up at them through the banisters' newels. The oldest black boy (certainly forty, possibly fifty—

10

at any rate more than twice the age of the others) said the least but was the one to whom the gray-hats gave most of their instructions. He conveyed them to the barefoot Irishman and the other two shod Africans by silent signals with roughened, gray-black fingers.

Finally we grew bold enough to mount behind them and follow them into our rooms—shockingly bare. They'd taken our toys—and the beds they had broken in pieces and carried down, they'd been ours! (I swear, I'd watched till then and hadn't realized it!) My heart began to bang again behind my ribs, as it had on the morning I learned of my father's death, but I didn't feel I could protest any more than my mother did. Soon, in that lingering state of fear, I began to fathom the headman's hand wavings: *Now, wait, faster, stop, get that, take this over there, the two of you move that, make a pile of those, load it, wrap those in that, use the rug for padding*—to which the other three—the Irish fellow and the two blacks—responded more quickly than they did to the occasional spoken orders from their human masters, lingering at the walls and watching, as we children watched.

I was both frightened and entranced.

At first I thought the old black boy was the only one who knew English. But as we learned the meaning of his signals, we learned as well their names—this one Sam, that one, yes, Paddy (but that's what everyone called pretty much every Irishman), the other Jupe, and the headman himself Jonah. His frizzy gray hair, his salt-and-pepper beard, stuck out about his head in tufts—as well as, from a word here, a phrase there, we learned that Sam and Paddy and Jonah and Jupe spoke well enough.

Only they preferred not to—

A cart passed so that I had to press back against the hall wall— "Watch it, boyo"—barefoot, the mick grinned as the thing trundled up—"or you'll lose a toe!"—and I glimpsed my alphabet blocks inside, red B, yellow M, black O, blue P went past . . . though they were Tommy's today, even if he was too young for them—

The cart porters' bosses, or their supervisors—the men in the gray top hats—or the lawyers (or their clerks) hired to superintend the unpleasant affair, once all was carried downstairs and packed in the pushcarts, made a quick apology to Mother, who still stood downstairs in the kitchen, then made a curt good-bye.

Then they wandered out the door—left open all this time, probably because of the carts in the house—into morning.

I glanced after them, wondering nervously if people might have gathered outside to watch our shaming—but (one) it was still very early, (two) it was not that sort of neighborhood, and (three) that's one reason some creditors had taken to bringing their carts inside, rather than taking the goods outside to pack them. It was faster, easier, and drew less attention.

In some neighborhoods boys threw stones at them.

As the porters were about to roll their barrows after them, Jonah called, clear enough, that he had to go back to get some box he'd left on the landing above, so that the other three, tired of moving beds and bureaus, stopped to wait for him in the front hall. The cart nearest was heaped as high as my head. It had two beds in it, disassembled to the slats, and I stepped up to look at what else it held.

Among the hundred fifty or two hundred fifty volumes at the barrow's back (each cart was almost six feet long), once stacked but now fallen over others beside a lot of linen, a carved sphinx that had stood on Father's desk now lay atop brocaded cushions. I fixed on a book and stepped closer. Green and brown and pink swirled over its cover board, like a bit of miraculous sea.

With its drawers stacked in another barrow, its stock in still another of the three-wheelers, and more books around and under it, the desk itself was in Jonah's cart. He'd gone back for his carton.

But I looked back and picked the book up.

It was small enough for me to think it was for someone my size and age.

"One you like, sonny?" asked Sam. Probably he was no more than nineteen, though his hair was the longest and fullest of the three Africans', and while I'd watched him roam our rooms, taking up this and that and packing it in at the verbal commands of his gray-hatted masters or Jonah's silent signs, I'd wanted to touch his tufty wool, to grasp it, to see how it took my grip or, when released, rebounded into its ruff. "Go on." Sam smiled over a mouth—full of yellow teeth? Seldom do those on that level of life show a full set past ten or eleven. "Take it. They won't miss it." And Sam was seven or eight years older.

Paddy came trundling up behind, pushing his great cart. (I glanced back.) "You blockheaded nigger," he hailed Sam over his load. "You can't do that! They're wantin' it all, not us handin' it around, like we was the Lords of the Earth and not them."

"Blockheaded nigger yourself." Smiling, Sam showed a *few* more teeth than the Irishman. "You know they're going to sell 'em a penny a pound to some Virginia gentleman who wants to get the bindings for his shelves—and won't read 'em no more than they will. You want it, son? Keep it. You don't? Put it back then." And, to the mick, "I was in service for one of that sort outside of Roanoke, when I was his age—'fore I run north."

"You run up here—you had a job and your own owner and a cabin roof over your head, no matter how leaky? I swear niggers don't know when they got a good thing. What'd you do that for?"

Sam held up his hand. I blinked at it. Most of his forefinger was gone. Somehow, watching the whole operation, I'd missed that detail. (I'd been paying too much attention to his hair.) "I had 'em all afore the week I run." Had he been keeping one hand in front—or behind him—through his work . . . ?

Paddy frowned deeply. "What happened?"

"Oh, my gentleman thought I'd snitched something not mine from one of his guests, and after that dumpy doctor had left he decided to teach me a lesson."

"Knowin' you, you probably took it as he thought—like you're doin' from your masters now, for that boy there." Paddy waved a soiled and implicating hand at me, at him. "Hey, if you were fool enough for that, you can't fault him."

"You can if it's your own finger he gets himself drunk enough to hack off with a hatchet on the choppin' block for his pork out back of the kitchen—then staggers off to throw up on the kitchen steps and leaves you screaming on the ground to bleed out." Sam looked at his hand unhappily, as if he didn't too often these days, then shook his head. "Two of his bondswomen, the Bible calls them—nigger bitches to him when he was angry, and to me too, when I wasn't— 'cause women and men, we'd learned our talk from him. Clucking, horrified, helpless, the nigger bitches picked me up, carried me back to the quarters, tied up my wrist so tight I gasped. They stanched my stub with pine tar and a bandage—and warned me keep out of his way. Once sober, see, he wouldn't like to be reminded of what his wrath had done—he'd paid good money for me when I was three—and would only get angry again . . . at me, for making him so uncomfortable, you understand, that he had to violate his own principles." He turned and looked as if he was about to spit on our rugless floor—but he didn't. "He was the sensitive sort. No, I'm happier with money in my hand at the end of a job and shoes on my feet when I start it. You'd be too if you'd been without both." (I wondered if he had forgotten Paddy was without.)

"Oh, I've had such treatment—or seen similar. Anyway, I still got all *my* limbs, if not shoes and gloves to cover them—though, who knows, someday I might not. But, no, I've not seen that yet in this country."

Sam snorted. "Today I won't even say the word nigger, unless I'm talkin' of my childhood, before I knew any other. Or to one who plays with it because that's the only way you can feel that you have some control of what flays you when it's wielded serious-like. I do it myself, and have certainly gotten my share of laughter and lightness from it. For the rest, bondsman will do. But I think there's a place for it and there are places that it's not for."

"Oh, that's daft!" declared Paddy. "It's just a word, boy. I used it all my life. I was just a little surprised to find I was one—when my grown sister brought me here on the cursed boat when I was ten. Sister?" He snorted. "Half the micks where we used to live before they done kicked me out said she was my mother and had come to this country to shake the shame of having a child by her own pa. *Ehhh.* I couldn't care less. By this time shamin's my bread and my water— I figure that's what makes a nigger. At least I guess so, at any rate."

"And that's why they call you a nigger as fast as they call me one," Sam said. "Because you're used to it, though, they think they can get you to do it again and be grateful in the bargain. That's a black thing to have in your history." Sam laughed. "Be glad that's where you have it. Believe me, the day you forget it, they'll win you over. So don't. The world itself has its ways of remembering what everyone in it forgets. That's one of the things my master explained to me he'd learned from his books, back when he still read them—before he grew angry enough to hack me into pieces. And did." His eyes snagged on his childhood mutilation—and he took in a breath.

"Today, they've started selling them cocoa leaves in the apothecaries to chew on for the pain—and they've always had that laudanum for ladies and light gentlemen. But that wasn't what they gave no nigger boy in Virginia who'd run afoul of his owner. Bondsman, if you like—and I prefer that, yes, even when I don't use it. Three days later, he called me in to apologize too. I stood there, with my bound-up hand throbbing, throbbing, throbbing with each heartbeat, as it had throbbed day and night for three days since he'd hacked my ability to work apart. My body was not going to let me forget what had happened, even while I stood and he sat behind his reading table and told he was now contrite. Under the influence, however, he'd simply been unable to think of any other punishment appropriate to a young thief. At the time, there'd been nothing else he could bring to mind to do. Did I understand?

14

"I smiled, holding my hand to the belly of my shirt, where, when I moved too quickly or had to use the hand anyway, blood still leaked from the bandage and stiffened it.

" 'Of course, sir,' I said. 'I know you didn't mean it.' And I smiled, while I wondered if I slipped half a cup—no, a whole one—of rat poison into his soup or his sauce, it might make him feel, perhaps, half as ill before he died as I felt in that room with him now, like I would pass out, unless I could sit awhile. Did I care whether he'd meant it or not?

"He'd done it!

"He smiled back and said I'd made him feel a great deal better, and thanked me for understanding his position. Oh, if I wanted to, I could go back to my work. 'Certainly, sir,' I told him, I who'd had only an hour off for my wound. Paddy, if I'd felt stronger, I'd have climbed into his bedroom window with a piece of fencing wire that night and strangled him while he slept.

"Only I wouldn't have wasted the strength I had left on him.

"The first time I woke—at two o'clock in the morning, it was—feeling stronger enough and better than I had been since his drunken fit had shattered me, I rose, dressed by moonlight, and took off through the fields in the direction I'd been told was north. Hey, I won't try to tell you what I suffered to get here."

More from fear of the fact that anyone should care what I wanted or, no, than from a desire to own it, I clutched the volume to the Sunday jacket Mother had made me wear because of the creditors' coming—though it was still Tuesday before noon.

"*Mmmm.*" Standing erect between the cart poles, Paddy grunted. "I was wonderin' how you'd lost it. But I decided I wouldn't ask." He didn't sound happy he had. "But now I ken it. Twelve, you say you was? Naw, that's a *little* young for cuttin' off body parts. Sixteen or over, at home I've seen folks do the same—but that was not in this country." He shook his head. (I was thirteen, but I hadn't been that much younger a year ago. Or had I . . . ?) "Hands and feet crushed and broken, useless for life." A small bull of a fellow, Paddy was half bald; reddish fur pushed from a largely buttonless shirt, torn at elbow and collar, white or ivory perhaps at one time, but now gray with what must have been six weeks' continual wear. (As was Jonah's fuzz; 'twas a different gray from that of the high silk hats. I began to wonder why we called them with the same word.) I could see stiff sections over his frayed shirt, which I thought might be splats of white paint—or, some of them, discolored to orange. "Come on. Let's go!" In a

15

haze of spirits and old sweat, he followed the darky, trudging behind his rumbling load from the house, as Jupe's, then Jonah's, own carts thundered up.

Then thundered out.

Helen let go her breath. (I think her foot still hurt.) "What awful things to talk about in front of children! It serves him right—that dreadful finger! " She looked at me. She looked at the book—I could tell she was about to say something like, *You're not going to keep it, are you . . . ?*

She looked at me, and for moments I thought she was going take it away. But she turned, intent on seeing to the needs of Mother, who, I realized, waited in the empty kitchen.

And we had two beds in our house where, that morning, we'd had six. Once, however, they'd tugged their loud barrows and our belongings out the door, I realized—even at thirteen—I'd acclimated enough to their stink so that I'd have to get used to the house again without it.

Deemed by the gray-hats unsalable, some bits of furniture remained upstairs. All the house's bookshelves were now bare.

As I blinked after the niggers and their barrows—still clutching my bit of the sea—fourteen-year-old Gansevoort stepped up and said, low enough so only I could hear, "I hate those black blaggards, Herman. I don't care whether they're from Africa or Ireland. They're all niggers and they come in like that to rob a widow blind. It galls me and I hope it galls you, too," while I remembered what it was like to be galled.

The evening of the creditors, after her own trip around the house— to assess, I suppose, this American calamity that had overswept us like a typhoon—Mother walked into the sitting room and sat in the older of the two remaining kitchen chairs Gansevoort had brought in earlier. (Along with the sofa, three armchairs had gone in the barrows; so had a painting, once on the wall where a rectangular discoloration remained. Looking at the wall, I remembered it had been a landscape. But though I'd lived with it in three cities, in five or six houses, I couldn't recall if, beyond the hills in the distance, there had or had not been a strip of bright ocean.) Gold and salmon light blazed through the naked panes and speared the room, to fall aslant the shelves, to bend at the wall's blue corner.

In the lap of her black dress, Mother counted twelve pennies. Two she'd found in the seams of one pocket, four more still at the bottom of her purse, and six in back of a slat-wood drawer bottom, still upstairs.

"Oh, Mother, *why* didn't you take some and hide it. Just a little— you *knew* this was going to happen...." Helen waved her fists around before her in frustration. "Oh, I'm sorry. You know I wouldn't accuse you. But, well, you *could* have—"

"Yes." She looked up. "Yes. But I ... because I'm ... I'm an honest fool!" She drew in a sharp breath. "You're right, of course. That's what I should have done." She looked down again at what chance rather than strategy had left us. "But I didn't."

"They probably expect you to," Gansevoort said.

Maybe you remember.

Back then a penny bought a loaf. (And I think I've spent my life since trying to restock my father's library, buying all the books I've bought and sold again or, who knows, writing the dozen-odd I did.) The first night's supper was another of bread without butter, but this time spring water instead of milk from the Hoydens next door—who sent as well some blankets—with slices of the last onion in the kitchen bin—instead of jam. Mother was pregnant with what would turn out to be Allan (Father's farewell gift)—and that he would grow up a serious, sober boy who would become the mayor of a small town and, yes, take care of her and, now and again, of all of us is, I expect, the reason I never killed myself, despite the times in one hemisphere or another I've thought of it, on those swoops through deepest depression.

So we ate after a fashion, but Mother did not have the fare we needed to take the train—all nine—to Boston and our own long-suffering grandparents. Two days later she did, though—borrowed, I believe, on an evening's visit to Lawyer Abernathay, who had been looking out for my father's foundering prospects and had a kind eye for the widow. She returned with the tickets folded in her shawl, having made whatever promise of recompense she had persuaded him to accept.

That night, save for Mother, Helen, and the girls, we boys slept on the floor.

Thus Hagar and her brood entered the lands of immiseration.

In Boston, at my mother's parents', in our first night in their house as fatherless orphans, I slept with that book, first in my hand, then under my pillow, as if it had been a favored toy. Green and pink and brown, with a leather spine, gold stamped, already too worn to read, inside it had type in two columns down small pages of India paper. The next morning, the moment I woke with the Boston dawn gilding the window, I slid it from beneath my pillow, opened its cover, and, with morning itself pouring across it, first read its actual title page:

Paradise Lost
and
Paradise Regained

by John Milton—an edition rather like Gansevoort's portable Bible.

I made a few attempts at it, but was a full fourteen before I got through its first two books. By sixteen, though, I'd read it all, and a fair number of others besides. I was, of course, in love with Satan, as what young reader of that tome isn't (Oh, if I ever wrote my own book, I'd make an equally hellish hero the center of my tale!) as he leads his dumb rebels to his and their doom.

And Mother got up in the midst of the night, sometimes even in the rain, to walk out into the fields and woods, making us wonder what we were supposed to do, and feeling more abandoned, till Helen and Gansevoort would go looking for her and most times bring her back.

Later I wondered if my grandparents hadn't been happy we'd quit them. They worried about my mother seriously, but not having her there was easier than being reminded of her eccentricities one to three nights a week. I was told in no uncertain terms I had to work. So, for three months, I was a boy clerk in a bank.

Once Allan got himself born, closer to Springfield, we ten moved into a house that would have been full with four. My grandparents could hope that, with all of us off in a farm toward the edge of the property of a Mr. Cowell of Amherst—the property ran all the way to Boston—Mother was at least in God's and her children's hands—and no longer in theirs. Fortunately, though, we soon forgot it.

Still, when she went wandering, most times they found her, Gansevoort and Helen. ("No, you stay here, Herman," Helen would say. "I don't feel right leaving the little ones alone, even if they're sleeping. . . .") But twice they came back from the moonlit fields and woods without her.

We didn't see her till she came back on her own, dress torn, face scratched. She said she had gone into the woods at night. No, she claimed, nothing untoward had happened.

Hair darker than mine and pulled back in a bun, Helen wore high-necked dresses and aprons without appliquéd flowers or frilled edging—in order to seem adult. She said shopping for flour and butter and getting what we needed for dinner and cleanliness was easier if she acted the eldest, which she was.

And so she rushed toward spinsterhood.

Between her and me was my big brother Gansevoort, *his* curls lighter, except in summer when the Dutch in us came out, tow in me, chickadee yellow in him, at least during our childhood. Had I been the proverbial savage, noble and naked (and when I was away on what became my *Typee,* I was for a month, though I left that out of the book with a few other things as a concession to damned gentility), it would have been the same on my butt cheeks, the backs of my thighs, my flesh burned red brown as an Indian's beneath the hemp and my hair gone gold above it—white gold.

Everyone said we Melville boys were bears.

If, in summer, I ran through the back fields without shirt or shoes, by the time *I* was fifteen, new and profuse on my chest and back, my shoulders and arms, the heavy hair went all but white blond. And what did I think as I stopped a moment, breathless, to stand, with the sunlight all around and gnats and midges swirling before and beside, and the sky limpid as spring water? Why I was the same age that Helen had been when, in Albany, we'd learned of Father's death. And within the same breath, I realized: My sister had had no childhood at all. Yes, she had chosen to work for us and give every aspect of her life for ours, but it was the choice of a slave who decides to work for the harshest of masters because she fears the world outside is even harsher, so that such seems simply the sanest option.

And what next did I think, feeling the dry earth under my bare feet, among the long grass my pants held away from my legs—save one spear that had got under a cuff to tickle my calf inside my pants leg—beside those woods from which Helen was always so afraid vagabonds would emerge in the evening who would do unspeakable things to our family, especially our wandering mother, in the night?

I must escape this maelstrom of guilt and find the world, the America outside these sun- and cricket-filled hills, this fecund farmland, which, because of the guilt of we who moved here, might easily have been a wounding wilderness.

In winter, from pate to merkin, my fur slipped back to Helen's hue. At sixteen I had a beard like a man's. Though he didn't come into his own bearhood till seventeen, Gansevoort would fight for me at the drop of an insult, and, only slightly more reserved, I'd tussle and tumble with Josephus and Zachary and that tomboy Lucy and Annekin—two lived in one direction up the road and three lived down the other—for Gansevoort's honor and rights. I'd even heard Helen screech like the mother of all banshees at one neighbor's brat, who she feared had hurt one of us.

Though Helen defended and more and more fed us, the five delightful nuisances (who doesn't see his younger siblings so?) were my personal responsibility, I felt. On Monday nights I cooked their dinners and confused their names, so that they giggled and sometimes even answered to the wrong one, and, anyway, the cooking was only once a week, Mondays. Gansevoort did it Tuesdays. Mother did it Sundays, so that, those nights, Helen could study. We were *all* our sisters' and our brothers' keepers—

Which is why you can't call me Cain.

Each of us idolized particularly the next oldest up and thought her or him our most perfect friend—Gansevoort in my case, Helen in his; down to little Thomas, who, through idolizing me, ended up far more of a sailor than I ever did, a captain of his own ship. But that was years later.

Mother was a wonderful woman—presumably, mothers are—but she was not the sanest in the world. Why go into it more . . . ?

Once, sometime after sunrise, Mother came wandering in on her own, as if she'd done nothing unusual—though she was tired and stayed in bed most of the day. Not Helen or Gansevoort or I had even woken that night, and spent the morning chastising one another for our own exhaustion before her . . . well, her eccentricities.

Indeed, that night she took all sense of parental security from us and scattered the ashes of her nocturnal wanderings throughout the country. We flayed each other for it—but never told anyone else about it.

As with so much else it was our secret.

Several times we switched farms. On one outside Troy we even built a wing: another sitting room, a small mudroom at the back entrance, and two more bedrooms that let Mother and Helen free up another room in the main part of the house for sleeping. And I was having those dreams that hound so many youngsters—I understand now—who live in several houses over a brief time, in which I leave a room in Albany only to step into a room in New York, or walk down a hall in Pittsfield and look out the upper Dutch door in the kitchen in Boston to see what I'd used to see outside on the kitchen steps in Albany.

In Troy, not far away, and less than a hundred years after our own revolution, we'd go sympathetically wild with the hope of freedom anywhere else in the world in July—on the fourth—in those days.

Back in '39, I'd first got to Shakespeare's plays, then Burton's *The Anatomy of Melancholy*, Macpherson's *Ossian*, Sir Thomas Browne's *Urne-Buriall*, *A Letter to a Friend*, *Pseudodoxia Epidemica* (only two books of it—and not the most interesting two, I later learned), and of course my Milton! And how does a boy that age who has already published his first set of newspaper *feuilletons* in the *Democratic Press and Laningsburgh Advertiser*, who reads *Paradise Lost*— for two more years, I confess, *Paradise Regained* defeated me, though I got through it finally—how does such a nineteen-year-old run away to sea?

Why, with his mother and three younger sisters accompanying him to the boat station at Albany, to kiss him good-bye (the girls were there basically to see that Mother, who'd insisted on coming, didn't get it into her head to wander off; by this point, whatever we said to our friends or relatives, they were more afraid of losing her than losing me), and with a letter of introduction to the family in New York of some college friend of my brother Allan, the Bradfords, with a request to put me up for the two or three days before the *St. Lawrence* left from Peck Slip for Liverpool, so that after a riverboat journey in which I felt as irked by my poverty as a boy could feel—I had two dollars with which to purchase all I needed for the trip—I spent most of it on the ferry moodily staring at passengers, whom I was sure had more money to eat with on board than I did, till they looked away.

But now you know what I ran from at nineteen, however I could manage it, when first I took off.

Once in New York—city of my birth, but how foreign it felt after the last five or six years—the Bradfords were as hospitable as possible. At dinner that first night Mrs. Bradford would not let my plate get more than half empty, as if she knew the appetites of young men.

After a night in their guest room, the next day I was off to the offices of Howland and Aspinwall at 55 South Street to sign my articles. The busy secretary got most of it right—except my name:

"Norman Melville," he put down. (Since my father's death, Mother had, indeed, added the *e* because she felt it was better for us all. And

21

we had been too young and too loyal to argue that it wasn't ours.) But they were not going to waste another form for something as silly as that—not for a simple mistake in a couple of letters. It went on, under the appropriate categories:

"Birth: City of New York.

"Country: United States.

"Height: Five feet, eight and a half inches," measured with my back against the rule painted up the wall beside his desk—

"Complexion: light. Hair: brown." I'd not spent a summer in the sun for it to get lighter—besides, I'd noted last year, it *didn't* lighten as much these days as it had when I was younger.

Then off again. On South Street, I managed to get a red wool shirt, a canvas hat, some stationery and writing material so that I could write Mother that I'd arrived safely in the city and my brother to thank him for the Bradfords, and other trifles for my duffle kit.

I had one penny left.

In a gesture to my own freedom, I flung it off the end of a pier.

New York Harbor received it in a burst of the froth it landed on, and that froth, a second past, once more untroubled, slid down the side of a small swell, the penny surely inches, feet, leagues beneath, twirling down through the water.

Back at my hosts', Mrs. B. was as generous with her supper as before, and however misanthropic a day in offices and the city's impersonal streets can make a man feel, as I've written in a book perhaps you've read, I've never felt so bad but I could eat a good dinner.

The next morning, with my kit, I took leave of the fine family for my ship, the *St. Lawrence*, Oliver P. Brown, master. I'd assumed—because it had said so in the advertisement—we were leaving that day. On board, I found an empty berth, but soon learned that our departure had been put off by at least twenty-four, if not thirty or thirty-six, hours. It just seemed awkward to return to the Bradfords'. So I slept in a bare berth on the ship that night—no one was there to mind. After all, "Norman" Melville had signed on. The next morning I was up and ambled onto the docks, wondering how I'd manage the day and when the ship would start meals for the crew. (Now I missed my penny, which might have gotten me a couple of rolls.) From a grocery just opening up along South Street, I begged a drink of water.

It must have been tainted, for twenty minutes later I was sick as a dog and, on a pile of cable chain, collapsed in the cool June morning and slept a fitful hour on the dock beside a piling, like some destitute drunk. (I'd assumed the disheveled men sleeping up against this wall or under that market cart were drunk. But maybe some were simply sick. And as hungry as I was—a sobering thought.) I got myself together. And wouldn't you know, it began to rain before I started for the ship. I went on board, still queasy, soaked, and already looking forward to anything I might eat to gentle my belly, with my burping and gagging. I couldn't be seasick already, I thought—before we had even sailed. Most of those lying about on the streets, of course, were more micks-n'-niggers—in those days you'd have thought it a single combined nationality, like Czecho-Slovakian, the way it was spoken, though here and there were some Italians, some bohunks, and squareheads recognizable under the dirt and the rags.

The niggers already knew where they weren't wanted, I suppose, but "No Irish Need Apply" signs manifested what was already rampant in the city's streets around us, more and more common around any neighborhood where hale and ordinary men might find work. (In my kit—a mick word they'd already loaned us along with the smell of their poverty—I had my Milton, but I hadn't brought my Browne, though by now I could recite the whole of the fifth chapter of the *Buriall*, as could most of the cultured men I'd known working for and around the *Laningsburgh Advertiser*—one of the differences between a boy and a man, I say. That's why I'd learned it myself. There's no better recitation piece, no matter the many times you hear it. Micks would inundate the American landscape during the famine of 1859—when Billy the Kid himself was born here in the same city as I had been, forty years before him. The signs even mentioned the primitive accordion and drum music of the Irish, becoming something to poke fun at in songs and to sing about. Most people don't even remember those signs from the years before, however—or, mostly, remember them since, now that they're willing to hire the Irish for the police force. But the signs were common enough in my youth for me to note.

With 356 on board and 920 bales of cotton, the *St. Lawrence* sailed on June 5 for Liverpool—where two men quit and three deserted and the most impressive thing I saw was the great Moorish Arch against the clouds outside the Liverpool Railway, with its two smokestacks at either side (though neither was puffing the summer I saw it). Before we'd pushed off from England, we had replacements for the men who'd run. Coming home, the cotton replaced by pathetic Irish folks who were longing for the freedom and work that was reputedly in my country for the having, we sailed by Cape Cod, while the sap oozed in the sun from the ship's planks to make trails, liquid for a

23

minute then, seconds after, hard as amber. We pulled into the New
York docks on October 1.

My first night back, because I had a little money with me, I went
to a bar and thought to enjoy some of the conviviality I had seen
between three men who had sailed with each other before they had
again found one another on our boat, and two others who clearly
had taken to one another and were already talking of signing on together again, there among the merchant marines. But though I en-
vied it in the others, either I did not know how to extend, or was
weary of extending, myself to do the same. Once we were docked,
perhaps, I thought, if the men were freed from the necessity of day-
time and nighttime toil, that conviviality might grow greater. But
in that South Street drinking establishment, what happened was
that, after half an hour among groups of friends, none of whom were
mine, some great blubbering, chestnut-bearded fellow, already half
drunk, caught me in an argument. "A sailor? You say *you're* a sailor?
You think four months on a passenger boat with cotton in her hole
makes you a sailor—?" and he staggered off, convulsed with laughter, as if he'd heard the funniest—and foulest—joke one might have
told him.

My next adventure was a trip out to Galena, Illinois, with my
friend Eli, brother of one of Helen's friends—Harriet—along the Erie
Canal, on the first leg of our trip to the Mississippi.

Eli had sold *his* first article to the *Advertiser* and was quite full of
himself about it. And he liked to read and had smart things to say
about what he read. But he was also always ready to take off on an
adventure, rather than sit at a table and work with his pen.

I figured farming would be better than the bank clerk's job I'd had
before I'd gone down to try out the merchant marines, and better too
than selling fur caps and fur gloves and arguing for my pay from
Mr. Allman, which is what I'd done after I'd come back.

I stood on the blackened boards of the barge deck, watching half a
dozen haws lines swoop out to half a dozen mules trudging the bank,
past the live oak and the willows and the sumac. On the far bank half
a dozen more swooped out to half a dozen more mules. The skinner
on that side was riding an unattached mule and smoking his pipe and
letting his boot heels flop as he jogged.

In his floppy-brimmed brown hat, Eli was talking to the head skinner, who now turned to tell him: "No—you may *not* ride one of the
mules. These are working animals—not for tourists. You wanted to
walk a while? So walk. When we reach the next station—it's only three

or four miles—get back on the barge, stretch out by the gunwale, and take a nap if you like."

I laughed. And so did Eli, then looked at me in humorous despair. Well, it had been his idea.

On my uncle's farm, there wasn't work, it turned out. So we sent a letter and came home. It got there three days before we did—we left our new Indian friends (who, for the perfectly silly reason that we'd wanted to kill them, had wanted to kill us. I hope you find that ironic). I'm surprised we didn't beat it. In November of the following year, 1841, I saw an advertisement for the whaling ship *Akushnett*, which would be taking on hands and leaving from Fairhaven, Massachusetts.

It seemed so easy to write the first book. I'd left a copy with Gansevoort and Allan, who'd taken it with them to their Wall Street offices in New York. The next I'd heard, they'd shown it to someone named Dr. Nichols, who'd taken the copy to England, and the next after that I knew, it was coming out from John Murray both in London and New York. It appeared late the following winter. Shortly, it was reviewed most praisefully by both Walt Whitman in the *Brooklyn Eagle* (though anonymously; I didn't learn he was the author until several years later) and Nathaniel Hawthorne in the *Salem Advertiser*. He signed his name, and through it we became great friends—till my side, perhaps, grew too intense for him to put up with.

On Bibliomancy, Anthropodermic Bibliopegy, and The Eating Papers; or, Proust's Porridge

Melissa Pritchard

BIBLIOMANCY: DIVINATION BY MEANS OF A BOOK OPENED AT RANDOM TO A VERSE OR PASSAGE

I HAVE BEEN PACKING in earnest, the sedimentia of four generations, strata of decades, the weight stone of things rolling away. I have sold, given away, disposed of by means of alleyway, obliging friends, strangers, and the Army that Saves, a third of my possessions. Another third has vanished into that public holding cube, the mini-storage unit. Contracting from 3,000 square feet of living space to 750 square feet requires an epic purge. Mostly, I welcome it, but for one room, a room I resist to the last. My library, my carapace, my identity: writer. A room with a view, three desks, one thousand books, and a reading chair decimated by the dog. Two of the desks have already gone, leaving the third, not a desk at all but a rough-made pine table. The sad-looking chair has been carted off to the upholsterer's. All that remains is books collected over a lifetime. Inherited, purchased, received as gifts, books signed by their authors, books stolen (my older sister's college paperback copy of Hardy's *Tess of the d'Urbervilles*, a 1959 copy of *Le Point*, "Univers de Proust," poached from a flat on rue Blanche in Paris, a copy of E. J. Bellocq's *Storyville Portraits*, never returned to the Taos Library), dilapidated hardback books from my father's Navy-brat youth (*Robinson Crusoe, The Last of the Mohicans, Robin Hood, 200 More Tricks You Can Do*). From my mother's Chicago girlhood (*Linda Lane's Adventures, Oriole's Adventures: Four Complete Adventure Books for Girls in One Big Volume, Daddy-Long-Legs*). A slim dark-blue-and-gold-lettered book, *SNAG 56*, about my grandfather's captaincy of a British hospital in World War II, books from friends, from auditioning lovers. Each book has had a place on my shelves. Now I am pulling them down, striking the set. This private library of paper, ink, and dust, these one thousand books in loose, friendly order, is the closest thing to an honest portrait of my life.

How to proceed? I call my publisher in Brooklyn, whose four-story brownstone feels entirely constructed of and held together by books, the air like old mucilage, tinged with shellac, rabbit glue. She suggests I break the process down, ask myself is this a book I could readily find another copy of, does it have sentimental value? If the former, let go, if the latter, keep. Armed with this system, I begin to sort and divide books into boxes. Initially tentative, indecisive, I turn discriminating, gimlet-eyed, ruthless. First to go are books I feel indifferent to, then ones I loathe but have kept out of guilt or a sense of obligation. Eight boxes go to the Perryville Women's Correctional Facility, three to my house sitter, also a writer, seventeen to the storage catacomb, to be shuttered into the rented silence of a metal unit, stacked beside a job lot of Christmas ornaments, children's toys, old linens, incomplete silver sets, stacks of furniture, and three centuries of family albums. The remaining books will be my companions in a narrow room with a pine writing table and a reading chair reclaimed by the dog.

In the art of bibliomancy, one allows the pages of a book considered sacred to fall open to a random passage. The Greeks divined wisdom from Homer's *Iliad*. Virgil's *Aeneid* was used for divination during medieval times, the *I Ching* is a current favorite with bibliomancers. There is a website devoted to literary bibliomancy, bibliomancy.org, "the wisdom of the ages at your fingertips." Enter the site with your life question, receive a reply from Dickens, Dostoevsky, Virgil, Hermann Hesse, Homer, etc. Type the question into a box, select a book from the list, and the answer, intended as insight, appears. I ask Charles Dickens about my future and receive this from *Great Expectations*, passage 406 of 1550: *Biddy turned her face suddenly towards mine, and looked far more attentively at me than she had looked at the sailing ships. "It was neither a true nor a very polite thing to say," she remarked, directing her eyes to the ships again. "Who said it?" I was disconcerted, for I had broken away without quite seeing where I was going to. It was not to be shuffled off now, however, and I answered, "The beautiful young lady at Miss Havisham's, and she's more beautiful than anybody ever was, and I admire her dreadfully, and I want to be a gentleman on her account." Having made this lunatic confession, I began to*

27

throw my torn-up grass into the river, as if I had some thoughts of following it.

I might have consulted Jane Austen, George Sand, Colette, or Mavis Gallant, but none of them are on the list. My diviners are solidly male.

As I relegate one thousand volumes to their fates, I ease my book ache with an invented subset of bibliomancy: epigraphancy. Choosing books at random, I flip to their epigraphs for more insights into my vague future.

Not every book contains an epigraph; a few have three or four. Epigraphs lend smart style, outfitting the author in witty, philosophic, or enigmatic dress. They also offer the reader a set of jeweled binoculars through which to view the distant stage, draw back curtains on the opening scene.

Here are random epigraphancies to reflect upon as I take slow leave of my private library, my Jacob's coat of many books, their ivory, deckle-edged, or smooth pages tattooed with ink both sumptuous and plain:

An oasis of horror in a desert of boredom.
—Charles Baudelaire
(Roberto Bolaño, *2666*)

My dear, these things are life.
—George Meredith
(Mercè Rodoreda, *The Time of the Doves*)

Novels arise out of the shortcomings of history.
—F. von Hardenberg, later Novalis
Fragmente und Studien, 1799–1800
(Penelope Fitzgerald, *The Blue Flower*)

I am accustoming myself to the idea of regarding every sexual act as a process in which four persons are involved. We shall have a lot to discuss about that.
—Sigmund Freud, *Letters*
(Lawrence Durrell, *Justine*)

ANTHROPODERMIC BIBLIOPEGY:
THE PRACTICE OF BINDING BOOKS IN HUMAN SKIN

Stones, clay and wood tablets, bamboo, papyrus, silk, bone, bronze, shell, palm leaf, flax linen, the earliest writing surfaces. Scrolls folded like a concertina, "butterfly" scrolls bound on one edge, scrolls with wood handles on either end, codices—the earliest books. (Jack Kerouac's *On the Road*, written in three weeks as a scroll manuscript, without punctuation, was recently republished in its original form.) During the first century AD in China, the earliest known paper was made from a mixture of mulberry, fishnet, and hemp waste. In the third century AD, a writing surface known as parchment began to be made from the skins of asses, antelope, sheep, cattle, pig, deer, horse, camel. Parchment consists mainly of collagen, and the highest-quality parchment, vellum, or *veau*, was made from the skin of stillborn or unborn animals. Finer still was uterine vellum. A vein network appearing in a piece of vellum was termed a "veining of the sheet."

From the fourteenth century, the most valuable books and documents were written on vellum. Due to its rarity and expense, monastery parchments were often scrubbed and written over, leaving faint traces of the previous writing, a holy palimpsest of gospels ghosting beneath a medieval sermon.

Early writing instruments made of bone or bronze marked moist clay tablets. Reed brushes were used to write on scrolls of papyrus, and the Romans used metal styluses to press Latin letters onto sheets of wax supported by tablets of beech or fir. Around 600 AD, the quill pen was invented in Seville. Long wing feathers of swans, turkeys, geese, crows, owls, hawks, and eagles were plucked, cleaned, sharpened, and dipped in ink, filling the hollow shaft or reservoir of the feather. Not until the eighteenth century was a machine-made steel pen point mass-produced.

The first inks were made from wood smoke and oil thickened with gelatin from asses' skins and musk. Sulfate and gallnuts produced iron-gall ink, tannic acid and iron salts, bound by resin, another. Tar, carbon, oil, honey, gum, the stuff of early script. Brown-black dye from cuttlefish too, and purple ink from squid, scarlet from madder, and from scale insects named Kermes vermilio and cochineal. Indigo ink was made from a mixture of woad, indigo, and gallnuts; books were bound with glue made from boiled rabbit skins, fish, horses.

(Secret or "invisible" ink, made from lemon juice, milk, vinegar starch, urine, etc., is a subtributary of ink history, filled with tales of wartime espionage, prison breaks, covert love letters, and children's mischief.) The Declaration of Independence was written on parchment or, as parchment is now called, to distinguish it from vellum, animal membrane. At the university where I teach, every classroom is required to have a copy of the Declaration of Independence, printed on faux animal membrane, tacked to its walls. The original Declaration of Independence, Bill of Rights, United States Constitution, and Articles of Confederation were all inscribed on the flayed, scraped, pumiced, and chalked skins of calves.

Ink from fish, grubs, plants, soot. Clay, stone, dried leaves, plants, silk, animal skins. Feathers engorged with ink. The yearning for permanence.

In our tenure on this planet, we have moved from organic to inorganic materials, from writing with earth's substances to writing electronically, with light. Scudding upon iClouds, bathed in iLight, the evocation *i* underscoring our devotion not to the planet, but to our disembodied, immortal hoped-for Selves.

> In my skin are the prayers and all the blessings made to Holy Church.
>
> And have not calves, goats, kids, Coneys, hares and cats skin? As vellum, they may be well written on. To be sure, their parchment is worth more than your skin, which serves you less.
>
> —Dialogue between two French monks, fifteenth century
> (Ronald Reed, *The Making and Nature of Parchment*)

In reading about the distinctions between parchment and vellum, animal vs. vegetable vellum, I stumble upon a term unknown to me—*anthropodermic bibliopegy*—the practice of binding books with human skin. My morbid self plunges on.

In 2007, a book entitled *A True and Perfect Relation of the Whole Proceedings against the Late Most Barbarous Traitors Garnet a Jesuit and His Confederates*, bound in the skin of Father Henry Garnet, a faint impression of his death mask on its cover, was sold by an anonymous collector to an anonymous buyer at auction for $11,000. While Father Garnet did not participate in the 1605 Gunpowder Plot to blow up the Houses of Parliament and assassinate King James I (now celebrated on November 5 as Guy Fawkes Day), the Jesuit priest willingly heard the confessions of those who were involved. Guilty by implication, Garnet was drawn, quartered, and a portion of his skin used to bind the account of legal proceedings against him.

Housed among other medical oddities at Old Surgeons' Hall in Edinburgh is a worn, unremarkable-looking pocket book. Brownish-black with a pebbled texture, it is embossed with faded gilt lettering: EXECUTED 28 JAN 1829 BURKE'S SKIN POCKETBOOK. The pocketbook, empty of pages, used for personal notes and money, is bound in the skin of notorious criminal William Burke, who, along with William Hare, his accomplice, murdered sixteen people, selling the corpses of their victims to Dr. Robert Knox to be used for dissections in his highly popular anatomy lessons. Burke was hanged for the murders, and his body was (ironically) dissected at Edinburgh Medical College, his skin used to bind this otherwise common-looking pocketbook.

The practice of binding books in human skin began at least in the sixteenth century and waned in the latter years of the Victorian age, the same era that memorialized loved ones with "jewelry" fashioned from the often abundant, shorn hair of the deceased. Books were bound in human skin for diverse reasons, including to memorialize, as a gift to loved ones, or to bind court testimonies against criminals in their own punished hides.

Human skin, tanned, looks indistinguishable from goat, cattle, and sheep but for variance in pore size, shape, and a peculiar waxy odor. The tanning process destroys DNA, making it difficult to differentiate between skins of human, goat, cow, and pig, but a new technique, Peptide Mass Fingerprinting, or PMF, has proven useful in determining whether a book claiming to be bound in human skin through inscription or questionable historical "evidence" is genuine. In 1935, a book was deposited in Harvard's Houghton Library by book collector John B. Stetson Jr., and given to the library in 1954 by Stetson's widow. In April 2014, this book, Arsène Houssaye's *Des destinées de l'ame* (*On the Destiny of the Soul*), was determined through PMF to be bound in human skin. "The PMF from *Des destinées de l'ame* matched the human reference, and clearly eliminated other common parchment sources such as sheep, cattle, and goat," Bill Lane, director of Harvard's Mass Spectrometry and Proteomics Resource Laboratory and Daniel Kirby of the Straus Center for Conservation and Technical Studies reported to the Houghton Library blog.

Melissa Pritchard

Sometime in the 1880s, Houssaye had given his book, a meditation on the soul and life after death, to his friend Dr. Ludovic Bouland, an ardent bibliophile. Dr. Bouland bound *Des destinées de l'ame* using skin from the back of an unclaimed female mental patient who had died of a stroke. A note penned by the doctor, inserted within the pages of the book, reads, "This book is bound in human skin parchment on which no ornament has been stamped to preserve its elegance. By looking carefully, you easily distinguish pores of the skin. A book about the human soul deserved to have a human covering. I had kept this piece of human skin taken from the back of a woman."

The female binding of *Des destinées de l'ame*, as reported by the *Harvard Crimson*, has a "greenish-gold hue as well as visible pores."

In the late nineteenth century, a French countess, dying of tuberculosis, requested that a strip of skin from her shoulders be delivered, upon her death, to writer and astronomer Camille Flammarion, so that he might use her skin in the binding of his next book. Compliant, perhaps flattered, Flammarion bound his 1877 copy of *Les Terres du Ciel, The Lands of the Sky*, a description of the planets in our solar system, with the countess's shoulder skin. Until 1925, the book was displayed in a library in Juvisy-sur-Orge, France.

A nineteenth-century English bookbinder of erotica used the breasts of deceased females, purchased from medical interns, to bind copies of *Justine* and *Juliette* by Donatien Alphonse François, better known as the Marquis de Sade, and in London's Wellcome Library, a seventeenth-century book on virginity, Séverin Pineau's *De virginitatis notis, graviditate et partu*, is currently on view, rebound in human hide and tanned with sumac by the same Dr. Ludovic Bouland.

This grisly legend persists: When Marie-Thérèse of Savoy-Carignan, Princess de Lamballe, an intimate of Marie Antoinette's, was executed in 1792, her naked corpse was pulled through the streets and the skin from her thighs removed to be used for the binding of a book. In whose private collection stands this rumored book, neatly bound in the marmoreal pallor of the Princesse de Lamballe's skin?

As Dr. Simon Chaplin, head of the Wellcome Library, says, "There may still be a number of books in libraries and private collections bound in human skin, not yet categorized or identified."

Each of us is a two-footed manuscript, a work in progress. Briefly bound in our own skin, uncataloged, unshelved, we form some seven billion volumes of the world's living library.

Within us too are digested libraries, cellular *bibliothèques* made of every book we have ever read. Writers fold sentences into crevices of the body, scratched in delible, sympathetic ink.

We are characters wandering, largely unaware, inside an inconceivably grand body of narrative, its scope greater than that of any novel by Balzac, Hugo, Sand, Dostoevsky, or Tolstoy, the plot a biomorphic field, an akashic record of all that has occurred and will occur.

If I kiss you, will you taste of all the books you have read or only the last one? If we are writers and we kiss, will we taste one another's unwritten, still dreamed, books?

> It ever was, and is, and shall be,
> ever-living Fire, in measures being
> kindled and in measures going out.
>
> —Heraclitus
> (Annie Dillard, *Pilgrim at Tinker Creek*)

THE EATING PAPERS; OR, PROUST'S PORRIDGE

Visiting a friend in Paris, I read her copy of Larry Dossey's *Healing beyond the Body: Medicine and the Infinite Reach of the Mind*, and learn that eating words inscribed on paper is an old, traditional folk cure for sickness.

When he became seriously ill at a conference in Baja, Dossey asked his friend Dr. Frank Lawlis to write words on a piece of paper and smash the paper into a capsule size that he could swallow with a glass of water. This would be his only medicine. He began to recover in three days, and though his friend considered the experiment a failure, since Dossey's symptoms lingered for weeks afterward, Dossey reasoned that had he not eaten his paper capsule, he might well have died.

As an elementary student at the Queen of Apostles Catholic school in Chicago, poet Jeanine Hathaway carefully wrote "aspirin" on the corner of a page from her notebook, tore it off, rolled it into a ball, and swallowed it. Faith worked. She felt instantly better, her sickness gone, as if she had taken a real aspirin minus the vinegar taste.

In France, Italy, Russia, and Germany, Bible verses, prayers, and spells were written down to be eaten as medicine—in Germany, these were called *Esszettel* or "eating papers." To drink these papers with water was to be cured by the power of words. In Holstein, the following words would be written on paper and given to a person with fever to be swallowed with water: "Fever stay away. (The person's name) is not at home." Reports from the fifteenth century describe apples being written upon and eaten, three almonds inscribed with words, squares of gingerbread imprinted with magical spells, and small pieces of buttered bread etched with a quill dipped in ink, to be eaten on three consecutive Fridays at sunrise and sundown. An epileptic might be helped by a formula written on a piece of paper using a needle that had once sewn something for a dead person, the paper then being warmed over steam from heated milk and presented to the epileptic on a piece of buttered bread. Even sick animals received *Esszettel* treatments. Today, a Bayer aspirin, a cross stamped on its round, white surface, is perceived by patients to be more effective than a smooth-faced, unadorned aspirin. And what of the Eucharist, believed by the Catholics who ingest it to be the literal body, the flesh of Jesus, healing the disease of sin, making them whole? What of the physician's scrawled medical prescription (RX being Latin for "recipe"), legible only to the pharmacist—does it have shamanistic power? Is faith a greater medicine than medicine?

In the 1920s, documents found in Eastern Mongolia described the Tibetan folk-medicine cure of eating pieces of paper with healing words printed on them. Approximately one inch by one inch in size, the papers had prayers or spells written in Tibetan, with separate instructions in Mongolian for dosage or use.

In Uganda in the 1990s, photographs of a Christian charismatic preacher and healer were dissolved in water and drunk by his followers. In the Catholic tradition, images of the Madonna could be dissolved and drunk with water, or swallowed as pills.

Bibliophagy is a rare disorder wherein the afflicted person compulsively eats books. Symptoms include feelings of relief upon eating books, and a reduction in anxiety brought about by the eating of books. Treatment consists of behavior therapy and medication. But if words can be eaten as magic formulae, *Esszettel* to treat sickness, cannot whole books be prescriptively dined upon and digested? If I eat a page of Proust a day, scissored up and stirred into warm milk, a kind of porridge, will Proust's words, his brain and style, over time, become part of my own? Might I compound a Virginia Woolf topical

34

ointment or swallow Shakespeare gelatin capsules before bed and again upon waking? Is there a Flaubert lozenge or troche? A smear of Chekhov for my buttered bread? Oh, dear Physician, will it add to the effectiveness of my long-term treatment, if I, poor ailing author, drink such august faces, snipped and floating, in water or wine?

May these words, eaten or drunk, cure all straying thoughts:

> *Mos gus yod na*
> *Khyl so od tung.*
>
> Where there is veneration,
> Even a dog's tooth emits light.
> —Tibetan proverb
> (Lawrence Durrell, *The Black Book*)

Please Translate

Edwidge Danticat

TRANSLATOR'S NOTE

We were asked to translate from Haitian Creole to English the following phone messages from Lina Philippe Guillaume to her husband, Jonas Guillaume, and father of five-year-old Jimmy Guillaume. We are professional translators certified by the city of Miami and state of Florida, license number CT09956 on file, if requested.

Message #1: Hi. Just calling to see how you two are doing. I'll call later. All right? All right then.

Message #2: Hi. Wow. Please call me back.

Message #3: Jonas, I wish you could call me back. I'm waiting for him. I have work tomorrow. I picked up an extra Saturday shift. Mama's going to watch Jimmy for me.

Message #4: Jonas, I just want to hear from you. I hope everything's OK.

Message #5: Jonas, is everything all right?

Message #6: Jonas, where are you?

Message #7: Jonas, it's almost midnight. Where are you?

Message #8: Jonas, I'm coming over there. That's right, you have my car. (*Muttering.*) Why did I let that thief borrow my car? (*Louder.*) Jonas, I only let you borrow my car so Jimmy could be safe in a proper car. Your car wasn't in the shop, was it? I can't believe I was fooled by you again.

Message #9: OK, Jonas, I'm very worried now. I'm going to call someone to bring me over there.

Message #10: Goddamn it, Jonas. It shouldn't take this long to get some ice cream. Where are you with my son? In the middle of the night.

Message #11: Jonas! Jonas! I want my child.

Message #12: Jonas. (*Sobbing.*) Jonas, please. Where have you taken my child?

Message #13: (*Inaudible.*)

Message #14: (*Screaming.*) JONAS!

Message #15: (*Calmer.*) Jonas, please bring my baby back. I promise, I won't leave you. I'll stay with you. We can go to Pastor David and get some counseling, for Jimmy's sake. Please, Jonas, just please answer this phone.

Message #16: You're not a policeman here, Jonas. You have to follow the law here. Just like everybody else.

Message #17: I wanted to avoid this, but this is your last chance before I call the police. You better call me, you illegal mother—. OK. Please, Jonas, please let me know my baby's OK.

Message #18: Jonas, listen to me. I'll take this as far as you want me to. If you think you have more balls than every other man in the world, I'll show you you're wrong.

Message #19: Jonas, I love you. I really do. Just please bring my baby back now.

Message #20: Jonas, is this about the car? I told you I paid for it myself. Marcus did not help me. You're jealous for nothing, Jonas. He's my boss, that's all, my supervisor. Yes, he promoted me at the hotel, but that had nothing to do with me and him being together. I mean, we're not together, Marcus and me. I'm not together with him. And I'm not together with you. Please just bring my baby back.

Message #21: Jonas, you were my first love. Ever since we were kids in Haiti. I have always loved you. I'm not going to stop loving you for someone I've just met. I would never demean you like that, Jonas. Please.

Message #22: My baby, Jonas. Please. (*Muttering.*) I should have never trusted that good-for-nothing.

Message #23: You're still sour about Marcus buying me that car, uh, Jonas? You're holding my child hostage over a man and a car. Then you know what, you're no man at all. The police are coming now to your place. The real police of this country. And I'm coming with them.

Message #24: Jonas, everyone knows I'm the one who bought that car. Marcus just gave me a ride to the dealership. He helped me bargain down the price. I bought it all by myself.

Message #25: Jonas, I'm never going to let you do this to me again. I'm never going to let you take my child again and just turn off your phone and scare me like this. It's the last time. I'm telling you. The last time.

Message #26: Jonas, this time I'm really going to call the police. You think I'm afraid to because I don't have my papers. Are you hoping they'll deport me so you can keep my son? Marcus is a better man than you, Jonas. He gave me that job even without my papers. Screw the papers, Jonas. Even if I get deported back to Haiti, I'm taking Jimmy with me. Screw everything, Jonas. Next time you hear from me, you'll hear sirens too. I'm going to be in a police car and I'll be on my way to your house.

Message #27: Don't push me, Jonas. You know I can do it and I will. You better just bring me back my child. I'm going to call Marcus too. He'll give me a ride to Fort Lauderdale and the police will get my baby from you. They'll arrest you and deport you, but not before I give Marcus a big kiss right there in front of your ugly face.

Message #28: Jonas, please. I'm sorry. I'm sorry. I just said all that to make you angry. I'm sorry, baby. I'm sorry, darling. Please forgive me. Please.

Message #29: Jonas, I'm still giving you a break. I haven't called the police on you yet, but if you push me I will. It's now 2:00 a.m. (*Inaudible.*) I am going to give you fifteen more minutes to bring my child and my car back.

Message #30: Jonas, can you hear the phone ring? Are you looking at my number and not picking up? Did you fall asleep? Is Jimmy asleep?

Message #31: Jonas, I'm calling the police now and I'm going to take a taxi all the way out there. I'm going to come and get my baby from you. Even if it costs a hundred dollars I don't have.

Message #32: Jonas, you're proving yourself to be a very low-class individual. If you think you're going to fuck with me, I'll show you. You're messing with me for the last time. You jealous piece of shit.

Message #33: (*Inaudible.*)

Message #34: (*Inaudible.*)

Message #35: (*Sirens blaring, mostly inaudible. Sobs.*)

Message #36: Jonas, how can you do this to our baby? (*Man's voice follows.*) YOU WORTHLESS MOTHERFUCKER, YOU ARE GOING TO DIE!

Message #37: (*Loud background voices. Sobs.*) Jonas, you should not have run and left Jimmy behind like that. Jonas, you should have killed yourself too.

Message #38: Jonas. (*Woman screaming.*) I WILL FIND YOU. WHEREVER YOU ARE, I WILL FIND YOU.

Message #39: Jonas, I will spend the rest of my life looking for you. (*Screaming. Sobs.*) Oh my God, Marcus. I can't believe he did this to our baby.

Message #40: Jonas, you stupid asshole. I can't believe you did this to our child. I knew this phone would lead them to you. It's like having a GPS on you, you imbecile. You can barricade yourself in there all you want, but they're going to get you. And if you try to run, they're going to blow you right out of this world. No court sentence will be enough for you, though. Even if you make it out alive and go to jail. One day I will kill you with my bare hands. I'm going to kill you, just like you killed our child. I will put your face in water and drown you the same way, just like I have now a thousand times in my mind. I'm going to show you, Jonas. I'm going to—

RECORDED MESSAGE: THIS CUSTOMER'S MAILBOX IS FULL.

END OF TRANSLATION.

Four Poems
Elizabeth Robinson

ON EDITING

Editing was the perfect recursive process—

to return to the thing and make it more itself.

As a child, she enjoyed the idea that she could think a thought

while thinking of herself thinking it, a predisposition

toward editing which understands it as

a kind of magical oversight on

immediacy

to thought. But never

was she able to be certain that she had actually

thought the thought while thinking of herself

thinking it.

To do this again and again, to strive for mastery

over the iteration that makes it pure.

Editing was never perfect, but it strove for purity:

recursiveness by excision. She edited and

she edited until it was possible

not that she thought, or thought herself into a thought

but that a thought existed, claimed

its site so that the mind could recur to it.

ON PAGES

Their purpose is to turn.

Literally,

against the clock.

The future, as read, is counterclockwise.

*

At last, alone or

singular,

the page measures its margin.

Creates the field, Janus-faced,

of the verso.

Time turns within its spine,

within its own signature, on itself.

*

Verso is to the clock as

signature is to time.

The page renounces itself in the turning.

Turning on its own rhythm.

Within its own leaf:

(Seasonal. Deciduous. Falling.)

If time accretes as pages—

If it sheds itself—

*

A field on which to fall, fall backwards, forwards, fall
into the spine.

*

Time, two-faced on the page, doubles back

to the imaginary, sans body, field, or time. What part means to whole,

spinning in the pivot of its own progress.

ON THE RED-LETTER EDITION

The Holy Ghost is garbed in white in honor of its invisibility.

For this invisibility

conveys immutable truth. Authority.

That the holy writ is literal. Is the white page imprinted with its

own transparency.

Except for the words printed in red.

The Holy Ghost, being, of course, male, has sex-linked red/green-related
color blindness.

And so its truth

is mediated.

White, remember, is the presence of all color. Except

when one

can't see the color.

The Holy Ghost—

it fails to recognize that someone else

said the red words. Said.

What is literal is incomplete because it cannot conceive the spectrum

from which it becomes itself.

Perhaps not the presence of all color. But a voice

that selects its own hue, and color recurring.

Partial

to the same truth. Glossy Holy Land maps.

Sheen of gilt enfleshing the edge

of its visual impairment, its vaguely white onionskin transparency.

ON TYPOS

Homer was a blind poet who resighted poetry.

In the woodland you were

dear and deer.

I might almost have said it simultaneously.

Where your

who are

you're

would land. Uncorrectable and

I might have said there

all at once

where

they're grazing

among wares, air and err.

It's these,

a thesis:

where made

to wear its self, it's

tangled in samenesses—a little

grove of the subtlest confusions and

a tune

I might have sung. A site wrung of

these is

a rung of sight
cited

synchronous. At once attunement

dear and recited unseeing. Whose words

might be there and theirs.

Some Episodes in the History of My Reading
Frederic Tuten

THE BED

MY MOTHER COMES HOME from work tired. We sit in the kitchen with my grandmother, who has prepared a frugal meal, and by nine my mother is off to bed. We do not have a TV, it is 1945, few do in my Bronx neighborhood, so I read a library book, a Jules Verne, maybe, or an abridged version of *The Three Musketeers*. The living room, with my wheezing grandmother sleeping fitfully behind the screen that separates us, my squeaky cot and the old, thin blankets, the winter coldness, suddenly vanishes. I'm carried into the richest worlds of life and remain there as long as I'm reading my book. And I'm protected from harm after I turn off the light as long as the book remains in my hand.

THE RAFT

My mother gave me *The Adventures of Tom Sawyer* and *The Adventures of Huckleberry Finn* for my tenth birthday. She had heard that they were what American boys read. I devoured the Twain books over and over again, finding myself in them—that is, my desired, adventurous free self. Finding in Tom and Huck the friends I needed and wanted, models to keep me in the hope of escape from my cramped world in the Bronx. I was raised by Sicilians and I may as well have been living in Palermo, where there was no vast Mississippi and no wide raft to ride it, no open sky and no territory ahead, no America.

I lived not far from the mighty ripple of the Bronx River and one afternoon I tied a small raft of planks I had plucked from a construction site close to the botanical garden—where the river ran through—then still on the wild side with a deer or two hiding in the brush. I left my shoes and socks on the bank and pushed off and sank. I got stuck in the river's soft muddy bottom and barely worked my way out of the muck. I was coated in watery mud and crying with fear on the grassy bank. I wonder what story I told my mother when she saw me mud caked and trembling. That was the early end of my exotic adventures. I consigned them to the safe regions of movies and books and, later, to putting them into my own fiction, in novels and stories located far from the Mississippi, far from America, and about artists, revolutionaries, and romantics, who, unlike me, burn and dare.

THE SEDUCTION

When I was young, I sought the more difficult books, the more difficult the better: I did not ever want to be led to where and what I had already known, to be guided in a language with words that seldom required a dictionary. At fifteen, I saw a beautiful older woman whom I had a giant crush on sitting on a park bench and reading as if nothing else in the world mattered. I was ashamed of my lustful thoughts and expected her to have read them in my stare. She finally noticed me and called me over and asked if I liked to read.

"Of course," I said and nervously began to name a few books I loved.

"Those are good books. You're my son's friend, aren't you?"

"Yes, I am," I said, not mentioning that we disliked each other, that he called me four eyes and a fruity bookworm.

"I have other books you may like," she said, "so come by for coffee." Her apartment jumped with books, shelves of them even in the kitchen, where we sat and drank coffee and where I burned for her. She lent me the novel she had been reading on the park bench, Djuna Barnes's *Nightwood*. "Let me know what you think," she said. I wanted to like it because she had. But I couldn't follow the story, I did not understand if there was a story, but there were passages of intense, mysterious beauty that made me tremble as I had on my first Holy Communion.

A year later, I broke my head trying to make sense of Joyce's *Ulysses*, another book she gave me, one she had a special passion for. Something extraordinary was going on there in that Irishman's ocean of words and I felt elevated, special, just trying to fathom it. But what remained in me was not only the novels she had led me to but the association of fiction with sexual longing, and with beauty and mystery.

My beautiful friend loved *Ulysses* so much that she left her husband

and children to live in Paris with a French scholar who had devoted his life to that one book. His passion to what she also loved was the magnet. Because of her, I'm drawn to every woman I see reading a book and curious to know what she is reading, snobbishly gauging her beauty to her taste.

Once, in a café in Paris, I saw an elegant woman, as Henry James would say, of a certain age, fixed on a book. She was at the same table over the following five days. Once, our eyes met and we smiled. I took the courage from that smile to approach her and ask in my most polite way, and in my crippled French, what she was reading.

"*Nightwood,*" she said, showing me the cover. "And you?"

I held back my surprise and my wanting to tell her how I had first come across the book, but instead I answered: "*The Third Policeman,* by an Irish writer. I'm not sure it's translated."

"I have read it in English," she said, adding, "I have wondered what you were reading all these days and wondered if you were a simpleton."

She did not appear the next day or the days after, which I ascribed to my intruding on her privacy. But the headwaiter, a man I had known for years and who was a friend of Lawrence Durrell's, said, "She comes here every spring and early fall for seven days and sits with a book, speaks to no one, and waits for no one. She is not French and she is not English or American. She leaves extravagant tips above the *service compris* so we don't care how long she sits, even when we are busy. She drinks kir royale. Anyway, she is beautiful." I imagined her world and wrote a novel about her called *The Green Hour.*

THE POISONOUS BOOK

A novel may just leave you where you were when you started it, and in that case it was not worth your time, the dear hours of your life never returned. Sometimes, and in the best case, a novel leaves you with a shudder of recognition—about what you do not know: It has altered you and you do not understand how or why, but it has. That does not mean it has changed you to be kinder or not to cheat on your lover or on your income taxes. But it has changed you: However alone, you are not alone.

W. H. Auden said that poetry changes nothing but the nature of its saying. That may be true for poetry, but fiction's power moves in mysterious ways. Some novels may elevate you, some may degrade.

At eighteen, I encountered such a "poisonous book," as the Huysmans novel given to Dorian Gray by the worldly Lord Henry was called. I was in my freshman year at City College and doing poorly—because I arrogantly, rebelliously read everything else but the required texts— and the final exams would determine if I was going to be expelled, which, for me, meant the street. I started to study four days before the exams. I liked the danger of it, the immersion of life at the brink's edge. Of course, I slept little and drank black coffee and smoked until my eyes popped; that was part of the ritual but one that deranged me. The day before the exam I lit on *The Fountainhead*, sitting on a pile I had taken from the library. I had been warned against it by my fellow bohemian students: It was a fascist book, an apologia for social Darwinism, an all-around rotten business with cardboard characters to boot.

It didn't matter. I started reading it in the afternoon and through the night and morning of my first exam. I slept for two hours and went off to the subway and down to the college, took the exams, and failed both algebra and biology. I had a semester of academic suspension to mull over my fantasy-driven crimes.

What had happened? Midway in my reading of *The Fountainhead* the idea grew that I was above exams and above study, towering above the college and above every demand made on me other than my own. And soon I was sure that I would not only pass the exams but that by my powers of concentration I would do brilliantly and win great praise. I was in the clouds of the grand Self. I was like the genius architect, Howard Roark, the superman of Ayn Rand's novel, one of the exceptions for whom rules were meant to be ignored or, better, to be shattered. My fellow students and my professors were the gears that made the System work, that giant academic factory that turned out standard bolts, screws, and solid citizens. I had a higher mission: I was an artist. I was the Howard Roark of the Bronx. I consoled myself with that idea for a few months after my suspension and while I was distributing mail from desk to desk in a large downtown catalog company.

ANOTHER BOOK, ANOTHER FOLLY

I suppose I descend from the line of those characters deluded by literature. Don Quixote rides off to save chivalry and the world, modeling himself on an antiquated literature of knights and their codes and adventures; the married Emma Bovary ruins her life in the pursuit of the kind of love she swoons over in the sentimental romances of her day.

My model for ruin was Hemingway. Nothing he could do was wrong. Not a sentence was off. His style was contagious and many in my generation caught the infection. I wrote shopping lists that read like his: "Buy a true bread. Be sure the *leche* is cold and its container true." His stories were perfect. His life was perfect. Everything Hemingway wrote and did I wanted to write and do. But not exactly: I did not want to fish or hunt. At eighteen, I went out on a day boat that sailed from Sheepshead Bay and moored some miles into the ocean. Within an hour I turned green and spent the excursion turning even greener below deck and pretending to show to the ship's crew—as Hemingway would have me—grace under pressure. As for hunting, at nine, I shot my Red Ryder BB gun at a squirrel squatting in my uncle Umberto's little Bronx garden and missed. I hit my uncle. My uncle was not hurt but the shot unsettled him, wounded his trust in me. I never again wanted to shoot at any living or inanimate thing.

At nineteen, I went to the *corrida* in Mexico City because of Hemingway's *Death in the Afternoon*; he had written about the drama of the run of the bulls and I was sure I would find, as he had, metaphysical courage acted out in the sand. But when the matador's sword plunged in and the bull fell and shuddered and died I felt ill. I was still sure, however, that the feeling would pass because I would come to see the truth and beauty in the bull's death and in the matador's union with the animal he had just killed. Back in my little hotel, I saw only the felled bull in the blood-soaked sand and I had to drink a lot of tequila before I could finally go to sleep.

From among all of Hemingway's stories, I was especially called to action by "A Clean, Well-Lighted Place," moved by its cadences and glamorous darkness. I liked the idea of a café/bar as a place of sanctuary and that to drink there was a mode of communion with the nothing, the *nada* of the story and of life.

I had learned from Hemingway that it is the writer's duty to drink. This was much easier than fishing or hunting or even sitting alone and, in total focus and purity of spirit, writing. Hemingway was not all to blame for this but he had given me a noble mission, an obligation to the profession, which I, as an earnest young man, was eager to fulfill.

I was fresh from meeting Hemingway—crashing his home outside

Havana—in the early September of 1958. He talked about writing and its need for discipline but he never mentioned the drinking part of the craft, which I assumed was part of the unspoken code that needed no mentioning.

That fall, as one of my experiments with the writer's life and duties, I went to an Irish bar, one of the few then remaining in Harlem, on my way to a morning class at City College. A long dark bar, a bowl of hard-boiled eggs, no TV, no radio, no music, as Hemingway would have wanted it. Just me and the purity of the bar and the bartender dozing by the window on the street, and the early morning still fresh with hope. I looked at myself in the mirror and, quoting from Hemingway's story, said, sotto voce, "Certainly you do not want music. Nor can you stand before the bar with dignity although that is all that is provided for these hours." At nine, I ordered a double shot of rye with a beer chaser. Then another.

I left for class feeling pleasantly woozy and glowing with dignity but, then, halfway there, I turned back for another round at the bar to secure the dignity. I missed my classes that day, and the days following when I renewed the experiments, but they too failed, like the raft that had sunk in the Bronx River.

It took me many years beyond my adolescence and adulthood to write my shopping list straight and to cease those and other such drinking experiments.

A NEW LOVE

Years ago, a noted writer asked: Who over the age of forty still reads novels? I did, and always with the hope of finding the innocent joy and impress of my early reading. For a while I took a vacation from fiction and turned mostly to biographies and memoirs and letters, to books on history and art. But enriching as they were, none had power over me or lived as deeply in my imagination.

Some few years ago I found for almost nothing all four volumes of André Gide's *Journals* at a library book sale. I had wanted them forever, for the physical beauty of the books alone and because of their echo from my youth, when Gide was a demigod of literature and whose novel, radical for its time, *The Counterfeiters*, I had loved. Gide's reading was wide and profound, and I came to value and trust his taste, a trust that grew volume by volume, and I wanted to read the books he so much cared about. I admired and felt kinship with him because he was not afraid to dislike what the world claims it reveres. He demolishes, for example, *King Lear*: "The entire play from one end to another is absurd" (*The Journals of André Gide*, volume 4). It was reassuring to know that someone else on this planet felt as I had. His praise for Steinbeck's masterpiece strike novel, *In Dubious Battle*, made me value his judgment even more.

So it surprised me to find his 1944 entry, "Have just devoured one after another eight books by Simenon at the rate of one a day." And then in 1948, the line: "New plunge into Simenon; I have just read six in a row." I had always thought of Simenon as a lightweight crime writer, but once I began reading Simenon it was curtains for me. I thought: This is why I still read, because without novels like this, life is just breathing.

Sometimes after a serious Simenon binge I feel sated, saturated, sick of myself, even, for being so addicted. My reward, as with drugs, is to receive less and less pleasure. I have been chasing the original high to no success, but like a true addict, I always relapse. I ask for little—a great opening, a dazzling seventy-five pages. I expect the letdown. But there is always another of his books to find the high.

Simenon wrote many novels, finishing them sometimes as quickly as in two or three weeks. You can feel the moment when he just had had enough. He speeds through the last third to get over with it and move on to write yet another. Classic seduction: charm, conquer, and flee. He jilts you but it's worth the ride and the disappointment. Better the inconstant but exciting lover than a faithful but predictable one.

No writer—not even Hemingway—opens his books with such economy and unadorned ease as Simenon does. No one draws you in as quickly on the first paragraph and holds you. No one creates or reveals a character in a phrase or line like him. In a 1955 *Paris Review* interview, Simenon says, "An apple by Cézanne has weight. And it has juice, everything, with just three strokes. I tried to give to my words just the weight that a stroke of Cézanne's gave to an apple."

In the novel *Madame Maigret's Own Case*, we see a woman turn down to the lowest flame a pot of stew she is cooking. She puts on her coat and hat and, before leaving, she quickly checks herself in the mirror and "seeing that everything is all right, rushes out." That little moment illuminates her pride, her vanity, her bourgeois correctness. Simenon makes no mention of her age, height, weight, no description of her hat, coat, shoes, her nose, her hair—all the ponderous, belabored detail that we are told is supposed to make a character vivid, real, and that we immediately forget. But in just a phrase, three strokes, voilà, Simenon's character has volume and personality.

What Simenon does so simply and brilliantly for character he also does in his creation of atmosphere or the mood of his novels. In that same *Paris Review* interview, he says that his sense of atmosphere comes from looking at Impressionist paintings when he was a young boy. I can't imagine how he transposed the sunny dispositions of those paintings into the musty hallways and the half-lit, creaking, dingy tenements, the smells of cooking wafting through a window in summer, the yellowish fog over the Seine in the wet fall, the evocation of Paris of another time before Malraux washed the grand buildings and sent their patina down to the gutters and sewers. Paris before the tearing down of the ancient market at Les Halles and its vans packed with produce and the little bistros serving onion soup at four in the morning. It almost makes you forget that Simenon is from Belgium or that Paris has changed. His atmospherics envelop his novels but never impede the velocity of the narrative.

When asked about Proust, Isaac Singer said, "Does he make you want to turn the page?" Of course, Proust does, but to turn it slowly. I'm not suggesting that velocity is the foremost quality that matters in a novel but the velocity of Simenon's prose sweeps away all the dross, clutter, and manicured verisimilitude of much contemporary fiction. And Simenon pushes aside the idea of writing only "likable" and "relatable" protagonists, the expected staples of standard-issue fiction.

Dirty Snow (published in English in 1951) is set in a small, grisly town in an indeterminate place and time—but clearly during the Nazi occupation of France and Belgium. The master image is of blackened snow, stinking alleyways, dens of steam, smoke, drink, and menace, where a teenager, Frankie, spends his nights. His mother keeps a brothel of two or three girls in her small apartment, where he sleeps and sometimes shares his bed with them. The boy commits murder and robbery and for no apparent reason, and tricks a young woman who loves him into sleeping with an older, slimy man. There are murderers in fiction that one can feel for, who indicate they are a recognizable part of the human tribe—Camus's Meursault, Dostoevsky's Raskolnikov—but Frankie is not one of them. There is nothing redeemable about him, not a shred of decency or feeling or devilish charm that even the most tenderhearted social worker can detect with a microscope.

There is no lovable Maigret, Simenon's famous detective, no welcoming cafés and domestic comforts, no Paris of quaint streets and interesting criminals. This town of dirty snow and gray cold is not even a hell crowded with tortured sinners. Here there is crime for which there is punishment, but there is no justice. Simenon's town lives outside of sin, of good and bad, and, like most life, has no boundaries but power. This is the grimmest novel I have ever read. And perhaps the most moral in its truth.

CODA

All my life I wanted to be near books, to have them close to me, by me when I eat, beside me in bed, and on the little shelf I built in the toilet—a trick I learned from Henry Miller's touching *The Books in My Life*. When a boy, I hated parting with books from the library and was always fined for late return. In my teens, I haunted Book Row on Fourth Avenue in Manhattan and could find the most important, beautiful books in the world for pennies. I did not need fancy bindings and hand-tooled covers; in any case, they do not enrich the literature they harbor. I would carry my newfound treasures in a brown-paper shopping bag on the subway, all the way to the upper Bronx, and imagine them piled up alongside my cot and in an already packed, unpainted pine bookcase. I read on the subway, on the bus, on lunch and coffee breaks from work after I dropped out of high school. I read when I got home and when my mother went to bed with one of her romances, usually a novel of pirates and the women they seized as booty and for ransom but whom they ended up loving instead. I read three or four books at a time, going from one to another like a Casanova on the prowl. I wanted to have friends but had few and none had a passion for reading. I wanted to have a girlfriend and go steady, as that was the height of sophistication for teenagers in the early fifties. I had a beautiful girlfriend but she was always busy. Busy with others.

No one was as sure, as steady, as magical, as mysterious, as sexy, as comforting, as life-giving as anything or anyone I found in the novels I took home. All my life there were disasters in the street, sadness on the subway, heartbreak and betrayals in and out of bed, the world was a disaster, but once I walked into my apartment and saw about me my books on their shelves, I was, I am, safe and maybe even brave.

Frederic Tuten

Among my books I still have some I bought or that were given to me when I was fifteen or sixteen. On those, I made a little drawing of my profile on the flyleaf, and wrote the date of purchase and in careful print the words: "Pelham Parkway, the Bronx." One was *The Magic Mountain*; another, Bowles's *The Sheltering Sky*. These and the others from the past I took wherever I moved or stored them for my return. As long as they were with me I had a history, one more vivid and palpable than a photograph could give me. The books brought with them the damp smells of my Bronx apartment and the spring breezes in the botanical garden where I had read them, the cigarette burns where the ashes fell, the coffee stains on the pages where they were read on the kitchen table, the echoes of the operas broadcast on radio WQXR directly from the Metropolitan every Saturday afternoon. I took *The Sheltering Sky* for Bowles to sign when we were teaching together in Tangiers in 1981. The book had traveled a long way from the fifties. Bowles asked, "Did someone pound this with a baseball bat?"

Suppose there is an afterlife and there are no books there, just waves of words with nothing to hold, no pages to turn, no aroma of paper and ink and dust. Even though there is an eternity of time to read, it would not be the same without the physical entity, the book and its earthly cycle from birth to decay, the once sunny, expectant pages moldering into dust along with the owner. I thought of the history of the burials of the great and the ordinary, and the goods taken by the dead for their future life, whole households of pots and pans and furniture for some, spears and axes for others. I want my books with me, the treasures I have loved and amassed along the way.

No simple coffin will do. I need a mausoleum, like that of the robber baron Jay Gould's mansion-size white pile facing Melville's headstone, up in Woodlawn Cemetery, the last subway stop in the Bronx. Mine would have floor-to-ceiling bookcases, carpeted floors, three or four comfortable leather club chairs, and reading lamps with rose silk shades beside them, and a skylight high above my marble sarcophagus. This is a library that I do not and never shall have in life but that I enjoy imagining will be built after my death. Open to the public, of course, twenty-four hours every day.

—For Jenny Diski

Bride

Julia Elliott

WILDA WHIPS HERSELF with a clump of blackberry brambles. She can feel cold from the stone floor pulsing up into her cowl, chastising her animal body. She smiles. Each morning she thinks of a new penance. Yesterday, she slipped off her woolen stockings and stood outside in the freezing air. The morning before that, she rolled naked in dried thistle. Subsisting on watery soup and stale bread, she has almost subdued her body. Each month when the moon swells, her woman's bleeding is a dribble of burgundy so scant she does not need a rag.

Women are by nature carnal, the Abbot said last night after administering the sacred blood and flesh. *A woman's body has a door, an opening that the Devil may slip through, unless she fiercely barricade against such entry.*

Wilda's body is a bundle of polluted flesh. Her body is a stinking goat. She lashes her shoulders and back. She scourges her arms, her legs, her shrunken breasts, and jutting rib cage. She thrashes the small mound of her belly. She gives her feet a good working over, flagellating her toes and soles. She reaches back to torture the two, poor sinews of her buttocks. And then she repeats the process, doubling the force. She chastises the filthy maggot of her carnality until she feels fire crackling up her backbone. Her head explodes with light. Her soul rejoices like a bird flitting from a dark hut, out into summer air.

Sister Elgaruth is always in the scriptorium before Wilda, just after Prime Service, making her rounds among the lecterns, checking the manuscripts for errors, her hawk nose hovering an inch above each parchment. Wilda sits down at her desk just as the sun rises over the dark wood. She sharpens her quill. She opens her ink pot and takes a deep sniff—pomegranate juice and wine tempered with sulfur—a rich, red ink that reminds her of Christ's blood, the same stuff that stains her fingertips. This is always the happiest time of day—ink perfume in her nostrils, windows blazing with light, her body weightless from the morning's scourge. But then the other nuns come bumbling in, filling the hall with grunts and coughs, fermented breath, smells of winter bodies bundled in dirty wool. Wilda sighs and turns back to *Beastes of God's Worlde*, the manuscript she has been copying for a year, over and over, encountering the creatures of God's Menagerie in different moods and seasons, finding them boring on some days and thrilling on others.

Today she is halfway through the entry on bees, the smallest of God's birds, created on the fifth day. She imagines the creatures spewing from the void, the air hazy and buzzing. In these fallen times, bees hatch from the bodies of oxen and the rotted flesh of dead cows. They begin as worms, squirming in putrid meat, and "transform into bees." Wilda wonders why the manuscript provides no satisfactory information on the nature of this transformation, while going on for paragraphs about the lessons we may learn from creatures that hatch from corpses to become ethereal flying nectar eaters and industrious builders of hives.

How do they get their wings? Do they sleep in their hives all winter or freeze to death? Do fresh swarms hatch from ox flesh each spring?

Wilda is about to scrawl these questions in the margins when she feels a tug on her sleeve. She turns, regards the blunt, sallow face of Sister Elgaruth, which nips all speculation in the bud.

"Sister," croaks Elgaruth, "you stray from God's task."

Wilda turns back to her copying, shaping letters with her crimped right hand.

At lunch in the dining hall, the Abbess sits in her bejeweled chair, rubies representing Christ's blood gleaming in the dark mahogany. Though the Abbess is stringy and yellow as a dried parsnip, everybody knows she has a sweet tooth, that she dotes on white flour, pheasants roasted in honey, wine from the Canary Islands. Her Holiness wears ermine collars and anoints her withered neck with myrrh. Two prioresses hunch on each side of her, Sister Ethelburh and Sister Willa, slurping up cabbage soup with pious frowns. They cast cold glances at the table of new girls.

The new girls have no Latin. They bark the English language, lacing familiar words with the darkness of their mother tongue. One of them, Aoife, works in the kitchen with Wilda on Saturdays and Sundays. Aoife works hard, chopping a hundred onions, tears streaming down her cheeks. She sleeps in a cell six doors down from Wilda's.

Sometimes, when Wilda roams the night hall to calm her soul after matins, she sees Aoife blustering through, red hair streaming. And Wilda feels the tug of curiosity. She wants to follow the girl into her room, hear her speak the language of wolves and foxes.

Now, as Wilda's tablemates spout platitudes about the heavy snows God keeps dumping upon the convent in March, the new girls erupt into rich laughter. They bray and howl, snigger and snort. Dark vapors hover over them. A turbulence. A hullabaloo. The Abbess slams her goblet down on the table. And the wild girls stifle their mirth. But Wilda can see that Aoife's strange amber eyes are still laughing, even though her mouth is pinched into a frown.

At vespers, the gouty Abbot is drunk again. His enormous head gleams like a broiled ham. He says that the world, drenched in sin, is freezing into a solid block of ice. He says that women are ripe for the Devil's attentions. He says their tainted flesh lures the Devil like a spicy, rancid bait. The Abbot describes the Evil One scrambling through a woman's window in the darkness of night. Knuckles upon pulpit, he mimics the sound of Satan's dung-caked hooves clomping over cobblestones. He asks the nuns to picture the naked beast: face of a handsome man of thirty, swarthy skinned, raven haired, goat horns poking from his brow, the muscular chest of a lusty layman, but below the waist he's all goat.

It has been snowing since November and the nuns are pale, anemic, scrawny. They are afflicted with scurvy, night blindness, nervous spasms, and melancholy. Unlike the monks across the meadow, they don't tend a vineyard at their convent. And when the Abbot describes the powerful thighs of Satan, the stinking flurry of hair and goat flesh, a young nun screams. A small, mousy thing who never says a word. She opens her mouth and yowls like a cat. And then she blinks. She stands. She scurries from the chapel.

After the Abbot's sermon, Wilda tosses on her pallet, unable to banish the image from her mind: the vileness of two polluted animal bodies twisting together in a lather of poisonous sweat. She jumps out of bed and snatches her clump of blackberry brambles. She gives her ruttish beast of a body a good thrashing, chastising every square inch of stinking meat from chin to toes. She whips herself until she floats. God's love is an ocean sparkling in the sun, and Wilda's soul

61

is a droplet, a molecule of moisture lifted into the air. When she opens her eyes, she does not see her humble stone cell with its straw pallet and hemp quilt; she sees heavenly skies in pink tumult, angels slithering through clouds. She sees the Virgin held aloft by a throng of naked cherubs, doves nesting in her golden hair.

In her melodious voice, the Virgin speaks of Jesus Christ her Son, his tears of ruby blood. The Virgin says her son will return to Earth in May to walk among flowers and bees.

When the bell rings for matins, Wilda is still up, pacing, her braids unraveling. Somehow, she tidies herself. Somehow, she transports her body to the chapel, where three dozen sleepy-eyed virgins have gathered at two in the freezing morning to revel in Jesus's love.

At breakfast, Wilda drinks her beer but does not touch her bread. Now she is floating through the scriptorium. She has slept a mere thirty minutes the night before. She has a runny catarrh from standing in the freezing wind with her hood down, and she shivers. But her heart burns, a flame in the hallowed nook of her chest.

You are all Christ's brides, said the Abbot this morning. *Do not break the seal that seals you both together.*

"I am the bride of Christ," Wilda whispers as she sits down at her lectern. She opens her ink, sniffs the bloodred brew. She has a burning need to describe the voice of the Virgin, the frenzy of beating angel wings as the heavens opened to let the Sacred Mother descend. She wants to capture the looks on their faces, wrenched and fierce. But there's Sister Elgaruth, wheezing behind her. Wilda turns, regards the sooty kernel of flesh that adorns Sister Elgaruth's left nostril. Elgaruth is one of God's creatures, magnificent, breathing, etched of flesh and bone.

"Sister," says the old woman, "mind the missing word in your last paragraph."

Elgaruth points with her crooked finger, deformed from decades of copying, too crimped to copy text.

"Forgive me. I will be more mindful."

Sister Elgaruth shuffles off. Wilda eyes the shelves where the unbound vellum is stashed, noting the locked drawer that stores the choicest sheets, stripped from the backs of stillborn lambs. She has never touched the silky stuff, which is reserved for the three ancient virgins who have been penning a Psalter for an archbishop.

Now, when Sister Elgaruth departs to the lavatory, Wilda tiptoes over to the old woman's lectern. She opens the first drawer, notes a pot of rosemary balm, the twig Elgaruth uses to pick dark wax from her ears. The second drawer contains a Psalter, prayer beads, a bundle of dried lavender. In the third drawer, beneath a crusty handkerchief, is a carved wooden box, four keys within it, looped on a hemp ring. Wilda snatches the keys, hurries to the vellum drawer, tries two keys before unlocking the most sacred sheets. By the time Sister Elgaruth returns, Wilda is back at her desk, three stolen sheets stuffed in her cowl pocket. Her heart, a wild bird, beats within her chest.

She turns back to *Beastes of God's Worlde.*

The goats bloode is so hotte with luste it wille dissolve the hardest diamonde.

In the kitchen, Aoife chops the last carrots from the root cellar, brown shriveled witches' fingers. Aoife is pale, freckled, quick with her knife. She sings a strange song and smiles. She turns to Wilda. In the Abbot's pompous voice, she croaks a pious tidbit about the darkness of woman's flesh—a miraculous imitation. For a second the Abbot is right there in the kitchen, ankle-deep in onion skins, standing in the steam of boiling cabbage. Wilda feels an eruption of joy in her gut. She lets out a bray of laughter. Sister Lufe turns from her pot of beans to give them both the stink eye. Wilda smirks at Aoife, takes up a cabbage, and peels off rotted leaves, layer after slimy layer, until she uncovers the fresh, green heart of the vegetable.

Wilda kneels on bruised knees. She has no desk, only a crude, short table of gnarled elm. Tucked beneath it are sheets of lamb vellum, her quills, a pot of stolen ink. She faces east. Her window is a small square of hewn stone. Outside, snow has started to fall again, and Wilda, who has no fire, rejoices in the bone-splitting cold. She's mumbling. Shiver after shiver racks her body. And soon she feels nothing. Her candle flame sputters. She smells fresh lilies.

The Virgin steps from the empyrean into the world of flesh and mud.

The glow from her body burns Wilda's eyes.

The words from her mouth are like musical thunder in Wilda's ears.

"My Son will return to choose a bride," says the Virgin, "a pearl without spot."

And then the Virgin is lifted by angel throng, back into the realm of pure fire.

Wilda sits stunned as the snow thickens outside. She prays. She whips herself. And then she takes up her plume. She tries to describe the beauty of the Virgin. At first, her words get stuck, stunned as flies in a spill of honey. But then she begins with a simple sentence, in tiny, meticulous script.

Whenne the virgin descended I smelde apples and oceane winde.

At Prime Service the Abbess keeps coughing—fierce convulsions that shake her whole body. She flees the chapel with her two prioress flunkies, eyes streaming. The Abbot pauses, and then he returns to his theme of Hell as a solid block of ice, the Devil frozen at its core. Satan is a six-headed beast with thirty-six sets of bat wings on his back. The Evil One must perpetually flap these wings to keep the ninth circle of Hell freezing cold.

Wilda frowns, trying to grasp the paradox of Hell as ice, wondering how this same Devil, frozen at the center of Hell, can also slip through her window at night, burning with lust, every pore on his body steaming. But it's morning, and the Abbot is sober. When he returns for vespers, his imagination inflamed with wine, he will speak of carnal commerce between women and Satan. But this morning his theme is ice.

Today is the first day of April, and a crust of snow covers the dead grass.

The chickens aren't laying. The cows give scant milk.

The meat cellar boasts nothing but hard sausage, ox tails, and salted pigs' feet.

The beets are blighted, the cabbages soft with rot.

But Wilda smiles, for she knows that Christ will return this blessed month, descending from Heaven with a great whoosh of balmy air. She has described the glory in her secret book: trees flowering and fruiting simultaneously, lambs frolicking on beds of fresh mint, the ground decked with lilies as Christ walks across the greening Earth to fetch his virgin bride.

*

On Sunday, in the kitchen, Aoife puts two bits of turnip into her mouth, mimicking the Abbess's crooked teeth. Crossing her eyes, Aoife walks with the Abbess's arrogant shuffle, head held high and sneering. Wilda doubles over, clutches her gut. She staggers and sputters as laughter rocks through her. Her eyes leak. She wheezes and brays. At last, the mirth subsides. Wilda leans against the cutting table, dizzy, relishing the warmth from the fire. A stew, dark with the last of the dried mushrooms, bubbles in the cauldron. Aoife, still sniggering, places her hand on Wilda's arm. Wilda feels a delicious heat burning through her sleeve. Aoife's smile sparkles with mischief, and the young nun smells of sweat and cinnamon.

Wilda's body floats as she looks into Aoife's honey-colored eyes, pupils shrinking, irises etched with green. Aoife murmurs something in her mother tongue. But then she speaks English.

"Man is a rational, moral animal, capable of laughter."

Aoife removes her hand and turns back to her bucket of turnips.

The Abbess is dead by Tuesday. Her body, dressed in a scarlet cowl, rests on a bier in the chapel. The Abbot, fearing plague, sends a small, nervous prior to conduct the service. The chapel echoes with the coughs of sickly nuns. The prior covers his mouth with a ruby rag. He hurries through the absolution, flinging holy water with a brisk flick of his fingers, and departs. Three farmers haul the body away.

That night, a hailstorm batters the stone convent, sending down stones the size of eggs, keeping the nuns awake with constant patter. Sisters whisper that the world has fallen ill, that God will purge the sin with ice. No one arrives from the monastery to conduct the morning service, and nuns pray silently in the candlelit chapel.

Contemplating the body of Christ, Wilda kneels before her little book, waiting for words to come. She sees him, torn from the cross, limp in the Virgin's arms. He is pale, skinny as an adolescent boy. His side wound, parted like a coy mouth, reveals glistening, pomegranate flesh. Other than the flowing tresses and silky beard, Christ is hairless, with smooth skin and nipples the color of plums. He has a woman's lips, a woman's soft, yearning eyes. Wilda imagines him waking up in his tomb, cadaverous flesh glowing like a firefly in the cryptic darkness. His groin is covered with loose gauze. His hair hangs halfway down his back, shining like a copper cape when he emerges into the sunlight.

The world is frozen in sinne, Wilda writes, *frozen until the Lammbbe descendes to walk among floweres and bees. He wille strewe his marriage bed with lilies. Hallelujah!*

Fifteen nuns have been taken by the plague, their bodies carted off by farmers. Not even a prior will set foot in the convent, but the nuns shuffle through their routine, sit coughing and praying in the silent chapel, their hearts choked with black bile. They pine for spring. But the heavens keep dumping grain after grain of nasty frost onto the stone fortress. In mid-April, the clouds thicken, and a freak blizzard descends like a great beast from the sky, vanquishing the world with snow.

Prioress Ethelburh orders the nuns to stay in their rooms praying, to leave only for the lavatory. Kitchen workers will still prepare food but the nuns will no longer gather in the refectory for fellowship. Victuals will be taken from door to door to stave off the contagion.

In the kitchen Aoife is bleary-eyed, and Wilda worries that the plague has struck her. But then the poor girl is weeping over her pot of dried peas.

"What is it, Sister?" Wilda moves toward her.

"Nothing," says Aoife, "just the sadness of winter and death."

But then Aoife pulls up her cowl sleeve, shows Wilda her thin arm—pale and finely shaped, mottled with pink blisters.

Wilda jumps back, fearing contagion.

"Only burns," Aoife whispers, "from Prioress Ethelburh's hellish candle."

Wilda allows her knuckles to stray across Aoife's soft cheek.

"I was out walking in the garden," says Aoife, "watching the moon shine on the snow, and she . . ."

Sister Lufe bustles in with a rank wheel of sheep's cheese, and the two girls jump apart. Aoife dumps melted snow into her pot of dried peas (the well is frozen). Wilda hacks at a black cured beef tongue (the last of it). Outside, the sun glares down on the endless white blight of snow. The trees are rimed with frost, the woodpile obscured, the garden paths obliterated.

*

Wilda kneels on cold stone, stomach grumbling. For supper she had three spoons of watery cabbage soup and a mug of barley beer. The crude brew still sings in her bloodstream as she takes up pen and parchment.

The Lammbbe will come again, she writes, murmuring the word *Lammbbe*, reveling in its deep, buzzing hum. She closes her eyes, pictures Jesus hot and carnified, walking through snow. Frost melts upon contact with his burning flesh. *Walking accrosse the barren earthe*, she writes, *the Lammbbe wille leeve a hotte traile of lillies.* When he steps into the convent orchard, the cherry trees burst into bloom. *Thirty-sixe virgines stand in white arraye, pearles withoute spotte.* The nuns stand in order of age upon the lawn, ranging from thirteen-year-old Sister Ilsa to sixty-eight-year-old Elgaruth. Jesus pauses before twenty-three-year-old Wilda. He smiles with infinite wisdom. He touches her cheek with his hand, peers into her eyes to look upon her naked soul. Wilda feels the heat from his spirit. At first she can't look at his face. But then she looks up from the grass and sees him: eyes like molten gold, lips parted to show a hint of pearly teeth, a tongue as pink as a peony.

"My bride," he says.

And cherubim scream withe joye, squirminge naked in the frothe of heavene.

The shrieks grow louder—so loud that Wilda looks up from her book. She's back in the convent, hunkered on the cold floor. She gets up, walks down the hallway, turns left by the lavatory. The screaming is coming from the sad room where nuns are punished, but Wilda has never heard a ruckus in the middle of the night. She peeks in, sees Aoife seated, skirts pulled up, hair wild, eyes huge and streaming. Prioress Ethelburh twists the young nun's arms behind her back. Prioress Willa burns Aoife's creamy left thigh with red-hot pincers. This time, Aoife does not scream. She bites her lip. She looks up, sees Wilda standing in the doorway. Their eyes meet. A secret current flows between them. Ethelburh turns toward Wilda, her mouth wrenched with wrath, but then a violent cough rocks through her. She shakes, sputters, drops to the floor. And Aoife leaps from the chair like a wild rabbit. In a flash she is halfway down the hall.

"Surely mockers are with me," says Prioress Willa, casting her clammy fish eye upon Wilda, "and my eye gazes on their provocation."

*

67

The next morning, Ethelburh is dead, her body dragged beyond the courtyard by hulking Sister Githa, a poor half-wit fearless of contagion. Twelve bodies lie frozen near the edge of the wood, to be buried when the ground thaws.

Aoife is singing in her mother tongue, the words incomprehensible to Wilda, pure and abstract as birdsong, floating amid the steam of the kitchen. Poor old Lufe is dead. Hedda and Lark have passed. Only Hazel, the girl who carries bowls from door to door, loiters in the larder, bolder now that Lufe is gone, inspecting the dwindling bags of flour.

"Prioress Willa has taken to her bed," whispers Aoife.

"God bless her soul," says Wilda, crossing herself.

Aoife chops the last of the onions. Wilda picks worms from the flour. And the soup smells strange: boiled flesh of a stringy old hen.

"Sister," says Aoife, her mouth dipping close to Wilda's ear, "I have heard that the Abbess kept food in her chamber. Pickled things and sweetmeats. A shame to let it go to waste, with our sisters half starved and weak."

Snow falls outside the kitchen door, which is propped open with a log to let the smoke drift out. The light in the courtyard is a strange dusky pink, even though it is afternoon. Wilda thinks of Jesus, multiplying fishes and loaves. She sees the bread materializing, hot and swollen with yeast. She pictures the fish—teeming, shimmering, and salty in wooden pails.

"Sister," says Wilda, "you speak the truth."

The Abbess lived in the turret over the library, and the two nuns tiptoe up winding stairs. The door is locked. Aoife smirks and fishes a key from her pocket. Aoife opens the door and steps into the room first. Wilda stumbles after her, bumps into Aoife's softness, stands breathing in the darkness, smelling mold and rot and stale perfume—myrrh, incense, vanilla. Aoife pushes dusty drapes aside, discovering windowpanes in a diamond pattern, alternating ruby and clear. The nuns marvel at the furnishings: the spindly settee upholstered in brocade, the ebony wardrobe with pheasants carved into its doors, several gilded trunks, and the grandest bed they have ever seen: big as a barge, the coverlet festooned in crimson ruffles, the canopy draped in wine velvet. Wilda wonders how the crooked little Abbess climbed into this enormity each night, and then she spots a ladder of polished wood leaning against the bed.

Aoife opens a trunk, pulls out forbidden things: a lute, a fur-lined cape, a crystal vial of perfume, and a bottle of belladonna. They find a clockwork mouse that creeps when you wind it up (a mechanism that Aoife, oddly, seems to understand). The girls giggle as the mouse moves across the floor. Aoife strokes the ermine cape as though it is a sleeping beast. Wilda leans against the settee, but does not allow herself to sit. The second trunk is chock-full of dainty food: small clay jars of pickled things, dried fruit in linen sacks, hard sausages in cheesecloth, venison jerky, nuts, honey, wine.

Aoife opens a pot of pickled herring, sniffs, eats a mouthful, chews, and then offers the fish to Wilda. They taste fresh, briny, tinged with lemon. Something awakens in Wilda, a tiny sea monster in her stomach, so weak and shriveled that she hardly knew it existed. She feels it stretching strange tentacles, opening its fanged mouth to unleash a wild groan. Wilda is starving. She gnaws at a twisted strand of venison, tasting forests in the salty meat, the deer shot by a nobleman's arrow, strips roasted over open flame. When Aoife opens a pot of strawberry preserves, she moans as sweetness fills the room—a kind of sorcery, the essence of a sun-warmed berry field trapped in a tiny crock. Aoife eats with her fingers, tears in the creases of her eyes. And then she offers the jar to Wilda. Wilda pauses, feels the monster slithering in her gut, dips a finger, and tastes the rich, seedy jelly.

"Hallelujah!" she whispers, smacking her lips. She eats more strawberries. Offers the pot to Aoife. But Aoife has discovered a stash of sugared almonds. Wilda tries them: butter roasted with cinnamon and cloves, a hint of salt, some other spice, unfamiliar, bewitching. The nuns sit down on the soft settee and spread their feast on a carved trunk. They eat smoked fish, dried apricots, pickled carrots, and red currant jam. Suddenly very thirsty, they have no choice but to uncork a bottle of wine, passing it between them. After shaving off teal mold with a small gilded knife, they consume a chunk of hard cheese. And then they discover, wrapped in lilac gauze, a dozen pink marzipan rabbits.

The monster in Wilda's stomach lets out a bellow. She can picture it, lolling in a hot stew of food, the scales on its swollen belly glistening. She pops a candy into her mouth, closes her eyes, tastes manna, angel food, milk of paradise. The young nuns drink more wine. And now Aoife is up on her feet. She opens the Abbess's wardrobe, rifles through gowns and cloaks. She pulls out a winter frock, thick velvet, the luminous color of moss, sable fur around the neck and cuffs. Wilda looks away as Aoife undresses.

"How do I look?" Aoife asks, still buttoning up the bodice, contorting like an acrobat as though she has pulled on fine frocks a hundred times before.

Wilda tries to speak, but the words will not come. Her throat feels dry. She takes another swig of wine.

The dress brings out the secret lights in Aoife's eyes, the swan-like curve of her neck.

Wilda feels ugly, small, though she has not seen her reflection in a good, clear mirror in seven years, not since her parents and brother died and her aunt sent her off to the convent.

Aoife chooses a fur cloak from the wardrobe, slips it over Wilda's shoulders. Wilda feels cold, but then a feeling of delicious warmth overtakes her, and her spine relaxes. Aoife picks up the lute, strums a strange tune, sings a song in her mother tongue that makes Wilda feel like she's dream flying, her stomach buckling as she soars too fast into whirling stars, the air thin and strange and barely breathable.

Imitating the Abbess, Aoife hobbles over to the bed, climbs up the ladder, peeks over the edge at Wilda, who can't stop laughing.

"It's a boat," Aoife says, crawling around like a child. Wilda remembers her brother, galloping around on his stick horse. Memories like these stopped haunting her two years ago, part of the earthly existence she has kept at bay. Now she remembers the two of them rolling in the garden, flowers in their fists, singing bawdy songs they barely understood, laughing so hard she thought her ribs would crack. She remembers the way her parents would scold them with stanched smiles, trying not to laugh themselves.

Wilda climbs up the ladder. She sits beside Aoife on the high bed. The stiff fabric of the coverlet smells of must and myrrh.

"Look!" says Aoife, opening a cabinet built into the bed's headboard. Inside is a crystal decanter encrusted with a ruby cross, a burgundy liquid inside it. Aoife sniffs, takes a sip.

"Wine," she says dreamily, "though it might be some kind of liqueur."

Aoife offers the bottle. Wilda drinks, tasting blackberries and brine and blood, she thinks, though she has never tasted blood, for the Sacrament does not transubstantiate until it passes into the kettle of the stomach, where it is boiled by the liver's heat, the same way alchemists turn base metals into gold. Some kind of matter floats in the liquid. Wilda feels grit between her teeth. The grit dissolves and the world glows, a fresh surge of pink light shining through red windowpanes.

Aoife's hand scurries like a white mouse over the coverlet to stroke Wilda's left wrist. Their fingers intertwine. Wilda marvels at the deliciousness of the warmth streaming between them.

The two sisters sit holding hands, leaning against thick down pillows, sipping the strange concoction at the very top of a stone fortress, snow falling in the eternal twilight outside—upon the monastery and meadows and forests, upon frozen ponds and farms and villages. They discuss beasts in winter, the mysteries of hibernation, the burrows and holes where furry animals and scaly things sleep.

"Do you think their blood freezes?" whispers Aoife, her breath on Wilda's cheek. "Do you think they dream?"

Wilda has the strange feeling that everyone in the world is dead. That she and Aoife are completely alone in an enchanted castle. That they are just on the verge of some miraculous transformation.

Wilda wakes to the clanging of monastery bells. She clutches her throbbing head. She tries to sit up, thinking she's on her cot. But then she smells musty perfumes, odors of pickled fish and honey, and her cheeks burn as the previous night's feast comes back to her in patches. How had it happened so fast?

Her swollen belly throbs with queasiness, the sea monster slithering in a mash of wine and food. She has no choice but to lean over the bedside and heave a foul gruel onto the floor. Bright sunlight shines through the windows. How long has she been asleep? She turns to Aoife, still dozing beside her. Not Aoife—where is Aoife?— but the Abbess's fur cloak, crumpled, patched with bald spots, sprawling like a mangy bear. She remembers a tale from her childhood, about a fair woman who turned into a bear. The she-bear scratched out the eyes of lovesick hunters and devoured them whole. The bear, like Aoife, had eyes the color of honey. She sang with the voice of a nightingale, luring hunters into deep woods.

Wilda climbs down from the bed, hurries back to her cell, and latches her door. She paces around the cramped space, feeling the rankness of the flesh upon her bones, the puffery of her belly, the sea monster roiling within. Her brow and cheeks are hot. She wants to check on Aoife, see how she feels, laugh about the previous night's feast—a whim, a trifle, nothing—but her skin burns with shame. She

71

pictures Aoife singing in her green dress. She imagines fur sprouting from her freckled skin, yellow claws popping from her fingertips.

Wilda vows to stay in her room without eating, without sleeping, whipping herself until the hideous sea monster ceases to squirm in her belly, until she has purged her flesh of excess fluid and heat and is again a bird-boned vessel of divine love—arid, clean, glowing with the Word. She has a clay bottle of water, almost full, the only thing she needs.

Wilda kneels on the floor, naked, whipping herself for the third time, bored with the effect, not feeling much in the way of spinal tingling, her mind as dull as a scummy pond. She sighs. Tries not to think of Aoife, the lightness of her laughter. She contemplates Christ in his agony—hauling the cross, grimacing as iron nails are hammered into his feet and hands, staring stoically at the sun on an endless after-noon, thorns pricking his roasted brow. But the images feel rote like a rosary prayer. So she hangs her whip on a nail and lies down on her bed. She watches her window, waiting for the day to go dark, the light outside milky and tedious. She hasn't eaten for two days, but her belly feels puffed up like a lusty toad. Contemplating the beauty of Christ's rib cage, the exquisite concavity of his starved and hair-less stomach, she shivers.

When she hears the giggle of young nuns running down the hall-way outside her door, her heart beats faster. And there's Aoife again, knocking softly with her knuckles.

"Sister Wilda," says Aoife, "won't you take some food?"

Wilda says nothing.

"Sister Wilda," says Aoife, "are you well?"

"I am," says Wilda, her voice an ugly croak, her throat full of yellow bile.

Her heart sinks as Aoife slips away.

When Wilda wakes up, some kind of flying creature is flapping around her room. A candle flickers on her writing table, her book still open there.

She spots a flash of wing in a corner. A dove-sized angel hovers beside her door like a trapped bird wanting out. An emissary, Wilda thinks, come to tell her that Christ is near. Wilda unlatches the door, peeks out into the dark hallway, and lets the creature out. The angel floats, wings lashing, and motions for her to follow. The angel darts down the hall, a streak of frantic light. Wilda lopes after it, feeling dizzy, chilled. They pass the lavatory, the empty infirmary. The angel flies out into the courtyard and flits toward the warming house, where smoke puffs from both chimneys. Crunching through snow, Wilda follows the angel into the blazing room.

The angel disappears with a diamond flash of light.

Fires rage in both hearths. And there, basking on a mattress heaped with fine pillows, is Aoife. Dressed in the green gown, drinking something from a silver communion goblet, Aoife smiles. Hazel lolls beside her in sapphire velvet, munching on marzipan, an insolent look on her face.

"Sister." Aoife sits up, eyes glowing like sunlit honey. "Come warm your bones."

Overcome with a fit of coughing, Wilda can't speak. It takes all of her strength to turn away from the delicious warmth, the smells of almond and vanilla, from beautiful Aoife with her wine-stained lips and copper hair. Hacking, Wilda flees, runs through the frozen courtyard, through empty stone passageways where icicles dangle from the eaves, back to her cell, where she collapses, shivering, onto her cot.

When Wilda wakes up, her room is packed with angels, swarms of them, glowing and glowering and thumping against walls. An infestation of angels, they brush against her skin, sometimes burning, sometimes freezing. She hurries to her desk, kneels, and takes up her plume.

A hoste of angells flashing like waspes on a summer afternoone. My fleshe burned, but I felte colde.

One of the creatures whizzes near her and makes a furious face—eyes bugged, scarlet cheeks puffed. Another perches on her naked shoulder, digging claws into her skin. Wilda shudders, shakes the creature off. A high-pitched humming, interspersed with sharp squeaks, fills the room as the throng moves toward the door. She opens the door, follows the cloud of celestial beings down the hallway, past the infirmary, out into the kitchen courtyard.

Wind howls. Granules of ice strike her bare skin as Wilda follows the angels toward the orchard. Her heart pounds, for surely the moment has come: The fruit grove glows with angelic light. Wilda can see skeletal trees sparkling with ice, a million flakes of wind-whipped snow, the darkness of the forest beyond. And there, just at the edge of the woods, the shape of a man on horseback. The angels sweep down the hill toward the woods and wait, buzzing with frustration as Wilda trudges barefooted through knee-deep snow. But her feet are not cold. Her entire body burns with miraculous warmth. And now she can see the man more clearly, dressed in a green velvet riding suit, a few strands of copper hair spilling from his tall hat. His mouth puckers with a pretty smile. His eyes are enormous, radiant, yellow as apricots.

Five Poems
Paul Hoover

THE BOOK OF UNNAMED THINGS

The house where he was born
fills with dust and birdsong.
Its rafters crash in memory.

She begs of the book of measure
a seam of restlessness and also
desperation. No title yet
for the book of names.

What to do with unnamed things
and the shadows they are cut from?
A sun for the book of origins,
moon for the book of sources.

He took the road of snow
to the house of exhaustion
where the book of ice was written
in the language of rain.

She sang in rain the ending
of a life too weary to speak.
The book of the sea was written
in the book of all that is.

He sang things into being,
recited the book of life
to a melon patch and dog days.

She was born and crawled sideways
toward a light she remembered.
She stands in the book of standing,

Paul Hoover

writes a page in the book of night,
sleeps one day and the everlasting.

He leans in the book of leaning.
Time, he knows, is on his side,
the vagrant house, wandering far,
hand of fire on the throat of fire,
the book of sand, its pages turning.

She unwrites what's before her,
keeps close what's gone away.
She asks the ceiling to oversee
what's spoken and what's silent,
a reason for the book of ending,
and just cause for beginning.

WRITTEN

The written stone rests
in the unwritten river;
unwritten rain is falling
over the written town.

Nothing written today,
but tomorrow you'll be written
as you sit in your room not writing.

Lo, it is written.
Pollen writes on the stamen.
The man writes a child
in the body of the woman.

Your eyes write the view
into the window,
but it doesn't stay forever.
It returns with you into the unwritten.

All that means is written.
Lo, a tiger of a word
has escaped its cage.

Our quiet words
wait beneath the stair
for a reason to speak,
an edge or fold or cause
to remark. *Oh*, we say,
no way and *no how*.

This is how the world begins,
dark branches written
against a white sky.

The written stone rests
in the written river;
written rain falls
over the written town.

HANDWRITTEN

this is handwritten
        touched by no voice

hand and mind moving
        in search of a dwelling

a form of resurrection
        the language rich in spoor

something like infinity
        plus the number one

sensations aren't fictions
        distances reach your skin

become the world you're in
        the scent of lemon peel

reminds you of the real
        summerbread, heartleaf

serve as "groundation"
      not intrusions but the basis

meadow comes to mead
      mountain to its scree

night wears night glasses
      feeling for its way

the deepest cut is absence
      its essences running in

forty-watt glamour
      of words upon the page

whose intentions are we
      call the night watchman

the pig from his pen
      our father in heaven

must have been dreaming
      impercipience please

not the gold standard
      eagles are not endless

and neither is resemblance
      a woman's green face

laughing in the painting
      matter, *mutter*, is only matter

it doesn't love or hate
      the bullet doesn't despise

the body it pierces
      it's only following orders

a hummingbird pierces the flower
      looks quickly into your eye

so busy it's hazy
        and where does it sleep

we are on our way
        never quite arriving

our words are only stations
        metaphysical weather

for an actual grammar
        summer seems to be slipping

back into the spring
        the shine on each leaf

knows what we're thinking
        it won't be long now

before all is known
        if not quite understood

squirrels fly
        birds swim

shadows don't lean
        their objects do

get out of paradise
        your pronoun knows

there's a sale on shoes
        at J. C. Penney

Paul Hoover

DEAD MAN WRITING

The dead man smells of cigars and roses,
of turpentine and persimmons.
The dead man yells, but only the cat,
grown far too thin, and a lonely child
named Moises can hear him.

Erect in a kitchen chair,
in the place where he had lived,
his hand moves heavily over the page.
The boy hears him scratching
and thinks the cat wants in.

Soon he has filled a page,
then many pages, but he is not revived.
His writing fills one room then another.

The dead man is not distinct
from the shadow of his hand.
The stain of his pen is great.
We believe the world was created
in a similar fashion.

In most rooms,
there is light somewhere,
allowing a face to be seen
or the size of a dead man's shoe.
Light insists more than darkness;
it can awaken a room entirely.

A mouse also lives there,
chased all night by the cat.
They move like breath in a furious circle,
like the soft liquid of an eye
intent upon seeing.

THE BOOK OF NOTHING

Nothing isn't empty.
It fills a room so completely
it spills into the street.
Everything comes from nothing.
Something, poor something,
stands vacant at the door.
A rose opens and opens
until its petals fall.
Then it seems vacant,
like a room with one chair.

Beauty is always fading.
We know an object best
when it starts to disappear.
Words are here but nothing,
meaningful sounds passing
then nothing but pleasure.
Light and space are something
passing through the trees.
A cry is heard in the distance.
It is something briefly
and then present absence.

A background seems like nothing
until a figure emerges, from what
seems the beginning.
But there is no beginning.
Something always comes before,
receding here, approaching there.
Only you remain
to bring it back from somewhere—
that shade of blue in the hallway,
black depths of the water.
Yellow fires, gray earth, and green
of wheat are something: actors
without equal, cock-crowing town.

Everything nature says
is ancient, careless, and cruel,
but it has no concept of nothing.
Leaning against a sunlit wall,
it projects casually something.
A mirror out of doors
catches the eye because
our eyes are in it, because
it seems to eye us
as part of its nature.

The overlord language resides
there, too: a stain, nerve knot,
with its incessant naming.
It comes into being, breathes,
then fades away again.
What was that? we ask.
Did you hear something?
It was nothing, says the cook.
A ghost, insists the chaplain.
It was dinner, says the hen,
so philosophical lately,
and always about one thing.

Three Found Books
Aimee Bender

ATTIC

SHE FOUND THE BOOK in the attic of the house she'd bought with the money from her parents' will. She was their only child, and they had saved mightily over many years and she paid for the house outright. It was blue, with a white door and a thatched roof. Inside, up a step-ladder, one could hide in the attic, which was surprisingly clean and open, without boards sticking up or spiderwebs growing. She suspected the previous owners had used it for some purpose, but she could not imagine what, as most activities required furniture of some sort. She did find the book, though, on the second visit. Leaning against a sloped wall. It was an old hardback book, and on the cover it said *Things People Say*. The author's name was not listed. The book had no ISBN number or publisher name but it seemed to predate the self-publishing industry so she did not know quite how it existed. It was blank inside, too. Almost like a joke: *Things People Say* and then the implication of nothing. Ah, she thought, turning the pages. I get it, she thought. Ha-ha. But she kept turning the pages, pulled on by some urge she could not name, and about a third of the way in, she found a filled-in page. "I say it's over, John," the page read, in ball-point pen. "That's what I say to you and your stupid gifts. I hate that shawl. I hate it, and the dinner, and the daisies. I am allergic. How can you not know that? Done. I am finally done." Three pages later, in a new and looser handwriting: "OK, Jean. It's over, then. I see this and I agree. I'm tired of apologizing and getting it all wrong. Just tell me how to go about it." Three pages later: "John, you are so passive. I can't tell you how to leave me."

Three pages later: "Jean, you have not left. We are going about our business as usual. Is it over?"

Three pages later: "It is over, John. I am going about our business as an actor now. I like the house too much to leave. You are still here for your own reasons. But it is over."

Nothing for about twenty pages. Then:

83

"You seem like yourself, like usual, lately, Jean. Have you been acting the whole time?"

Three pages later: "No."

"I can't seem to tell when you are acting and when you are not." (Also three pages later, for this and every subsequent entry.)

"This is why it is over. You can't tell? This is exactly like the daisies. This is exactly my point."

"Can others tell?"

"To what others am I married?"

"Can you tell?"

And that was it for the rest of the book.

The new owner sat in the attic quietly. It was just so clean, the cleanest attic she'd ever seen, and the floorboards were a golden pine color. The walls leaned in to form a peak and someone had built a skylight into the northern slant leaving a stretched square of sunlight on the rug sample left behind that was the shape of Utah. It was, the woman thought, probably the most peaceful place she had ever been, despite what she'd just read. She leaned the book carefully against the wall again, went downstairs, and made herself a dinner in the kitchen using the old but functional appliances.

As she ate her dinner, she thought about the owners whom she'd met briefly when she bought the house. They were older, pleasant, chatted without tension; the woman wore a bun that made her resemble a woodcut. That's what the buyer had thought: I've never met a woman so close to resembling a woodcut, she remembered thinking. Even the wrinkles on her cheeks seemed less like skin creases and more like someone with clear skin who had been roughly etched. The man looked like a regular man. It was the woman who seemed at once drawn and real. So she knew the book belonged to them because it was the same problem raised in the book itself. As far as she could tell, they were still together when she'd completed the house purchase and had moved as a team to another smaller house about thirty minutes away.

The light dimmed outside. She drank a glass of wine with her dinner. Brussels sprouts and a ham sandwich.

She, once, had lived briefly with a man who reminded her of a sculpture. At first it had been a compliment—that he was so burnished and beautiful, his skin and his musculature. But then she started to see him as inert when he would lie there with her in bed, his muscles frozen in some way, his tautness no longer attractive but seeming to indicate a person who could not relax. And come to think of it, there was her best friend in grade school who had the eyes of a watercolor, whose tears even seemed pale blue, whose features were unformed, washy, whose parents instructed her every move until her face itself began to lose specificity and when they were no longer friends the woman had trouble even locating her friend at school, even spying her in the hall. That friend had almost drowned in a neighbor's swimming pool and people had wondered if it was deliberate. Drowned? She hadn't ever put it together before. It was too perfect. Of course it had been a suicide attempt. She had nearly washed away already and was only taking one more step. For the first time in years she thought she ought to reach out to that girl, hoping she was still alive. I'll do that, she thought to herself. I should've been a better friend. She returned to the kitchen and retrieved a brownie she'd bought for herself, cutting out a square so she could eat it over several days. She looked out the darkening window thinking of all the people she'd met who were made of art and not life. And here I am, she thought, a single woman eating a corner of brownie sipping wine in a house bought from grief, she thought. Be careful, lady, she told herself. Or you will become a Hopper or a lonesome black-and-white photograph from Beginning Photography Class in no time.

She got busy with cleaning and forgot to reach out to the grade-school friend.

It would be months before she ventured into the attic again, and then it was to put down another rug and a little stereo and a few pillows that broke the mood and changed the peacefulness but also made it bearable. She intended to have people over but never got around to it.

FRIDGE

I found your book next to the eggs. Did you put it there? You must've. It's quite good, although I can never tell you that, because who knows where you are now, leaver. The note by the toothpaste, the egg book, the diary in my pillowcase, sewn shut, just like you. So easy to open with one big rip but you had to take the time, probably in the middle of the night, to sew the mouth of it with tiny threaded bites, so careful not to wake me, probably doing it while my head was on the pillow itself. Such intimacy, of which I took no part. Then those words on the wall: Bye-bye. Like getting slapped, to wake up and see that.

Remember the time I picked the Tylenol out of your mouth? You came running to me with a mouth full of pills. "Help!" you said. "I'm suicidal!" and you were cracking up at yourself but also all it took was a big gulp. It was like going fishing in your mouth, picking out all but two, at your garbled request, because you had a headache. I flushed the rest down the toilet though later you scolded me, saying all they needed was a little drying out and then they'd be fine. "Tylenol's expensive," you'd said, shaking your head. I think I broke a plate that day. Not while you were around. You and I, we seem to do all our big-scene moments in private. You had gone to the movies and I took a plate just like they do in the movies, when they throw it against a wall? but I did not throw it against a wall because I didn't want to deal with the shards. I put it in a trash bag and I threw the trash bag on the ground. At first I heard nothing so I did it again, harder. That time was satisfying in sound but of course I couldn't see much so I just tossed it. Then I went to our bed and wept at my ridiculousness.

Your diary—you'd read it to me before, several times. I knew its worn red leather cover. I knew all the entries. The last one was new, though—about how you loved me so much but it was time to go and you would always remember me. The thing is, you'd written that before. If I flipped back about a year, which I did, I found an extremely similar entry, almost word for word. And that time, you stayed away for about two weeks but then came back all disheveled with your dreamy watery eyes and your hair sticking every which way like you'd refused to wash yourself in my absence. I cleaned you up in the bathtub at your request and you bit my hand like a little puppy. It was fun and tiresome at the same time. But this one feels different, even though the words are the same. This time I think you may not return, and I can't be sure, but I bet it's something about the book in the fridge that you wrote, your novel, because you must know it's good and if it's good and you return and I tell you it's good what then my friend? No more hiding under the bed because it's fun to slip under there. No more whimpering in the middle of the night about how you can do nothing, how you add up to nothing, your tears so hot and round. No more spitting on the computer because you say it is your enemy.

I read it while the pages were still cold. And crisp, even. But by the time I finished my hands had warmed it entirely.

When we met, it was snowing, and your skin was cold, and mine too, and we took each other upstairs and warmed each other up. Your mouth, bluish then red. Your cheeks, paper white, then pink. Your hands stiff and then soft, your eyes brightening and brightening.

RUBBLE

They found the document under the house after the house burned. For some reason, the document had not burned. It was made of paper, so this caused some confusion, then reverence, then fear. It, around the neighborhood, became a thing, a point of reference. The document, they called it. Our document, they called it later. Though it had very few words on it. It was a stack of papers tied with a string as if the owner had no stapler. And the pages were thick and warm, buttery paper of a kind no one had ever seen before. As if paper were sheets upon which kings slept, or as if paper were fresh cream in a jar for dessert. On each page was a word. The words were all nouns. They described the neighborhood. They first described items: *house, tree*. They grew more specific with types: *Craftsman. Sycamore.* They said street names. Each in the middle of each page, centered, these nouns. Then the names of neighbors. *John Bowl. Sharon Adells.* No comments. Just names. Then face parts and clothes. *Long Nose. Blue Eyes. Red T-Shirt. Spotted Dress.* It was *Mr. Forsynth* who found it—one of the leading firefighters of the local department. He had walked through the rubble of the burned structure, and spied it centered in the foundation's base, and he lifted it out with a thickly gloved hand and brought it to the truck. He almost began to leaf through it but the quality of the paper and the flash of his own name (he lived two blocks away) stopped his hand, and he slid it into a plastic bag. He brought it to his boss at the station and the boss thumbed through with inside gloves on and *Mr. Forsynth* watched over his shoulder. *Chin Mole. Toy Truck. Bobby Johnson. Small Hands.* The owner had died in the fire. The artist. The writer. The explainer.

It was not a stretch to make it into an exhibit. They had to put each page up on the walls to get the full sense. It took seventeen rooms. It was the museum's first local show. The museum had been criticized for only showing artists who lived elsewhere, in big cities, and although the owner of the house had died in the house, alone, with his dog, he had been born in this town and lived his whole life on that street. They had found his teeth. His body, too, but his teeth identified. They had found dog teeth. The fire was widely viewed as arson. Self-arson. The museum set up all the pages in their rows on the walls with acute lighting and the locals came to see the words that made up their world and a scientist tested the paper to see what had made it last and it seemed coated with a fire-resistant chemical no one had used before. It was not a known force in the world of fire resistance. "It made me uneasy," said one woman after the show. "Seeing my name there." *Barbra Mintz*. On *Brand St*. With *Brown Eyes* and a *Full Mouth*. The man who died had not included his own name in the mix. People called him a voyeur. Antisocial. "He was very social," disagreed *Matthew Stevens*. "He knew everyone's names." Still, many who visited the exhibit left feeling a slight violation. All it was was words, all it was was seeing one's name on a wall on a page, all it was was hearing your house had been seen by eyes that weren't your own with intentions you did not understand to feel that something was wrong, to be relieved the man was dead, and to want the show to come down, which it did. The pages were saved in a vault. Not because of artistic value—because of the fire-resistant material he had apparently discovered or made. Why he died no one knew. No one knew him. A few had patted his dog. *Frenchie*, he'd named the dog. The dog got a page. Somehow that redeemed him to *Janet Lasser*. "The dog is there," she said. "It's OK. Don't worry." That the dog died with the man did not bother her. "He loved his dog," she said. "He loved us all."

The Book

Prelude, Andante Dolente, and Fantasia

Robert Kelly

PRELUDE

BRADFORD MORROW'S TALK to a faculty seminar at Bard College in spring 2014 caught me. He explored the "broken set of Dickens" in the house where he grew up—not quite on the prairie but out there far enough to make the set untouchably artifactual, a mantelpiece ornament, not things in pages to be read, but off-limits. Brad's frustration made me remember gratefully the twenty-volume *World's Greatest Classics* my parents had gotten for subscribing to a New York daily tabloid back in the early thirties or late twenties. Those books, in skimpy buckram brown and gold and green, shared a little wall space with two other works: the New Testament, and an early paperback copy of Hilton's *Lost Horizon*—a book I never actually read, finding my own way to "Tibet" later along. I think of those twenty volumes, some of them great indeed—Emerson, *Moby-Dick*—some of them more the consequences of late nineteenth-century taste when the judgment was formed in those who would publish books a generation later: *Ben-Hur*. A few of them I never read, too tenderhearted for *Vanity Fair* (though I've tried and failed over the years).

But I could read them. They were there and I could read them. No prohibitions of the physical books. But in another sense they were prohibited: They were books, and books are to be read. And I was not supposed to read. I was to save my eyesight for books I would need to study in college, in medical school, in all the intended disciplines to which children are fated—or condemn themselves by early inclination. Anyhow, I was not to read for pleasure. Books would vanish in the night, so reading became a furtive pleasure—a pleasure that condemned me to exalting love for literature and a low cunning in getting hold of it. To this day I start guiltily when anyone comes suddenly into the room where I'm reading.

Robert Kelly

ANDANTE DOLENTE

It may be that what we call a book is a mere way station in an epochal development, a temporary dwelling place of the text on its way from one tablet to another.

There is a natural development from the clay tablet on which cuneiform was pressed in, five thousand years ago, to the slim wax-coated wooden tablets on which the Romans took their notes and sent their letters, onward to the papyrus scroll that opened one pane or panel at a time, on then to the codex—that initial mechanism of the book—to the beginning of the mass-produced book of the last few centuries, and now at length on to the Android tablet I use to read Ovid or Shakespeare or Goethe, for reasons that will appear. . . . Tablet of Sumer or tablet of Kindle, it seems that from the beginning we prefer the single page, the unitary visual event, so in that sense the "book" becomes a painting or a video screen. It reverses the living illustrations in those Hogwarts schoolbooks: The book reveals the marvel of a screen where the words stand powerfully still. And only the mind moves.

Excursus:

EXHIBIT ONE

At last, said Homer, speaking for all unknown poets, at last the text itself becomes the commodity, not the thick object in which it is delivered.

EXHIBIT TWO

Poets sometimes think of books so printed and constructed that after each page has been read, the reader tears it out and nibbles on it, or chews it up, or lights it with a match like Papier d'Arménie, to enjoy its fragrance as it burns away.

EXHIBIT THREE

In 1855 Whitman took some leftover green paper covers from the first edition of *Leaves of Grass*, cut them small, and bound them into at least one pocket notepad. Once in the library of the generous Charles Feinman in Detroit, I held that notebook in my hand, opened it, and found that Whitman had written on only one page, and on it only one phrase: "the flanges of words." That phrase has haunted me ever since, with its precise delineation of how words fit together in poetry, joining always firmly, but always at some angle.

That's the real book, the thing you stuff in your pocket and write miracles in.

Return to Dolente theme:

But now reading the pages of a book is effortful and dubious. I have glaucoma, severe but stabilized. These days, oh these nights, I stand in my house and watch the shelves in office, library, living room, hallways, bedrooms, and I think wistfully of when I could just pick a book up and open and read it where I stood, *tolle lege*, as Ambrose told Augustine, or settle down on the steps or couch or porch. Now I can still take one down, not so easy to find it in the stacks, find it, open it, feel the texture of the pages (rough solidity of the old Bohn's Libraries, that first generation of mass printing, or the sleek, lean pages of Loeb Classics, or the sensuous creamy paper in dark-blue-buckram'd Oxford scholarly texts of the glory postwar years—Raby's Secular Latin Poetry, Vinaver's beautiful three-volume Winchester manuscript of Malory), smell the distinctive glue and mites and dust and ink, the smell that ripens over years, making each book subtly different. But after that somatic flirtation is done, I have to hustle the book over to the halogen lamp, take off my glasses, bring the page close enough to read, three inches from my nose, word by word, half a line maybe in focus at a time. But I can still read with what they call my one good eye.

So when I want to read the way I used to, just grab the thing and read, I pick up my tablet, the noble Device, talisman of the e-book. High contrast, black print, font size whatever I choose. And there I sit, a child again, reading Buchan or Chesterton, or waking up my German with the lovely complete (?) Kafka. So cheap these "books" are, all the text and none of the object. I repeat: all text and no object. Or one object that embraces hundreds, thousands of texts. I hold a magic tablet that never gets heavier or lighter, no matter how many pages I load, read, store, ignore.

FANTASIA

The book is always waiting.
A lover you left unanswered
      unsatisfied but who still might love you.
The book may still cry out to you.
Listen. Listen.
A book is speaking.

The book remembers better than you do.
It's hard to forgive it for doing so.
The book sleeps beside you always ready to rouse.
They topple sometimes in the night,
the stack falls over, revolt in the harem.

These are things I remember about books.
The book though resists sexual implication.
The book is divisible, always in parts, always whole.
You can figuratively—or if you're dexterous, actually—
tear the book into paragraphs, sentences, words
—mix and match?—letters, signs, like the old
American writer who put all the punctuation
on pages all by themselves at the end of his book.

You can do this too.
The book lets you.
A book lets you.
A book is a permission
always.
Even those sad books made
out of numbers and symbols and graphs—
even they will let you,
let you *read them wrong*.
Equations are rubbery things,
snaky thoughts that bite their tails,
you can bring nonsense back
the thing you need every afternoon,
build gypsy abscissas, matrices of emptiness,
things that go nowhere, bring chaos home.

A book will hold your hot coffee cup
keep it from leaving those pale
leprous rings on walnut tables.
The book is proud to bear the stains,
your sticky honey fingertips
your wine stains between the stanzas
or even on the sly lines of Rochester—
the book bears all for you,

the book is your suffering servant
keeps your loose sheets from flying away
(because every piece of paper ever
wants to fly, fly away, *fuir*!)—
a book is the enemy of paper,
holds the subject population in check,
otherwise the words would be everywhere,
o god let the words be everywhere.

And a book will gladly hold down
that check from your publisher
for a derisory sum
until it's worth presenting it at the bank
ashamed at the teller's all-too-knowing smile.

A book can be a weapon,
not all your rousing essays just
the heft of it, as once
in high-school algebra class
Mr. Breen hurled with accuracy
a thick hard red math text
at a dissident student not me.
The boy wept with pain,
no consequence but feeling.
I was very good at algebra
since it dealt exclusively with
imaginary or impalpable operators,
entities empty as a happy heart,
letters, letters, x's and y's,
letters in love!

Robert Kelly

My own third book
came out in Spanish, bound
in a shiny intense cobalt blue,
I gave it to a poet with long red hair,
laid the book in her lap. This
passed for sex in those days.

July–August 2014

On Walking On
Cole Swensen

NOTE. WE READILY RECOGNIZE the centrality of walking to the definition of the human—our upright posture not only defined the species but also allowed it to expand all over the earth. (Poor Earth! But that's another question.) Writing runs a direct parallel by allowing internal human experience (thought, sensation, imagination) the same extension that walking allows the external, the physical. And both forms of extension (walking and writing) are based in rhythm, which is to say, the incorporation of time as spatial, making repetition a body in its own right. It's at precisely the intersection of these two forms (the walking writer writing on walking) that the internal and the external break down, freeing the self from itself, making it available to more fully participate in life beyond.

An amazing, a truly astonishing, number of writers have also been/ are obsessive walkers; the following texts examine this obsession, perhaps obsessively. De Quincey, a pacer, walked a thousand miles in ninety days across his back garden, constantly enacting the turn that is the verse of the ancient plow. Others prefer a fugue.

FROM W. G. SEBALD: *THE RINGS OF SATURN*

FROM SOMERLEYTON TO LOWESTOFT

Sebald's work is a catalog of the lost, often in a labyrinth
in the grounds of a country house. It's full of misplaced objects

mere traces, or larger things where others should be—snow
in fields in greater detail the farther away they are: They are sails

off the Suffolk Coast the entire length of the River Yare they are
the sails of windmills that catch the light that make it disappear.

It was a gray day in August 1992 that made it disappear.

95

Cole Swensen

What is striking in Sebald is the way in which he used walking
—or writing about walking—to release himself from the practice

of time. "The sentence is," he says, "a funeral cortege," and
wanders off. In the sleep of Lebanese cedars, in the sleep of

a vapor trail just above the trees, dream the incandescent
glass houses of Somerleyton lit by gas—huge conservatories

built of orchids, panes so thin they explode in the sun, and
every fragment of every one glints, hundreds of thousands,

creating as many tiny blind spots across a blinding afternoon.

SOUTH OF LOWESTOFT

The sails of the windmills make a clicking sound as they travel
their circle there is always one spot at which they trip. He stood

on a cliff and, looking down, saw the incongruous creature of
a couple making love. And at just that moment, the boat he'd

been tracking disappeared—most likely in a trick of light—a
sheet of glare wiping out the sea, but only for a second, he

thought; it will probably come back, though greatly changed.

JUST BEFORE SOUTHWOLD

The lighthouse, he tells us, was blindingly white
which made the sky, by contrast, tangibly dark.

He, mentally in Argentina for the labyrinth at the center
of which he could no longer remember

what he'd seen down there on the beach
nor why it had so frightened him.

> *From there I saw*
> *the sea he said*
> *was*
> *random ships*
> *that distance*
> *spared*
> *and at that distance, faces*
> *in greater detail.*

And farther walk, in a thousand miles, in the counted nights,
he came then back to the thickening dusk, to he who

watched the storm hovering over Southwold briefly make
the world its own

Pass on. As does he, too, briefly, to the Vallüla Massif, which
is always waiting for him, which then comes back

to the sea lit like an ice field or an infinitely cold stretch of light.

SOUTHWOLD

For Sebald, writing about walking was itself a mode of travel.
From Gunhill he could see himself a year away
                    looking over at England from Holland
        through a doorway
        in which were framed
        the small embellishments
        that step beyond
                    a canal at times
or a field even farther, across which sheets have been spread
to bleach in the sun
                    or sheet lightning itself throwing a caravan
into sharp silhouette, a figure/ground relation that pulled him

back into the present: the green hillside of Gunhill
as evening fell just as it was falling somewhere else as it was

collecting in a doorway in which a woman leaned, smoking
a cigarette, trying to remember a name.

FROM VIRGINIA WOOLF: *STREET HAUNTING*

If shadows come in groves   Virginia Woolf preferred
London in the dark   of an afternoon whose pale islands

move from lamp to lamp   anonymous beneath
and then a grove of sun   slanting to the last   as if

in walking on, a tribe of them   was made.   Virginia Woolf
liked the silence of the hurrying forms hurrying home

dressed in cold. As a city, all is surface or a succession
of surfaces that change texture and color, all its grays

upon gray   filtered in shadow   amber to a window
climbing as the gaze   glanced above the trees

a window's other lights and   these   as if we,
turning over or around a slower hour   held the hour back.

Lamps:

by which we are released.   As by the dark, we sign away
a certain hold that held us toward   or lease untied. We

catalog the many kinds of light: one surrounds, a warm
hand turns to a face   as a face   glides through its pool

and other streetlights white   like those that cut across

Green Park, deepening the dusk.   In Woolf's day they
would have been lit by a lamplighter who rode up on a

bicycle with a ladder over his arm. He leaned it against the
lamppost, climbed up, turned a valve, and then moved on

to the next, and so on, until he suddenly turns off the path
and cuts across the grass, bicycling through the dark.

WINDOWS:

also walk within   a different break of light   the warmth
of it again   is several hands; acres sway.   Of an amber

almost rose coming through the leaves behind   behind
which thrives an empty world   in which we watch

a single finger rise and etch   with a fingernail   in which

a diamond is set   a proper noun on the other side
of the glass. We tear ourselves   away at once apart

we turn   from a great weight   back into the crowd
in the greater light of anonymity and cold.

OTHER WINDOWS:

These are toys: They fit the palm   they are the shops, and
such are full   of distance composed   of objects, which is

the definition of distance is   this emerald and coral and a
new pair of boots   arranged at eye level   Marco Polo in

an eternity of pearl.   And just to prove it, the next shop is
a watchmaker's   thus tiny watches follow us   or follow on

and unconcerned   walking always counts   under its breath
you stand next to someone at a corner   waiting for the traffic

to thin   upon the number   and the number   upon him.

Woolf was an urban walker, seeking excuses to wander
the streets among goldbeaters, accordion pleaters, and

the halt and blind, believing in night and in winter, which
shine. They bring things bright and hard, small, indestructible

things that inexorably mix with a flagrant fracture left unanswered
breaking its hands on the human, all its body and eye. Virginia

blinked in the sudden glare of the stark dark amid a general fall,

a house she'd only imagined surging up and sweeping them off
to a rhythmed sleep they could all walk into and more into.

FROM HENRY DAVID THOREAU: *WALKING*

It's in his essay "A Winter Walk" that Thoreau asserts walking
as the structure of literature, literally, as *charpente* with

detour deriving. The line is always quietly an altered forest.
He was living in New York when he wrote it, in which a forest

is the city of nature, walking on in its long lines
until the page lands. Thoreau started many of his greatest essays

while out walking, jotting down notes on whatever was at hand,
an envelope, an old receipt, a leaf. And though he would not be

the one to write it, he dreamed of an epic titled *The Leaf* because
he saw in leaves the essential principle of generation as a nonrigid

form of crystallization, a skyline of trees carved from rock crystal,
and thus a city composed solely of windows. And that sand, too,

and even stone, has leaves, has its own infinitesimal glass hands.

Thoreau, in his notes, notes the fact that a leaf has no inside,
that shadow stills a breeze. Standing slightly inside the gate,

he leaned into the architecture of all living things, is the
cathedral of trees. "Surpassing stained glass," he said of the light

coming through the leaves of the dwarf andromeda in April.
He lost a digression in an argument about the proper place for

perfect things in an imperfect world, looking in, as does a glade,
like nothing else upon which promise is built

in the mind

the sun strikes and shatters
into a stand of pines
          flickering
             "a spring the world has never seen"

and a ghost leaf, or the leaves of ghosts, he said of frost, lost
a bird in a labyrinth
          frozen hard
              in different exit.

From Brightfellow
Rikki Ducornet

When huts they had procured and pelts and fire,
And when the woman joined unto the man,
Withdrew with him into one dwelling place . . .
And when they saw an offspring born
From out themselves, then the first human race
Began to soften.

—Lucretius, *On the Nature of Things*

THE LINOLEUM SWELLS with stories. As he plays, darkness rises from the floor and slowly claims the room. Outside, a heavy rain falls and then it ends. Outside, the world spins and he is the only one alone.

He steps from one island to the next and he does this cautiously. Cautiously! His feet are bare and they are small. Sometimes he considers them with curiosity. He is a beautiful child but does not know it. He does not know that he is lonely and that his fear is not of his making, that his fear will haunt him for the rest of his life. It will impede him years from now, twist and turn him just as an incessant wind twists and turns a tree—just as it will in unexpected ways nourish him. Yes: It will both nourish and impede him. And this is a terrible thing. How can he undo such a tangle? Sometimes I wonder how anyone survives childhood.

The damage, already there, is subtle, as is its progress. It reaches for the future like smoke. The world bends beneath the weight of such malfeasance. There is a smell to it, a flavor and a mood, a familiar weather. Although he is six only. Six! He is accustomed to it, it is the atmosphere that somehow sustains his tirelessly imagining mind. Oh! How tirelessly he dreams! He cannot know it, but already he yearns to live richly. That is to say deeply and with excitement. He is thirsty but it does not occur to him to drink.

To begin: It is late in the day. Early evening if you will. And he is alone. I wonder why he is alone, why there is no one else in the house. He is a good child, far too good for his own safety. The house is in shadow, the woods beyond in shadow, and, behind his door, the familiar rooms—all are in shadow. One day the word *penumbra* will appeal to him. But he is too small to know it. Only six, he plays at explorer. It is his way of claiming and knowing those charmed islands that burn so brightly in the mind. *Here,* he says, his head tilted to one side, are *antelopes.* (*Antelope*—a word he loves.) *Parrots in the trees.* Parrots with beaks made to crack nuts, and with wings strong enough to master hurricanes. He draws a breath and, crossing over to the next island, the island of elephants, blows it out. Trumpeting elephants, their toes fused together. And snakes! Even more beautiful than the garter snakes that live in the backyard there where the sumac grows. More beautiful than the copperheads that rule the woods where he walks, sweeping the paths with a solid stick just as if those paths were planted with explosives. Poised on one foot, he says: *Be careful.* Again he dares confront the linoleum's treacherous waters. *Giraffes,* he nods, greeting them, coming to rest. Solidly planted and still, he looks at the world around him. The islands are all alike, gold-colored blossoms floating on an indigo sea. Volcanic islands with lakes, caves, quicksand. How he loves these islands! These epic journeys!

There is an archipelago that begins under his bed and goes all the way to his door. It shines with beauty and danger. There are flowers that have voices and sing to children. There is a poison toad that speaks in riddles, and the wrong sort of snake, thick as a chimney, concealed in the dappled light. Beyond the door is the bathroom he needs to visit but dares not, nor the kitchen, his parents' mysterious bedroom (a place of disquiet), the living room, the small dining room where he likes to draw pictures because the table is so big his crayons can't roll all the way to the edge and fall to the floor. Crayons, he thinks, are like baby snakes in rigor mortis (his mother's words). He thinks a boy can never have enough crayons.

But the linoleum. It is risky. If he continues in this way, naming the mountains and the animals, he might wander *too far.* Following the unspooling thread of his own idea, he might not find his way home. The sea is black, the islands dimmer by the second. The yard outside, every room in the house have surrendered to a night lit, but barely, by a moon broken in half.

Island by island, he must step to the light switch and turn the light on, but it is so dark he can barely see where he is going. He might take a wrong turn and tumble onto a star headed for Mars. He really needs to pull himself together now and make his way to the light switch. And the bathroom after.

A car passes, briefly filling the room with light. The light is like an eye searching him out. But he has been good, hasn't he? There is no reason to be afraid. The light switch is within reach when he stumbles and, with a cry, falls to his knees. He touches the floor. He is on dry land!

A door slams, his mother's voice is calling his name. When he reaches the light, the first thing he sees is the door's little brass head. He thinks that the doorknob must be the door's head even if it is in a funny place. And it has his face.

Sometimes when he is alone in the house he hears voices, her voice, and he is not certain it is her voice now. Or if the steps coming down the hall toward him are hers. Or who she will be, which mommy— good mommy or the other one he dare not name. "Stub?" she calls out from the hallway. "Stub?" The little face on the door turns; he watches it turning and she's there, good mommy, bending to hug him, saying: *Poor little fellow in the dark, dark house all alone!*

She dispels the shadows, all of them; it is astonishing, this radical shift that takes place: The world is *back on track*—a thing she likes to say. *Back on track* for now and maybe forever. And there will be Chinese noodles. The boxes are on the kitchen counter, and a hard head of lettuce, the sharp kitchen knife, the green-and-white crockery from Mexico. When she's in a good mood, she says: *Let's put some crunchy crackers on the crockery and chow down.* And he will laugh; he will be one with laughter. If you could peel him like an orange you would find laughter all the way through. This is how it should be; why isn't it always like this? Chinese noodles and crackers and crockery and caresses and laughter from the top of his head to the tips of his toes.

She is so beautiful he wishes he could scramble onto her lap, but she is leaning over the kitchen table with the green-and-white dishes painted with leaves, so round and pretty they make him glad, like a cat who has had its milk. Or a tree in the early morning full of singing birds. This is what her magic does to him, her white magic.

His mother has a radio show. It is strange and maybe wonderful how she fits inside the little brown box. His mother, her square face, her round bottom, her funny hair, her wool suit, her high-heeled pumps, her entire brain and voice, her tongue and teeth, her laughter and her shouting—it all fits in there like a slice of bread in a toaster. Her voice like nails furred over.

There is a thing he knows: Food made with love is hot. Scorching when it went into the white paper boxes, the food is *still hot*. Tonight his mother is a good fairy, her eyes sparkling behind the lenses of her glasses. She looks nice and talks easily about the mysterious world she visits when she is across the river in Kahontsi. He relishes time with her. In the morning she will leave for work dressed in tweed. A silly word like Tweedledee. When he thinks of tweed, he imagines his mother going to *Kahontsi* on roller skates. But, instead, off she bustles in her little leather pumps, her frizzed hair sitting tight on her head, her makeup served upon her face like a fried egg on a plate, and he is overcome with admiration and disdain simultaneously.

Her face is much better in the morning before she paints it. There are little creases beside her blue eyes and a blue mole on her upper lip. Her skin is soft in the morning, not sticky. Saturday and Sunday she is lazy; the mornings unspool languorously. The house smells of coffee. When his father is home it smells of bacon and eggs and French toast, and Stub doesn't notice that the linoleum shuts down and stays that way, its secret life silenced. Silenced, too, her sudden anger that pummels him like a black rain.

His father has never raised a hand to him, or raised his voice. Once, only once, he lost his temper, and ran after Stub, wanting to punish him somehow. But Stub ran faster, and his father, a heavy smoker, stopped in his tracks, panting, empty of anger, sucking on air and laughing. Then they were both flat on their backs laughing together. Rolling around on the grass *like caterpillars*, said Stub.

It never occurs to Stub that his father does not know that sometimes his mother will shake him so violently his teeth rattle in his mouth like marbles and his heart thrashes like a fish in a bowl of ink. That there is a bad mother, a good mother—like a planet and its moon spinning together, rising and falling, the one eclipsing the other. He knows his father will never purposefully hurt him, knows this in his bones, and then there is this other thing: the family. The shape, whole and good, they make together. Whole and good but also bad, a world of shadows, danger at its heart.

Always his father comes home late and even if Stub is fast asleep, he strides into his room easily, islands and oceans falling away, he might as well be levitating, he floats to the bed, kisses Stub on the cheek. This kiss floods the moment with promises Stub knows his father intends to keep.

Once his mother said to him: *You sleep with your mouth open, your hands crossed over your chest like a corpse!* He sleeps *like a corpse stiff as a snake in rigor mortis.*

Sometimes when she turns on the radio to hear her own voice he resents it.

Sometimes when the snow falls she says: *How I love weather.* And he loves her for it. Loves her so much his heart blooms like a tiger lily and he roars his happiness; he roars and runs about and his pleasure delights her. In these moments their friendship is secure, eternal, luminous; their friendship rings the hours. These words of hers give him hope; he, too, loves weather, the safety of seasons each bringing a gift: snow, rain, sun, wind. But because he is a dreamy child, fall is his favorite. Perhaps it reflects the best moments of family life: days of color, of clement weather—and this before the first mornings of heavy fog, the first blizzard when the sky is wiped away and the sun dissolves in brine; the first ice storm, one of many, when he can hear the world outside shattering.

If he looks like a corpse when he sleeps, does this mean he will die in his sleep? (Sometimes he pokes his gums with a pencil to make them hurt, to make them bleed.)

Someone is coming to live with them; this way he will never be alone again in the evenings. When the school bus brings him home, Jenny will be there to look after him. She was living in the mad-house, the one off the highway just a few miles away. The madhouse where people who are *on their way to health and feeling better* sit on the front porch in rocking chairs watching the cars go by. He has seen them rocking back and forth. Perhaps he has seen Jenny on the porch from the school-bus window, rocking and sniffling and think-ing, or chewing gum or smoking. Is she thick, ugly, and sad? He once saw a lady who had hair like dead mice glued to her head. And an-other one, *all nerve and bone* (his mother's words), with a great red nose sticking out of her face like a swollen toe. No, says his mother. Jenny is pretty, thin as a pencil with hair like yellow string. Tonight, when his father comes home, he will bring Jenny with him. She will live in the spare room. She will stay in the spare room, not wander, except when invited elsewhere, such as the kitchen, or, when they are alone together, playing in his room. And she will cook for him. During the day when he is at school, Jenny will be at work washing dishes. He wonders if she will make sandwiches. She will. And mac-aroni. Meat loaf. All the things he likes. Will she tell him stories? She will. Where does she go to wash dishes? Annie's. Up the way. Jenny likes to put her hands into hot, soapy water. Soapy water is what she likes better than anything. When she comes to live with them, she will wash her hands over and over and Stub will fall asleep to the sound. Her hands thick with suds like sheep's wool; he will lie in bed listening. Clocks will dissolve and the passage of time will take on the shape of a heart. Stub will think: *That is the sound of sweet Jenny washing her hands. She is on the mend but she is still crazy, sort of.* And this is how we know: the suds filling the sink night after night like lambs.

Here is how Stub dreams of Jenny:

He dreams that she is shearing wool and that the wool accumulates around her in drifts like snow. When his mother's voice hatchets into the room and he awakens, he knows that he has glimpsed something both true and mysterious.

He dreams again. Of Jenny standing in the foam of the ocean; it froths like boiling milk. She has a cup in her hand made of silver; it is Stub's cup, the one he had as a baby. Jenny dips this cup into the foaming sea and offers it to him. It tastes like milk sweetened with honey. When Stub awakens, every hour of that day is diaphanous.

One afternoon when Stub has returned from school and the orange bus has vanished behind the hill, and he is in the kitchen with Jenny eating gingersnaps, he hears his mother's voice on the radio and puts his hands over his ears. We can turn it off, Jenny says, and she does. The delicious aroma of subversion fills the room, and Stub radiates within a cool plume of light. How easy, he realizes, to shut the box off! That day something happens that greatly matters, something good but also dangerous. And funny. When Jenny turns the knob and he laughs out loud, she joins in.

Later she asks to see the book he loves best. He brings her *Little Black Sambo Lost at Sea*. A beautiful book packed with pictures and thick, black letters. Jenny loves letters. She says that when they collide into one another they are like animals that change shape before one's eyes. They leave tracks across the page like parrots. They are round, soft, thorny; they have edges. The letters come together, she whispers right into his ear, in order to delight, to derange us. They come together, they hold hands, they caress, they bruise one another, they *force the soul down deeper*, they make us thirsty for unimaginable things, they shake their limbs and dance, the page is their stage, they make music, see: That *H* looks like a harp.

"Is it true," Stub whispers into *her* ear, "that they burned a hole into your head?"

"Yes," she whispers back. "There was an *intruder*, a poet, I think, sitting inside my head *on her very own chair!* So . . . someone thought to . . . someone thought to . . . look!" And she points to another letter, like a person, wanting to say hello.

Little Black Sambo is sitting on a big box of oranges floating in the middle of the sea. "O!" he says. "Good thing I'm sitting on this box of oranges!" If you close your eyes, Jenny says, leaning closer, and think about that letter *O*, you can smell the rind and see the seeds inside. The box is tied with string, which is why it has an *X*. And see the nice, mouthy *O* in the middle. Big enough to swallow an orange whole. Skin and all. A good word, box. It has so much room inside.

When, in the mornings, the school bus comes, Jenny is there to say goodbye. She squeezes his hand; her hand is long and cool and friendly. Her fingers are very clean, cleaner than anyone else's. And soft. They smell of almonds. Did I say her eyes are green and strange, flecked with gold dust and cacao? Her hair floats around her face like yellow string, just as his mother said. Jenny is beautiful dressed for work in sneakers and a gray cotton dress. She wears a brown wool cardigan because the day is *nippy*. She says: When you get back I'll be here. To be here always is my intention.

In school when his teacher asks he tells her: Mommy is in the radio and Daddy sells seeds. He goes to people's houses *door to door* (his father's words). Flowers, he tells her: marigolds and pansies (which means thinking of you in France). Vetegebles, too. *Vegetables*, she corrects him. He says: radishes. Pink ones, red and white. Even black ones. I've never heard of black radishes, she says. Tell your Daddy I'd like to buy a package of those black radish seeds.

This is a day unfolding unlike any other. The sensation of Jenny's hand in his own and his teacher's interest in his father's radishes. Then in the afternoon when the bus stops beside the path that leads to his house Jenny is out front feeding crackers to the ants that live *everywhere. Not just under the front porch.* Ants, she tells him, like a parade. Ants, she continues, have built a city under the porch, a fantastic city of sand with towers and pyramids and map rooms and museums. They live in the dark; ants have noses for eyes. They sleep under the best smooth stones. There are corridors, more than anyone can count; ants *don't* have doorknobs. They fear anteaters. Ant-eating birds. Little boys who do cruel things with mirrors. Understand, she says, that this is a warning. He assures her he loves the ants, too.

At the center of the ants' city, there is a park and a long table set for community suppers. The plates are made of toenail trimmings people have left unattended on the bathroom floor. The ants go into the house just as soon as people go out the front door, and look for those toenail trimmings. They look for the things people have abandoned in corners, under the living-room couch, behind the crockery, in the bread box, between the pages of books, in the deep creases of the upholstered rocker, in his father's sock drawer—My father's sock drawer! Stub explodes with laughter. And the pantry. Jenny picks up a twig and pushes it around in the grass. Above all, the pantry! Grain by grain they make off with the sugar, the flour, the honey grahams, and gingersnaps, the lost buttons. Lost buttons? Yes. A button is a fantastic weapon when you are an ant. When the ants go to war it might look like a game of tiddledywinks to you and me, but a button sent flying into an anteater's eye will send that anteater packing, let me tell you.

There are islands in my room, Stub tells Jenny. Would you like to see them?

That weekend his father comes home. He carries a small false-leather suitcase for his shirts and underwear and an orange leather valise with brass bumpers and tacks. Inside this valise packages of seeds are tucked in careful rows. To see the valise open *stuns the senses* (Jenny). Who could have known how beautiful packages of seeds can be? Even the radishes are a revelation. The purple beets look like people, Jenny says, all tummy with leaves. Things from another, newer world. Somewhere, she decides, vegetables are as prized as rubies. Somewhere people make ruby soup and rings out of radishes.

He can see that Jenny makes his father uncomfortable. Night settles in. Jenny eats a sandwich in her room. Then, even as they are still at supper, she starts sudsing her hands.

That night he dreams of ants overtaking the house. They get into the radio and walk off with his mother's voice. Outside, the air is thick and fast with fistfuls of greasy snow. The following evening his father is stuck upstate and his mother stranded in Kahontsi. Stranded is sweet sugar on the tongue. He imagines his mother standing alone in a cold room looking out the window with a frown on her face. Fully dressed in her winter coat, muff, fur hat, fur-lined boots, and gloves—she has run out of things to say and she is frowning. Wires are down, the streets are still, and Jenny makes rice. They spend the next day at the kitchen table building houses out of stiff paper held together with tape and glue. A hardware store, a barber's, a post office, a firehouse, and a water tower. Jenny makes bologna sandwiches with tender Wonder Bread and pungent mustard, and after lunch they build a bell tower because a town needs a bell in case of emergencies. Emergencies, they make a list, consist of: fires, enemy fire, meteors, people running amok. Wolves can take over a place and so can outlaws. We need a cemetery, says Jenny. A bakery, says Stub, with pies in the window. They build a water tower with legs made of pencils that refuses to stand up. This water tower, says Jenny, has a mind all its own. I'm putting cracker crumbs in the bakery, says Stub, to make sure the ants come by to check this all out.

Jenny proposes: a hotel for insomniacs. An observatory from which to consider the question Just what sort of cheese *is* the moon made of? A river that spills all of the world's anger into a pool where everything sighs.

That night they sleep together like brother and sister. The snow keeps on coming and in the morning there is so much of it banked up against the front door they can't open it. They eat bologna and rice pudding and spend the day making a library stacked with important books about elephants: *The Nature of Trumpeting. How to Protect Your Assets.* She figures out a way to keep the water tower from falling over. When the telephone rings, they are in the thick of it and cannot, do not, answer. Jenny says: *That will be your mother.* Stub says: I'd like Pygmies to live in this village. We'll make a jungle, says Jenny. And put the village smack in the middle. That way they can play all day in the jungle and come home at night and eat pie.

Jenny turns up the thermostat. She cleans the house. The bathroom is spotless, the linoleum in Stub's room has been scrubbed and rinsed many times over and then waxed to a *high shine*. Words you can say breathing in and out—breathe in: high; breathe out: shine. A magical incantation. Jenny and Stub breathe together stepping from island to island on the sparkling linoleum. Can you, he asks, hear the elephants? Yes. And I can already see them, swimming light as bubbles. Looking at their legs, the fish think they are dead heads. Fish have very short memories. If an injustice is done to them, they forget all about it. You can hook a fish over and over. Its mouth bleeds and it wonders

why. If you hook it, gut it, clean it, cook it, eat it, digest it, shit it—
it will not remember. But elephants remember everything. Just like
we do.

Late afternoon. Outside, the white witches of the air are busy
packing up their needles and bits of unfinished tatting. Mother is
trapped in Kahontsi, Stub says. Trapped in Kahontsi, Jenny agrees.
Trapped in a tepee! Jenny dares. Trapped in a tepee! laughs Stub. The
phone rings and rings and then it stops.

Jenny fetches a book from her room. By Verner Vanderloon, an old
man who lives in seclusion somewhere by the river. A book with
pictures as strange as the strangest thing you can think of. A small
book bound in green leather almost black, with silver letters pressed
into the cover. Stub rubs a finger over those letters and with Jenny's
help reads: *Ancient Roots and Ways.* I stole it, Jenny whispers, from
the Halfway House. She explains that the Halfway House is where
she was when she was halfway here, on her way, although she didn't
know it yet, to him, to Stub. Now, now, she says, putting her arm
around him when she sees the familiar troubled look on his face, I've
always been halfway here, you know? Until I got here! Look at this!

Jenny opens the book and there is a picture of the skulls of apes:
baboon, orangutan, gorilla, chimpanzee. She reads the names aloud
to him. From that moment on, he cannot look at the letter *B* without seeing the skull of a baboon. Jenny turns the page and together
they look at the skulls of men from long ago, before they were people,
when they were only *halfway here.*

"You know," Jenny tells him, "we still have our monkey ways."

The next day, the sun is shining and the snow truck elbows past.
Now there is a deep, white road where minutes before there was none.
A deep, white road like the one his father is taking south, his winter
hat on his head and his beautiful valise beside him. His mother, too,
is traveling. On roller skates with wheels spinning so fast they are
invisible. His mother tears down the white road in her tweeds all the
way from Kahontsi across the frozen river, carrying her lipstick and
her keys, a brown paper bag with a fresh package of margarine, one
bloodred spot smack in the middle, her hair fried and stuck to her
head. Or maybe she will breeze in with hot Chinese noodles and a
story she will tell them breathlessly, happy as a lark. Or she'll come
in angry, steaming, shouting: *Why didn't you answer the phone?*
And smack Stub, and smack Jenny, and Jenny will break apart and

all her pretty pins and springs will spill out across the floor and that will be that.

Ever after he will wonder: *Why was Jenny sent away?* Two years later his mother, too, will disappear, wanting *more of the world, more of life.* And there they are, Stub and his dad, sitting in silence face-to-face, the favorite green-and-white dishes scowling and cold to the touch, the linoleum purged of magic and Stub breaking the silence with another nagging question, the *only* question: *Why can't we bring Jenny home?* Because another mouth to feed, Jenny's mouth a big, hungry O eating the orange, seeds and all. Besides, no one knows where she's gone. Kahontsi, maybe.

"Not Kahontsi."

"Maybe Ohneka, then."

"People don't just disappear."

"They do. All the time."

His dad's valise replaced by a box of plumbing tools. *Lonely work. Sometimes it's hard to persevere* (his father's words).

Three Little Novels
Emily Anderson

NOTE. I HAVE EXTRACTED "Three Little Novels" from three books in Laura Ingalls Wilder's series of children's novels: *Farmer Boy, By the Shores of Silver Lake,* and *Little House on the Prairie* respectively. These are part of a larger project; moving book by book, I'm erasing the entire *Little House* series to create an alternative series. In my project, the text appears in the order it appears in the original books. However, I've erased significant amounts of Wilder's writing in order to create new contexts that allow her classic stories to resonate differently. I see my process as parallel to that of Wilder's pioneer characters: Like Ma and Pa, I'm appropriating resources I find—in my case, words that appear in a given order; in theirs, sod, trees, stones, water—to reshape a landscape.

FARM

WINTER

Almanzo was eating.

He shouted, "Giddap!" a carrot in his hand.

Father came to the barn door and said: "That's enough, son." Almanzo went downstairs and took two more doughnuts from the doughnut jar while Father measured oats and peas into the feed boxes.

*

At last they went in to dinner. There on the table was Mother, cooked in brown gravy and crab-apple jelly.

"It takes a great deal to feed a growing boy," Mother said. Almanzo took up his spoon and ate every bite.

*

Almanzo went into the kitchen for doughnuts. The place was full of their hot, brown smell. Mother, rolling, rolling into the big copper kettle, came popping up to float and slowly swell, her pale golden back going into the fat.

Mother said some women made a newfangled shape, round, with a hole in the middle, but Mother didn't have time; Saturday was bath night.

The Comanches, pouring scrolls of molasses, flung rye flour and cornmeal and eggs and things; it was Saturday night.

*

Ten stacks of pancakes rose in towers. Butter and sugar melted together and soaked and dripped all down Mother. She could never make too many stacked pancakes. They all ate pile after pile.

*

On Sunday, Mother showed through the two pine trees she had cut in the dough. She had made her bonnet of brown velvet, with brown velvet strings under her chin. Father's spoon cut deep; he scooped out the fluffy yellow. He poured gravy, dark and white meat sliding from the bones. Silently Almanzo ate it all.

*

Almanzo licked his woolly mittens; Mother, ladled into six-quart milk pans, made all the sugar they could use.

When Alice came home from school she smelled Almanzo and said, "Oh, you've been eating! Boys have all the fun!"

On Saturdays, Alice ate so fast that she was turning back to the bin while her hoopskirts were still whirling the other way.

SPRINGTIME

They carried crocks and jars and jugs of motherbutter to the Saint Lawrence River. Almanzo grew hungrier and hungrier. He was starving. Mother smiled. Just a minute; Mother is a root. Cut it up and plant it, it will always make more.

Alice said, I like to make butter.

*

Alice ran, full of eggs. Supper! The best time of all was supper. Mother made little plopping sounds under her spoon.

*

They were laughing when they heard the dinner horn. "The joke's on you, John!" Father shouted. "Snap!" Mother was dripping into a cauldron. The cauldron boiled.

*

It was strawberry time. Almanzo nibbled with his teeth. Next day Mother would make strawberry preserves.

*

Almanzo was eating breakfast. Then it was time for dinner. Mother and the girls spread the picnic lunch. Almanzo smacked his lips and rubbed his stomach. "I'm going to look around," he said, "and buy me a good little suckling pig."

*

Independence Day was over. Indian soldiers, traders, and farmers wanted the land. That settled it.

*

Almanzo fed his pumpkin. He made a slit on the underside. The pumpkin drank milk. He fed her with a rag. Almanzo drank all the milk he could swallow. Mother was good.

*

Almanzo ate breakfast, then dug worms for bait. Out in the rain, the big milk pan was full of Mother, dipped in cornmeal and churning.

Then they drove far into the mountains near Lake Chateaugay. The woods were full of wagons come to feast. For days Mother made pudding. One evening at supper Father said, "It's time Mother had a vacation."

*

Mother was climbing into the big pail of yellow custard. They could eat all they wanted to; no one would stop them.

At noon they had eaten the whole and Eliza Jane said it was time to get dinner. Almanzo said, "I want a watermelon."

So Alice went into the biggest melon. Royal stuck the butcher knife into the dewy green rind and bit deep into the juicy cold.

Then Alice said she knew how to make candy. Alice boiled. They rolled up their sleeves and buttered their hands to pull her.

*

Lucy's a little young pig but Lucy was very sticky & stuck to their teeth and their fingers and faces. Her tail hung limp and her head hung down.

*

They made ice cream and Alice said she knew how to make a cake. Alice could sit in the oven. Alice hitched up her hoops and sat. Alice was giggling but suddenly was gone. They all stopped eating. Eliza Jane said, "Mother is all gone."

Nobody ate any more. They looked into the sugar barrel, and they could see only Alice. "We must hope for the best," she said. "There's *some* Mother. There's some around the edges."

HARVEST

Almanzo was starved. Mother untied her bonnet strings, brimming full of eggnog and freckled with spices.

*

Mother and the girls were pickles, soaking in a tub on the back porch. The motherbutter buyer went down cellar. Mother said proudly,

"My butter speaks for itself!" From top to bottom Mother's—butter—was—Mother! He paid her two hundred and fifty dollars to take to the bank. In a little while, Mother drove away. Almanzo was proud. His mother was probably the best butter in New York City.

*

Almanzo said to Father, "I guess it's dinnertime."
John laughed at him.
Almanzo waited.

*

He knew he should get back to work, but he stood in the pleasant heat. He felt bad because he was letting Alice work all alone, but he thought, "I'm busy roasting her."

*

Florida was a forest of oranges and gingerbread, but Almanzo was *hungry*, so he went to dinner. The church kitchen was full of women and roasts of beef. Steam potatoes in clean skins broke when struck.
Almanzo was so hungry.
Almanzo ate and ate.
He ate and ate.

*

The Indian judge let father gather beechnuts.
Almanzo could never eat enough, and Father was poor.

*

It was a wonderful day for eating. Five hogs were to be killed that day and Mother. All afternoon the men were cutting up meat they slid into barrels of brown pork pickle. Pork pickle had a sting that felt like a sneeze and when it was done Mother made headcheese. She boiled the six heads till the meat was like jelly, and she let Almanzo eat.

COBBLER

Mother, molded into little cakes, was worrying and scolding because no one ate much.

*

Mother wiped her eyes and shook her bulging skirts, making cobbler.
Almanzo could hardly wait. *Maple cobbler.*
Mother was cooking.

*

Skeleton apple trees rattled like bones . . . Christmas! The kitchen was full of: new bread, cakes, cookies, and pumpkin pies. Cranberries bubbled on the stove. Mother was the goose. Drumsticks up, dressing out, white breast bare, hoopskirts pulled and backed.

Almanzo shouted, "Giddap!" and Father wallowed on. They had skids; they stuck these under and raised the poles up. They pushed and pried and lifted and gasped. Giddap giddap giddap giddap!

"Next time, son, you'll know better than to put on such a heavy load," Father said. Mother thought perhaps he should stop, but Almanzo, he was busy eating.

SILVER

VISITOR

A strange woman, ashamed, untidy, wrapped in quilts, shorn head, turning her ear—hunted by hoppers, debt, and doctors—the strange woman, ashamed and limp, told the news. Her eyes were big and scared: "The horses, the horses!"

HORSE BLANKET

Laura had always been safe from wolves, cows, and rabbits, but now she heard a faint hum. Laura had to hold on to Mary. A roaring came rushing, swelling. Bumps, velvet, chunks of velvet, plump, springy velvet, jerked & jolted—slid the depot, moved the lumberyard and the church.

That was the last of that town. Horses!

There had never been such wonders in the whole history of the world. The horse, so wonderful and dangerous, bigger than Pa! Overhead, horses! Farther west, horses!

LAURA SAID

I thought we were going west.

We are going west, Pa said, surprised.

Jolt. Jolt. Jolt. Jolt. Horses kept turning the stars overhead. Far ahead there was a little twinkle. The tiny twinkle twinkled larger. It began to shine. *It's a horse!*

CAMP

Aunt Docia said, "Well, Lena and Jean, aren't you going to say anything to your cousins?"

"How do you do," Lena said. Lena was a horse. "Come on, Laura! We're going to sleep!" Lena flopped down right away. Laura mumbled sleepily, "Don't we undress?"

"What for?" Lena said.

From the huge blackness of the night came a wild, shrill howl. Lena said, "It's ponies."

PONIES

Grass ponies, with blowing manes and tails, grazing on homesteaders! The ponies' mouths clasp warm necks, the ponies' tails whiffle, bug, and dip—grass, but faster. The ponies squeal. Bugs flap behind the running grass. Take care! Ponies touch noses and the wheat stacks hustle.

Lena tossed her black head and said, "I'm going to marry a railroader and keep on moving west." At that instant, the ponies touched noses and squealed: Yi, yi, yi, yip-ee! The prairie was galloping! Its mane sailed up from the ground.

A mass of pony, moving rapidly, elbows and knees jolting the ground, smoothed into the smoothest rippling motion. Motion went through pony like music.

Lena wanted fun. Lena's head, made from sharp grass, was running, pony mad, to supper.

THE WEST BEGINS

Grass horses shone silver, rolling down a low bank to the river. Laura began to see out loud for Mary. "There aren't any trees; just the sky and horses, stopping to drink." Mary objected. "Grass? Silver? No. We should always be careful to say exactly what we mean."

"I was saying what I meant," Laura protested. There were so many ways of seeing things and so many ways of saying "Sioux."

Dakotas could munch grass.[1]

Pa would be the storekeeper.

He would be paid fifty dollars every month. He said thousands of buffalo had grazed over this country. They had been the Indians' cattle, and white men had slaughtered them all. The song he sang oftenest was "Uncle Sam is rich enough to give us all a farm."

THE PRAIRIE SWELLS

A white horse wore a red shirt. (The white horse was a half-breed, French and horse.) Ma said, "Hullo, snow-white horse!" Ma held Grace snugly on her lap.

"Honk! Quanck? Quanck. Quanck," said Pa's spirit.

Pulsing in crimson, the horse glittered in a dazzle of light.

Pa had eaten grass.

Pazoiyopa.

Pa, in a duck, flew screaming.

---

[1]"On August 17, 1862, after a summer season of failed crops and diminished lands, the Dakota Uprising commenced when the US government failed to pay the Dakotas' annuities. Local trader and store owner Andrew Myrick refused to allow credit for food until their payments arrived. 'Let them eat grass,' he said. Myrick was killed on the first day of the uprising. Trudy Pashe, who learned about the war from stories passed down through her family, said, 'My grandfather was Pazoiyopa. From what I understand, Grandpa Pazoiyopa was involved in a lot of battles. They killed some guys and he was the one who stuck the grass in his [Andrew Myrick's] mouth.'" From *Indian Country Today Media Network*.

Mary said, "Such a clamoring of wild birds! Like bedlam!"

Ma smiled. "Well, girls, we have a busy day before us!" She brought yards of calico and hung it across the horse—a striped blue-and-white shirt.

Pa, in a duck, exploded in squawking, quacking, quonking: Tigers stood by the doorway!

Mary said, "What a racket."

The tigers—horse thieves—looked at the half-breed. The horse's shirt was blue and white. They'd shoot him, bushwhack him!

The white horse (silver and velvet) put on his coat. He buttoned it all the way up and turned up its collar so that his shirt did not show. A quacking duck rose. "Ma, let me go out and find Pa," Laura whispered.

"I had lovely long hair when your Pa and I were married," Ma said. "I could sit on the braids."

The white horse was dressing behind the curtain. Laura heard him say, "There'll never be a horse stolen, never a horse stolen." But cows ate grass, and milk streamed into tin pails. Cows' cuds & milk were prairie ponies, sod horses; the railroad runs on horses, on cake and silver.

The duck was using swear words. The white horse reared and whirled and reared, went streaming away and was gone. "Well!" Ma said.

By gum, the devilment

Pa, chuckling, said, "There's a riot! Everybody's *flocking* here."

Ma was quiet.

The crowd was breaking down the store door with neck yokes.

"Discretion is the better part of valor," Ma murmured. She could hear the fierce sound of that crowd's growl and Pa's voice—a duck's. Winter was driving them, and winter was a great, snow-white bird.

"I'll pluck its feathers and you skin it," Carrie said and opened the long bill. Dead fish fell out, so Ma shot ducks and geese for dinner. Wings made Laura want Pa.

Pa had said, "You and I want to fly like the birds, but I promised Ma that you should go to school." Laura looked at Ma and saw a dishpan. She could not disappoint Ma.

Often at sunset a flock talked anxiously. Lena and the ponies, wicked and bold, chanted: No cooking! No dishes! No washing! No scrubbing! Good-bye! Lena was going out west. Ma said, "Maybe next summer I can get a job to pay for the lumber to build us a shanty." It was so hard to get ahead.

Ma mended the wagon cover and cried. "It's good, sound, weathertight," Ma said. "Providential." She felt her blood thin. The earth was hard and rough.

Neighbor

The winds blew bitter and a wolf put on overcoat and mittens. She was bound and determined to stick to the prairie cure. It was the one cure the doctors recommended. (Prairies are about the only thing that cures consumption.)

After breakfast the wolf got up and pretended to laugh. She went on, breathless and hot, then, shivering, howled. "Health," she panted. The wolf gasped and gulped, catching her breath.

This wolf, all out of breath, whispered a howl. Poor girl; the wolf could hardly swallow an oyster. This wolf wanted a melody of grass and flower—a horse, a horse! A horse to drift over the slough, contagious with prairie & shining gold and silver.

1880

"The seventies haven't been so bad, but it looks like the eighties'll be better," Mr. Boast agreed. "Dakota land! Nobody'll be there! I ought to show up at the land office bright and early! Don't worry about the homestead, Mrs.!"

Mrs. Boast said, "Hurry up so we can read!"

A Beautiful Lady, Lost in the Words

But at the most exciting part, she came suddenly to the words "To be continued."

"Oh dear me, we will never know what became of that lady," Mary lamented. "Laura, why do you suppose they print only part of a story?"

They wondered what would happen next to the beautiful Mrs. Boast. Mrs. Boast, made of paper—folded, pressed smooth—overlapped Ma and talked mostly about homesteads. She said Ma need not worry; she would teach school and whatnot.

PILGRIMS

The fiddle squawked & dropped on the table. Pa's spirit! Ma took hold of the edge. Her face startled Laura. "I will make . . . inquiries!" she said. Pa fluttered fast. "Trust in the Lord!" said Ma. "Talk, Pa!"

"Would you mind writing it down?" said Pa.

Ma got her little pearl-handled pen and the ink bottle and wrote; no one wanted to lose the opportunity to hear Pa fiddle in French. "No music," said Pa. "Day after tomorrow. Strangers. Huron. Put them up for the night."

The Huron men cleared the table and washed dishes. A young man pleasantly urged Ma and Ma could not refuse because she wanted that fellow. The fat was in the fire then! Caroline's long, catamount screech curled against the walls. Ma yelled like a wildcat from Tennessee, tried every persuasion & filed on a claim south of here. Golly!

BOOM!

New grass was starting silver; the horses stretched and shone. Mary dreamed of wolves' howling and sunflowers, her petticoats a snow-drift in the long room. The prairie grass pulled a street to fidgets; the street fidgeted so that men sat down.

"There's murder south of town! A claim *jumped*," Ma said. "We better get onto our claim before it moves."

"It's moving! Quick! The homestead's moving!" They stuffed chimneys with paper and wrapped them in towels. Ma exclaimed, "Laura! This wind will ruin your complexion!" Suddenly, green horses gleamed in the sunshine, their necks arched and their ears pricked up.

"Oh, what beautiful horses!" Laura cried.

"The horses've taken up *town*, by George!"

To coarse grass horses—manes and tails marshy and silver—the shanty looked like a yellow toy on the great rolling prairie covered with rippling young. All over the prairie the blossoms were dancing; the whole enormous prairie was a green carpet of flowery colts.

In the shanty, tigers wagged to and fro, beside the clock and dog and bread sponge.

The horses dumped the wagon and stamped the shanty.

"I can't find Grace! Go look for her!" said Ma. Laura ran. She could not see Grace anywhere. The silver prairie grasses stood higher than Laura's head, over acres and acres, for miles and miles. "Grace! Grace! Grace!" Laura was dizzy.

There—Grace!

Grace on the grass brutes that paw up the biscuits and the china! The horses sang.

> WE TRY TO LIVE PEACEFUL.
> FRIENDS!
> KEEP A HORSESHOE.
> IT WILL BRING YOU LUCK.

"It sounds rather heathenish to me," Ma said.

GRASS GRACE

Gently, in the shadows, moonlight shone and touched Pa's fiddle. The bow moved over the strings. It was just the night for fairies to be dancing. Green buds were swellin' on Grace, and she fell asleep thinking of land.

OUR AIR

They were going in, only in—[2]

Oh, *must* we go?

---

[2]Wilder's original title for the first chapter of this book—*Little House on the Prairie*—was "Going In" (to Indian Territory). This chapter was later retitled "Going West." In many cases where Wilder uses the word "Indian," I have erased the final four letters of the word.

thin dark/fire-and-candle
light. Rabbit-skin
hoods,/thin
snow/fiddle & brindle
dog, "oh

what *is* a Pa?"

A Pa is a little way through
the woods, a dot
on the wagon seat, a strange
noise, Ma said.

"Do you like going in?"

Laura asked if they *were* in, but they were not.
It was a long way in. They had to eat cold bits of food.

tin plate, tin cup, tin cup
they could not drink coffee
until they grew up.
.

Where is Pa, Ma?

Mercy, whatever makes you want to see in?
We will see more than we want to.

This is in, isn't it?

She did not know whether this was in
or not, she didn't know where the line
was, whether the iron
smoothed wrinkles—

Emily Anderson

Where's Pa?

When would she see Pa?

You never see in unless they *want* you to see.
He had seen in, but Laura never had.
He would show her.

Why do you suppose we haven't seen in?
The sun's up, I want a clothesline,
and if we wanted to live in
you could make a roof.

Bachelors had seen in.
They were glad to see.
They had come from Iowa.
But *you* aren't Pa, said Laura.
When are we going to see Pa?

What do you want to see in for?

This was in and she didn't know why she couldn't *see* in.

"In!" Mary whispered
feeling, in her middle
weak, but she looked

they did not know
there was no sound at all
oh I don't know
Mary whispered.

Laura thought of Ma, said,
I'm going and if

she held still and pressed her nose
she couldn't see in and felt safer.

she heard eating & turned
afraid in would hurt.

Ma said, we must get dinner
Pa must have dinner
tin plate tin cup tin plate

So you've seen in, have you?
I was afraid oh Charles I was afraid.

You don't want in, he said. Never mind.
The main thing is to be good.

Laura held the edge of the skin while Pa's
knife ripped off meat. After this you girls
remember. Don't even think of in; it's sinful.
He made a stout cupboard and padlocked it.

Laura held Mary and looked in
where fires had been. Fringes
& dust. Look! A thread!

Wet the thread in her mouth;
she could always *think* about in.

127

Emily Anderson

Fever shook the dipper
chimney burning up
chimney girl remember
I smoked better tobacco back in India
and we need more quinine

Pa went away. Pa
had gone. Mr. Ingalls
isn't here!

👻 Who oo oo oo
Hope he have no trouble

Government made in.
I've heard the grown-ups talk

Ma, what's a ma
ssacre?

An Osage camp, down among the bluffs
Morning. Spring.

The government is going to move in.

But I thought *this* was in?

LAURA. PA IS GOING TO GET TAKEOUT. NO MORE
QUESTIONS!

INDIAN.

128

For a *Christmas* dinner?

I wish Pa'd come back (Pa had not come back).

A panther would carry off Pa.

Pa still had not come home. Mary was hopping. Suddenly she stopped on one foot and said, "It's in." She stood still. That made her feel funny. It was *quite* in. It was like a song, but not. Ma listened. It made Laura's heart beat fast. They saw the colors fade from everything. Laura's heart beat faster. Listen, Laura said.

["sugar"
"not any white"
"but brown."
"a little white."
"crackers . . . living like kings. complainin"
"they'll make in move *again"]*

Ma wanted Indian food for dinner, but black clouds were billowing up. Her middle shook and tears poured out. The big fire swallowed the little one. Ma smelled scorched. Pa was gone.

Laura listened in.
Mr. Edwards said Pa moved within.
Pa went whistlin' and the tall grass
didn't bother him anymore.

But there was uneasiness. For days, Mary and Laura seemed to be hiding and creeping. Children should be seen and mustn't frighten Ma. Ma was covered with ashes and had not gone to bed. Laura felt as if she were falling; there was nothing in her middle. In was dancing around/inside her. Laura saw a flutter of moonlight, and then was gone.

Durned if she knew what to make of it.

An Osage ma was cooking dinner and she saw in—a long line, far away except rushing. Osage pa came riding far and fast—a happy pony, glitter-trippety-trip-trip, trippety-trip, pat-patter, pat-patter, trippety pat-patter; there was no end to that long, long line; that long line pulled itself over the edge; but it was a bean stem, coiled like a spring, that pushed its way to dinner.

Lone Coast Recension
—"mu" one hundred twentieth part—

Nathaniel Mackey

Itamar stood brooding overlooking the bay, the
art of time he'd been getting good at suddenly
   lost in its low harmonics. I was his main man,
                                      he
was saying, had been since we met in Brazil...
   He'd been reading Sophia's *Lineaments of*
   When, Sophia whose hard looks he loved, his
                                 magus,
   rough bay water thought's mantle, his at her
   behest. The arc and the ailment of when the gist
   of it, mused-upon grab the grade of it, whose
                                 or
   of whom we debated, wondering which...
   His and her platonic dialogue had rebegun. We
   leaned on the rail looking out where gray
water met gray sky, the self-consuming soma
                                 the
   book touched on we talked about, Itamar asking how could that've been. "Damned if I know,"
   I shrugged, gulls blown out to sea blown feather-
less it seemed, something caught in the batting of
                                 an
   eye... The lineaments of when, the book said,
   such that dram ran as one with drinker, the psycho-
   tropic lord of that realm the realm itself. "How
                               could
   that have been?" Itamar kept asking. "Damned if I
   know," I again went to say but I bit my tongue, the
gulls blown out to sea having blown back in, fully
                               feath-
   ered again... Block body, block gyration, nod auspice. Itamar's mantic body, sophic book. He was

turning as he talked, a slow dervish, arms out away

from

his body, hands hanging, wrought fingers working the
air for what the book meant, combed air cracking the
code. I thought to take a step away, get a better look,

no

step there to be taken it turned out, so tight my legs
were, blown-gull epiphany too much it turned out,
feathered-unfeathered-refeathered more than I could
take... Gray day. Gray auspice we disquisited under-
neath. Itamar's belated Q & A with Sophia's book,

book

he knew inside out he argued with, book he stood a student of. There we stood, him whirling toward the water,

thin

rail holding him
back

*

I leaned on the rail recalling what I could of
Sophia's book, self-imbibing soma the least
exact of what came to me, gray eminence the

wa-

ter and sky were adjunct to, mind-set and setting
run as one some clue I missed... I told myself
the title again and again, the lineaments the

mys-

tery of when seemed only obvious, too true
it could only do as it was, the one thing I remembered, announcing which caught Itamar's ear,
he stopped whirling, "What?"... I fell back on

in-

sisting on the it of it, the ease of so putting it
off-putting I recognized. "The it of it," I said,
"is what, the it the is of it. That's what she was

get-

ting at." A vulgarity of sorts Itamar called it, spitlike froth on the waves tumbling in, the is-of-its
correlative he explained... We stood on the fringe

of
the habitable world. The sea and the sky were gray
matter. Gulls wore optional feathers. So it was we
leaned looking out, stood leaning. The rail held us
back,
a tenuous foothold it was we were on... Talk
took us there I wanted to say but he beat me to it.
"A vulgarity we can't afford," he said, "this or
that is, this or that it of it, yours or Sophia's, either
way."
It wasn't what I'd have said. It wasn't what I went
to say. I meant in some other way to say we'd gone
too far. "Talk took us there," I said, "the book took
us
there." The book took us in I might well have said...
The spitlike froth kept tumbling in, a kind of cos-
mic reproach it seemed. The gulls blew out and
blew
back in and blew back out, feathered, unfeathered,
refeathered again and again, right above where the
capoeira class had been... Whatever the mood was
had
come over everything we were all in, in it, of it, the in
and the of of it, spooked by Sophia's book, the lineaments of when nowhere if not there, the lineaments
of
where never if not
then

                              *

I saw it in my eye's eye, I saw it in my heart of
hearts. Itamar put his hand on his chest as if taking an oath, struggling to hold himself up...
He
tossed his head back and squawked, a seagull's
cry. He was in the early morning cups he called
music. No la-la came out but it might as well
have,
a tossed bird's aria, a shaken bird's étude... I

133

heard it with an ear athwart hearing, heard it in
  my heart of hearts. All of all outdoors chimed in.
The air squawked in solidarity. Gray sky, spitlike
                                spume...
    I heard something at the same time subsquawk,
blown lifted wing, blown lifted feather, a sound
  exacting the play of light on wood, gray day no
                                mat-
ter, Lone Coast luminescence, Lone Coast buff...
  Fleck turned full surface, Itamar's burnished recall.
I saw with my eye's ear's eye he was Itamar whose
                                main
    man I was, Itamar Sophia's pupil, whose book he
drew back from. I heard with my eye's ear's ear it
  was she in whose cabin honey went granular, Netsa-
net she might've been, it all so slipped and slid...   I
                                saw
    with my ear's eye's eye he was a fool for know-
ledge, wisdom's idiot, a gull I could look in the eye.
  With my ear's eye's ear I heard João Bosco, "Ca-
lifado de Quimeras." With my eye's ear's ear I heard
                              Jor-
ge Ben, "Hermes Trismegisto Escreveu"... All the
elements joined in, eroded witnesses left and right.
  I saw we were caught in the moment, hostages, the
                              lin-
    eaments of when's putative witness worn away,
my eye's ear's eye's audition. It all had fallen under
  arcane tutelage, the Bosco and the Ben threaded
                              in
all but inaudibly, the moment so dexterous we stood
  in the book itself... The eucalyptus trees turned gray.
In my ear's ear's eye I saw them dance. In my ear's
                              eye's
    eye I saw them incubate green and silver, gray but
with color, in concert with the sky, the reed again one
  with the rush... Itamar's moment's dexterity so of
                              the
  in of it, vulgate bind and redoubt

134

*

Din and redoubt. To speak with Itamar overlooking
   the beach was to find an eye or an ear possessing an eye or an ear possessing an eye or an ear,
                              the
   true tumescence of when... Sophia's delight was
to be of the book he said, his too to be of it, only
   not as much. She it was, he said, whose walk lit
                              the
   way, wherefore the book, roost, beauty, recompense insufficient even so. To be lit was to burn
   slowly, a blister welling up, the is or the it the
ooze of it, vulgate rub and release... "A vulgarity
                              of
   sorts," he'd say every now and then. The phrase
   came loose from what it was stuck to at first,
an ictic insolence the more he repeated it, the thing
   whose name it was if it named anything... "A
                           vul-
   garity of sorts," he all but spat, consonant with
   the waves tumbling in. He went back to the book but
   came away from it, back as though the break were
                              the
   book, which it was. Where was it if not in a break
   we stood I wondered, herons and egrets lifting up
from the marsh nearby, reeds and the like right at
                              the
   water's edge, where was it I rhetorically asked...
The low rung of the river lay to our right falling
   seaward, no way to be where we were unalloyed.
                              Bro-
   ken water, collapsed hatch. Fallen rung. Sunken
   lock. Flank we were shadowed by... Wherefore the
   book, there being more than one where, would-be
containment, step fallen out from under. There we
                              stood
   on the next rung down, dust on our feet from the
   summer, step we stood abreast of, caroling more
   than one when... The tumescence of when was our

book outside the book, a see-thru hymnal we sang
                                                  from,
   andoumboulouous dust in our throats. The tumescence of when was part Philomena, part filler, a
   book we coughed our throats out reading from...
                                                  Thus
   the *ta'wil* he worked, sublime substrate, query, quib-
      ble, quirk, platonic two-step, *a vulgarity of sorts*
   titrated, sublime sulfate, lexemes lined in a row. He
                                                  re-
      collected the log he'd sat on hatching balloons to-
   ward the back of the beach, the grain of Sophia's
   neck, hand, face, the closing up of when a dry suc-
culent, a pressed ice plant, a stain on the page... To
                                                  what
   end I wasn't sure except to say it had hold of him,
      Lone Coast recension a kind of pixie dust, breathy
   book his wish blew thru. Lit precipitate, something
                                                  a
   smile brought to light, something the sun, outdone,
backed away from. Lit remnant the new epiphany,
   gray day, gray water, gray sky... He said it was the
                                                  book
   of being there, he called it the book of having been
there, there but for looking on and also by looking
on, there but not all there, no matter where, wherefore the book... Sophia sat him down he said, her
                                                  book
   sat him down. Sat him down on the learners' bench
   he said, sat him down on a rotting log... Sat him
down on a smooth, round rock he said, sat him down
                                                  on
   a rock-hard zazen pillow, sat him down on what felt
                                                  like
   a throne

                              *

Itamar was a ghost haunting the spot on the
    beach where he'd met Sophia, the house they'd
eaten couscous in, the cliff the capoeira class
                           prac-
    ticed on... They'd lain in the sand one night,
bored but for the book that came after, a lighting
  up as latency rose, a lightening up, hot stuffy
                          room
    the world had become... *Clothes on, off, on,*
platonic either way, knowing what wasn't might not
  suffice, each toward the other's loins' bouquet,
                        there
    they'd lain, blasé. This the taunt song running thru
                          them
    as they
lay

            *

    (slogan)

    It wasn't what he thought it was, no matter
    what he thought it was, a ravenous ghost
  gorging on crumbs... Sand mixed in, no
                    mat-
    ter. Salt mixed in, good as gold, sweet
    savor. It wasn't what he thought it was... A
    swing or a swell, sweet riches not so rich,
                      all not
    lost like-
    wise

Letters Inscribed in Snow
Laynie Browne

WE ARE STANDING in a gallery looking at the floor. Embedded, sunken, is a four-foot-by-four-foot-square slab of ice, opaque white. Around the slab is a rope, officially cordoning off the area. A plaque on the wall upon entering the small room reads "A Book Inscribed in Snow." The ice is blank, bare. The artist did not show up to the opening. We find out later that the artist used a pseudonym. An agent had installed the piece, and departed. Failed to answer questions. The artist clearly intended an unwritten and therefore open book. Surely the real author or the real artist would come forward. But what does that mean—the real author—of snow, of the found, of letters, of invisibility. Bodies standing on frozen ground in winter. Trying to divine what is written beneath. Upon which inscription do you stand?

*

dear—

I want to be writing my new novel. But I have not begun. Though I've taken notes many times, beginning with a series of dream letters, inscribed in snow. My thoughts are still too unformed. When the right fictional story (which I plan to steal) falls in front of me I will begin.

And one of the central questions will be:
Is the writer writing to /obsessed with someone living or dead?
Imagined or real? Or is the one writing the letters the construct?

And another will be, what is a letter? Or maybe the book is made up entirely of journal entries, found on the pavement. Or about to be published by one who has died or vanished, or fictional accounts of dying, or dying as an impetus for correspondence.

Yes, I love you.

How will the book begin?

138

*

Sitting in a café, I put down the chain of dream letters I had been reading. They were published under your name but I was doubtful. You have many names and this was one encoded, an anagram of your enclave, but also a symbol used by a collective of writers who write nothing. You say, in a multiauthored statement, that writing now is lifting, recontextualizing the abundant texts already existent. You say that writing is amplifying, that writers perform as a modern circulatory system. A nervous system, testing impulses up and down avenues, axes, venues of ether, and performative bodies.

*

I was supposed to meet you at the café. I put the chain of dream letters back into my bag and tried to concentrate, my head bent over my laptop and piles of papers. I kept looking up to the plate-glass window, beaded with rain, each time the door opened. In came many faces covered with water, and coats buttoned tight. But each time I looked up it was not you who entered and after a while I lost track of how long I had been waiting. What an endless chain of persons who are not you. Suddenly when you did appear I closed my eyes for a moment because I disbelieved what I saw. How could it be you? You were smiling and suddenly there was no distance between us but even though I recognized you, what I recognized was not your person. Is that possible? The moment furled and unfurled. I was standing to greet you. Distance closed around us, the enormity of having never before met in person, unless once years ago. Or was that imagined? I'm not sure because in our correspondence once, when I was brave enough to mention it, you behaved as if I had said nothing.

*

Later you sent me a message I did not entirely understand. I had wished for a spectacular meeting and instead I wondered if I had been speaking to a blank composition book. The message relayed an unsolved mathematical problem, which you noted as the most notorious problem in theoretical computer science. You summarized the problem like this: P=NP? You mentioned that the problem would be difficult to paraphrase, but practical applications included cryptography. If the solution to a problem can be verified in polynomial time, can it be inscribed in polynomial time? In order to find a solution, one must first locate a book of exponential time. But your words disorient my meaning. What is your meaning? You try to overcome the difficulty of unsolved problems by breaking down the separation between the body of the known and the unknown. You tell me that this is how you define art. You ask me to join you in this project of decoding the absent book of dream letters. I agree, though I do not entirely grasp your motives.

*

We are standing in a gallery looking at the floor. Embedded, sunken into our memory, a four-foot-by-four-foot-square slab of ice, opaque white. The space is still surrounded in rope. A plaque on the wall upon entering the small room reads: "Here was once installed A Book Inscribed in Snow." The ice has been removed. You did not show up to the meeting of the enclave. I was surprised that when I looked down into the sunken space, I saw a pile of papers. Who had left them? Whoever it was clearly intended for us to find them. Was it the original artist or someone else? But what does that mean—the real author—of letters, of intent, of anonymity? Bodies trying to determine which hand should reach in and retrieve the letters. Above whose inscription do we stand? The letters were white, opaque, eroding. Around one notion of already published texts, now another set of letters might continually enlarge us. As we stood examining the bundle, once absent, now actual.

*

dear—

What I really want to know is (that is what the character in the book will want to know) why am I writing this fiction when I have a perfectly reliable life? I have a perfectly remarkable problem I cannot solve. A dream is transparent only to me and is the safety of that which cannot be taken. I must reverse. It takes a very potent illusion. Why now, am I addicted to abandonment, hidden to my motives? Where is the one who walks into the light, across a frozen letter wearing only a smile? And that is enough.

*

dear—

I will go and visit my fences now, the ones that keep me sane, such as the borders of any body or book, the borders of time and light, borders of what is said and unsaid. I like to mess with these borders, to know they are in place to some extent but then to stroke or subvert them.

Everything is a lie. There is no separation of bodies. We are less than a myth of ourselves. And aging is another lie, what we look like, how we rely upon ideas of ourselves. Humility comes later, when we work harder to keep ourselves intact.

I try to forget pain through pleasure, through trying to break down any separation between my body and the body of my lover, who is willing and brilliant, but does not entirely grasp my motives.

*

When I ask about the chain of dream letters inscribed in snow you pause from your calculations and look up at me. We are sitting in your studio, on cement floors. All around us are printouts of statistics, long vertical equations. Letters I have sent to you. Poems created by formulas. Exquisite corpse drawings. The bed is unmade, covered in star maps. Texts by Kepler, Einstein, Archimedes, Euclid. You look at me as if some deterministic polynomial time has been thrust between us. You look at me as if to solve for "x" were comparable to violence. You must have known that I was not asking if you or your enclave had written or found the letters. You looked at me as if to say, how could I possibly ask to whom the letters were written? In this moment of nonspeech between us I saw clearly that I was being accused, but of what I was being accused I had no idea. A book of silence instantaneously arose. Did your gaze communicate animosity that I did not know what I should certainly know? Either I was the "you" to whom the letters were addressed, or the mentioned lover, or it was someone else in our small circle I probably knew. Probably

141

it was someone who had been standing around that night at the gallery, looking at the blank slab of snow. This was in fact the real reason why the publication of the letters, their circulation, had gained so much attention. The letters were an endless source of speculation.

There we were at all hours of the night, groping on hands on knees, with pencils and pages, tall glasses of tea. We were turn machines, binary representations, working on this question of completeness, nakedness, on conditions, positions that might satisfy a question. We had become the question in episodic wanderings. We knew nothing about integers or time, but we became an architecture about the mathematics of nondeterministic futures.

Two Essays
Adam Weinstein

BRIEFLY CONSIDERED: SUB-PLOTS

> *Then there were the sub-plots, being pleasant things, which dreamt below four of the six gardens of the parish. Mr. Tyros and the elders, however, preached against the plots with such effect that their manufacture was abandoned.*
>
> —*The White Rose of Chayleigh*

1.

BEFORE CONSTRUCTING THE GARDEN, the sub-plot is considered. It is never spaded, dug, or trenched, but caved using dynamite, or any such potassium *lumen*. The charge is laced along the bare ground and exploded downward until the correct depth is confronted. Thus the process is also called *lumination*: from Latin, "light," but also "opening." When installing a new garden, the boom indicates that the process has begun—the boom, the first language of the garden space, its *pneumaphon*: breath + sound. This is a holy sound:

> Again a dart, the Wind-God's own,
> Upon his string he laid,
> And all the demons were o'erthrown,
> The saints no more afraid.
>
> —Canto XXXII of the *Ramayana*

2.

In his treatise on lumination, Viollet-le-Duc notes that the sub-plot "is the artificial foundation on which the garden will rest" (*C'est sur ce roc-factice que repose l'immense cathédrale*).[1] In his original

---

[1] *Dictionnaire raisonné de l'architecture française du XIe au XVIe siècle*, Volume 4.

French, *factice* ("artificial," but also "dummy") plays on both the creation of an a-physical space—a hollow upon which the garden rests—and its *dumbness*, or silence. The insistence on the garden as *cathédrale* suggests the sub-plot as crypt. Yet here is an empty crypt, loss without origin:

> What bitter blanks in those black-bordered marbles which cover no ashes! What despair in those immovable inscriptions! What deadly voids and unbidden infidelities gnaw upon all Faith.
>
> —Ishmael

Its *phon*, the primordial sound, is an impossibility: a body that never was, which simultaneously calls from within the coffin, "But I am here." It is a silence (σιγάω) that lusters.

3.

For every six shovelfuls of dirt, exploded by lumination and collected in a barrow, one shovelful of ripe manure or humus is mixed in. Water is added until the resulting mash is the consistency of heavy mortar, and enough mortar is pasted along the newly plumbed walls until they are completely resurfaced, preventing them from crumbling. A light raft of branches or sticks is braided over the dig, and then shoveled over with dirt.

In his commentaries on lumination, Origen indicates that the branches for the roof of the sub-plot should be those of the palm tree, "instead of branches cut from the trees or stubble brought from the fields and strewed on the road." In the Greek, Origen uses the word *poi* (φοι), denoting branches from the date palm (φοῖν), which also suggests the particular color of the branches: purple or crimson. Origen also plays on the etymology of Phoenix (Φοίνιξ):

> When this bird completes a full five centuries of life straightway with talons and with shining beak he builds a nest among palm branches, where they join to form the palm tree's waving top. As soon as he has strewn in this new nest the cassia bark and ears of sweet spikenard, and some bruised cinnamon with yellow myrrh, he lies down on it and refuses life among those dreamful odors.

Poi is both the Phoenix's feathers and the color of its death. It is the nest it builds in the top of the tree, *poin*, and also the Phoenix itself. *Poi* is a tapestry of contradictory notions, which both affirm and deny that the Phoenix did, or will ever, exist. When one points to the bird at any particular moment, one has only a slur of colors, states of being, textures, ontologies, and irregular spaces. It is fitting, then, that *poi* seals the sub-plot. This is the perplexing beauty of the non space, the hidden heart that refuses to be defined. Once its roof is broken open, for instance.

4.

The history of gardens is a history of order. Consider the Persian *chahār bāgh*, which is divided into four quadrangles to represent the four corners of the earth. Here the garden's order is an analogue to pure, universal geometry. Or the Japanese *kaiyū-shiki-teien*, which uses *miegakure* to guide the visitor along a carefully chosen path. And finally the Victorian garden, whose special order is that of imperialism and conquest.

> The garden is a rug onto which the whole world comes to enact its symbolic perfection.
> —Foucault

The sub-plot, on the other hand, refuses order. Once the space is constructed, it signs an impossible ontology. Thus the sub-plot is marked with the image of the *obolus* (ὀβολός), which carries a double meaning. On the one hand, the *obolus* is the shell of a clam. Although the lines of the shell are drawn in radiating concentric circles, they end at the crustacean's lip. Yet here begins the clam's double, its second half, where the radiating turns back toward its source, from the largest circle to its most minute at the hinge—and again, and again. It is fitting, then, that the *obol* is also the coin given over to Charon. We cross the river Styx clutching empty space, a shape that mirrors itself in hollows of calcite. We return to the place from which we perpetually depart.

But *obolus* is also *oubliette* (in Latin, *oblīviscī*): absolute interiority. Closed and locked, it is a room without language. One cannot speak *of* the sub-plot, but only its skin. Once it is covered with palm leaves, laid with fresh soil for seeding and planting, and then grown thick with vegetation, the sub-plot is dream, and the dream is always already *obliterated* the moment it is enacted—*oblīviscī*, forgotten.

Instead, we may lie down in some garden and close our eyes and test the space by thunking upon it.

5.

The sub-plot, then, reminds us that the garden never draws to a conclusion. It is the perpetual question *When?* Whereas the garden will proceed chronologically, the sub-plot may exist *kairologically;* that is, it has always already existed, and in doing so, it is always already forgotten.

6.

At the end of the season, say, in late summer, when the kale begins to yellow, the tomatoes are touched with frost, or the broccoli has been cleared of its crowns, we pull the stalks and rupture the soft soil. When the pulled roots are especially deep, one might get down closer to the soil and peer at the earth as it is carried away in bits, both clinging to the excavated roots and also as it piles concentrically around the new lack. From the fissure arises static, an aggregate noise (Latin, *nausea;* Greek, ναυσίη). But one realizes that the static is unsourced—it seems as if it was already there, somewhere in the color of the excavated plants, the garden itself, maybe the space around the garden.

Soon snows begin to fall. The ground is covered in a fine white sheen. When the first deep freezes come, the grubs and nymphs bury themselves deeper in the soil, protected by the blanket of snow. It is the season when all things kneel before Boreas, who dwells in the cave of Mount Haemus in Thrace. He is god of the north winds, bringer of winter. "By force I drive the weeping clouds," says Boreas.

> I whip the sea, send gnarled oaks crashing, pack the drifts of snow, and hurl the hailstones down upon the lands. I, when I meet my brothers in the sky, the open sky, my combat field, I fight and wrestle with such force that heaven's height resounds with our collisions and a blaze of fire struck from the hollow clouds leaps forth. I, when I've pierced earth's vaulted passageways and in her deepest caverns strain and heave my angry shoulders, I put ghosts in fear, and with those tremors terrify the world.
>
> —Ovid

146

Adam Weinstein

* * *

In spring the garden is reseeded. We plant spinach and kale, collards, turnips, carrots, parsnips, lettuce, radishes, and peas. Sometimes the nights dip to freezing, and in the morning the seedlings are a deeper and more fragile green. But if the day is warm, the plants recover, and by late afternoon it is as if the night never was. Soon the fruit trees bloom, the apricot a thousand buds of white. And then, when the promise of frost is forgotten, the tomatoes and peppers and eggplants and squash are sown. Sunflowers are already a foot high. Scapes are clipped from the garlic and onions. Soon summer will be upon us. The cycle is replenished.

And yet: There is always a lurking space, neurosis of the *terra*. It is there in the night. In Aeschylus, the seven warriors sacrifice a bull; "touching the bull's gore with their hands," they swear an oath to Phobos, god of fear, who delights in blood. But their promise is false. Gore will not undo gore. Tautologies, which are intractable, cannot be undone.

  Gaia, earth and mother, daughter of primal Chaos, has her secrets. When we draw the space below the garden, so do we pay tribute to the silence from which all life springs.

> The sub-plot is an infinite sphere, the center of which is everywhere, the circumference nowhere.
> —Judah Moscato, Sermon 31

The sub-plot is the song of our bodies. Always already lost, it refuses us. And we embrace it in discomfort.

Adam Weinstein

TABULA RASA, OR, SOME VERSIONS OF THE ICE

> *I try in vain to be persuaded that the pole is the seat of frost and desolation; it ever presents itself to my imagination as the region of beauty and delight. There the sun is forever visible, its broad disk just skirting the horizon and diffusing a perpetual splendor. There snow and frost are banished; and, sailing over a calm sea, we may be wafted to a land surpassing in wonders and in beauty every region hitherto discovered on the habitable globe. What may not be expected in a country of eternal light!*

—R. Walton, Saint Petersburgh, Dec. 11, 17—

1.

At the South Pole, three oceans converge: the Atlantic, Indian, and Pacific. In contrast to the immense sheets of ice and bergs, the waters are a profound blue. In his 1772 journal recording the crossing of the Antarctic Circle, Captain James Cook writes that the color can only be described as a tautology: "Blue is that blue is."

Cook's words echo the *tetragrammaton* of the Hebrew Bible: *'ehyeh 'ašer 'ehyeh* (היהא רשא היהא), "I will be that I will be." Rabbi Moses de León, a thirteenth-century kabbalistic scholar, notes that *'ašer* (רשא) is a mere anagram for *rosh* (שאר), or "beginning." Secreted in the *tetragrammaton*, then, is the origin.

Thus, in Cook, the eternity of the ice.

One hundred and twenty years later, when Robert Falcon Scott successfully lands on and explores areas of the Antarctic, he carries the words in his pocket, written on a scrap of paper. Scott's 1910 journey was his last. The entire crew perished of starvation and cold. Some years later his journal was found, and the record of the tragedy is clear and hopeless. Near the end, the rations are gone and the men starve; blizzard upon blizzard pummels them, erasing any hope of exiting the icy, barren maze: "Oates' last thoughts were of his Mother, but immediately before he took pride in thinking that his regiment would be pleased with the bold way in which he met his death. He slept through the night before last, hoping not to wake; but he woke in the morning—yesterday. It was blowing a blizzard. He

148

said, 'I am just going outside and may be some time.' He went out into the blizzard and we have not seen him since." Says Scott: "We all hope to meet the end with a similar spirit, and assuredly the end is not far."

The men had made their way into the interior of the Antarctic, where three oceans converge and disappear, the beginning and the end, themselves disappearing into the most profound blank of space.

2.

Since the time of the ancient geometers, the arctic regions were the boundaries of the world. The North Pole is Arktikos, after the constellation Ursa Major: Arktos, the bear. Arktos is the guide, never dipping below the horizon and always visible to travelers:

> the Great Bear, that some have called the Wain,
> pivoting in the sky before Orion;
> of all the night's pure figures, she alone
> would never bathe or dip in the Ocean stream.
>
> —Homer

The South Pole is Antiarktikos, the beginning. There, in the caves of Nox, sleeps the dreamer Cronus,

> confined in a deep cave of rock that shines like gold—the sleep that Zeus has contrived like a bond for him—, and birds flying in over the summit of the rock bring ambrosia to him, and all the island is suffused with fragrance scattered from the rock as from a fountain. And the prophecies that are greatest and of the greatest matters they come down and report as dreams of Cronus.
>
> —Plutarch

Over the South Pole rises the constellation Centaurus. Half man, half horse, the centaur is the symbol for transition, existence posed on the threshold of two worlds. Beyond the gates of Cronus is the timelessness (*aiónios*) of the gods:

> For you are infinite and never change. In you "today" never comes to an end. And since your years never come to an end, for you they are simply "today." But you yourself are eternally the same.
>
> —Augustine of Hippo

149

*

In Aristotle's *Physics*, the poles become a model for the universe. The ice is *entelecheia*—a combination of *enteles* (full) + *telos* (purpose)—and *dunamei*—potential or power. The ice is possibility. In *De Anima*, Aristotle uses the unwritten tablet (*grammatei*) analogously. Suspended between the poles of birth and death, we are coming-to-be (*genesis*) and ceasing-to-be (*phthoras*). Mankind is time (*chronos*), the unceasing perfection of the ice.

When Cook wrote "Blue is that blue is"; when Scott, carrying the words on a scrap of paper, perished in the abyss: There was the absolute confronted.

3.

> He was the first man who desired to break the
> close-barred gates of Nature down. The vital force
> of his intelligence prevailed, and he advanced his
> course far past the blazing bulwarks of the world,
> and roamed the whole immeasurable Cosmos.
>
> —Lucretius

Tracing the forgotten paths of the alchemists, Victor Frankenstein pursues nature to her hiding places. Says Frankenstein, "They had left to us, as an easier task: to give new names, and assemble, in connected classifications, the facts which they in a great degree had been the instruments of bringing to light."

With only the moon to gaze on his midnight labors, Frankenstein collects the bones of the dead, and disturbs, with profane fingers, the tremendous secrets of the human frame. "A churchyard was to me merely a library of bodies deprived of life," he says, "which, from being the seat of beauty and strength, had become food for the worm. I paused, perusing and analyzing all the minutiae, until from the midst of this darkness a sudden light broke in upon me. After days and nights of incredible labor and fatigue, I succeeded in discovering the cause of generation and life; nay, more, I became myself capable of bestowing animation upon lifeless matter." His is the power to command the thunders of heaven, to mimic the earthquake. More, to rewrite the visible world with its own shadows.

Yet at the conclusion of his work, Frankenstein finds the beauty of the dream vanished, and breathless horror and disgust fill his heart: "A cold dew covered my forehead, my teeth chattered, and every limb became convulsed. By the dim and yellow light of the moon, I beheld the wretch as it forced its way through the window shutters." Like the Arabian who had been buried with the dead, Frankenstein finds a passage to life; aided only by one glimmering, and seemingly ineffectual, light, he authors the dream that poisons sleep: the monster.

As one who has come breech through Cronus's threshold, the monster is neither time nor timelessness. Scarred by his own liminality, he is cast abroad. Where he seeks protection and kindness, he is despised. He is an object for scorn. He is profoundly alone.

And so, united by no link to any other being in existence, the monster flees to the everlasting ices of the north. Says the monster, "Everything is related there, which bears reference to my accursed origin; the whole detail of that series of disgusting circumstances which produced it is there inscribed to mock me; the minutest description of my odious and loathsome person is written, in language which painted your own horrors and rendered mine indelible."

Formed from primordial *chaos*—known to the alchemists as *nigredo*, the shadow within—it is to *chaos* that the monster seeks his return. At the threshold of night, where sleeps the dreamer, the monster will build his funeral pile and ascend it. He will exult in the agony of the torturing flames. The light of that conflagration will fade away, and his ashes will be swept into the sea by the winds. From the ice he will be absolved and unwritten: "My spirit will sleep in peace; or if it thinks, it will not surely think thus."

Yet in Arktikos, desire is anathema. Hope is made grotesque in darkness and distance. The monster burns himself on the pile, and his ashes form hieroglyphs on the ice. His bones are masked by frost. Borne away in his glacial coffin, he is carried to the sea; and with the mighty shock of an earthquake, the ice splits and cracks and the monster is cast adrift, one of the numberless bergs in the frozen Arctic waters.

*

Perhaps, one day, the monster will be revealed to himself. One day, deep in his forever dream, the monster will hear the whisperings of a stranger. It is a voice that will come to him from beyond the threshold of time. "You perceive, now," the voice will say, "that the life you've dreamed of is impossible except in a dream. You perceive that it was pure and puerile insanity, the silly creation of an imagination that is not conscious of its freaks.

"Strange, indeed," says the voice, "that you should not have already suspected that your universe and its contents were only dreams, visions, fiction! Strange, because they are so frankly and hysterically insane—like all dreams: a God who could make good children as easily as bad, yet preferred to make bad ones; who could have made every one of them happy, yet never made a single happy one; a God to whom you ought to have been Adam, but were, rather, the fallen angel, driven from joy for no misdeed. Everywhere you have seen bliss, from which you alone have been irrevocably excluded. 'Make me happy,' you have said, 'and I shall again be virtuous.' You were benevolent and good; misery made you a fiend.

"Yet you are not you—you have no body, no blood, no bones. Frankenstein has no existence; he was but a dream—your dream, a creature of your imagination. And you are but a thought, dreaming at the threshold.

"Some day you may realize this. Then you will banish Frankenstein from your visions and he shall dissolve into the nothingness out of which you made him. On that day you will be free—to dream other dreams, and better!"

Until then, the monster is blind in his grief. He is a vagrant thought, a useless thought, a homeless thought. By his nature he is inextinguishable and indestructible, dreaming forlorn among the empty eternities of his solitude.

4.

At the still point of the turning world. Neither flesh nor fleshless;
Neither from nor towards; at the still point, there the dance is,
But neither arrest nor movement. And do not call it fixity,
Where past and future are gathered. Neither movement from nor towards,
Neither ascent nor decline. Except for the point, the still point,
There would be no dance, and there is only the dance.

—T. S. Eliot

Between the years of 1903 and 1905, Roald Amundsen became the first explorer to successfully traverse the Northwest Passage, a route that traces the southwestern coast of Greenland, and the northern coasts of Canada and Alaska. In December 1911, he reached the Polar Plateau. When asked how he was able to accomplish his many feats, he replied that he owed a great debt to the indigenous peoples. It was from them that he learned Arctic survival, using sled dogs for transportation and animal skins for warmth.

On June 18, 1928, while attempting to rescue part of an Italian exploration team that had crashed on their return from the North Pole, Amundsen's plane disappeared in a fog near the Tromsø coastline. Focusing on a forty-square-mile area of the seafloor, the Royal Norwegian Navy's unmanned submarine, *Hugin 1000*, searched for the wreckage. Nothing was found. Amundsen was the last of the Heroic Age of Arctic explorers.

In some versions of the ice, it is the unbroken silence that attracts and repels us. Says Aristotle, "as someone waking is to someone sleeping, as someone seeing is to a sighted person with his eyes closed, that which has been shaped out of some matter is to the matter from which it has been shaped." In Aristotle is the hope of the unwritten, the coming-to-be.

At that certain hour, however, when solitude overwhelms us, we may try to make the ice speak. We author a demon, who, alone and anguished, kneels before his creator and asks, "Why did you form a monster so hideous that even YOU turned from me in disgust?" His ruined cry evaporates in the frozen absolute. The ice is mute.

Each year, as the earth grows warmer, the polar ice caps begin to melt. The oceans rise. Various species disappear or alter their migratory routes, and villages are in danger of flooding. Soon the earth may again become the hourless tranquillity of unbroken seas. Mankind's destiny will be fulfilled, and the page, itself unwritten, will reveal its sublime secret. "Heartless void," says the poet: "The ice is the fantasy our own annihilation." And here, perhaps, is the true terror of the ice: It is *duma*, silence. Called "the wielder of fiery judgment, the destroying angel," Duma is eternal death.

> Unless the Lord had given me help, I would soon have dwelt in the *duma*.
> —Psalms

Among the descriptions of his South Pole expedition, however, Amundsen records another version of the Arctic:

> It is some hourless moment in the early days of the world. The sea, absolutely still, so perfectly mirrors the night sky that I cannot tell where the universe begins and ends. And then, from amid a ring of stars, some *thing* appears to me. Soon it comes near to me. It might have once been a seal; but now, touching the fine hairs, and staring into lifeless eyes, I only see death.

As the thing floats before him in the abyss of starlight, Amundsen watches ice crystals sprout upon its body. Time moves at a great pace. Soon the thing is nothing more than a dark kernel within the ever-growing mass of ice. Aeons pass, and the seed is lost to him. "In those far-off days when the mighty mass of ice pushed on with awful force," he writes, "without meeting hindrance or resistance, it met a superior power that clove and splintered it, and set a bound to its further advance. It was a frightful collision, like the end of a world. But now it is over: peace—an air of infinite peace lays over it all." Where there once were placid seas, Amundsen now gazes at the great expanse of the Arctic.

In Amundsen's vision, the ice is neither the beginning (*rosh*) nor the end (*ehyeh*); neither in time (*chronos*) nor eternal (*aiónios*). Instead of gods or deities or magic, the ice is a cocoon, inside of which is a *thing*: the sad opacity of flesh, robbed of spirit. It contains no secrets, nor does it proliferate them. Deep within the ice is death all the same, but it *is* death: unspeakable perfection.

To know the ice, then—*tabula rasa*, the unwritten—is to know silence, complete and absolute. Says Scott: "We will make unto ourselves a truly seductive home, within the walls of which peace, quiet, and comfort reign supreme. The word 'life' is struck out and 'window' written in." Perhaps we might call it eternal death. Yet it is to be empty of desire in perfect repose, the profane spectacle of eternal bliss and the machinations of extinction abandoned.

NOTE. Appropriated text in section IV from *The Mysterious Stranger*, by Mark Twain, and *Frankenstein*, by Mary Shelley.

Ravished

Chris Tysh

NOTE. *RAVISHED* IS THE CLOSING section of a three-book project, entitled *Hotel des Archives*, consisting of verse recastings from the French novels of Beckett, Genet, and Duras. It is a deterritorialized type of literary translation I've been calling "transcreation." Taking the French prose of *Le ravissement de Lol V. Stein*, Marguerite Duras's 1964 novel about female voyeurism, as a point of departure, I operate a double shift: one of language and genre. Consonant with postmodernism's practice of appropriation and *détournement*, this tactical move away from ground and origin directs me to writing as a site, passage, or arcade, where the lyric opens up to the endless traffic of signs. Ultimately, transcreation signals to both the first text and its afterlife, the graft that lives on under a new set of linguistic and formal conditions. This regeneration is a participatory, dialogic communication beyond continents, languages, and temporalities. Duras's admittedly always-already poetic narrative is carried into prosody as a mode of expression, that, without entirely losing the novel's diegetic arc, travels along its border ever so nimbly, and yet always retains the libidinal shadow that haunts her lines.

V. AS IF STITCHING A SHEET

As soon as she sees him
come out of the theater

Lol recognizes the man
in the dark valley of her mind

155

Chris Tysh

something incendiary no doubt
rapacious leaps out from the eye

the way he looks at women
wanting more with each gaze

enough to recall
the one she'd known

before the ball?
Maybe she's wrong

What heat and fatigue!
She'd gladly slide

this heavy brooding
right here in the street

I see the following:
The man has a few

minutes to kill
before his rendezvous

Chris Tysh

scanning the boulevard
a vague hope Lol finds

divine
of meeting yet another girl

than the one she spied
in the garden

in tune with his step
she tails him at a distance

intent on placing her feet
in the same black prints

as if stitching a sheet
with big hasty needles

She must be wearing
those flat ballet shoes

I imagine or invent
a gray coat maybe a hat

that can be taken off
any minute to pass

out of sight   indiscernible
like a blade under the tongue

Roving eyes he ferrets
the teeming square

mourning every woman
in advance of the one

who doesn't exist yet
for whom he could

at the last minute ditch
the very lover they both await

Given the black and vaporous
mass of hair   that

small triangular face and
immense eyes outlined

by the ineffable guilt
of this adulterous body

given unlimited funds
of soft round hips

as she steps down from a bus
against the crowd

golden combs to the side
of a dark *voilette*

he will be the only one to free
in a single gesture that goes

snap around the shoulders
inside a minuscule cry

They are together—trains   winds
heartbeats   a summer solstice

come to as if pushed
by the same high tide

Chris Tysh

on the surface of an inlet
sensation of thirst misread again

Lol will have easily guessed
the name that trails there

spell or apparition
had known it for weeks now

the round vowel sounds
dance on pursed lips:

Tatiana Karl's migratory
beauty approaches the Forest

Hotel past waving alder trees
and a large naked field of rye

Sheets of ice one could say
where she'd gone in her youth

with Richardson   forgotten
about   crystal cup

Chris Tysh

she spins under her footsteps
No use to shadow them too close

since she knows where
they're headed

How she lowers herself flat
out barely visible dark stain

In milky-green shadow
a few feet from the light

that just went up
on the third floor

At this distance she can't hear them
and only catches a glimpse

if one of them crosses the room
up and down a bluish shape

holding a cigarette
elbows on the sill

Chris Tysh

smooth as a stone
Tatiana reappears in the frame

Night has come mixed with lies
about a greenhouse on the edge

of town accounting for Lola's
return at such a late hour

Husband and children pity
her numb hands—can't help

believing her tall tale
almost lost the thread

VII. TOSSED FROM SELF TO OTHER

What happens next
at the Bedford house

is hard to explain even less
form a contiguous shape

that curves around the guests
wavy and restive

162

balls on a pool table
about to break

It's a question of who sees
whom outside the fan

of windows skirting the grounds
The women are poised

by French doors   voices
loop together like an *étude à quatre mains*

In truth, it's the husband's violin
we hear bursting from the upper floors

Jean has a concert tomorrow
Lol explains   stroking Tatiana's hair

Something strange a sudden proximity
of opposites begins adrift

an arc that cuts flower beds
tears apart what's left of truth

Chris Tysh

I hide bent over to better hear
oh sweet venom

"Not sure I can visit as often
I have lovers, you know"

Tatiana's pink mouth pouts
velvety phonemes

In this blind man's bluff
it is Lola Stein who is "it"—we think—

and maybes
infinitely translatable

language   temporal and deictic
as "here" and "there"

When I look up again
from behind the bay window

Lol's eyes seek mine
belying a certain gaze theory

164

the consoling fiction men wear
like an armband

Here I am again stepping
into a bayou   deep mossy folds

where love changes hands and color,
over black and blue skies

On the periphery of her lie
I shall howl and be quartered

in the wide sense of the word
she utters to prove she's back among us:

"I've met someone recently"
Having just smelt a burning house

Tatiana feels like shouting, "Watch out, Lola"
instead she turns toward Jacques Hold

"Shall we go?" He says, "No,"
like a convalescent stretching his long legs

Chris Tysh

IX. THE LONG SPOON OF FEAR

That Lol is not yet "cured"
shows up in the way guests

hang on her words
when she laughs

too much or stops
midsentence

They pass the long spoon
of fear   ever so polite

not to spill a single drop
of the old belief

that women rarely come back
intact from such passion

All want to know more
about this act of translation

where one language
picks up someone

staggering
in an empty street

only to precipitate her further
into a gorge of substitutes

in the other—faint thumbprint
of alarm about her temples

Now radiant amid the seated
company   she draws

a pattern on the tablecloth
as if plants and meaning

shared a common plot
I look down at my shoes

any minute now the ship
will break into pieces

and I'll be swallowed
by the whale of a lie

Chris Tysh

But the moment passes
and Lol's husband drops

the stylus on a record
that sounds like rustling

skirts or footsteps
on dry leaves

I whirl Lola away
in a zigzag dance

toward the bay windows
"You went to the shore"

I say like a detective
coaxing a confession

Almost pitching
against my shoulders

—a cargo I've stolen before—
we'll go together, she says

tomorrow very early
meet me at the train station

Like a border guard
Tatiana takes up her post

but the noise of the phonograph
blurs our words—a fence

she squeezes through
on the edge of tears

She begins to understand
an intimation of things past

that a sudden explosion
has altered the grammar

that is to say binding agreement
between I and me   she and her

When Pierre Beugner appears
at her side I know for a fact

that should Tatiana cry even once
I'd be out of a job on the spot

Superb in her new dress of pain
she almost faints at the idea

as if death were a sheet
come to cover our nakedness

I invite Tatiana Karl to dance
"What does Lol mean when she claims

to have found happiness?"
Her hair cascades so close

to my lips I should start
running

Instead like every rake
I simply say, "Je t'aime."

On Translation's Inadequacies
A Personal Essay in Two Languages with Interpretive Translation

Minna Proctor

PIO

—COSA FA UN pulcino di 40 kg?

—Non so. Cosa fa un pulcino di 40 kg?

—Fa PIO PIO PIO.

Anche se gli uccellini parlano la lingua di fede, non vuol dire che è una lingua semplice. L'uomo Pio che conobbi, non lo era. Pio non fu pio. Tutt'altro. Noi ragazze lo chiamammo Il Lupo. Cose così:

—Com'è andato con Il Lupo 'sto weekend?

—Bene. Andato veloce senza freni.

Freni . . . Non frenare. Parlavo cosi perché ero principiante e Pio me l'aveva insegnato. Ero giovane, semplice, piena di fede nel domani. Una gallina, piccola, tenera, preda di notte agli avanzi del lupo.

—*WHAT DOES AN eighty-pound chickadee say?*

—*TWEET. TWEET. TWEET.*

Birds speak systematically. The bigger the bird, the louder the voice. The louder your voice, the more love you find. The more love you find, the more love you give. Whence love whence faith. With faith, you leap. With faith, little bird, you fly.

Birds, I learned as a young woman, speak differently in Italian. As do dogs. Dogs say "bau bau." Roosters say "circhirichu." And birds, chicks to be precise, say "pio" to mean "chirp" or "tweet." Pio also means pious. And Pio is a proper name—as in Padre Pio, the beloved saint who came from Campania, a region in southern Italy. I knew a man from Naples named Pio—not a saint. Not even a little. We called him The Wolf. Wolves ululano. Pio was a wolf—all Drakkar Noir

171

*and a fussily groomed five
o'clock shadow.*

*Pio and I both worked for a
small company that ran LCD
subtitles at film festivals and
one weekend ended up
together alone in a hotel in
Pescara, a battered cotton-
candy beach city on the
eastern coast of Italy. My
Italian was crummy. Although
I'd lived in Italy for almost
two years, I was only just
beginning to have the courage
to say things. I was eighteen,
courage was capricious and
often more reckless than it
was impressive. For some
reason that wasn't clear to me
in the moment but became so
later, Pio spent a great deal of
our first meal together that
weekend trying to teach
me the meaning and
pronunciation of the word
"frenare"—to brake, like the
squealing brakes of a car. It is
astonishing how long perfectly
bright people can discuss the
meaning of words with
beginning speakers and have it
pass as actual conversation.
Really, you don't need small-
talk skills if you're an
American abroad. Especially
if you're pretty, blonde,
innocent, so young you don't
know the difference between
reckless and courageous.
Between faith and falling.
Between braking and breaking.*

BETWEEN TRANSLATION

Se c'è fosse solo un modo unico dire una cosa, non ci sarebbe bisogno degli scrittori, ovvero il bisogno ci sarebbe già stato, compiuto, tempo fa nella C'era una volta. Detto. Fatto. Non c'è da dire niente di più. Finché le cose non si cambino da se, senza l'intervento linguistico.

Invece siamo noi tutti esperti dei varianti, noi traduttori delle esperienze della vita e dalle ombre, di quello che è e quello che viene detto su quello stato. Sia meglio. Sia diverso. Io lo capisco così. Tu lo capisci cosà. E così vanno i verbi. Senza di che ci troviamo in compagnia di uno scrittore di discreto fama in sua casa gentile in un elegante quartiere della città, noi due, volte intense, insieme seduti davanti ad una scrivania d'autore molto ben curata, le pagine scolte dappertutto con degli appunti nelle margini in due anche tre lingue fallite. Chiedo. Ascolto. Che angoscia per lo scrittore, che fatica l'essere preciso ed evocativo. Lunga pausa e lo scrittore e la moglie ballano una bellissima danza stile Portoghese. Il consumato non ha traduzione. E se non questo . . . Che angoscia l'essere imprigionato dall'idea che ci sia solamente un verbo. Ed è verbo suo.

My mother and I argued at length about the translation of the word alma, *which appeared in a line of poetry she was setting to music. She set poetry to music all the time, but it was often instrumental and so she didn't always use the poetry itself in the final piece. The words themselves were inspiration and incidental. But she always included the poetry in her program notes and often consulted me about the Italian translations. We disagreed about* alma, *which has several meanings in Italian but in English it's just a proper name that seems derived from* alms. *In the end we agreed that all translations were inadequate but settled on the English word* sigh, *because that's what the music it had inspired sounded like.*

I worked once with a famous author on a translation of his short stories. People kept asking me if he was an asshole, because that was his reputation locally. I found him instead to be charming, respectful, dedicated to his art and his beautiful wife. We labored over his lush, baroque stories, stacked with literary references that spanned

E se ho capito bene, vorrei
sapere che cose succeda quando
muore?

periods and languages,
complicated by his impatient,
roguish, and ambitious mind.
We spent many ten-hour days
comparing texts and choices,
confirming variations and
testing the implications of
every English decision I made.
We'd break for strong sweet
black coffee and one day
instead of coffee he and his
wife danced. They twirled
gorgeously and easily around
the living room—as if the
word intricacy *had never*
been invented. Piteous Fado
on the record player turned up
to a deafening volume. All
translations are inadequate
and just before the book was
sent to press he fired me.

I stopped translating. And
more recently he died. There is
no trace of the stories I wrote
from his stories. My version is
gone and so there is one less
reading in the world of his
immutable words.

ALMA CHE FAI?

Da una lingua ad un'altra
cambia il cervello, dai ritmi,
sensi, colorature. Questo è il
perché alma può significare
anima spirito nutrice sospiro in
Italiano ed in Inglese no. Alma
era una parola che discutevo
molto con mia mamma prima
che morì. "Spirito" dissi.
"Sospiro" disse. Ma in verità
lei non doveva mai scegliere
perché lei si esprimeva in
lingua musicale. Spesso
componeva musica ad una
poesia italiana senza neanche
usare le parole della poesia
nella musica. La parola ispirava
la musica. Un passo oltre
traduzione andava la mamma,
un passo che esprima tutti i
valori di una parola. Eppure io,
andando un passo oltre in
un'altra direzione faccio conto
ora che parlare italiano, scrivere
italiano, pensare italiano, è
quello che facevo da ragazza.
Ed ora non la sono più. Se
traduco da italiano attraverso
non solamente la lingua ma
anche un tempo. Se parlo
italiano mi esprimo nella voce
di una ragazza, con pensieri,
spiriti, sospiri da ragazza.
Giovane io sono in italiano.
Sciocca pure. E beh. Per lo
meno sto qui, a visitare un po'
con la mamma.

*Something I always resented
about Italy (at least the Italy
I lived in as a young woman)
was that if two couples went
out, the men would sit
together in the front of the car
and the women in the back.
God forbid a woman drive
when a man's available to do
it better. No chance at all that
you'd want to spend any part
of the double date talking to
your boyfriend. Less chance
even that you'd want to spend
it talking to your friend's
boyfriend. Obviously, if it was
just the two of you alone, you
always got to ride up front,
and routinely as if he were
engaging a parking brake, your
boyfriend would stick one
hand between your legs and
drive, shift, and smoke with
the other. Because Italy is like
that (at least the Italy I lived
in).*

*One night we were out with
Fulvio, who was an actor,
and his date, who was
English. Her name might have
been Rose or Alma. Either
name works because we only
ever met her that one time—
like so many of Fulvio's
passions. Rose and I gossiped
together in the back seat
because that was the friendly
thing to do and Fulvio, the*

175

*actor, who had briefly and
uncharacteristically stopped
talking, suddenly remarked
that I spoke entirely differently
in English. He insisted that
based on the few moments
of conversation that he'd
overheard from the back seat,
I was an entirely different
person in English. I
volunteered that I might be
smarter in English, though
maybe less precise, and he
said he thought instead that
I was softer, heavier somehow,
more intense and a little
scary. Not at all like a
screeching cat. Because
otherwise American girls the
way they talked were all
screeching cats.*

*I often thought I was happier
in Italian, because somehow
there was less riding on it. I
didn't have to commit. At
eighteen, nineteen, twenty
years old, Italian was a
costume I'd hide in for
months at a time, smartassed
and awkward, full of
wonderful sounds that I
disgorged as if they were the
most sophisticated and
viscous primal scream therapy.
And when I was hiding in my
Italian costume, English was
transformed. It became my
private refuge, the language of
silent thoughts, puzzles*

*of abstractions I never needed
to solve because there would
never be a need to express
them. I said* Ti amo *to a man
long before I could bring
myself to say* I love you. *I was
even able to say why I loved
you in Italian, because, I said,
it's the only thing in my life
I'm sure of.*

*There are pictures in my
mother's photo album from
when she was a young woman
studying composition in
Florence in the late 1950s,
black-and-white photos of her
and a beautiful young man on
a bench in the Boboli Gardens.
His short dark hair is putty
thick and unruly, his big
almond eyes cut back like
knives along languorous
cheekbones. My mother is
glamorous, perfectly turned
out in a trim little suit dress
and patent leather pumps,
her freckles standing out
exotically against her pale
skin, one eyebrow cocked
ironically, her curly dark hair
sleepily crooked as if she'd
just woken up from a nap on
a flower bed. My mother's
Fulbright grant went very far
in postwar Italy, she felt rich
for the first time in her life.
She had clothes made to order
and said sometimes she'd
have four stuffed artichokes
for lunch, just because she
wanted to. For many years I*

177

*thought the man in the picture
was a boyfriend she called
Claudio, who she said was
always cross at her for being
late.*

*Everything untranslatable
belongs to her—both young
women in Italy, both shedding
oppressive American selves,
running a little, and flying a
lot—we trespassed the same
foreign refuge together
decades apart. After she died,
I sat for hours looking at those
photographs, trying to conjure
and consume the brilliant
years of my mother's youth by
sheer effort of staring. And I
suddenly saw for the first time
the wedding ring on the hand
draped around my mother's
shoulder and realized it
wasn't Claudio in the picture
at all.*

Fragments from Lost Zoroastrian Books
Eliot Weinberger

There where the sun rises

*

The edge of a razor

*

Of knowledge, not love

*

The several kinds of wheat

*

All good thoughts I think willingly; all good words I say willingly;
all good deeds I do willingly. All evil thoughts I think unwillingly;
all evil words I say unwillingly; all evil deeds I do unwillingly.

*

The skin on the head
[. . .]
The head of a man
[. . .]
One bone of the skull
[. . .]
All the blows that [. . .] the skull are counted

*

179

Eliot Weinberger

One whose words are accepted

*

As much as the earth

*

Fifteen sheep, their hind feet

*

Libations offered by a liar

*

All the agreements in the world

*

The smallest of those stars is as large as the head of a man of middle size

*

He makes himself guilty of the sin of breaking a man's leg

*

thwam khratus
[*Meaning unknown.*]

*

A place that gives pleasure, though not absolute pleasure

*

The column of life made marrowless

*

From there they come to kill and strike at heart, and they bring locusts, as many as they want

*

The ox rose up, the land bore

*

Soon he changed this to death by the fault of his tongue

*

Of the same thickness

*

For the first time he comes near to her, for the first time he lies beside her

*

What is between the kidneys and the spleen?

*

The shortest *hathra* is of three words
[Hathra: *a measurement of both space and time.*]

*

The dead shall rise up, life shall come back to the bodies, and they shall keep the breath

*

The man who [. . .] does not [. . .] anything, be it ever so little

*

badha idha afrasani danhubyo
[*Meaning unknown.*]

*

It becomes more violent than that

*

Give lawful, well-examined wood

*

Another man, of a steady leg, [. . .] glory

*

stavano va puiti paidhi davaisne va
[*Meaning unknown.*]

*

Even uncovered and naked he will chant

*

How many sorts of plants are there?

*

If their fathers at once

*

In such a way that death should not be produced by burning

*

As much as a fly's wing, or of a wingless

*

He calls him

*

Let no man alone by himself carry a corpse

*

By two fingers, O holy Zarathustra!

*

Of the dog-kind

*

Than the nose is to the ears, or than the ears are to the mouth

*

For all of them shall a path be opened across the Kinvad Bridge

*

As large as the top joint of the little finger

*

He has made the good waters and the good plants

*

And Paradise, boundless light, undeserved felicity

From the Dung Beetle's Perspective
Edie Meidav

> *I grew up thinking there had been a war, and that our soldiers had gone to war to guarantee the democracy. And that there were no disappeared people, that it was all a lie.*
>
> —Victoria Montenegro

THINK ABOUT BECOMING A PARENT and you consider consequences. When you came into our life, we thought about what a world stretched and all we wanted to teach you: we must hold tight to the faith that this document I am now composing will stand the test of history's reckless habit of making virgins out of everyone. Others call it amnesia.

Never forget you were always our hope, your mother's and mine. That your mother died when you were young, that she remains in your recall a shred beyond what you know from photographs is of course unfortunate, but who among us controls fate? Consider the strangeness of antibodies' passage through a vein, and how dimly we perceive this, just as we see the stars, great and mighty: mere pinpricks. So much of our knowledge operates in this manner, tempting and as irreproachable as it is unreachable.

Did you know dung beetles navigate by the Milky Way? They roll balls of dung before placing on their heads little dung caps that let them perceive the stars. So many things come down to this sort of magnetism and gravity. Equipped, the beetles make their way as best they can.

From their perspective, family rites make perfect sense. And of course it also makes sense, in a fashion that remains eternal, that the young regard their parents with accusing antennae. It did not take Freud to invent this trick: generations increasingly turn on forebears with the rage of new life in them, the unbent grass using the decomposed dead from which to derive vigor.

You are on your way toward becoming a mature young woman and are, moreover, with child, so I thought it important to hand you now, our faculties still intact, a sense of what might be most important as you continue forward to becoming a parent yourself.

184

Once I had a lover. I hope this does not embarrass you, now that you are of age, since what child fails to cringe at what an old fuddy-duddy does with his unit after the military dress has long been retired, so to speak, becoming a jolly roger only brought out for special occasions, but I have always been proud of how you have conducted yourself, both as a student and at home, not to mention as a girl and a blossoming young woman. I believe I can speak honestly. Why? From early on I knew you were special, a prodigy, most especially at the harp but in so many other domains: you a daughter whom I could press forward to my associates and have you read aloud for them particular words, at one of the many parties your mother and I loved to have, parties filled with associates and colleagues—and what beautiful words those are, words that say that a person exists.

To you, our colleagues and associates may have been insects stretching forth long scratchy arms from one of our many overstuffed armchairs, aiming to tug you close to their cobwebs—visuals of nose hair and an aroma of reminiscences tinged with wet dog scent—but to us they were our cherished company.

For them, and blame me for this still, I would sometimes press you to play the harp. You say now you winced as your wrists turned one arpeggio after another. Yet to me you had the face of an angel, reminding us of better, simpler times. When no harp was handy, to our colleagues it is true I might say: Ah, look what sophisticated words our daughter can read, how proficient she is. Often, it is true, I'd pick up a random book and there you would be, a shock to the system. You told me years later you hated this, that I made you feel like a performing monkey, but who would not be proud of an eight-year-old pronouncing such difficult words in such a mellifluous voice, yours carrying such strange and great authority? It surprised all of us.

Argillaceous. Autochthonic. Erumpent.

Your eyes would flash afterward, rating your audience. Since you could read any word from whatever technical book I happened to have handy, it is natural you wished to gauge whether we were worthy.

Were we? What I can tell you is that at a young age you happened to be proficient. I do not share this bit with you merely to inflate your ego. Of course not! Nor do I preach speed for its own sake, the burden of the prodigy. Of what use is it to arrive at an end sooner than others? Who are the leaders of today who appreciate speed because they do not wish to acknowledge their past? Nor should we disguise the fact that your mother and I were proud, I most especially, that you could read so young.

Of course later you blamed us for having encouraged you to skip a grade, but what were we supposed to do with you when already in kindergarten you were reading? The teacher with the mole and slit skirts told me she often left the classroom with you in charge, reading to your fellow pupils. To that kind of child, what can something as mundane as first grade offer? You blame us for how you hold your pencil, never trained in mundane cantilevering. And for the shyness in your second-grade classroom that made you find it less embarrassing to sit in your seat and urinate, a small puddle spreading its shame, rather than leaving to sign your name outside the bathroom that both boys and girls used. That you were shy about signing your name surprised me. This was hardly a trait associated with my family line or the daughter I knew, the one with whom I now share so many fond memories. I never had any trouble with you. How surprising then to learn from your mother that you carried your wet balled-up underwear back and forth in your satchel for weeks before stowing it in the back of some drawer marked *miscellaneous*, a word you knew even back then how to pronounce, this a mark of your greatly advanced state.

But to return to the point, once I had a lover, before I was with your mother, of course, for all that your mother liked to tell me I was often an admirer of other women, to which I would reply that women are set down around us so we may admire them. Would you tell someone in a rose garden to hold his nose? If someone walks on a beach, do you tell him to stop breathing the salty air? Everyone ends up with a particular menu of tastes. My own point here is that this woman, the lover to whom I am referring, liked me to slap her a bit and also to yank her hair when we were between the sheets. I suppose the direct phrase to use here would be when we made love, since in your current state it is quite clear you are at that unblushing stage where you have acquitted yourself with one of the young men with whom I have seen you disporting yourself, boys with such large Adam's apples it is apparent you must have, as a girl growing up, appreciated one of your neighbors, one of those gangly boys for whom all energy seems to collect at the throat.

To return to the point: I concur, making love is nothing to blush about. Of course in my era we were idealists. In folk songs, girls and women were flirty but during our meetings so impossibly near and earnest, and how hard it was to understand these two aspects living together: suture together a red-hot, wriggly bonobo bottom to the bespectacled head of Karl Marx and you can imagine how we boys felt. If we rookie surgeons managed the suture, we enjoyed what came of it, the fruits offered once we had executed enough healing on that pesky mind-body dialectic. All that consequent wriggling around seemed a healthy enough part of the new philosophies with which we stuffed ourselves.

At such times, if one connected to a flitty girl who turned out capable of earnest delivery, one could feel oneself a lion of the nation, the loin of its future. This line of reasoning may be hard to understand if you didn't live through our time. But our flutes and guitars, the fitful gyrating along with our chatter about the new world order, all of it a direct ladder toward the bedroom, made us know we helped a good system ascend toward its historically inevitable triumph.

The funny thing, and not to linger on this point too much, is that if you are a man with full-blooded sympathies and you lie with enough Trotsky admirers, you do start to feel you form part of the national pride, so admirable and sporting in any moment that you need promise little to any female. The assurance made us was that one day each of us would find a fertile seedbed into which we would lay the pearl of possibility. Such patrimony we could bequeath, such a feast promised all of us. None of us thought seedbed or pearl could betray our good faith, none of us thought we'd have to take matters into our own hands.

Of course you can imagine how hard it might have been for a young man like myself, on the cusp of full masculinity, who already guessed what sacrificing to the dedicated commitments of adulthood might mean. Grow older and all branches become more singular. As if to become older means you start climbing an upside-down tree only to realize you now cling to one hefty trunk: the trunk has become your fate and *amor fati* will be your limp consolation.

So imagine that I was still early in my climbing, on one of the branches of that upside-down tree, still foolish in feeling this branch could lead anywhere, much as one begins a document like this, something particular to both writing and life: one begins and thinks the branches could lead anywhere only to find oneself on the trunk of a particular conclusion. I climbed since I was an ambitious corporal, to be sure, and I had a lover, a bit older than I was, more experienced, not that her flesh was any the less supple, only that her experience was so much greater than mine that I wanted to plant a flag in it, to conquer and swallow it whole. And she, too, wanted me to conquer, this woman who liked me to do her like a dog. Does this seem a quaint notion, now that people are into, as they say, so many different sorts of activities? She needed me to yank her hair back and then mutter words from our former dictator, the one from whom publicly we were happy to be free but who privately still ruled our bedrooms.

I do not mention this to make you wish to throw down this guide in disgust, though I begin to realize that this might not be a story I should follow to its logical conclusion. Again, it is merely that as a man of advancing years it has become incumbent upon me to share with you the wisdom I have collected in my time, especially now that you find yourself with child and may need some advice about parenting, one of the horrible new words to which my generation has had to accustom itself. We did not know about parenting, we just became parents.

Suffice it to say, of course, as I rose in the ranks, aspects of my position became distasteful to me. It was announced to me, for one thing, that I had to leave the older lover in the dirt without ever seeing her again: she never believed that such injunction came from directly above and not from the greater above, that of mortality, or a man's distaste for anything reeking too much of it. Paradoxically, soon after the discharge of my yanked-hair lover, it happened, as a condition of my particular role in the administration for that period, that I came to be in charge of how people disported themselves between the sheets. Of course we didn't refer to the duty in this way. Rather, having ascended to a post in one of the more cultured ministries, a post I had coveted, I found myself tasked with nighttime behavior. You see how readily I took to how people spoke there. So many of those around me liked to say that particularly ugly phrase, that people were tasked. Be that as it may, wishing to prove worthy of the new nation we were all creating, I stood ready to be tasked and would show myself through the tasking.

And in one of my new roles, I was asked to come up with a new code of morale for the nation, something quick and slangy enough that people could recall it easily, something they could use as a dowsing rod when making a choice that might affect our national hygiene, if you will, and so of course I said: Remember Our Traditions, since one of the first logos we had as a nation back when we were first forming ourselves in the more modern way was the man in his broad hat taking the woman in the peasant dress by the waist to swing her about. This man in his elegance, our fellow of the logo, looked as if he would have voiced such a motto to his sons as they prepared to take leave, heading out to storm the world, just as the woman, the mother of our nation, appeared with the cant of her head and outflung arm to have advised her daughters in similar fashion. Remember our traditions. What those traditions were did not, in truth, need much plummy articulation: enough to invoke this glorious house of the past in which we were not peasants married to the dirt but rather gallant wielders of tradition.

And it is not just that this motto now appears on all our billboards and official correspondence, it having been taken up with a spirit I could not have foreseen, even if there is that unfortunate resultant acronym, ROT, given the gothic cast the designer gave the first of each of the letters, so that we are ROTting away on every official communication and children see this ROT in their classrooms, but rather I see now that as a father I might remind you to hold tight to our traditions.

A few years ago you began asking in a manner I can only describe as querulous about some inconvenience in the fact that we maintain no photo albums of you in your early years, in contrast to the tottering weight of those we have amassed ever since you were three.

Every child feels the indignity of what a parent does or occludes, and what can I tell you, dear one? Your mother was a great one for amassing photo albums in general, to be sure. But what comes to mind is that you never asked me about other items probably more relevant to your future, such as the unfortunate case of Michael A., a man too kind to a group of infidels in our government. What happened to poor Michael A.? He let dissidents dine at his table, his children playing with theirs, and then one day, Michael A. failed to show up at his office. A hint of poisoned chicken was bandied about, a mention of foul play by a maid, and still one could find no trace of him, not the slightest whiff. What do you say about someone like this?

He was duped into his end, a state of mind that, in our family, you have never had to fear.

As I consider it, our troubles, yours and mine, began the day recently when you looked at me strangely. Middle of an official lunch you had attended with me, you sprang the question on me like one of the feral cats you so pitied as a child, your look so biting. "What if you were not my father?" What kind of thing was this to say as I was about to ascend to my magisterial functions, soon to walk up the stairs that wiggle so inopportunely, up to the podium where I would place a ceremonial wreath around the neck of an important man, a popinjay, of course, the kind of strutting man whom it is hard for me to celebrate, whose tailfeathers have always been too hefty for the scatter of thoughts in that vain little head, while it occasionally falls

189

upon me, in my position, to celebrate the undeserving.

The opposite of such moments of unworthy celebration—and I could string a wreath with them—was always you. Do you know that I could have had a birthday for you every day of every year we had together? Do you know all the times I have held your head to my chest and stroked your hair? That I so painstakingly learned after your mother's death to use my brute thumbs in braiding your fine girl's hair, no easy task for a man who, back in our darkest decade, had his hands hammered by an unscrupulous interrogator?

How can you then turn to me and ask me such a question and at such an inopportune moment?

Do you know that your question stayed in my throat, a choke, and as I aimed for equanimity, I tripped on those stairs, and as I looked over my shoulder, thought I saw you choking down, in strange symmetry, a giggle, your face a mirror of what I saw in the popinjay's smirk.

The next day, as you know, you pressed upon me a photo of two rebels you believed were your parents. That awful friend of yours gave you the photos and the misinformation. What is more horrifying is that you chose to believe her fairy tale.

Is it a parent's job to instruct a child in what to believe?

You came upon me in the kitchen where I was having the maid make the kind of soup you once loved, the one I made whenever you were sick. The one for which I had to go to the local butcher's, where he knows me and owes us some favors, his house having been passed over in many recent storms, where he now bequeaths us massive bags of bones he promises come solely from grass-fed beasts of our plains, the bones with an architecture oddly large and misshapen, truth be told, now taking up all the room in the freezer another fellow in our district gave us as a small gift at your last birthday.

Is it true—you dared ask, as I was telling the maid how to stir the soup from the outside of the pot toward the center—were my parents those journalists who criticized you?

The maid, an alley cat who speaks only the indigenous language, someone with whom I communicate in a pantomime that gives me no little pleasure, averted her eyes. Even she knew something disgraceful was transpiring.

I should have asked you back a more serious question: Do you wish to defile the memory of your mother this way? Or, rather, do you know how many have been destroyed by the carrion who alight on the memory of what our nation wished to become?

The heart doesn't kidnap you, it doesn't hide you, it doesn't hurt you, it doesn't lie to you all of your life, you said, love is something else.

Brush your hair, I told you, we're going to be late.

This is incredible, you said. All those times you threw your gun down on the table to tell us about subversives being tortured or killed?

Is there something you really need to say, I asked, my posture stiffening. I have long believed every man has something he can offer any scene of confrontation, yet it had not become clear to me what I could offer.

Argillaceous. Autochthonic. Erumpent. If I could only hear you with the sweetness you once had speaking those words again. What could I say back to you.

Popinjay?

You stole me! And then the final straw: It was good your wife died young. You kill everything!

I would not have any more of the vileness you were trying to stuff in me.

Instead, I grabbed the soup ladle from the maid, gave the broth a determined stir, and turned on you, modulating my voice: You know, dear, ever since certain friends came into your life, they have sucked out your sweetness. Is what you're saying something they have pressed into you too?

It's not my friends, you said, it's you!

You flounced out of the room, leaving me with the maid already turning back to her soup, making one of those horrifying indigenous gestures that could mean benediction, protection, curse.

After you spoke, I decided I could no longer stomach the official function to which we were meant to go and instead went to my room with its comforting morocco walls and gold-studded chairs, a room in which one can pore over a secret black book, because of course there does exist one concerning you, with all supporting documents neatly folded, tabbed, placed in archival lamination. And so since one day you will find this black book, after I die, unless I were to burn it, which seems an inhumane course of action, I thought it might behoove me to write you now, to help you understand some of the issues parents have.

For one thing, as any parenting book will say, the one I intended to write at the outset of this branching narrative, parents must act as containers for the emotions, violent or otherwise, of their children.

191

Hence it falls to me to gently entertain and then correct your version of events. Were I to abstain from this function, you would not qualify as my daughter and I not your father.

To begin with, we did not steal you: we saved you from an unfortunate situation. What in your temporary blindness you call an abuse of power was to us a righting of collective wrongs. I ask whether you would have preferred an orphanage, which would otherwise have become your upside-down tree trunk? Little life would have cleaved to such a trunk.

In your eyes flashes an anger I can recognize. Know that this document is the best way I have of letting you know some of what you wish to know. You have not spoken to me since our conversation. You believe it an admirable use of your life energies to keep on smoldering. And if you still think you should call those other two your parents, I am sorry for you. Every person will go to a heaven or hell made of their beliefs.

Why is there no birth announcement, you kept on, your eyes black holes.

The maid might as well have not been there in the room with us. As you leaned toward me, I was all that mattered to you. And if I loved you with great heat in that moment, with something I have never been able to conquer rising up, it changed nothing, especially not how you smelled then, such a clammy and dank girl, my daughter a girl so much of the grave, one could almost say argillaceous.

Memo to My Muse

Paul West

LOOK, SWEETHEART, I KNOW we are living on borrowed time that we have been borrowing from life since 1984, when we heard from that pliable humanist of a doctor we should not expect too much longer a life. Well, as DHL said, we have come through, two golden retrievers of the mellow soul, stronger than ever because I the vehicle (you the tenor) am partly bionic, a fine howdy-do for an ex-athlete who played as a pro for years. Clearly, honey, it's the words that have saved us, neither of us recognizing they had no limit, could be parlayed to the top of their bent, and then some further. So many old chums actually goners, among the mothballs and lilies, rescued by no navy, vouch-safed no warning (some). I can only conclude we are still being called upon, not by embossed cards on a silver tray (as in the officers' mess of long ago), but by word savorers who must have heard that farcical conversation when my publishers told my deans, *Don't let him retire, he'll flood everything.* If I did, it was only, honest, because I was going slowly, honest: a couple of pages a night, or on a satin Bermuda beach with pink in the ink of a Luddite—just long enough to indite one of these samples of a life's exhaust, except for ours. Hence this.

Taken literally, any stethoscope's an instrument for listening to sounds produced within the body, but your average Boy applies it to the TV, the radio, water pipes, woodwork, even a roach trapped in a typewriter-ribbon box. Dum-di, dum-di. I listen, lick my lips at, the sounds of the red jellies churning and wobbling within chest cavities. Given opportunity, I would listen to Lenin's tomb, the Pyramids, the Rock of Gibraltar. I've heard trees growing, limestone creaking, roadways humming, cigarettes crackling, even the stereo (when the machinery adds its whir to the sound of a symphony, like technicians getting in the way during one scene of a movie shoot and, thanks to some astute director, being left in, not as a novelty but as a specimen of the truth-behind-the-truth). With some fore-boding, I've listened to silent things—the air, a pound of fresh-ground coffee, the phosphorus head of a match—and have thereby developed a dismal sense of what ignores me. Take this thought even further:

If you slash your wrists, the blood doesn't look at you, doesn't heed you at all, but goes about its business according to known laws. I sometimes lose sleep when I get to thinking about how much of each person is merely *stuff*, without which he wouldn't be alive, but which has nothing of his personality stamped on it. Put Napoleon's heart alongside Stalin's, on a clean, white tray, and you don't know which; or Byron's penis alongside Casanova's, Helen of Troy's twat alongside Sappho's, Abraham Lincoln's bladder alongside John Brown's. You never know whose from whose. And that's partly why I'd like, although from what surgical-supply store I know not, a stethoscope for listening to identity, something regular and measurable as a heart's beat, something that persists, can always be eavesdropped upon. But then what would you hear? A heart makes a succession of beats; an identity, according to David Hume, is only a succession of perceptions, so to speak, and the mind is a theater that is its own play. So why bother? All you would hear is a series. You'd be none the wiser than the Chinese Chuang Tzu, who dreamed he was a butterfly and, on waking, wasn't sure if he was a man who'd dreamt he was a butterfly or a butterfly who now dreamed he was a man. The other night—was it night? I'm unsure, but it was a black time—I dreamed I was myself, and now I don't know if I was An Other dreaming or if now I am another. I can't sustain this for much longer: The mind's fidgeting, forever in fact in recoil from this or that, it won't obey, it never did. Worst of all, even at my most vehement instigation, it won't dismiss the conceit that I have been *taken over* by the Tesseract Fund in ways other than financial, so much so that my dizziest imaginings have come to be just as "real" to me as, say, the hives I've been plagued by, or my spondylitic neck, or migraine or dyspepsia or postnasal drip.

For example, in one of my books *I* am the planet Mars, I no longer laugh at such a fatuous swap. I'm accustomed to my body temperature's varying from 80 degrees Fahrenheit to –300, which is mighty upsetting to those reactionaries of etiquette who still insist on shaking hands. A friendlier frostbite they never had. I no longer mind my diameter's being only half that of Earth or my mass's being only one-tenth of same; after all, my pressure is only 1 percent, I've no oxygen at all, just carbon dioxide, argon, and water vapor, oh it's a serviceable mixture, it cuts down on my smoking and those violent keep-fit runs across space I used to fancy myself doing, and it tends to keep visitors away, they so much dislike wearing suits, it makes the whole affair so damned formal. By now, I've grown accustomed to those space paparazzi who zoom past with cameras at the ready, hoping to catch me scratching at my scrotum or leering at Venus. Nobody sees much of me, that's a fact; a flyby's only a fleabite, I conveniently blush for them and it's over and done with. Once, before I evolved a philosophy, the slanders used to bother me: being linked up with (and made responsible for, in some cases) war and agriculture, which was like attributing peace to that mountain of exaggerated presence, Everest, and razed-ground activities to Mount Etna. Most intolerable of all, though, has been the comparatively recent downgrading of my intelligence: Mars, once thought capable of intelligent being, they have now decided has nothing but rocks in his head, in the cracks of which there may, here and there, be a plant or two. It's true that 30 percent of my complexion is discolored—a bruised blue green, as if I've been swatted in the face by micrometeorites—and this they used to interpret as arable land, or something just as gross. Little do they know that these are camouflage areas known locally as Anoxybiotic Biblianths, in which, instead of men's writing books, there are books busily writing men, the rationale for this activity being as follows: gaping at my blue-green regions, but virtually writing off what of me happens to be ocher red, such men as Schiaparelli, Lowell, Archenius, Kuiper, Tikhov, Dollfus (unfortunate name!), and Oepik planted labels on what they thought significant—quotable—features of the Martian style. Thus I find myself saddled with (to name only a few) a Scandia, an Ortygia, a Mare Boreum, a Tempe, an Ascuris, a Cydonia, an Eridiana, all of them names having an unmistakable leftover flavor. I don't mind this too much, you can give a dog a bad name and it sticks, but not a planet, certainly not while the so-called experts in Martian Environmental Medicine are still fooling around with such stray concepts as anaerobic bacteria, glycerol, waves of darkening, perma-warm spots, and subsurface water tables. What truly got my Martian goat was the imposition upon my surface (no doubt by astronomers with such names as Bill Posting) of the following quasi-literary allusions: Amazonis, Nix Olympica, Dis, Elysium, Electris, Hellas, Ausonia, and Atlantis. In retaliation, which I myself regard more in the nature of a red-shift pastiche, the Martian mind is returning these concepts to their owners marked Sentimental, Trite, and Neoclassical. There are, however, a few other names inflicted upon me, which have necessarily been given other treatment, to wit the following, with Anoxybiotic-Biblianthic rendering as described:

Arabia: The Seven-Pillars-of-Wisdom is about halfway through writing his novella entitled *Gordon Lawrence*, publication dates

1833, 1885, 1888, 1935.

Eden: East-of-Eden, who seems to suffer continually from razor nicks, is doing one thousand words a day on *John Steinbeck's Pelvis*, the legs and spine already having been written. No date.

Arcadia: A professional hiker and passionate ecologist, Arcadia is hard at work in a mountain shack on his *Sir Philip Sidney*, having already completed the courtier and the soldier and half of the essayist, there being only the poet to go, and he mostly in paper cups. Tentative date 1586. Tentative price: thirty-three terrestrial.

Khaos: an immigrant writer from Belblin, Khaos has already finished off his treatise on gas in *The Body of Hermann Broch*, whose adventures with a potato—in both a race and a stew—will be recounted in detail with a strong Irish flavor and some small attention to the efficacy of gaslight in procuring suicide. Date uncertain. Price: five cogitos, three sums.

Both Aethiopis and Dis I have decided to reserve for myself, the one being a fiction about a black-power fanatic named O'Thello, born in Dubfast, the other a lively tale entitled *George Merde*, in which a girl called Dis will alienate a man called Dith with her cross ways. No date, no price; these books will be handed to the next ancient Mariner who flies by.

The group of us—Seven-Pillars, East-of-Eden, Arcadia, Khaos, and I—spend most of our time by one of the seas—Sirenum, Hadriaticum (a name that we think some Martian joke), or Chromium—writing with felsite on lava, going underground only when the dust storms occur, when we repair to a Mars bar and drink marsala while singing the "Marseillaise" to keep our spirits up. Seven-Pillars, mind, he likes to walk out in the worst of the dust storm, so we tend to be deprived of the best conversation he has (he addresses the particles and listens to them howl), whereas East-of-Eden, born under Pisces and a graduate of the Mare Tyrrhenum School of Marine Biology, likes to drink and be friendly, his nickname being Len. Arcadia's a bit standoffish and snobby, claims he has blue blood and a pedigree going back to Planet X, the matrix planet of the asteroids, that was guillotined some three hundred million years ago, but he answers to the name of Pimpernel or Cad and can always be made to cry quite openly if you tell him the story of the Lafayette Escadrille's expedition to Mare Australe in the year (-Q) or of the governor of MNC (Mars Narrowcasting Corporation), who once landed his private fun jet in Tempe, thinking it was Xanthe. As for Khaos, he's a morose, taciturn type, an inveterate late riser, so your chances of talking with him are slim unless you call him Jim, and then he cracks up with laughter, protesting he isn't Jim at all, Jim was a Memnonian whereas he, Khaos, happens to be an out-and-out Thaumasian. One can easily lose his way up here, even though the place is only three or four hundred million years old, with the water table not even set yet and the volcanic ash always getting into your eyes. Dark years ago, we sent an envoy to the Blue Planet—his name was Jail Borgias—requesting immediate cessation of Mars's labeling and complaining about the monotony of labels already affixed—most of them, in fact, terminating in those fusty old suffixes -is, -ia, -us, -um, -ium, et cetera, whereas the Moon, according to our observations, seems adorned, nay embellished, with such a varied pageant of names that (as we see it) the only healthy future Mars can have will come through cross-breeding with such eugenic paragons as Tranquillity, Boscovich, Wilkins, Flamsteed, Sharp, and Caroline Herschel, the main problem being to get them together. Borgias, it now appears, never made it to his destination, perhaps having overshot into the Magellanic Clouds, whose diameter those who measure have measured in light-years, or, having taken en route a subsidiary post as chicken inspector on Antares, three hundred times the size of the sun, or as head librarian on Venus, where books weigh only a little less than they do on Earth, although much more than on me. Whatever happened, no good has come of it, for daily we are affronted with fresh names. There is now Kosyginium, between Deuteronilus and Niliacus Lacus there is even Nixonia, and, saddest to mention, pseudoapocalyptically east of Khaos (which makes him insensate with rage) a Regio Jesus, which seems to have no bounds at all.

The only thing we can do—Seven-Pillars, East-of-Eden, Arcadia, Khaos, and I, Mars Apparat, to give for once my full name—is to shift this planet through sheer willpower nearer to the Asteroids, come what may. Our plan, if so desperate a maneuver may be anything so ascetic as a plan, is to have our moons Phobos and Deimos strike up a nodding acquaintance with Ceres and Eros. Meanwhile, we are circulating the rumor that Mars is indeed a dead world, as S. Arrhenius of Stockholm said in the early twentieth century. Appalling rumors from the Moon strengthen us in our resolve: When molehills come to be named Bardot, Westinghouse, Cola, Vatican, Capone, Sol Estes, Oswald, and Sirhan, you can expect anything on Mars.

And when it arrives I shall not be here.

The "Lost" Chapter of John Jourdain
Ranbir Singh Sidhu

SCHOLARS OF SEVENTEENTH-CENTURY literature of the sea have yet to fully take up cudgels in the debate on the veracity of the purported "lost" chapter of John Jourdain's journal. In the published account (as reprinted in the venerable Hakluyt Society edition of 1905) of his visit to the island nation of K., *The Journal of John Jourdain, 1608–1617, Describing His Experiences in Arabia, India, the Malay Archipelago, and Lands Nearby*, Jourdain wrote scathingly, describing K. as "hotte, uglie, and wythoute even those accomadations anye beggar mite finde agreeable."

Little more was said for some two hundred years, the location of K. left a mystery, which it remains to this day, and the subject thought of little interest; until, inside an old seaman's chest abandoned in a Kent attic, were discovered the yellowed pages of what appeared to be the entire original manuscript, which included the never-before-seen "lost" chapter. This seaman's curiosity was passed among a group of self-described "enthusiasts" for many years, and has only recently entered the broader realm of scholarly interest.

Though many consider it a forgery, the fact remains that the handwriting matches verified contemporary samples from John Jourdain, and the spelling matches his own quite unique form, which meandered among possibilities as much as he meandered across the globe. That the seaman John Jourdain, or his original publisher, would want to suppress this version seems more than likely, as it touches upon topics that might well have been considered inflammatory in its age: the hot-blooded whimsy of a traveler obviously affected either by fever or alcohol or, as is suggested in the account, other substances. As such, it can be placed next to Cyrano de Bergerac's account of his journey to the moon or the adventures of Hans Jakob Christoffel von Grimmelshausen's creation Simplicissimus in his flights of unfettered imagination.

But such poetical whimsy from so otherwise as obtuse a seaman as Jourdain seems unlikely, a fact that the considerable number of supporters of the veracity of the lost chapter never fail to point out.

The weight of testimony on both sides of the argument thus stands quite strongly, and the debate, as noted above, has only begun to be argued among scholars and the more learned professionals of the sea. In the meantime, it is up to the reader to decide for him or herself as to the credibility of events, places, and individuals described.

A MOSTT CURIOSE SOJERNE INN THE LANDES OF K.
BY JOHN JOURDAIN

Att my cominge aland upon an Unnamed Shore I found the Kinge and his Unkle both together, with many Others; of whome I demanded Leave to rest for several Daies for the Heate had strucke myself and my companions alsoe siche that wee knewe not some among us our verie Names and walked the Deckes like Ghosts unto ourselves and unto each one the other; all of us terriblie affrighted by the casualtie to our Common Senses. At one time I would calle my Chief mate by the Name of the most common Seeman, even of the Boy, and he would looke att me as though I had become one of the verie Natives that had soe affrighted us manie Daies before on the Ilandes wee did lande upon. At another time the entyre Crewe would not knowe me and calle me by siche strange Names and speake with siche curios Tonges that I guessed not who I myself was, holding the Beliefe that they who knewe me not knewe some larger Truthe. The Heate was the verie Devile Himself for it would leade oure Sense one way and when we felt the strength of Certaintie it would knocke all wee knewe downe and wee were but required to Build up again oure Worlde from Senses recentlie attacked. And then when again wee felt a common Beliefe growe among us, that wee each knewe the Name of each other, that wee knewe our owne Selves, the Devil in the Cloake of the Heate would come at us againe and knocke at our Certainties and Knowledge. Sailing aboute like this wee were at the edge of Great Blows and Violence wiche, had notte we landed at the Unnamed Coaste and there mette with soe kindlie a Kinge, wee would without doubt have become the Servantes of the Evile One in his Designes upon this Worlde.

The Reader maye wonder thatt in oure Flighte from the hordes of the Devile wee meerlie founde our bodies at the Mercie of a Pagan, though he bee a Kinge, and thatt then our Deliverance was of the kinde that sentt us from Pott to Flame, as the sayinge goes. Wee did not first see this and founde in oure Host everie Kindness that wee would bestowe upon a fellowe Christian mett in Distress, and onlie later did wee have cause to question the motives that wrote upon his Face and upon the Faces of the Kinge's Servants siche pleasant and welcoming Smiles.

The Kinge, upon oure coming aland, made readie a Feast of all the Fruite and Fowle and including anie Animale that walked upon four legs within his Dominion, wiche wee were led to belive singularlie Expansive for hee did compare himself to no other figure than the Great Mogul. All nite the fesivitie continued and wee were all much pleased for the beautiefull Daughters of the Kinge did serve us in most delitefull waies that many a dream of mye tired Crewe was thatt nite fullfilled by the site of siche lovely Faces. The youthfull Damsels did plaie and cavorte with us, singing and dancing in most Liberal a Fashion that my poor Christian Heart was much blushed butt my Bodie, wiche bee onlie Christian in the waie our Philosopher Platoe spoke of a Chaire being not a Chaire, but a reflection of an Chaire in the Heavens, and here I confess my Bodie bee butt an Earthlie Chaire and a sad reflection on thatt Heavenlie Bodie thatt wee all strive towards, did nott blush att all butt took full Part in the Festivities and their necessarie and most sweete Conclusions.

Siche a nite was hadd bye all thatt come the Morninge and again the dreadfull Heate wee but laye there, oure dear Damsels by oure sides, and slept untill no later a time as when the Sun rose direct above us and wee feltt the verie Skin on our Faces too bee on Fyre. I was the first up and seeinge my Men in so sad a situation I immediatelie sett to wakinge all. Soon they were gathered with their Maidens and I feltt again some reliefe to see noe Harme had come too anie in the Nite at the Handes of our Pagan Host.

The Heate did not abate and for manie Daies we played with the beautiefull Damsels that the Kinge gave us siche kinde Libertie of and oure sore Heartes were much healed by this Interlude thatt came upon us in oure dire Neede, soe wee eache thanked the Lorde fore His Generosities. Wee all believed thatt noe Force other than thatt of the goodeness and kindeness of oure Lorde did offer us these Heathen Pleasures, though the Reader maie thinke it Improper to give Credite to a Lorde for siche License as wee enjoied I awnsweare and saie I presume nott on the waie and manner of oure Lorde's Bountie butt take that wiche He offereth withe a Open and Gladd Heart. I knowe the Lorde onlie through that wiche Hee giveth and Presume nott on his Will as soe manie, or soe it seeme to mee, of oure fine Preachers doe who seeme to knowe the verie Thoughts of the One whose Name Men cannot Speake. Siche greate Powers are nott myne and though I reade His Book and knowe He is the Worde I will not speake for Him and do instead reade the payle reflection of his Grayttness in the Faces of the Maidens who gave my selfe and Crewe siche humble Pleasure.

After some dayes I gaind the abilitie to converse in the Language of the Native, haveinge learnd severall wordes of their Tongue from the able wymminn who accompanied us everyewear. With these wordes and much use of a Gesturall Language, one common to all Men, I was able to speeke with their Kinge and his Counsailors. Learnd Men speeke of the Tower of Babbel and how ever since siche Tyme everie Nation has had its own Language and theye speeke of the inabilitie of Man to talk to Man as the Roote of Much Evile. I saie Not Soe, for do wee nott have a Common Language, one even an unschoold Childe must knowe, in the Produckt of oure verie Hands. Do not oure Bodies speeke for Us as well as oure Tongues do. Is this nott howe the famed Venecian Marckoe Polloe first spake with the Grate Khan. Perchance the Bodie lackes Civilitie and the Daintie wordes that mayke a Parlour home of Genteele phrases but if one Man needes mayke himselfe known to another and the Twoe lacke onlie a Common Tongue then the Bodie speekes as cleerlie as anie Grayt Oratour in oure Howse of Parliemantt. No doubt thatt if oure Statesmenn were allowd to use onlye this Gesturall Tongue their Straininge to maike their meeninge cleere would avoyd us manie Battles and the loss of muche unnecessarie Bloode and far fewer Widowes would bee Cursinge the foolhardiness of Olde Men that bringe Countryes intoe terrible Conflagracion.

The Kinge tolde mee that the Heate which much affected my selfe and my Companions was alsoe newe to him and to his Countrye, afflyctinge terriblie his Subjeckts. He asked if perchance I mite offer some Respite through the Magicke of my Lorde, of whome I alreadie had spoken, butt I said I had no more Voice with Him than the Kinge himselfe, an Unbeliever. The Kinge was muche Distraut by siche News and sayd hee knewe nott howe to bring Reliefe to his sufferinge Peeple and askd if I mite accompanie him into the Highland where a Grayt Ceremonie was too bee held in severall Weekes. I agreed gladly for I was happie to repaye the Kinge for all the kindenesses he had offered us. But then his Face went Darke and I thought him angrie with mee and he spoke with a havie Voice telling mee that I must never speeke of whatt I see att the Palace or the Ceremonie for itt is all of a verie Private and Secrett Nature. I agreed reddily and sayd I would accompanie him alone and att this he smiled and the Darke stare left his Face and wee dranke sweete Wine and tooke of daintie Victualls.

Wee departed thatt same Daie. I told my Companie thatt I would bee bye Necessitie awaye some manie Weekes and for them all too mayke whatt Pleasant use theye mite of the ample Generositie shewed to us by oure Hosts. Theye were much gladdenned too Lerne thatt oure briefe Visitt would nowe extend indefinitelie. Manie had made among the Maidens serveinge us whatt in oure Nation we would call a State muche like thatt of Man to Wife, and sayd all would feele a sore Loss if oure Departure was deemed Imminentt. Among them I saw severall whoe passed up the most Beautiefull of Maidens and tooke as their Companion a handsome young Lad for whiche purpose theye Employd muche like anie Man employes his Wife. The Seeman in his Travells sees manie Sites, bothe Strange and Wonderfull, and of these the Man who lies downe with a Man is noe stranger than manie others, and the Thought should nott disturb the Reader. Is not the Estate of Marriage thatt made betweene a Man and his Wife and is not a Wife that Personne who is said to bee married to a Man. Then if a Man does marrye a Man, the one becomes, in the Eye of oure Lorde, the Wife while the other is the Husbande or Man.

A long Procession led up into the Hills and as wee Climbd the Heate onlie grewe Worse and I coulde see on the Face of the Kinge a grave Consternacion at siche unpleasante Climate. I was carryed in a coverd Palanquin similar to thatt of the Great Mogole in Hindoostan and feltt my selfe to be held in a Position neere thatt of the Kinge himselfe. Oure Journye was plaeasant and the Kinge tooke everie Opportunitie to tarrye and to followe those Pursuits naturall to Kingeshipp. I talk here of Hunttinge and Converseinge with his Subjeckts on their Troubles and Joyes. I was much touched when one Forenoone a young woman appeered whoe had recentlie lost her Husbande to a Disease cawsed bye the Heate and whose Lande was then stolen by the Brothers of her Late Husbande. She and her three Children weare leftt withoute Propertie or Livliehood as is Necessarie for the Comfortable Enjoyementt of Life. The Kinge ordered that the Brothers bee brought in frontt of him and so Brothers came, their Heads bowed and shewing much Obeisance to his Magestie. When the Kinge learnd the Truthe of the Womann's testimonie he ordered the Brothers bee putt to Death and soe they wear thatt verie Daye by the agencie of a swift Sworde.

I was too see muche of the Kinge's Justice in bothe its Terrible Anger and in its Gentle Kindeness in the weekes we made oure

Slowe Progress through his Dominiones and I was thus able, through his Naturall Trust of my selfe, the Cawse of which I could nott wholly fathome, to dispute with him about the Proper Function of the Kinge and wee passed manie an Eveninge drinking sweete Wines and comparing the Guvernmantts of oure Twoe Nations. I have alwayes enjoied an uncommon Speede at the learning of Languages and my enlargeing Vocabularie, combined with the aforesaide Gesturall Language common to all the Races of Man, gave us much Reason for Merrimentt and Joye.

One daie wee tooke oure Reste in a Towne where onlie faire Wymen appeerd to greete us in the Streete. Att the arrivall of the Eveninge no Men had shewed themselves and soe I askd the Kinge howe it was thatt we had encountered no Men. Were theye awaye Huntinge or carryeinge on other Activities proper onlie to Men thus giveinge Explanacion to their Absence. The Kinge tooke some Minutes to Respond and att firstt seemd quite Perplexed. This is a Towne, he explaind in due Tyme, where onlie Wymen lived. Haveinge said this he thought itt Sufficient and began to talk on other Matters. But I found no sufficiency in his Explanation and demanded of him the same Question. Hee then sayd thatt before even oure Enteringe he had beene Requird to aske Permissione of the Towneswymmin to Repayr here for the Nite and again, believing his Wordes enough, moved on to other Matters. The Kinge askinge Permission of his owne Subjeckts! The thought greatly troubled mee and I demanded whatt neede did a Kinge have to aske Permission. I asked whether here lived a Religious and Righteous Communitie much like the Nuns who live a Spare Lyfe in the Convents of deare England and soe requird Proteccion from the rowdie Entourage that ever followd the Kinge. These were nott Religious wymmen, the Kinge told mee. Indeed, they lived all together, eache beeinge Wife to everie other one soe if I asked, as I did at the Kinge's request, to whome a faire Maiden was marryed, she would smile like a Cockette and Pointt to everie Womann in the Towne. I was muche Startled by this News and then Demanded further awnswear to my firstt Quescion. Whye did the Kinge require Permission. Though hee was Kinge, he tolde mee feeling muche abused by continuinge Questions, he was still subjeckt to the Wymmin of his State. Above him the Queene ruld and she had decreed that whattever Towne be filld with onlie Wimmin shall live untoe its own Lawe, even above thatt of Herselfe or of the Kinge. I was muche surpirized and Pressd for further relacion of these Curious Lawes.

After muche Explanacion, of which the Kinge grew earlie Tired, I learnt that Wymmin held prescednce in many of the Relations and Activities of the Land. Indeed, he sayd to mee that though I believed on oure firstt Landinge my own Men had chosen Maidens for their Companie it was the Wymmin whoe chose the Men. No Man chooses a Woman here, he explaind, and even hee the Kinge was pluckd by his faire Queene. Whatt use are Men, I then demanded, butt hee would nott awnswer sayinge the Time for siche Questions was over for the Daie. And then appeared manie Wymmin in oure Tentt who tooke Great Command of oure and their Pleasure thatt I was to tell the Kinge nextt morne thatt though a Lande ruld by wymmin did seeme Strange its Distracions were quite Considerable. Whatt happenned in that Nite I cannott Relate for itt would make the least Christian of Soles blushe soe deeplye that their Bodies might be taken for a wounded Man on a Battlefield.

Wee passed through manie Similar adventures in our Path, too numerous to Relate here, and manie strange Sights did cross my Vision that I had manye opportunities to Question all I knewe of the Worlde and its Peeple. Had I been of a Philosofical nature I mite well have founded a Newe Schoole of Thought. In terms simple enough for any mere Labourer to understand, I would saye that in this Worlde wee Judge others by that which wee knowe, yett all we knowe is the tinie Worlde of oure Upbringinge. To base upon siche Knowledge a Condemnacion of oure Peeres whoe knowe as littel as oureselves and further, to Condemn Others whose Wayes wee knowe nott by oure own small Standardds, is to take upon ourselves the verie Mantle of the Lorde and claim wee understand His Wayes, though siche Wayes are veiled in Grate Mysterie beyond our feeble Vision and Comprehencion. Why did nott the Lorde strike downe these Pagans a Centurye agoe. I knowe nott and presume nott upon the Plann of oure Lorde or His Desines, and saye onlie thatt I enjoye and rejoice in His Bountie and Mercie.

Wee came upone oure Destination in the Night and as iff in Expectation grayt Fires were burninge to Welcome us and there was muche singing and dancinge and sweete Musicke of Tabour and Pipe and manie other instruments. After taking of manie Victualls wee Repayred to the Palace where the Queen waited to greet the Kinge.

The Kinge approached her in the manner of a Subjeckt and on his Knees did present his Personn and spoke Timidly of all he had done in the Service of her Magestie. She abused himm muche and her Tongue was Round and Large in what few Insultts I did Comprehend. She even sayd that once the Kinge was in their Chambers she would give him a Violent Thrashinge. I was muche Angered at firstt for I hadd become a Friend to the Kinge and believed the Queene owned no Rite to Abuse him in siche Manner. My Thoughts were thus sett against the Kweene and when itt came Time for the Kinge to present mee to her Magestie I approached the Throne with Haughty Aire and little Regarde for her Position and when the Kinge's Counsailor bidd me kneele I refused. There was muche Stirringe in the Hall at my Impudence that I felt everye Eye upon mee. The Queene looked sharply att mee and I believed that then and there my Head would bee lostt as I had seen so manie lose their Heads on my Journee to the Palace.

But then the Queene spake Sweetelie, sayinge, Why do you Dishonor me in siche manner. And I, not knowinge whatt to say, said simplye that it was because she dishonored her Husbande, the Kinge, and I hurriedlie abused her for her sharpe Tongue and the Threats of Violence she poured upon the Head of my Friend the Kinge. And then a strange thinge happened, for everyone in the Halle began to Laugh, and to Laugh most Riotously. Even the Kinge and Queen fell to their Knees in such Amusement that I believed this must be some Final Torture before the Executioner arrives.

Onlie after manie Minutes of suche Abandonmentt did the Queen compose herself sufficiently to Speeke siche thatt she sayd, quite plainly, that she in no waye abused the Kinge, but that hee, on returning Home after siche Long Journeys, loved nothinge better than to be Whipped and Abused both by Tongue and Lash and contrarie to dishonoringe him she was in fackt succumbinge to his most Deepe Desire. And then, after askinge Humblie for Permission, the Kinge explained that his onlie Desire at that Moment was to bee taken from this Halle to a Private Chamber where the Queene would bounde him with Strips of Animall Hide, spitt upon him, and Conduckt upon his Personne the mostt Fiendish of Activities, siche that I have nott wordes to fully describe them here. The Queene then requested my Presence at this curieuse Rituall and sayd to mee thatt iff I should soe Desire similar Pleasures could bee arranged for my selfe.

I thus spent an Eveninge with Distractions passing strange that iff I place but a Cupfull on this Page the Reader will nott onlie call mee Liar butt think that I have made some Packt with the Devil himselfe. But whether dear Reader you believe or do nott believe, I place heer before you an Accountt of my Activities that Nite soe thatt youe may Judge mee by my Accione upon the Balance of your owne Lawe.

I was led to a Roome that cann onlye be called a Dungeon for around aboutt us in this damp and stone-lined Chamber were all manner of curious Instruments that on initial Inspection defied all explanacion cept that which applied to them the Function of producing Payne. The Chamber was litt by an huge Fyre in its Center casting uponn the Walls such a Tangle of menacing Shadowes that I feltt upon enteringe a flutter in my disturbd Hart. The Queene quickly placed a Hood over the Head of the Kinge and tied aboutt his Necke a rope soe that itt seemd he was an Prisoner standinge on the verie Gallowe that would Hang him. The Kinge, rather than Remonstrateinge againstt his Queene, lett out a sounde of Delicate Joie as one heers when a Little Childe is rubbed upon the Bellie by the hand of a caring Mother.

Butt rather than take this Sounde as Invitation to lett fall from her Lips wordes of Care and Love, the Queene sett aboutt abusinge him with her Tongue, sayinge ghastlie Phrases and castinge upon his Regale Head a number of Curses that would chill the verie Bones of an Enemie. On heeringe so Sharpe a Tongue cast att him the Kinge did nott Defend himself or cast similar Aspersions upon his Wyfe butt fell to his Knees and brought his Mouth to the Feett of the Queene and there did Lick the verie Ground, which even in siche Darkenesse was cleerlie a Field of Filth and siche Matter as is Deposited by Animalls in their dailie Activities that I would faine touch itt with Glovd Hand. But the Kinge wentt to his Task with unseemlie Abandon and soon was Rollinge to and fro while the Queene, unsatisfied with meere Curses, began to Kicke mostt Violentye att his Person. I was here att the Pointt of Makeinge a loud Objectione when the Kinge lett out so shrille a Screame that I was stoppd, certain now that siche Behaviore would have its Proper Punishmentt and that the Kinge, regaininge his lostt Sense, would bring downe uponn the head of his Wyfe siche Punishmentt that she would never think to act in siche Manner again.

Sadlie I was wrong for the Queene grabbd him roughlie by the rope around his Necke and made him Crawle to one of the Contrapcions already mentioned. Here she tied him bye the Hands and Feet soe that his Bodie formd a large Cross, though knocked onto its side, and I thought he resembld the Savioure in His Passione, and his Cries were siche like that more than simplye foregivinge his Tormentore, he calld her bye sweete Names and lett fall upon her siche Complimentts that strangely onlie served to infuriate her More. What Monster was she that she dealt soe with the Man she called her Husbande and her Kinge.

206

I was nowe in siche a State of Surprise that even iff I soe desired I could nott raise my Voice in Protestt. My Bodie and my Eyes felt a Compulsion thatt made me wantt to Stare and lerne the Outcome of these Darke Practices. The Queene, with Violent Hands, tore from his Bodie his everie coveringe soe thatt he Hunge there like a Newborne Childe and I was Amazd to see that his Maleness stood Alertt like a Flagpole upon which the Union Jack will soone be Raised. She then tooke a Whip and struck him fore and aft so thatt the Kinge lett out siche Yells I was forcd to cover my Ears with my Hands. I thought then that I must be regarding a Pantomime or Playe putt on for my Amusement and thatt all I had seen was simply a kinde of Actinge. Once the thought was upon mee itt seemd the mostt Naturall solutione to the Puzzle of these Practices and I Congratualted my selfe on looking through the Joke of which I was certainlye the Butt.

But itt was the Buttock of the Kinge that freed me from beinge the Butt of an Imaginarye Joke. Upon it I spied what were cleerlie Lacerations cawsed by the Whipp the Queene lett flie soe Unceremoniouslie, and soone thin Fingers of Bludd were running along his Buttock and Leg. I sawe soone across his whole Bodie similar Cutts thatt forned the Origin of manie tinie Tributaries of Blood thatt, if the Queen's actions were to go Unchecked, would quicklie Gather into their owne Thames or Nile. Butt just as mye Feare for the Life of the Kinge grewe to its Height and I was againe pushed to Act upon his Behalfe, my goode Intentions were Ambushed by a Totale Change in the Manner of the Queene. She quitt her Rough Treetmantt and dropt the Whipp and threwe herselfe down at the Feete of her Kinge, asking Forgiveness and Begginge that she bee freed from soe Uglie an Activitie.

Here is the True Nature of the Queene, I told my selfe, for surely some Demon mustt just the Minute before have Released her from its Darke Gripp.

Butt as this thought came over mee the Voice of the Kinge emerged from under the Hood, begginge her to continue with the Terrible Activitie and claymeinge thatt she must Give Up her gentle Strokes and move on to more Harsh Punishmentt. That hee called these Gentle Stroke did surprise me Greatly for the Whipp did Crack loudlie through the Air and everie Time it came downe upon his Naked Bodie he would lett out the mostt terrible of Cries as though he were an Animall in an Abbattoir undergoinge its very last Breaths upon this Earth.

The Nite continued in siche manner and if I had nott been there to see with mye own Eyes siche Peculiar Occurences then I would never have Believed them from the Mouth of Another. I watched as all manner of Instrument was applied to the Bodie of the Kinge and even those that had been cookd in the Fire untill their Tipp did burne to an unseemlie Scarlett notifying mee of the Great Heate to which the Metall had been brought. All Nite the Screames of the Kinge continued yett through out his Manhood did Stand ever to Attention and if I did nott heer on Occassion the Sweete breaths he uttered I would nott have believed itt possible. For it grewe cleere to me, as though a Myst rose that had earlier coverd mine eyes, that the Kinge did enjoi this Activitie and that, as the Queene had earlier assurd, he lookd forewarde to it upon his Retuorne to the Palace.

I was at one pointt in the Nite sorelye Tempted to followe the Example of the Kinge. I believe that whatever Activitie wee ourselves have nott Tried lies beyond the View of oure owne Judegementt, and so feltt, thinkinge my selfe a Friende of the Kinge yett consideringe his Activitie close to Madness, thatt I my self mustt take a Partt if to Judge truthfullie is my Desire.

So, on sayinge siche like to the Queene, she Smiled mostt Diabolicallie and within a Minute I too was Tied up like oure deare Savioure, a Hood stitched from the Skinn of a foul-smelling Animall upon my Head, my clothes torne violentlye from mee, and my own Manhood, to my great surprise, pointinge up to the verie Heavens themselves. She tooke no Mercie upon my Greene Nature in her Wayes and the Whipp flew as Violentley at mee as it had at the Kinge. I too Screamed butt alsoe, I must tell the Reader, that after a short time, perhaps under the Influence of the Rare Beautie of the Queene who betweene the Strikes of the Whipp lett her Gentle Hands run over mee, feltt a certaine Kinde of Pleasure thatt is beyond the Qualitie of my Pen to Describe. And soone, I too, like the Kinge, demanded when she lett the Violence of her Stroke slacken, that she Whipp mee with the Full Force of Strength in her and I cried out like oure Savioure on the Mount of Olive, thatt she bee Forgiven for her Sins.

Thus the Kinge and I became Brothers of a Sorte, sharing a Passione for the Punishmentt that his Wyfe was wont to mete out upon us. At anie Tyme of Daye or Nite the Queene would change her Countenance entirely and Demand that I perform the mostt Diabolical of Tasks. I mite be Talking with her in a Crowded roome when suddenly I would see in here Eyes a certain Flash and I would know that

soone, if nott immediately, I would be Charged with a mostt humil-
iatinge Function. Sometimes I was ordered to Strip bare in the
Presence of all and then to Run my Tongue along the Floor from
Foott to Foott untill I had licked a Path from every single Person to
everie other Person in the Chamber. At other times, she would order
the Kinge to do upon mee siche Unspeakable Acts thatt I dare nott
Write them here, butt only State thatt the Twoe of us would Perform
Deedes thatt nott even the Devil and his Consort would Imagine.

Siche was my Life in the Courtt and though to anie Reader it
mustt seeme a Most Damnable Existence I found in itt to the
Contrarie a kinde of Sweetness thatt in my Previous Life I had not
ever encountered and began to believe thatt I mite yett Live outt my
Daies as the Curious Servant to the Passions of the Queene.

Butt throughout these Dayes the Heate continued to afflyct us
most mercilesslie and whatt Joyes we mite find in the pursuit of
simple Pastime was as soon devastated against the Rocke of Dailie
News that spoke at everie Houre of Families whose Cropps had been
Destroied by the Climate or who had lostt manie Members to the Ill
Humors that proliferated under soe Harde a Regime. There seemed
everie Daye to passe through the Palace a groweinge Procession of
those seekinge either the Charitie of the Kinge or his Protectione,
and on everie Lip their was a Clamoure for the Kinge and Queene to
hold siche Great Ceremonies that would bringe Favoure from the
Gods on the Countrye and the People.

I askd the Kinge whyy had the Ceremonie nott yett beene Helde
and hee did tell me that the Queene, uponn whome the Stars shone
siche Light that gave here Eyes into the Future, whiche I tooke to
meane the Queene was alsoe something of a Cabballistt or Astrologer,
had deemed that the Daye propitious to the Ceremonie had nott yett
arrived. But when he said this I could reade in his Face a certain
weariness, if nott an anger, at her Refusall to signal the Openinge of
the Annuall Ceremonie, siche that when I pressd him further he
turned awaye as if in sudden Fright att mye wordes and said nott to
speake further of this matter and never to bringe it upp in the Presence
of the Kweene.

In the following Dayes he shewed more than an ever a groweing
Melancholia and oure Nightlie Pasttimes held in thatt Darke Chamber
alreadie described became quite dulle of interest, for even when the
Queene did whipp most wildlie at the Kinge untill she fell to the
Floore with Teeres of Exhaustion showering her face, and soe thatt I
expected him close to Death Himselfe, he shewed little Enjoymentt

Ranbir Singh Sidhu

for our Game and in the morne would turne to me a mostt Sullen and Disaffected Face, yett saye nothing of the Cause of this Great and Troubleinge Lassitude.

One Eveninge I heard him in his Bed Chamber pleadinge with the Queene to Holde the Great Ceremonie within thatt weeke for, he said, hee could nott hold himself in check anie longer. I did not understand his wordes and so endeavoured to Listen again everie Night with the Hope I might learne more of his Ill Humor and thus affect a waye to Aid him in his Distress. The nextt nite I againe heard him Pleade and was able to Heare the awnswere of the Queene, where she told him without Reason that the Ceremonie would Waite and then Laughed most Cruellie at his Abjectione. Over the Nites he continued to pleade, sometimes makinge the Case for Himselfe and other times for the Peasants whose Life and Livelihoode laye within their Handes. Butt everie Night she refused him and I grewe mostt angrie at her Heartlessnesse and determined the Nextt night to burst in upon their Discussion no matter whatt the Kinge had ordered.

Soe whenn I heard them Whisperinge again the Night followinge, with the Kinge pleadinge for his Subjeckts and the Queene laughinge haughtilye in his Face, then I knocked openn the Doors of their Privatt Chamber and thundered loudly in, exclaiming uponn my Soul what grave Injustice the Queene did to her owne Kinge and Subjeckts by withholdinge from them this mostt Precious Ceremonie.

Butt both Kinge and Queene gave mee a Look of siche Astonishe-mantt thatt in the Middle of my Oratorie I began to stammer and to haltt. The Kinge was Smilinge mostt broadlie and his Face had uponn it none of the Dejection I expected. Indeed, he seemed to be in mostt Light a mood that I began to wonder if my poore Suffieciency in their Tongue had led me into a wide Blunder. It was the Queene who explaind to me in mostt kindlie Termes that for the Kinge the con-tinued Sufferinge of his People in deede produced muche Joye and that his Pleadinges everie Night was simplie a Game that theye played together. Butt then I demanded to knowe why out of this Chamber the Kinge displaied so Melancholie a Face. This was partt of the Game, the Kinge did saye, and that hee for the purpose of his Greatt enjoyementt did like his Subjeckts too think that he did Care after their Well Beinge. Yett I protested that I had seene him acte with siche Benevolence towards soe manie Subjeckts that this Joye hee tooke in sufferinge mustt be a Shield to hide some other Awnswere. But Noe, the Kinge did saye, for he claymed I mustt have seene howe whenevere hee did mete outt Justice a far greater sufferinge was produced than was alleviated. Did I nott wonder, he asked, whye the punishements for even the smallest indiscretions were indeed huge. I doe nott care for the Well-Beinge of my Subjeckts, the Kinge declared, butt onlye that through seeminge to alleviate the sufferinge of a fewe I can give my selfe great Pleasure by cawsinge the sufferinge of the Manie.

I was again muche amazed and wondered iff anything that I sawe in this Countrye was what it was, or thatt if ever I was presented with Mirage within Mirage and I seemd, as I leftt the Chamber, to bee walking Blindfold in a Labyrinth of the Kinde the Ancients in their Pagan wayes had followed. I knewe nott what was whatt or whoe was whoe and everie Motive held behind itt a Greater Lie soe thatt though the Kinge did muche to Persuade mee of his Hatred of his Subjeckts and his Joye in their Agonie I could nott believe it, butt I knewe that if hee told mee the verie Opposite and claymed after all a Love for his Peeple then I still would Questione and seeke with-all a greater Reason for his Stark Behaviore. Yett seeing his Apparent Gladness in the Sufferinge of his Peeple I decided to joyne him in his Emotione and soe looked upon Payne as a source of Happiness where before I had looked upon as a State needing Succorr or Amelioracion, and in deed I did finde that in another's Sufferinge muche Joye was to be had.

Butt I had little Tyme for siche Peregrinations of the Minde for the Nextt Morne the Great Ceremonie was announced to Beginn that same Nite and the Cittie was overcome by the Preparations that seemed to Require the energies of the whole Populace. I could write muche of the Sights I sawe that Daye butt will pass them over to give the Reader an Account of the Ceremonie and how, through curious Meanes, I did finallie departe this Lande.

The Ceremonie did last manie Dayes and if asked to give a full Account of all I sawe and did in those dayes, or even if asked to give an exactt Account of the Number of Dayes I passed in these Festivities, I would Faile for muche I sawe and did Remains beyond my own Understanding and the Wordes of this Language do not hold in them a sufficient Pliability, the waye strong Wood bends to form the curved Hull of a Shipp, to describe all I did see and do.

Upon a Field there were arranged manie and strange Machines which I tooke to be the Devices of War and Destruction. Siche things as great Batteringe Rams or Catapults with which to laye Siege to Citties and to Terrorize a People. Fires burned across the Open Plaine and manie Figures moved in the Night, dressed in Clokes of Rough

211

Materiell and manie Voices cried outt, shriekinge into the Aire in Tongues I had never before Heard. The Great Machines made Awefull noise, like Monsters rumbling in the Darke, and I feltt a grewing Terror as I walked that first Night of the Ceremonies among the Crazed Peeple. Everyone drank from huge Urns a Libation whose Taste I still cannot Describe but which Cawsed an Odd Effect upon the Minde, not like Drunkenness att al but perchance close to its Opposite, a sense that one could see all in the Worlde with a Startling Cleerness.

The Machines, when finally I sawe them closelie, were not at all the thinge I had expected. Rather they were Inventiones whose Purpose was beyond mee. Some resembled, in huge forme the Contraptiones that the Kinge had hidden in his Secret Chamber whereat the Queene performed terrible Deedes upon his Bodie, yet others recalled the forme of Animalls I had seen in Life or in Bookes on the formes of the Great Beastes that walked upon the Earth before the Deluge of oure Lorde. I seeked out some Face I knewe for an Explanacion but could finde none as all Men and Wymmen wandered with their Heads lost in Hoodes or shrouded by Maskes. There was one Machine made all of Wood that was a Birde with Beake and Eye and Winges out-stretched sitting as though waittinge for some signal to lett go the Earth and Flye up into the Heavens. Whatt purpose these Machines served I could in noe waye guess and though they moved and made Greate Noise, some of them Issueing from themselves Balls of Fire and Rockets that Sped up into the Night with a Terrifyinge and Shimmering Brilliance, theye Acted withoute Mover as though Imbued with a Lyfe of their Owne.

The Heate seemed ever grater, beateinge downe upon us even in the Night and as the Strange Ceremonies continued, I stood aboute like a Watcher nott knewing the whye off anythinge I sawe. I encountered Men and Women naked, jumping up and down straight into the aire while letting oute howles with everye Jumpp, and others crawlinge on Hands and Knees and Barkinge like Dogs, and others still who Danced without stopp until they found them-selves inside a Frenzie that seemed to tear at their verie Sanitie so thatt they threw themselves onto the Hard Earth, their Limbs kickinge at the Ground and att eache other, and others who seemed to intone solemn Hymns as might anie Monk in our Sacred Monas-teries yet all the while they hunge upsidedowne like Batts suspended from Trees by Ropes that helde their feet, and even others who fought all night and daye with Blindfoldes over their Faces, and others who

212

hauled Great Boulders across a Field onlie some Minutes later to Haule them backe to that verie Spott they had originallie acquired the Rocke, and those whoe tooke a Sworde to their owne Extremities, slicinge off Hand or Foote while shewing no sign of Payne or Agonie, and others who leapt Wildelye hither and thither as though their Bodies were taken up by some Elemental Force, and soe manie other Sights thatt if I were to Catalog them heer theye would take upp the Whole Remainder of this Narrative and I would telle nothinge else exceptt this Listt of Odditties, exceptt that I will add that behind my Visione there was Constant Sounde like the Earth groaning, tearinge open, as though a Riftt were forming belowe oure own feet and that at anie momentt we all might sinke downe into a Netherworlde and falle forever intoe the Domains of Satane and his Disciples. The Noise was made by the Machines that movd aboutt us with a continual motione, clanking and banginge and shootinge out Jets of Flame into the Aire and more than once into Groups of Peeple who would then Burne and Screame. This Sounde is the background to my everie Memeories of those Nights, an Infernal Sounde that even nowe when I sleepe I faile fullie to Escape.

Howe the Dayes passed I knowe nott except thatt I owne a strained Recollectione of Daye followinge Night and so on for manie siche Cycles though if asked howe manie I cannott saye but knowe that in this Ceremonie I passed more than a single Night and less than a Monthe. For my selfe, like all others, was soone caught up in the Madness that surrounded mee. The Drink that all tooke Liberallye of produced, as I have said, a ceratine Effect so that the World became singularlie Cleere in a manner beyond the Abilitie of Wordes to Conveye. I sawe all arounde mee with the Utmost Detaile as though I was a Watchmaker lookinge at the world through the Prism of his Glass. I too bayed at the Night and threwe myself at the Earth and at times Jumped up into the aire straight up and downe without controlle and even tooke to crawling on all fours like some animall and slicing my Bodie with a knife, thoguh I did nott lose anie Appendage but meerlye cutt my selfe across Chestt and Arme.

At one time I crawled up into the Great Bird for it had in itt manie Seates like Pewes in a Church and if my Memories is nott false a mostt Strange thinge did then take place. The Bird, crowded with manie of us, includinge the Kinge and Queene, did begin to move as though Alive. It made a grate Roaringe noise like the Lyon of Darke Afreeka which I have Heard in the Jungle of Ethiope and then began to Shake mostt violentlie and soon I felt a Wind against mye Face and the Fires that had a Moment before surrounded us were nowe far belowe and soon were like the Heads of Pins so that the World seemed to Shrinke awaye. I was afraide it might disappeare forevere, but as the Worlde belowe was shrinkinge, the Worlde ahead Grewe in direct Proportione, and the Mountaines, which had been soe far awaye, were now Close to us. I feltt I could touch the Heavens and expected thatt att anie moment the Face of the verie Lorde would showe itselfe.

Then the Mountaine, which had been Groweinge, began to Shrinke and I looked downe and sawe that my Feere was cominge aboutt. I couldd see the verie Curve of the Worlde, its Land and its Oceane, and above us, what had been Skye began to Darken and I knewe we were entering that verie Realm of the Stars, the Empyrean it selfe, and before us the Silentt Moone hovered, groweing with everie Breath. We were climbing into the verie Vault of the Stars, like Thieves smuggling into Eternitie.

We landed in oure Shipp withoute Captaine or Saile upon the Surface of the Distante Orbe with all the Gentleness of a Swann cominge down upon a Still Lake. Lite Dustt flew aboutt us and whenn it cleered we could see faraye like a Ball that might fitt into a Hand oure own Azure Globe hanging over oure Heads. I reached outt an Hand butt could nott touche itt. Then we all departed oure Craft and began to forage across the Strange Surface which showed to us everie Color of the Rainbowe. The Rockes were greene and blue and scarlett and purple and the Skye, unlike oure Sapphire on oure owne Worlde, was a Burninge Gold studded nott with Stars but withe Diamonds that shone and glistend and some hunge soe lowe that I could stande upon a Hill and reache up and plucke them from the verie Heavens, like Fruite pluckd from a Tree. With siche like I filled my pockets.

When I looked downe again I was surrounded by Figures whoe were short and gray and showed thin Limbs but large Heads the shape of Almonds with wide, round Eyes that stared intently at me. They made curious noises I could nott decipher and began aboutt my Bodie a Dance that circled and then led away. I followed with my Bodie everie Motione, thinkng that beinge on the Moone I should doe what Lunaticks doe, as the sayinge advises aboutt the Roman. They sang a Strange song that I could neither understand nor imagine how anyone might call it Musick and thought it only a loonnee Tune, and I watched as they pushed their heads into the loose Dirtt and soe did I and then they pulled their Heads outt butt since I could nott see when finally I pulled my selfe free they were some distance awaye. I hurried after them but they grewe no closer and soone I had lost them entirelye.

I found the Shipp againe withe all on Boarde, prepareinge to Depart and when I spoke of the Lunaticks I had encountered all said I must be Dreaming for no one Lives upon the Moone, that everyone knowes.

Soe the Daies of the Ceremonie passd and when itt was over I woke one Morne to find aboutt me a most curious Vision. Bodies laye everyewhere, none moving, lit by the brilliantt morneinge Sunne and when I stood and began to stumble from Figure to Figure I sawe on everie one the markes of a Terrible Violence. Across their Chestts and Faces, their Legs and Arms, were deep and bloodie Cutts. Some had lost their Heads and others their Limbs. Everywhere was the Scarlett Blood from their Veines. Mye owne Hands were stained with itt and I wondered iff I had taken a Part in this Massacre.

Thenn I found the Bodie of the Kinge similarly Killed and close bye him the Bodie of the Queene withoutt Head. I found no one Alive heer and when I returned to the Cittie there were onlie Cattle and Dogs but no Subjeckts. The Great Roomes were Hollow of Peeple.

I searched in my pockets for the Diamonds I remembered plucking from the Moone and to my grayt Surprise founde there a pocketfull of the moste Fantastick rocks. Diamonds, rubues, stones that shonne from an Inner Lyte alle there owne, and I was thus further Confusd by my Peculiare Remembrances, for I had Believed itt but a Dreame.

I tarried in the Palace some dayes hoping too seeke outt an Explanacion for these Strange Deaths, but in all thatt Time I came across no other Living Person. A greate Silence hovered over all the bildinges and the trees themselves did seeme to Weepe in greefe. Finallie I gave upp all Hope and tooke to the Roade that led downe to the Ocean, and after some Dayes of Travell I found my crewe still there in much the same State I had left them weekes or monthes earlier, I knewe nott, except that nowe all were Gladdened to leave and come closer to the Prospectt of seeinge again their Families, those that had them, and a Familiar Shore for those without the Connexion of Blood Relatione.

And the next daye, the Heate havinge muche Abated, we did leave that Unnamed Shore, wich I named in my memorie K., for the Wide and Azure Oceane. As our shippe took saile, I looked one laste time upon this lande of Manie Curiosities and thought I sighted, high on a hillocke, the Kynge himselfe standinge with his Kweene, their

hands high and waving farewell, and all around them, equally un-
molested and unmarked, their greatefulle happie Subjeckts.

I thoughte then, as the wind carried us on the first stretch of oure
Journee Homewarde, how the Worlde we see is butt one Idea of the
Worlde that is, and even that Worlde is but an Idea of Others, and our
Dreames are but the Fancie of other Dreamers who spend their Nites
dreaming Us.

Three Poems
Maxine Chernoff

It's easier for reality to imitate the dime novel than to imitate art.

—Umberto Eco

PLOT

The book of books

is too heavy to hold.

My Nazi falls out

and Victoria Falls.

No one in bedrooms

Leaking green light

or under the shadow

of sails at full mast.

Where is Homer's

wine-dark sea

in pages filled

with remedies

and half-baked plans

for future books

in which gold weaves

words and birds

Maxine Chernoff

fly off and guns are heard

in a distant version

two miles from the

Hopperesque diner.

The same old story,

the oldest of tales,

we don't want to tell

where her face

appears to the awkward

boy who sees a rose

and nestles in clover,

gets tangled in

lies and lost in

beginnings. The book

of books is asked to

dance around evil

but can't select

the magnitude.

History comes

to lend its heft

as the book

closes its pages and

retires to a shelf

bearing the burdens

of all mankind.

So many chances

are not enough.

Time to fail

has too many rooms.

TOLD

But that's another story.
—Ray Ragosta

Here stands Jules
without his Jim, there an
an old man weeping
for his wild fruit.
An innocent daughter
has gone to the woods
where the story encloses
her ultimate day. You hold
a spoon, its glacier
of salt, a loaf of bread,
its mushroom-cap top.
And he is with her
at the blue beach house
where only silence enters
the space. The heart, too, a book
that nothing escapes,
not even the dust on the frontispiece
he won't read or the yarn
that was destined to be a hat.
Still, you know the tragic
outcome. Haven't
you read it in a book?

Maxine Chernoff

WANT

... *a stage between bent and mistaken.*
—Rosmarie Waldrop

A painting carves the rescue

and the drowning

in cubes of light which

language cannot hold

as lovers' arms reach

for the story you create

to punish time. Distraction

gray and ghostly

in pale November light,

a moment teases grief

to sit beside you at

the window where darkness

stains your face as fresco.

You forecast endings

battered by your fears.

Please, wind, be merciful

to what sums the morning

leaves at margins of our want.

Offworlds

Anne Waldman

HOW COME UNTETHERED back to command or plan, the cult of glitches. How may your book be written? Disperse boss of all patterns, organize your original beauty. Civil engineers as angels don the DNA on slip, Fez on nightshift, invader leptons, themselves in the comedown. Not body-based theory but another accounts for dignity, the greatest moments in Russian history as told by an activist, for example. Her century needed her.

Or your medieval cities arise. Not privative pathology not a performance in arms that becomes flammable, an essay of twin truism and survival. No no not that. Not that, the clericalisms, the nails of martyrdom, bullets come in sizes. Not flag signals to make our deletions work, how you might live on expanding your code from stress points of memory. How this is normal. I dreamed this. I drugged this. I was an anthology considering conceptual possibilities in the economic downturn. I carried many others. Where shelter? Between the pages mercy and struggle. To leave a record behind.

A mind stream presents itself, cool water. A tidal pool of future entity. An intellectual conundrum on "micro ouvert" consciousness. A makeshift abbreviation or torrent of semantic power that may be translated into delectable things to imbibe as our journey continues. Consider immateriality, its textures, its playful corridors. How secular can you get before you are back in cement, on the floor praying release.

It was a city built from the bottom of a bowl, then tipped over the edges. It built itself an ever-flowing a warren of pathways an echo of neural exchange in medina power. You could buy, you could sell. You could buy-buy, you might sell-sell. You could study and be the subtlest thinker of all past and future times. The future was struggle, the future was taking off if one could scribe and fasten around the old days, the old codes. Could fashion a fluid Arabic that no crimes be committed. Do not poison the Nazarene. I swear this. And I and the one-writes-this visited many holy books. A Torah housed in the Mellah made of skin of gazelle. Koran in its inestimable illumination that was untouchable to a non-fellaheen but singing out muezzin of ecstatic devotion. The Bible curling, swirling in glory, books of the dead with many iterations of mantra and prescription, recipes for afterlife travel with swirling mandalas of incumbent power. Offworlds.

Crush identity? A Marxist creature too never irrevocably in error, never perfect, victims in the long performance of an afternoon, cruelty we will escape from, I promise. Escape autocracy, plutocracy, blind adherence. I am just the blockbuster for you.

To Deleuze you say *Gracias*, to the other you whisper your need for cross-cultural genres to slide into the semantic mix. I will spell it right this time, You say biting your ADD tongue, your autistic nerve reversal. You are unwilling to walk alone on hot sand. You want a new cosmology, cooler, less insistent. Even demand of "instant" becomes obsolete. Though moment still be grand. This is "our moment." Be uttered as in a cone of archive. Can you work without sun over you warming you or survive deep in the red luminescent ocean floor without a bell jar? How will you be recognized, human without a war? Chaos meant "without a library."

The "not knowing one language one knows all the possibility of sensation of instant relays" suggests a story. Tell me what it is. Tell me your tactics for this liftoff, this send-off as they wave their multi-activated tentacles. One for every day of the year although that calendar resists use when the frequency marginalizes all those old strategies. You were an octopus or saint of imagination. Take your pick. But not planning. That was a word that we dismissed long ago: strategy. It was male, it was war, it was not making progress, it was tied to scheming and a miserable plot of critical lingo takeover. A book of mere tactics. It was tied to male artists singing to themselves in a circle howling to have the moon take notice. *Please cold dead moon take notice as we imitate your borrowed light.* It was a drumming ritual, it was a plaintive wail for more nourishment of the woman who wasn't coming to the ringside. Don't get me wrong I love the men, the poet-men of linguistic enterprise. Put your weapons in the meltdown.

She was busy at the inexplicable, she was busy at the ready, she was still arguing but in a new psychic way: in silent screaming. And her story was not confusing. It was simple. Tell me what it is. Tell us what it is. It is a pedagogy in itself. You can carry it anywhere. The Reds were coming.

A bifurcation. A city. Parents with wings and a pantry. A fourth-floor walk-up window, a *fenêtre* on the stars, a defenestration often recorded by women although frequently performed by men. They would do this blindfolded so as to avoid their mothers. Throwing the girl a bone. A bone with a trigger. But the girls write the ritual down on animal skins. It will be studied later in a cave. Trying to distinguish between a cave down low and an independent window high on the fourth floor. That's not enough to jump from, making a metaphorical leap is the magic. Masking a disillusionment with your culture, its city-living-transportation problems unsolved. But going up? Yes, up it is. Maybe it is like poetry, a long thighbone. It was incised with tiny runes that give meaning to perseverance, to walking with children slung on back. And a bone considers the other animals, your relatives, not strangers and the use the others' bones have. Don't get me started. So she is never tamed. She is swinging it over her head as a cheerleader with baton. She is trained as a cheerleader. Then she is taken under a desk to drive the demons down when the Reds might be coming. And sirens wail and tell of meltdowns. Let's go offworld, she thinks, this is it. How will I travel, how will I be? I want to cheer. She was suddenly in the upside-down cup of her life. Held and safe and covered with cloth. A blue blue cloth. And it was a bowl she could see out of surrounded by glass it was. Other world looking in.

Then there's a jaded relapse and shatter and another war. This is pedestrian. How can we ever return to the complex thighbone meditation? The tableau changes all over the planet as coasts give way, as empires tremble and fall or reconstitute even more implacably. And powers build towers to organize by. But that changes, you know that changes. And she dreams that there will be a waking up to everyone speaking in an unfamiliar tongue that even the trillionaires won't recognize. When you no longer digitize the spoils.

A brilliant reprisal. But being young years the girl dreams in a way you never quite understand. How big is vocabulary? Did you know it all already? What creates the image of language in a dream? What is it you really hear? The sweet bruit of offworlds, the collective searing whispers of all you could ever hear in your spare time beyond ploy and seizure. You memorized this to say it down. Travel through this and be healed.

From The Book of a Thousand Deaths
With a Foreword by Salvatore Hobson
Brandon Hobson

NOTE. THREE MONTHS FOLLOWING my son's birth, I received the following short manuscript in the mail from my father's unpublished book, *The Book of a Thousand Deaths*, which he had evidently written somewhere in Mexico when he was living with a young woman he'd met before he left the States and, eventually, disappeared. There was no return address. Even stranger is the foreword written by an uncle Salvatore I never knew I had, who addressed it to me and my four siblings.

My father went missing somewhere in Mexico in the summer of 1998. The case is no longer under investigation. I know nothing of the details, what he was involved in, what kind of people he dealt with—nothing. He was very private. Of my four siblings, my sister Veruca and I kept in contact with him the most, mainly due to our interest in his art. After receiving this manuscript in the mail, we have since tried to track down our mysterious Uncle Salvatore with no luck.

I have reproduced the manuscript I received here, brief as it is, in its entirety.

—BH, Tulsa, 2014

Dear V., Z., A., B., S.,

When I spoke to your father in the weeks prior to when he went missing, he mentioned he'd never told any of you about me. We laughed about it then, but in truth I don't blame him: Your father was known for his certain eccentricities, among them his rage, isolation, and silence concerning personal issues. We reconnected a few months before he disappeared after years without speaking to one another for reasons too personal and unimportant for me to go into here. I should tell you I was hospitalized and treated for many years due to my bipolar disorder. I'm currently living alone with my two dogs in California. I've aged much in the same way as your father, as he's

225

several years older. Brandon, I've sent the only remaining pages from *The Book of a Thousand Deaths* to your address since your father gave it to me and mentioned your interest in his writing. Veruca, he mentioned your daughter might be interested in his drawings, so I will be sending these to your address soon. There are also numerous photos, postcards, and memorabilia he collected over the years that I will be sending to each of you.

I'm sure you're aware that before his disappearance, your father took a lover, a young woman named Inez, whose art led him to begin sketching various nudes. I'm sad to report that Inez passed away recently at only thirty-nine. She spent time in a rehabilitative facility for addictions to prescription pain medications, and ultimately committed suicide by overdose on October 11, 2013. If the following text gives any sort of indication as to why your father detached himself, I would like to think, under the current unfortunate and odd circumstances, that he would want each of you to read it.

Yours,
Salvatore Hobson, January 2014, CA, USA

THE BOOK OF A THOUSAND DEATHS

His father raised pigeons in a chicken coop with an aviary attached to the front. White homing pigeons quick to fly and return. Though he'd lost several to hawks in the area, he was still able to breed the pigeons and use their eggs. When he was a boy, his father had told him to watch out for hawks. Once, they went into the woods and he saw a hawk dismantling some sort of rodent with a long tail.

"Demons," his father told him.

The day fell dark. His father drank whiskey and moved slowly, wielding a butterfly net. There were strange noises all around them—the wind in the trees, voices of ancient mystics, the sky crying out.

"Demons," his father kept saying.

Later, at home, they listened for mice in the walls.

In his childhood his mother developed a rare disease of the blood coagulation system, causing blood clots to form. Her kidneys and brain cells grew weak and she needed plasma to survive, so she spent a lot of time in hospitals. His father kept drinking and disappeared for days at a time.

"He's with that whore," his mother said weakly.

He put his hands in his hair and scratched. He kept scratching and scratching his head.

"Go to your room," his mother said. He stayed up late into the night, searching his soul. After everyone was asleep, he went down into the basement, where a few pigeons cooed from the dark windows. He fed them angel cake from his hand. He sang a pirate song about ship rats. The entire room filled with rose-colored light.

His father drank in the middle of the night. He drank to forget about the woman he was in love with, but the more he drank the more he longed for her.

He built tiny replicas of cities and small towns with colored construction paper. Nights after his mother was asleep he worked in the attic, by a dim lamp, sometimes all night. He built streetlights, trees, automobiles. "When I'm done I'm writing love letters," he said to the dog at his feet.

He wrote notes on tiny slips of paper: "I will be in the bar downtown, where the beer is good." Then he went downstairs and outside to the chicken coop and aviary. He tied the notes to the legs of pigeons and released the pigeons from their aviary, and they flew into the night sky.

A few days later, when the pigeons returned, their messages were gone.

They called him mentally deranged. Still, he wasn't bothered by accusations or judgment.

He loved prostitutes. They were the only women who would sleep with him.

The first woman brought him photos of missing children. He couldn't bear to look at them, so he sent her away. She returned with a glass of red wine that lit the entire room.

"To relax you," she said.

She was really a bag lady with missing teeth. Helen of Troy, she said. Aphrodite! Venus, goddess of love! She put a finger to her lips and pointed at the wall, but there was nothing there.

The next woman brought a paper sack full of fruit and vegetables. She removed her dress and bit into a ripe tomato. The juice ran down her chin and onto her breasts. He started pulling off his shirt when he saw her lift her arms.

"You can shave my armpits," she said.

He took her on the floor.

The next woman wore an Afro. She pulled off his shirt and blind-folded him. Then she led him by the hand downstairs to the basement, where there were loose pipes and exposed wires. She tied him to a chair. He stared at the wall while she lay on the floor, moaning and touching herself. This went on for six hours.

The last woman was young and very thin. She wore heavy make-up. She brought him a piece of paper and unfolded it. "It's a map leading us to a place where we can find ourselves," she told him.

"Where?" he asked.

She didn't answer. She smelled like the chickens out in the barn. She broke down into tears. She told him her name was really Paolo and she was a Puerto Rican boy from the south side of the city.

He complained of a sore tooth all day. He didn't do anything about it. In the afternoon he went to the flea market and bought a record player. He took it home and played his records, which consisted of Latin guitar music. While he listened, he unfurled a piece of paper that was wedged into the back of the record player. He read aloud: "She will be in the bar downtown, where the beer is good."

He spent the rest of the night drinking old bourbon from a paper cup. Later, when he was very drunk, he used a bottle cap and a spoon to extract his own tooth.

"Water is afraid of dying, too," his right hand told his left. "Look how quickly it freezes to ice."

They fasted for thirty days. They saw fasting as a type of healing, like sleep. They believed fasting brought miraculous things for their health. Their neighbor quit having Tourette's outbursts when she began fasting. Another neighbor developed a stronger sense of smell and taste. The boy with braces on his legs took a few steps without falling. His mother always talked about the spiritual benefits, claiming one could see the manifestations of spiritual beings.

On the day the fast ended, she told her husband, "I'm making a pot of stew. It's full of rabbit and squirrel." He took the plates and set them on the table, where everyone was waiting. They could hear mice in the walls. The dog was licking egg yolk off the floor.

"There are a thousand souls inside you," she told him. "A thousand dying souls."

For him, the world was transient and opaque. It brought a lethophobic panic the moment he watched his father, a victim of Alzheimer's, sit on the edge of his bed, drooling and staring at something on the back of his hand. He never stopped worrying about losing his mind, his memory. He'd always wanted to be a scientist. Often he imagined himself leaning over a microscope, studying dendritic structures and dorsal root ganglia. Living an entirely different life than the one given to him. Yet things would turn out differently.

The world was indifferent to him, transient and opaque.

After she died, for weeks he sat alone in the room upstairs. One evening as the sun was going down, he looked out the window and noticed a leaf twirling in midair. The leaf fell from the tree outside the window, and it was as if time stopped and nothing else existed in that moment except the leaf twirling in midair under a branch. The sounds he heard coming from another bedroom upstairs sounded like something had gotten into the house, maybe a squirrel or a rat. But when he walked into the room he saw someone sitting on the bed. It was a woman, and she was looking down at the floor. She was small and very old. He waited for her to look up but she didn't, so he spoke to her: "Who are you?" he asked.

"Who are you?" she said.

"Talk to me," he said.

"Go home," she said. "Go home to your children."

He waited for her to move or look up but she never did. Then darkness spread across the room. Soon he fell asleep on the floor and dreamed his hair was three feet long. When he woke, the woman was gone, and the house was silent and dead again.

*

Outside, night had fallen and bled away. In the days that followed her death, he found himself grieving alone and in horrible ways. In the attic he sat at the desk by the window and began writing his auto-biography in the form of fiction. This was only the beginning. This was not the end. Then he wrote a letter to his five children in the voice of a stranger.

The Watteau Poem
Donald Revell

Life in heaven not alto, but the freight
Trains' higher register a shriek of couplings
In the February night air bedside
Table bedside telephone 1982
Resembles her, resembles the two of us.
We are an old married couple in Corinth,

Tennessee. How is any child's
Eyesight a heaven? Any soprano
Stepping down out of the cars onto?
The color of periwinkles not yet
Came very soon afterwards, palette.
Be easy in your mind. Read yourself to sleep.

Into a train-yard cauldron one man,
Watteau until later on, looks again.

Corinth, Tennessee, is a township northeast of the city of Knoxville.

Symphony No. 4 of Gustav Mahler includes the song "Das himmlische Leben" for solo soprano.

Periwinkles, in French, *pervenches*, blue flowers of the dogbane family, Apocynaceae.

Jean-Antoine Watteau, October 10, 1684–July 18, 1721. Rococo.

Donald Revell

A sudden river to the clown of roses,
S-curved presidency, the letters too
Are letters, and I mean to say Pierrot
Run among the roses suddenly red.
What's to be said for understanding? Too
Late, too late. Those saints won't hunt. These flowers
Understand nothing of the waking sleep
Makes poetry. How many red letters
In a country mile? We cross the river
Simply to rest in the shade of things, curved
In a flash and onrush I can feel,
Sleeping with you. Almost sleeping. I see
A garden scripted beneath our breath and noise.
See here, Johanna, Joachim, and Watteau!

Another will entice me on, and on
Through almond blossoms and rich cinnamon;
Till in the bosom of a leafy world
We rest in silence, like two gems upcurl'd
In the recesses of a pearly shell.
   —John Keats, "Sleep and Poetry," ll. 117–121

Let us cross over the river and rest under the shade of the trees.
   —Last words of Stonewall Jackson, May 10, 1863

Yes, I can hear it. Inside

The tiger lily bent double,

What I'd taken for a soft breeze:

Bee mouth, behemoth, sips. It is

For you to decide. The beauty

Bent to the breaking point, is she

Sad? Is she Cythera? Turn, turn,

To me, and I shall honestly.

What Watteau? If ever I once

Breathed the fine air, Dumbarton Oaks,

The world premiere of another

Country, June 1984,

The waitress is in love with us.

Are we the exact pilgrims? Yes.

The Embarkation for Cythera by Watteau, 1717, The beautiful pilgrims, have they only now departed? Have they only now arrived?

Another Country, a British film written by Julian Mitchell and adapted from his play of the same title. Part romance, part historical drama, it is loosely based upon events in the early life of Guy Burgess, spy and double agent. Betrayal is a sacrament of the last man, of the priest unto himself alone.

Dumbarton Oaks, Bliss family estate in Washington, DC. The house is now a museum and research library. The gardens, designed by Beatrix Farrand, are open to the public.

Donald Revell

If the horse any longer . . . it *was* you.

Ride it. Restore the original word

Inside an only. And here it comes clattering,

The matter once only and, afterwards,

God.

I'd arranged a shelf of animals.

At the center was a clear space,

An ark for snow, dust, and adagios.

Comes a time you must understand, you two,

I did it for you. I left my lover

On the far side of the swimming horses.

Chincoteague, Cythera, the summer house

I never saw builded, although I am

The spook of the builders, Antoine Watteau.

Chincoteague Island is a coastal island in Accomack County, Virginia. The feral horses known as "Chincoteague Ponies" actually live and graze on the salt marshes of nearby Assateague Island, and are descended from animals released into the wild by seventeenth-century colonists. On the last Wednesday of every July, mounted riders herd some of the ponies and swim them across a narrow channel to Chincoteague, where they are auctioned off in aid of the local fire department. Once, in Colorado, a cowboy poet asked me if I'd ever seen horses eating fish out of the ocean. I think of the Chincoteague Ponies as of angels, as of tireless commuters, as recovering alcoholics in a story by Cheever. I would like to walk beside one across the Tappan Zee Bridge some early morning, whistling the adagio from Brahms's Violin Sonata in G Major. In 1861, the residents of Chincoteague Island voted *not* to secede from the Union.

Donald Revell

A place of quiet nor of such consent

Never any of it turning to say

The perfect life is ourselves this evening

Once the weight the desperation of it

Intoxicated as the mountain lights

Nearest buildings some distance away mark

Events of such glamour loves our waitress

Wanting to care to bring us the mountain

Alphabet of which your green eyes show

There is no cutting corners in color

The heaven-sent harries our evidence

Each sign each second of extremity

All rescued by the Lord gives freely

Unhappy we cannot say He

In celebration of the three hundredth anniversary of Watteau's birth, a major retrospective of his works was assembled. It traveled to several of the world's great museums, including the National Gallery of Art in Washington, DC, where it was on display from June 17 through September 23, 1984. I saw it there. Betrayal hung upon the face of Watteau's Pierrot (sometimes known as Gilles) like a cloudy veil upon a weathered mask. Earlier that summer, in New York, at the Whitney Museum, I'd seen a major retrospective of the paintings of Fairfield Porter. The clouds in Maine, the houses beneath them, the lawns running down to the ocean, shone separately, each from the other, in distinctive, pious illumination. The parts of a world are alone with God, crowded together. I can never separate the Watteau exhibition, in memory, from the Fairfield Porters I'd seen a few days before, some distance to the north. Columbine might have been a dog asleep in Maine. Harlequin remains hidden somewhere in an upstairs bedroom.

Blaze of fir along the ground, I mean

Needles in a finger-splay showing

God's direction to the wind, why now?

Could it not have saved the boy sooner?

Colin to Cuddie: Blow the fire.

Love to liking: Lullay my dear one.

Rummage the odes for a fir tree more,

A black finger-mark on pitch-black sky.

I will lug my son into the light

Soon. Blaze me then. If the ground envies

The wind, despair's a fine thing. Mine eyes

Etcetera will lug my son soon.

Pagans were underfoot always, Watteau,

Heavy to me and not a boy for you.

Colin Clout, a shepheardes boy enamour'd of Rosalinde, is Edmund Spenser's own avowed persona in *The Shepheardes Calender.* A rural musician and lay prophet, Colin is the conscience of English pastoral poetry, evermore.

Cuddie, an unhappy Heardsmans boye, is the main character of Spenser's "Februarie" eclogue.

Lullay, myn lykyng, my dere sone, myn swetyng, | Lullay, my dere herte, myn owyn dere derlyng.
   —Fifteenth-century English Christmas carol

Then you, the burlesque of our lust—and faith, | Lug us back lifeward—bone by infant bone.
   —Hart Crane, "National Winter Garden"

Of smoke in Bethel no solitude can say,

Or archangel. Said Christ to me a wisp

Tilted into the trees to meet mountains,

Palm trees. Company of losels and pricks.

Say it again, Lord. We are not lonely.

Asking girls at two o'clock in the morning

Stabbed through the heart, joy's absolute only

Saying, will you be married all these years?

Bejeweled, yes, where the dog was sick.

Heaven's gate, yes, made of pearl and jasper.

Also I had in my mind the fountain

Wept a crazy glass into my birthday.

A new car is another Christmas morning

Farther on. Further, Antoine, my roundelay.

Bethel, literally "House of God." In Genesis, Bethel is the site of Jacob's dream, the one of a ladder thronged with angels ascending and descending. In my Sunday School, we read very little of the Old Testament, and so it was not until I came upon Denise Levertov's beautiful 1961 collection that I knew anything of that dream. I never met Denise, but we did have a good correspondence over the course of several years, from 1986 until her death. Her letters seemed always to arrive when I most needed them. They were like windows in houses in paintings by Vuillard.

Losels, scoundrels, good-for-nothings, rogues.

Jasper, Revelation 21:18, "And the building of the wall of it [Jerusalem] was *of* jasper . . ." Among the secrets of why and why now, I ask you to number the death of our dog Jasper, a giant schnauzer.

A space between clockwork and the rainbow
Wrapped in wads of hay, happens a child.
Whose? Mary would say Cupid's. Venus would
Paint rainbows across my Christ, the soar
Falcon I should learn. And so it is
Star's lief to wander, murdering as far
As the next animal—hind, bee—nightgowned
For the fayre election, calling itself
Queenie. Children hurt one another
And themselves. Between the clockmaker God,
Combing the beaches, and His joy fell a truth
Like thousands of wounds. Watteau, it's Christmas!
The elementary school playgrounds
Behave the night sky as if they owned it.

Covenant below my eye, self-made
Something, dread awhile to frighten rabbits
Out of the snow, but no, nothing like that.
I went to the window today nearly blind.

Christ promised me American catastrophe
All my own. My erst friends, beloved,
Would hurry away down the white, white snow,
And I would pound into the windowpanes

White names, their names. Below the eye, self-made
Imagination of a colored spree
Plays hangman. Wretched man. Wretched tree.
Ermine of the coldest kind, says Watteau.

Into my heart to write a Christ did, once,
The whole way go, on the off chance.

Windowpanes, facing into the little square of garden, Blackburn Street, 333
Blackburn Street, 1984, a letter on my desk from Terry K., thanking us both for
happy days in Washington—Dumbarton Oaks, the Watteau exhibition, the screening
of *Another Country*.

Wretched tree, I am thinking, of course, of Judas. Betrayal is the good health of
human helplessness every time, every time, and also of its hair.

Donald Revell

A fold field chose   The rightest boy

Something to wings   Well accustomed

So that so that   A long woman

Finding him nude   Would love and know

The carrying   Beneath her heart

Was his was he   A fold field chose

In the Grecian   Epigraphy

Muddle is made   Of a plain truth

As if two girls   Climbing a hill

To some ruins   Were not two girls

And the long boy   Trailing after

Were not the Christ   But one Greek more

Christ's epigone   Clownish Watteau

Painted for them   A hilltop home

Epigone, an undistinguished imitator or follower; also *Epigon*, one born after; in the plural, *Epigoni*, as in the sons of The Seven against Thebes.

... *Time is the steward of decor.*
In auctioned fittings that no longer are,
Persists the image that forever is:
Ease, class on class, and in the distance, war.
—Turner Cassity, "Epigoni Go French Line"

I met Turner Cassity only once, at the home (27 Chestnut Street, Binghamton, NY) of Patricia Wilcox, sometime in the spring of 1974. His patter was devilish and keen and kind: "Why do the wicked prosper, Patty? *Because* they are wicked!" Patricia Wilcox was the first friend my writing ever had, and certainly the best. She perfectly loved this world of which she perfectly despaired. God's truth was an oxalis growing in her kitchen window. I last visited her and her family in June 1984, right around the time of my thirtieth birthday.

Very light snow of smalls. The last one,

Time at last to praise intervals when

Nightclothes speaking of angels begin

In cold beloved bed one flannel,

Falls. Afterwards there must be skating.

Lately, Watteau, I've found you often

Painting flannel and periwinkle

In the Twenty-Third Psalm. Is it me?

It is small enough to pray, and cold

In bed. Cupped in blue flowers, needle-

Sharp as winter starlight, the breasts of

Skating you know. The musics will stray.

Periwinkle and dots of fire

Praise Christ Cupid on snowy rapier.

This morning of the small snow / I count the blessings . . .
   —Charles Olson, "The Songs of Maximus"

The Bishop's Wife (1947), a film directed by Henry Koster and adapted from Robert Nathan's novel of the same name. In the scene I'm remembering, the angel Dudley (played by Cary Grant) is seated on the floor beside a child, the bishop's little daughter. He tells her the story of a shepherd boy's fight with a lion, and the story becomes Psalm 23. The scene is so deeply focused, so clear and clean edged in every direction, it could only have been photographed by Gregg Toland, as indeed it was. Cinematographer of *Wuthering Heights*, *The Grapes of Wrath*, and *Citizen Kane*, Toland died in 1948 at the age of forty-four.

Tan-ta-ra, cries Mars on bloody rapier,
Fa-la, fa-la, fa-la, cries Venus in her chamber.
Toodle loodle loo, cries Pan that cuckoo,
With bells at his shoe, and a fiddle too.
   —Thomas Weelkes, 1608

Donald Revell

How near would you dare to row? Revisit

Your island now after so many such

Mornings, mornings the rabbits set to burst

Cornflower blue, is it smoke, is it frost

So makes the color, and you would surely

Never leave. Her. You once together set

The lintel askew from a ship's last timber.

Her. And the animals came to your hand.

The color of foam is sound, not color.

Swale, gunnel, swamp Andromeda, choose, man,

You must choose your parcel of imagined

Land and live in it, dry, berry-brown dry.

Dressed as a clown Antony, Antony

Rows for home. Christmas, they said. Come Christmas.

. . . But one of my most frequent expeditions was to go from the larger island to the smaller one, disembarking and spending the afternoon there, either walking in its narrow confines among the sallows, alders, persicarias and shrubs of all kinds, or else establishing myself on the summit of a shady hillock covered with turf, wild thyme and flowers, including even red and white clover which had probably been sown there at some time in the past, a perfect home for rabbits, which could multiply there in peace, without harming anything or having anything to fear. I put the idea to the Steward, who sent for rabbits from Neuchatel, both bucks and does, and we proceeded in great ceremony, his wife, one of his sisters, Therese and I, to install them on the little island, where they were beginning to breed before my departure and where they will doubtless have flourished if they have been able to withstand the rigours of winter. The founding of this little colony was a great day.

—Jean-Jacques Rousseau, *Reveries of a Solitary Walker*, trans. Peter France

Entirely forgotten they the license, hame and sky.

To manage a fine staircase, turning one's eyes

To his angels of no help, needing any, they

Have forgotten. Take this engine now from me.

Beloved rib cage and poverty hame.

Bell. Bell. Steeple that buried my parents

Under the hill was a staircase too.

Psyche had two sisters. Of women, a man

May speak to facts but never to opinion.

I was given a flag at my father's grave.

Beside him, my mother in death has made

A baroque staircase, a variance, a rage

Brighter than archangels. Take it from me.

Totty as busy rain, climb it, climb it.

. . . no unearned income | can buy us back the gait and gestures | to manage a baroque staircase, or the art | of believing footmen don't hear | human speech.
—W. H. Auden, "Thanksgiving for a Habitat"

"Psyche Showing Her Sisters Her Gifts from Cupid" by Jean-Honoré Fragonard, 1753 (collection of the National Gallery, London)

Yes, I will be thy priest, and build a fane | In some untrodden region of my mind, | Where branched thoughts, new grown with pleasant pain, | Instead of pines shall murmur in the wind . . .
—John Keats, "Ode to Psyche"

Busyrane, a wizard in Spenser's *The Faerie Queene*. Busyrane was associated with lust and with sexual love in (and out of) marriage.

Donald Revell

Watteau in rags: Climb! For only far is
Free. The difference between a rag and a rapier
Catches fire at extreme of sky,
Disappearing just then, sex then, leaving
Adam there, Eve until a long time
Mother mine. The baroque smiles across me.
Edna Davis pray for me and my good conduct.

Sainted depth of focus undercroft pray.
All over again shall we manage
The staircase, Watteau a ways ahead,
Rags becoming rage, brightness falling through
Busy rain. June 18th, 1961.
The final license of a final day
Says you. And of the two sisters, one says I.

At my right hand, always, when I am writing, sits *The Hymnal of the Protestant Episcopal Church in the United States of America* (1940) inscribed, in delicate blue handwriting,

For good conduct
From, Edna Davis
      (Teacher)
June 18, 1961

World Book
Carole Maso

For A is the beginning of learning and the door to heaven.

—Christopher Smart, *Jubilate Agno*

ONE OF THE THINGS I LOVED most when I was a child was to read from the children's encyclopedia (*the ice age, the oboe, the migration of birds, the origin of oceans*) and hours would pass in an instant as time warped and warbled and space seemed to expand into an elongating oval shape and I would vanish into those pages. Often I would find myself lost in the many wonders of the world then: an abacus, an acorn, an airplane (*the silver world*), falling into a half trance I have never quite been able to lift myself from since (*the velocity of light, the theory of tables, the point of indiscernibility, a logic of wings*).

The volumes had been ordered by my parents from a man they said had come to our door. I see him still in the gloaming, sitting on a park bench, gathering his courage and tomes; evening. Curiously my parents had understood these books to be a crucial, even urgent addition to our universe, a fact that has always fascinated me, for who among us would have guessed how insightful they were. They were beloved creatures: Mother, with a bird's nest on her head, and Father holding a burnished trumpet (*peace in our time*) but to me they seemed utterly out of touch. How could they have known, I wonder—so removed they seemed from the secret life of children (*a fossil, a blue striped feather, a carapace, a chrysalis, a sarcophagus, an apple*). We imagined we roamed another world entirely. Our parents some distant totem toward which we vaguely yearned.

It strikes me now on reflection, and perhaps I see it better in retrospect (*the house gone to archetype: crimson, roses, summer . . .*) that even then it was I who was the one who was out of touch—only imagining a pack of wandering sibling comrades at my side. A clamor of children, a din—receding already back then.

I look to the ceiling where the German airship the *Hindenburg* hovers. The cat recently deceased in the air like a gray dirigible.

After word of the acquisition of the encyclopedias, weeks passed without another mention of them and it seemed as if we had invented the whole thing as a distraction. It does seem preposterous now: a little man selling books in the night, every letter on every volume embossed in gold to light his way, wings attached to his back.

What an odd time, that suspension between the knowledge of the existence of such books and their arrival, weeks or perhaps it was months later. It seemed like forever. That eternity strikes me, especially now, as we verge on something like World's End, as one of the sweetest and most hopeful of my life. Who would I become? What was I to be?

How to describe their strange presence, their weight in the end? I watched the boxes that October accumulate in the hallway, until at last the set complete was ceremoniously opened one evening after Father returned from work. We placed each on the shelves made especially to hold them. These tomes I would become so devoted to. Hold one of those shiny, strangely thin but sturdy pages and a universe (*foxglove, parallelogram, cupola, indigo bunting, Tunisian basket weavers*) would open. The blue butterfly we sought. *World Book*. Before me the blossoming of all human knowledge.

How quickly after that my classmates turned to shadow: their games, their edicts, their petty clubs taking on a kind of pallor and quiet until they receded altogether. Gone their whims, their exclusions. My vertiginous free fall into beauty had begun. The great continuous world ocean is commonly thought of as five separate oceans lying between the continents. (*How could I have imagined, swaddled like that?*) The Pacific is largest and almost round. One can be farthest from land on the Pacific than anywhere on earth.

How to describe the mind's immersion? I found myself submerged as if under that great vast, singular sea, lucid but helpless. I bobbed and wove toward the siren's song deliriously (*fish inflected, sea soaked*). Few things could cause me to lift my dreaming head anymore, caught as I was in the sway, the fray of information and thought and dream. From the margins Post-Einsteinians, tipping their hats, bade me on. *Hello*, I call out, but who can hear from this darkly lit distance?

I want to live. Let it be said as the world this afternoon teeters on the brink of ruin. I feel indescribable sadness when I juxtapose the children's encyclopedia with the world we have made.

The Hanging Gardens once flourished on the east bank of the Euphrates River, about fifty kilometers south of Baghdad. Fruits and flowers, waterfalls, hanging from the palace terraces. Engulfing, inviting, entranced, we move toward their splendor and darkness, for who has ever seen such a thing, rising into the air? Said to have been invented by Nebuchadnezzar to please his concubine homesick for her green land, even those historians who give detailed descriptions of the Hanging Gardens never saw them. Longed for by poets, embellished by all who heard of them. It is said that when Alexander's soldiers reached the fertile land of Mesopotamia and saw Babylon they were mesmerized by the climbing gardens. In splendor high, high into the air. *Look!* It is quite possible, I have since learned, that those extraordinary pleasure gardens were only dreamt, invented, and that this wonder, not unlike other wonders, existed only in the mind.

I try to navigate a path from the hanging gardens to the school and back, but school, with the occasional exception—*Mlle. Trent, Mr. Sea Bream*—was a horrible bore, which, after the arrival of the *World Book*, became entirely without purpose. It is said that in the 1670s, a French locksmith named Besnier flew by means of paddle-like cloth wings, which he attached to his shoulders and feet.

Who's there? A knock at my door. Oh, it's my brother tapping out his code—an indication that there might be something of importance happening, and so, lifting myself from the charms of that world, those swells (*more like music or shadow*), I descend one of the interval of stairs that are scattered throughout our suburban split-level house.

Yes, my brother is right. There she sits, Aunt Lorraine, strange and dangerous on the couch with my mother. She has come in from the country for the afternoon. Each of us vying for the position closest to her so as to best observe this, our ghostly relation (could she really be ours?), fashionable and thin, flawlessly performing her concise magic. First she would tap tap tap the little blue box, then slowly open it, first unfolding the foil, talking all the while, then, slipping out a slim, cylindrical treasure (*a kind of mummy*) and lighting a match (*phosphorus*), she would put a tiny flame to it. We sit rapt (*five children on the couch*) and watch her talking and laughing while breathing in, inhaling (*that small brilliance at the tip*), then exhaling. We were inside the stratosphere. We never got to see such a thing up close. That pyre of plant and paper, insinuating its way into our eyes and hair, and lungs; a dalliance of the highest order. We are mortal and immortal on that green couch in the New Jersey summer. The world on fire. As many times as we bear witness, we

247

never tire of it. My mother and my aunt talking, oblivious, in this, their stolen time together, laughing and levitating in smoke up to the chandelier. Their lovely bits of conversation falling from the strato-sphere—*not Isabel really, who would have dreamt?* They were buoyant and beautiful and we craved beauty, and we craned our necks to see.

The grace of their exclamatory gestures seemed to me a kind of miming, part signal, part lamentation, missives to a heaven where their impossibly young mother already resided. A lilting figure pre-sented itself in a high corner, a wound would float through any day they spent together, a feeling that would inevitably tinge the after-noon. We sat transfixed. A hand on the heart, a hand on the head, sisters joining hands. As the smoke accumulated and we breathed the illicit air more deeply. The baby's head obscures the view for a minute. A baby's hair on fire burns at desire's wayward periphery. Get out of the way! The world is too dangerous to live in. *Daddy does seem a bit under the weather*, my aunt sighs, looking to her sister and exhaling. Never did they seem to notice our awe or ad-miration or alarm. It was, we assumed, just another of those chasms that exist between adults and children. (*I stand on a great coral reef; it is composed of a billion organisms. Who can see me?*) Only now that I am a mother myself do I understand how my daughter, Rose, must view me: shuffling around with stacks of papers, glasses of wine, worried, singing, telling nonsense stories, distracted, a consoling, benevolent, but fundamentally clueless figure in her universe.

Many experimented with the idea of balloons, but the Montgolfier brothers of France made the first successful airship. The cigar-shaped craft carried a steam engine and had a speed of six miles an hour. In 1783 they built big balloons filled with hot air. Women (*sisters*) in baskets attached to these balloons floated freely through the air for the first time in history.

I was as lost then as I am now. *Father, can you let us in yet?* we children would ask. The red light outside the door where we stood. We had found ourselves on the wrong side of the magic this time. My father, in the silver world. *Father, can you let us in yet?* My father in his darkroom pulling images from the chemical bath. *Can we come in yet?* The trays, the silence, the sensation of being at crea-tion's edge. My father's shadow face in half-light, following a child down a dirt road near a lake, on gleaming paper. The sway of the trees . . .

Intrigued by a world I felt too intense to live in, I immersed myself

248

in those encyclopedias, a safer place, where I might stave off the green ray of the television, the Sunday procession of saints, the wine turned to blood, the floating sisters' sorrow, my distracted father in darkness. No, I remained engrossed by those pages: the origin of stars, the migration of birds, the transit of Venus, peace in our time, ancient Egypt, electricity, the great inventions up to then, a century, at that time at its midpoint. I thought that I myself might become an inventor one day, but that dreamy child in the end has only invented a handful of figments: unstable, reluctant delineations—shadows on the page, characters in my novels. A novelist—how peculiar. In my life so far—a life well past its own midpoint, I have done little more than chase ghost figures, intimations, inklings, glimpses of what I once thought I might see in full. Charting voices both within and without. I bow my head to the passing entourage. My grasp on them so fleeting, so tenuous—it was always the case—I do not presume to hold. These figures of such haunting obscurity, simultaneously completely present and utterly absent, right before me and already gone. That drift, that flickering, that delirious procession—here and not here. I try to reach them through the flickering. What in me longs toward them, and their uneasy consolation, these apparitions, strangers risen from my psyche? An odd way to have spent one's life.

The three-lined paper, with the broken center line. The gray of the pencil mark, the smell of the eraser. A girl is handed the key to the world—in a handful of letters. So be it. She's lived a long time now with the secret.

There, resplendent in the imagination's dark light these characters gather again: Ava Klein, my dearest creation, mortally ill in her hospital bed, Francesco at her side; Anatole, perpetually stepping onto the small plane, taking flight. They come and go. Carlos: He's cut himself on the punch bowl—he's furious, angered by my whimsical summons, he wonders why he's been called back again, after all this time. . . . That drift of figments, that procession before me, having traveled unfathomable distances to get here. Handing us in the end their indecipherable messages. How strange to be alive.

All those who have populated my solitude. A bleary chemist takes the center of the dark stage for a moment. It's Ava's father, Phillip, looking on. In the white corridor he holds the black coat for his wife and she slips her arm into the soft hollow. She's back to make her grave donation. She holds her precious bone marrow in a silver cup. Mother, Ava says, *I'm over here.* Such sweet abandon—one scarcely knows how to bear the innocence of these creations. Gathering now for the year's longest night under the winter sky. From what longing were they created? These configurations of language, arrangements on a page, stilled and in motion, this motion within my stillness, this world without end. Anatole, leaving the solstice party, heady with death, scrawls a note and heads for the airfield. These lovely accommodations to my sorrow and to my hope. *Off you go.* How are you feeling, Ava Klein? She stares into the distance. Guglielmo Marconi sits on a hill in Newfoundland waiting for a sound. Above him dangles a kite, with an antenna attached to its tail. Across the Atlantic in England sits Marconi's assistant. At twelve o'clock on the twelfth day of the twelfth month of 1901 electromagnetic waves carry the first sound over water, a *dit, dit, dit,* Morse code for the letter *S.*

How are you feeling? She points: It's her aunt Sophie standing at the ditch she will be shot into—seven months pregnant and about to die again despite my best efforts. And here now Francesco perceived through this shaped feeling—*I love you*—this retreating figure about to leave once more. *Out the door you go then.* His serene and perfect indifference—like those two sisters, encapsulated in dream time, laughing right before me and utterly out of reach.

My brother and I floating on a dock at my grandparents' lake house those interminable summers—now locked in time. Two figures you could not get to again no matter how hard you tried. Why such melancholy tonight? The sky is on fire.

What is this mission I find myself on now? Resuscitation, retrieval, resurrection, rescue of all kinds, my life's work. To compensate for a loss I cannot even begin to fathom. Though certainly today there are intimations.

I hear sound over water as when I was a child bent over that encyclopedia. My novels. Those characters. Have I said it—their consolation, their weight, and the eerie feeling that I do not exist at all except when I am with them? We create each other. *Where are you?* I do not close the manuscript too soon, fearing disappearance, but finally lifting my weary head from the page I say, *Yes, yes, I shall come to bed.* What was it I had wanted of them? *One more minute.* Who hears me? Perhaps, I conjecture (*birds migrating make black patterns on my studio wall*), I am one of the already dead. *Are you there?*

Gilles Deleuze describes a principle, a point of indeterminability, of indiscernibility, when the distinction between subject and object loses its importance. We no longer know what is imaginary or real, physical or mental, not because we are confused, but because we do not have to know, and there is no longer even a place from which to ask. It is as if the real and the imaginary were running after each other.

I am trying to reach you S, S, S on this terrible afternoon as clouds descend. A boy points to the sky. Ava calls for Sophie, Francesco, her parents, all.

And what in the end will it have meant? A question ordinarily beyond asking yet at the cusp of this sorrow today, this strangeness all of a sudden. . . . (*The United States begins a preemptive war in Iraq.*) I am scheduled to teach Chris Marker, and begin Godard this afternoon. One does ask what cannot be answered—expecting—expecting what?

I write to you from a faraway land. I write to you from the end of the earth. I write to you from the end of childhood. I write to you from the land of obscurity. This flawed and mortal document I call a novel. And if no one else recognizes it as such—what will it have mattered? As bombs begin to fall.

Voices emanate from the open page now. It shall be a record of our vanishing, one of the voices offers. A book of scraps, last messages left on answering machines, trace elements, an unfinished book of hope, a sort of reliquary, a dome, a memory of bread, a dormer, a basket, the rabbit path. It shall be a cradle that holds time. A prayer. More and more a prayer. It shall speak to what mattered most—as much as it was possible to do so. It shall be a pageant, a celebration, a mourning grove, a history of our suffering, both intimate and epic. At the limits of narrative—as we go (*dit, dit, dit*)—last ways of reaching each other. A confection, lighter than air, a wish, a hope, a dream, a pageant, a lark—the flurry of existence. My mother's voice, the way the swing swung, the way he looked that night. And bells. Birds. Migration. Peace in our time. A philosophy of wings will emerge.

It shall be our lives, eclipsing the darkness. Our lives passing brightly before the darkness, and obscuring it for a moment.

This small offering that is song. On the horizon, the revelers. Weaving slightly, lifting a glass to another century as it passes. A book for all that is precious and passes—must pass.

It shall be a catalog of all that has been lost. And of what survives. A record of what somehow, for now, still survives.

Dear Grandfather,

The day of the week is Tuesday. The season is autumn. You are living in the United States of America.

Carole Maso

"Has the Sea Given Up Its Bounty?" the melancholy headline read in today's paper. "Most of the earth's surface is covered by oceans, and their vastness and biological bounty were long thought to be immune to human influence." ". . . in the dim hint of the ocean's former bounty . . ." swordfish once three thousand pounds. Cod, once six feet in length, have essentially vanished. The place we still call Cape Cod—for the fish that once flourished—like the Indian names for things we have decided to keep. Mattapoisett, Narragansett. Manhattan. Having decimated the tribes.

Our great-grandchildren tell their great-grandchildren: shrimp. They laugh at the word. And when cooked they turned pink . . .

". . . like a ring of fire burning on paper, as one ocean, then the next, and then—uses itself up."

"There's been too much short-term vision. You look at all that water and think there's no way you could overfish it."

Living things are among the most interesting wonders of nature. That is one reason why you enjoy going to the circus or the zoo or a farm. Almost everywhere you go you will find living things of one kind or another.

Look! Someone points to a lighter-than-air creation passing over our head; it is shaped like a lozenge.

The *World Book* reports that it was 1300 AD before anyone tried to solve the problem of flying scientifically. Roger Bacon, scientist and writer, studied the problem seriously. One of his ideas was that very light objects could float in air just as somewhat heavier objects could float in water. The idea of balloons filled with "liquid fire" that would be lighter than air. He also suggested a flying machine that would flap its wings like a bird.

Such a machine is called an ornithopter, but no one has ever succeeded in making one that would fly.

What did you think was beautiful there? At the edge of the abyss it feels more important to know. Simply to have some sort of record before separating into random strands of narrative and sound. Incoherence, bedlam. Scraps of voice left from cell phones all over the debris field. P, are you all right? I am trying to reach you. What in the end will I have been?

I would often find myself on Sullivan Street in Soho—after a day's writing I liked to roam. There at one particular spot I could stop and see to the north the gorgeous Empire State Building and then without lifting a foot, turn the other way downtown to see the Twin Towers. It was astonishing—in one neat swivel I could see it all. I

252

must have done it a thousand times.

And then not again. And then not. And the expectations adjust to the given, as if we were made for that—or so it seems: One's expectations shift with some illusion of ease: to first see the sky through those ruins. Those waffles of steel. The accommodation to survival. And even though those towers are still there in my mind's eye I force myself to see only empty space.

Nothing more. Your heart could break. The pivot now made silently in dust. A habit, I know.

Of our ingenuity, and our resourcefulness, and our folly. That smoking ruin. And then nothing. That utter presence in absence. To see and forever what is not there.

The French woman, suddenly back alive again before me who once whispered: *I too would like to make the walnut wine but am never able to, for walnut trees are always too far from me on St. John's Day. It is important for the success of the wine to have soft, milky walnuts picked fresh on that particular day in June, and to marinate them in red wine and sugar for long months so that the flavors and colors blend.*

What was precious, fleeting, most beautiful and ordinary—a woman on St. John's Day contemplates the distance—and if not the real story, then what the story was for me.

This transit that was our lives, these glimpses: a young wife doing an interpretive dance with rattle and rabbit head for husband and newborn, a sort of scamper. Another mother doing an asparagus dance for her daughter who has just eaten five tips. Her hands above her head in a point.

And that other mother-to-be gesturing at the ditch.

Messages difficult to decipher: "The cloven-footed animals are at risk." They feed from her open hand on this hospital bed.

Let me know if you are going. The park inside us widening.

A reverie: fragile and fleeting. Our lives: We used to take the rabbit path. Our lives: what opened to us as children on that bridle path. The Swedish Pavilion nestled in the park. The Marionette Theater. That crystal palace by the sea. Our lives: *I too would like to make the walnut wine.*

A Book of Intimations. It shall be our lives.

Andrei Tarkovsky: "My function is to make whoever sees my films aware of his need to love and to give love, and to be aware that beauty is summoning him."

And what does it all mean? If you asked we could not tell you. The park in afternoon shadow. That vast expanse of purplish green.

Our lives: Dearest Carole, You ask how I am now that Zenka is gone. The truth is, dear friend, I am really only half alive without her.

Our lives: the way the dark waves brightened on that windy day, late afternoon, Brighton. What is retained—why that afternoon out of the thousand afternoons—having driven for hours in the rain.

Deleuze as I have been reading him for my film class will speak of the "crystal image" as the most fundamental image of time, since the past is constituted not after the present but at the same time, one aspect of the present of which is launched into the future while another falls into the past. We cannot tell them apart, and the crystal where this divided time resides makes these moments one indiscernible from the next. The immediate past that is already no longer and the immediate future that is not yet. A mirror that endlessly reflects.

That drift, that delirium—that procession of figments—here and not here—right before me and already gone. Life indeed is but a dream as you, Ava Klein, as you wander out of reach now.

Our lives: Where are the St. Jean's Fires of my youth?

Fall—the autumn light—the feeling of a whole way of life waning, the smell of slight decay, we burned enormous bundles of dried grape vines. The fire flared up dramatically and in such essential brightness. I can't begin to describe that brightness etched in my mind, even now.

As a child's delight in front of a birthday cake: one candle, two candles, three, then suddenly there are seventy. The fires went down as fast as they had flared up. They flame then sputter, extinguished by a breath.

They used to say that the girls who could cross the blaze in one leap without scorching their skirts would find a lover within the year. . . .

The bombing begins. The children ask, in Arabic, in Farsi, in German, in Hebrew, in Kurdish, in French, *Où est la porte?*

Windows on the World:

See how the Staten Island Ferry looks like a bath toy from this vantage point. The United Nations like an upright deck of cards. How small the door. We press our hands against the glass.

My father points to the sky: It's the *Hindenburg* in flames. It's New

Jersey and it's 1937 and he's six years old, and it's just another one of his hapless collisions with history—my father walking through the exploding world.

As infants in Paterson, New Jersey, every boy was checked as the search for the kidnapped son of the aviation hero Charles Lindbergh continued. In the evening, a knock on my grandmother's door.

Who knocks (spoken in Italian)?

Is that you, Salvatore?

Marconi and the first sound over water.

Where is the door? She opens the children's encyclopedia. A is for Antarctica, the explorers fumble through white, through ice. Where is the door?

What color bird will you be today? Rose asks.

The bombing begins. I will be a bluebird with a rose breast, she says. How are you feeling, Ava Klein?

Under cover of night, from this dreamy bed, thousands of calls may be heard. Most songbirds travel by night. The air is more still, the temperatures lower. Most night-migrating songbirds fly below two thousand feet. Before migration there's something like dread in them and nothing can quell it but the flapping of wings.

Shadows on my studio wall:

Sisters enveloped in smoke on a pale-green sofa I think circa 1965. I seem to always think of it, floating through smoke—an insinuation, a strangeness—a world unto itself—an island among the mod Swedish blond furniture of that room. They are laughing, and my aunt is blowing smoke up toward the chandelier. The bright bell rings and now another visitor comes to the door. My mother simply by virtue of her charms (*a bird's nest, polka dots*) could lure anyone, it seemed (*driven by wind, the current of oceans, the stars, the sound of her voice*) to that, yes, now definitively green couch. The bell rings and we run to it. It's the good Dr. Jehl, our great friend, and all the children jump up and down, up and down, and he is in his uniform and he is carrying his black doctor's bag with compartments (*the way it unfolded*).

Dr. Jehl, how happy I am to see you once more! His calmness, his reassurance, his intuition—a healer, one of the gifted, our salvation sitting on our couch. The world is a safe place as long as he is near. That much is abundantly clear. He opens the book he has brought for us, the *Peterson Field Guide to Birds*. It had a green cover. I held it that day a long time.

Let me know if you are going. Dr. Jehl walking down the wooded path and pointing to things: a boletus mushroom, a lady slipper, a jack-in-the-pulpit, a tufted titmouse. Dr. Jehl, once an American Army doctor in the Second World War, who came some days in his uniform, donned in medals, I cannot think why. The good German doctor who named the world and all its birds and stars and clouds and trees. Who showed us the places animals made their homes. He was in love with my mother like everyone else, tramping through the woods near our house with the five of us children pointing out the many wonders: edible berries, blue-jay feathers, cocoons, mushrooms, the purple finch, the goldfinch, the bluebird.

Over the radio in the last two hours I hear the Desecration of the Birds. Their names used for machines of war: the Black Hawk, the Raptor, the Falcon, the Eagle, the Osprey, the Raven, the Shrike.

He loved dahlias, digging them up every fall they lived in the dark and all was well with the world. Dr. Jehl, tromping through the forest. *O Tannenbaum*, we five children sing with him, he with his walking stick and knickers, in that dappled, that flickering light of the mind. O Sacred Tree.

We hear the song of the lark, he points to the sky—coming in and out of range, on Lake Erskine so many years ago—*Dr. Jehl, come back!* How have I so misplaced this time? Encapsulated; it has broken off and floats, autonomous, serene, without any concern for me. Having detached itself from its dreamer—*come back*, I whisper and grasp what light it leaves behind. I touch the edges of the glass globe where the German doctor and the little girl in radiance reside.

After almost everything else has left, there, there I am back with him, age seven again, improbably risen from the Fatherland, the Europe of Sorrows.

We will fight the Americans, the Iraqis are saying, *even with sticks.* A country posing no threats.

Rose loves the goldfinch and the robin and the bluebird with the rose breast. The mourning dove is shy. It is larger than a goldfinch. Its tail is tapered with white tips on the edges of the feathers.

Rose alights and I wonder whether (*this tentative spring*) she will need a sweater or a juice box—and I think of this child I have been chosen to be the custodian of and how every nuance of her being and every aspect of her becoming is my concern. She smiles, walking to me through the war. And inside that bird's nest: eggs. She walked with perfect posture so as to protect them. Five.

I think of the children of Iraq and realize they too—and it is not a great leap—might, in another life, have been mine—and at this minute shivering in the atrocious heat, hungry, frightened, tired. They too belong to me. Think how frightened the children must be—as all of Baghdad is blacked out. We have allowed our most basic human contract to lapse: to see to it that the children are not harmed. They were for us to protect.

Why had we handed over our obligation so readily? We were obliged to have brought these things close to us—to not keep a distance.

I think of Michael Lu, a child in Rose's kindergarten class. Struggling his way with fury toward English. Wrenching himself out of Chinese. *Broken* is the only word he can say in English. Everything you ask of him—his name, his age, how is he today, where do you live. Broken, he says. Broken, broken. Where is our fury?

The world is broken. We left it carelessly as if it were a toy. We thought it was something we could casually replace. We lost our way.

I walk from one room to the next.

Children of Iraq, how is it you stay alive?

At the edge of that green couch, my parents stare blankly ahead at the television set that in my memory sits on a low platform and down a long tunnel at the opposite end of the room. The president is talking and he sounds something like a billy goat, bathed in that blue cathode ray, trying to act as if everything were perfectly ordinary, but we children know better. A bay filled with pigs. How horrible. I walk to my mother's side—though I am big, I sit on her lap.

It is not then—though they meld in my mind somewhat—but the next year, the same couch, the television emitting its darkness, when I recall my first sense of terror. I am less numb this time and more panicked, in fact. I gauge the world this day by my parents' responses—I have never seen them look quite this way, and we wait together, for what I do not know. In my father's face: World's End. My parents are unreachable, inaccessible—and we children are left completely alone—I am the oldest and must take care of the rest of the little ones now, as we roam the extraordinarily dangerous terrain of our suburban living room. A week in October. *A poisoned rocket is pointed at us*, my brother says. Really? Wow. Duck your heads! The world is nothing like you had supposed. Hauling your children's encyclopedia (*Antarctica, Africa, aster, air*).

At the edge of that couch, in my father's face, an unreadable emotion. Seeing the president's head (from which emanated the voice of a billy goat) as if from a far distance in the blue light of the television set. *Rockets are pointed at our house.* Quarantine. Just the word

257

haunts. This was the same fall that the *World Book* arrived. I had only opened the first book: A.

Apple. Abacus. Albatross.

Red floods the desert, in shock and in awe you stand.

And where children once swam in the Euphrates—

The theory is, as its title suggests, to shock and to awe Iraq by dropping as many as eight hundred "smart" cruise missiles on the country in two days—

The earth is a rocky planet in the habitable zone. This zone is an area where liquid water, which is essential for life, can exist. Unlike gas planets, rocky planets like earth have surfaces where water can gather in pools and seas.

The world ocean covers seven-tenths of the earth. No one standing on shore or sailing on water can help wondering how large the ocean is. Even on a large steamer one may cross the ocean day after day and see no other ship. Men in lifeboats have floated for months without being found. The ocean is not only large, it is also a very lonely place. I think about the melancholy encyclopedia writer who wrote this introductory paragraph to the ocean for children in 1963.

The great continuous world ocean is commonly thought of as five separate oceans.

A woman says *plage* just above the line of her breath.

In shock now, and in awe.

The children's encyclopedia reads: *The Middle East, located at the juncture of three continents, makes it a region second to none in the world of tracking, research, and study of the phenomenon of bird migration. More than five hundred million birds pass over the Middle East twice a year in the autumn and the spring.*

In Baghdad the children say, *I'm thirsty.* And make the universal sign for water, their hands cupped in the air—and thousands of birds cover the sky.

My sixth-grade teacher, Mr. Spreen, stands now before the darkening blackboard where he has written "The Cradle of Civilization." He pulls down the map. Everything begins here, he says. With his pointer he reaches and his black jacket lifts up slightly from his hip. This is the Mesopotamian Circle. The word "Mesopotamian" comes from the Greek for "between the rivers," and he points to the Tigris and the Euphrates. Now mostly present-day Iraq. Everything starts here, he says, pulling down the map: the first cities, the centralized state, mathematics, astronomy, the wheel, the sail, the measurements of time: the sixty-second minute, the sixty-minute hour, the 360-degree circle. The written word. Our first stories. The way we think of who we are.

Fancifully, we girls called him Sea Bream. . . .

Pillaged, the cuneiform tablets that tell us of the invention of writing, the creation of the first cities, legal codes. The Cradle of Civilization—our deepest memories engraved there.

Destroyed a clay tablet. It bore a few simple marks. At the top was what seemed to me to be a fingerprint, and below it a stick-drawn animal, perhaps a goat, or a sheep. For the first time ever, a transaction of animals conveyed, by drawing signs on earth. Recently discovered in Syria. Sheltered in the museum in Iraq. The tablets survived until today.

Witness to the moment of our beginning.

Missing: a vase, a book, a bird, the counting of sheep, so begins our sleep and our forgetfulness.

Ten thousand years of human history.

Missing: tablets from the *Epic of Gilgamesh*, the world's first literary work, from the culture that invented writing.

The child draws the letter *C*.

I go to the children's encyclopedia, that record of the great wide world and all its wonders and all its charms.

When I was a child I liked to go to the children's encyclopedia and millennia would pass in an instant.

A bird is an animal. It has a backbone, it is warm-blooded and walks on two legs, the same as a human being. It flies, as do insects and bats. And it lays eggs like salamanders, some snakes and turtles. But a bird is special. Birds are different from all other creatures, for they alone have feathers—and a wishbone.

At night I dream a goldfinch alights on the head of a child.

The Armenians say that this means there will be one thousand years of peace in the kingdom.

Missing: a small carving of a bird, one of the earliest stone sculptures in existence. The archaeologists had found it literally in the hand of its ancient owner, who had been crushed to death when the roof of his burning house fell on him, evidently as he tried to save this piece.

The priceless library now ash.

Unlearn the world with me, I say to that dreaming, studious child who is bent over the children's encyclopedia at night with a flashlight reading about—what—I cannot see anymore. Unlove the world,

259

I say to that child. But she does not hear me.

The child draws the letter *C*.

Destroyed, disseminated, or left to be sold on eBay.

At her small table, the child writes. On her three-lined paper. Her first marks and words—her private cuneiform.

A bird is warm-blooded and has wings.

Unlove the world with me.

I close the children's encyclopedia on bird.

That night when my dream resumes, the air is already in flames.

Dear relinquished future, dear sadness, dear regret.

A bird is an animal. It has a backbone, it is warm-blooded and walks on two legs, the same as does a human being. It flies, as do insects and bats. And it lays eggs, like salamanders, some snakes and turtles.

Unlove the world with me, Rose.

Unlove the world, but she is blue now with a red breast. Rose and I walk through snow, looking for the Lenten rose. It's still too early, I say to her, and my voice echoes strangely against the gray mountains. Inside we open the Book of Roses. Two-to-three-inch cup-shaped flowers in deep maroon, green, cream, hues of white and pink. Deeply lobed evergreen leaves, they are valued for their late-winter or early-spring flowers that appear when little else is in bloom.

The Lenten rose floats resplendently by with its melancholy message: Take refuge.

I was happy to be on this earth with you and the flowers.

I ask her to unlove the world with me. Even the flowers. Even the snow. She made a snow cat, a snow girl, a snow rabbit, that interminable winter. She was learning to write. Her name in snow. Even the birds.

She reaches in her toddler body from a place passing, then passed, already passed with her palms up: Great news: It's snowing! And snowflakes collect in her open hand and on her tongue: cherry blossom, ash. Preserved in this crystal of time, eternally five, there in my mind's eye.

Unlove the world.

She leafs through the children's encyclopedia.

My parents seated on the edge of that green couch in front of the flickering box.

Dr. Jehl holding a fallen baby bird. My mother walking with a nest on her head. My father blowing a moody bugle. *Unlove the world.*

But she is just learning to count. Mr. Spreen holding my model of the solar system. Wire and clay. A clod of earth. The fluorescent head of the president. We look out the window and see a loping deer, a hedgehog, a red fox, horses in fog, Saturn, Mars, the wobbling of stars.

But she says no. If she understood what I was asking she would certainly say, as it is one of her new favorite phrases, I refuse.

She loves me tonight as far as Pluto and back, times infinity.

At what point do we accept the reality of loss, that brevity is part of the butterfly's beauty?

Our lives passing before the darkness and eclipsing it for a minute . . . All human longing, all human ingenuity. Dear relinquished future, dear regret. Dear smoking ruin. Shall summer come this year and go as always?

I recall last August. Rose in blue light: "This won't be the last hot day of summer?" she begs. She makes me promise as I try to coax her out of her princess pool.

Crooning to the tilted earth—brevity of the day, lighting candles on that longest night—throwing sparklers—we were a strangely hopeful lot right up until the end. What was that in us, as a people— this collective assumption—that the good would prevail, that there would be plenty of time? Despite all the indications to the contrary. From the severed arms: a philosophy of wings. From the broken heart, hope.

Let us croon to this earth, not entirely in tune, before we fall back into forgetfulness, into nothingness escorted by the president, the silent congress, the senate in evening clothes, into our annihilation.

When shall the next catastrophe strike?

Unlove the world and all its wonders and all its charms (*the oboe, the ice age, the invention of writing, the origin of oceans*).

Before we are delivered back into oblivion. Let those of us who still can, sing.

From the fragments: a beautiful songscape.

Begin this book in gentleness, dear Reader.

I send Rose out to school through the war and she reaches back to me through the first green of spring. It's March 1993. She says I will miss you. I wonder if she will need sunscreen today (she will) or a hat. Goodbye. And she turns back one time to look at me—a receding figure in her bright eye.

Rose makes her way down the path to school. She is learning to

261

write. I will miss you, she says, singing as she goes. Promised today at the Winter Bear Montessori School: the ten board, word lists, the pink tower, carrot work, the binomial cube, the movable alphabet, the abacus. She can't wait.

Mystery Poem
Elaine Equi

1.

I'm compelled to read mysteries
as the murderer is compelled to murder

and the detective to solve righteously
and the mystery writer to inscribe

the lonely night with his existential moonglow.
A mystery is musical, mathematic, precise.

Wittgenstein famously sought solace
from the rigors of philosophy

in the pages of mysteries. But what if
the mystery writer simply got bored or distracted

along the way, and forgot the investigation,
and began to fall in love with the suspect Antonioni style?

A poet is someone who goes out of her way to preserve
a mystery, and can be led astray by ignoring or distorting

certain evidence, while willfully harboring poetic illusions.
Then there is the type that always answers a question

with another question. I confess I'm guilty
of having done that myself on more than one occasion.

It's an easy way to avoid the stigma of closure and say:
"Let's keep the case open and see what develops."

2.

In spring, when trees and gardens begin to bloom
a woman—refined, artistic—a professor I know

licks her lips and announces: "It's time for a lot of dead
bodies to start piling up. That's what I want to see."

I couldn't agree more. I don't believe people addicted
to mysteries like to solve puzzles. I believe they want to kill.

At least part of them does, and in order to entertain those fantasies,
they must insure that that part is eventually apprehended

and put away, disposed of like a cheap pulp novel.
People that travel often tuck a mystery or two in their suitcase

(or now on their iPad). What better way to escape the monotony
of a sunny day than to sit on a beach, daiquiri in hand, and dissolve

mentally into the mind of the grumpy Swedish detective Martin Beck?
To follow as he trudges through rainy Stockholm streets, coughing

and sneezing, running down one false lead after another, as if to assure us
crime solving is a job, not a frivolous indulgence.

Such passages remind me of how some sci-fi writers go out of their way
to portray space travel as boring, claustrophobic—time spent

playing solitaire between the stars. Yes, unraveling a mystery is a form
of travel in and of itself. I feel at home in California, having been driven

up and down the coast so many times by the likes of Raymond Chandler,
Ross Macdonald, and the incomparable James M. Cain. During long insomniac

nights, we'd stop for a cup of coffee and ask the locals what, if anything,
unusual they'd seen, then jot down their answers in a notebook.

A two-headed turtle; a three-legged dog; a white sock tinged
with red, forgotten in a Laundromat; what looked to be a skeleton

slow dancing in the corner of a tavern to a popular song.
Wait a minute, these clues are starting to read like a poem.

3.

My heart races. My breath is shallow.
Why do I care about these fictitious lives?

Why sweat as if I'd committed the crime?
The dragnet is closing in with its inevitable inevitability.

I close my eyes, not when there's blood or mayhem,
but when order is about to be restored—can barely stand

to read the preposterous (and believe me it always is) ending
which resolves everything but hardly ever explains a thing.

OK—it's finally over. I'm calm, as Mayakovsky once said,
as the "pulse of a corpse." How finite everything suddenly looks,

moving slowly or quickly toward its own demise.
No wonder I must return to poetry for traces of, if not eternity,

a largeness of spirit and voice—some quality of being
less easily exhausted. Even those who disdain the metaphysical

can marvel at the ability of words to overflow their meanings;
even a rigorous materialist like Oppen was not immune to awe.

From The Book of Spells
Andrew Mossin

THE LANGUAGE

We bleed and burn with thirst, our blood is strength.
—Tristan Tzara

The world is exiled in the name. Within it there is the book of the world.
—Edmond Jabès

1.

Begin somewhere, somehow
Begin with "effects left blank"

Begin "the weight in want"
"the loss the order in destroy"

the way that language folds up unexpectedly
and we're left unsure how to proceed . . .

Assign risk to mornings clear and cloudless
empiric understandings that have become habit

the collar of red seen from your last window
the emphasis that "she" acquires spoken silently at the
     circumference of thought.

To begin here is not to begin there
where yesterday another myself stood, another

imposition of the self that rendered the first
version mute: *I was sitting at a table*

and through the lens of my left eye saw
a man, not far from me, his horizon

spiritually blank, I couldn't say what it was
that drew me to him, the way he

hunched over his table and appeared to be
writing, the writing he was doing I

can't say it was anything, there was a legibility
to his hand, I couldn't see the words

as they formed, his wrist moving
across the pages of notebook paper

arranged on the table before him
as if light itself had been drawn away from every object

leaving only this: a circle, wordless
inside another circle of words.

2.

Is our task, then, like Darwin's
to find in language expression for what

follows, "modifications consequent
on other modifications"

the virtue of which is to understand
cause and effect in the world

assignations of the natural surface
where we walk without effort

unable to acknowledge
how at odds our beings are

with what is around us, the play
of light in trees that doesn't

allow us to form words for
the "struggle for existence"

that is, like a hand's sudden wrapping of itself
around another's hand,

both portent and apprehensive
grasp of the visible: *I moved*

away, I saw it was isolation
bordering another form of isolation

the language I was looking for
wouldn't allow me to say what I needed

to say, one tree
blocking the light, another

affording me great depth.

3.

As if streaming from one
river and the woman at the other

side calling out to us, "Bring us back
to you," the versions

of a woman's contiguous being
that acquired meaning only after

she had long vanished.
Is there one calling out to one calling?

Is there a reason
why in the mornings we can hide

ourselves in the prolixity of language
its habits and conciliations

writing in our notebook *the very noticeable*
difference awaking without one, awaking

in the throes of memory, not oneself, apart
from all who came before, throat and chest

I retrace, finger knots, nods up against
my finger bones, prodding, as they must

go, band by band, into a circle of light
offered again—

A tool like that
blackened, hard-hitting

striking back in language
when it is so often

the other way: formless
grappling for the speech of another

to complete what needs
saying here, black spirals of ink

down a margin: voiceless.

4.

Even pity has been
removed from us, *pietàs*

that gave us ability at first
to see

not without difficulty
our mother's body raised epitaphic

above our own. There was always
the dutiful distrust

of language, as if it could
impoverish us all over again

the way Merleau-Ponty
describes that interaction between selves

at the rim of experience
a kind of border opprobrium

encircling the "I" speaking
to the one listening: "Whether speaking

or listening, I
project myself into the other

person, I
introduce him into my own self."

One can say *I was pulled by you*
into myself, you pulled me back

from who I was and gave me
back myself

even as the words we give
each other—awkward, banal, bittersweet—

can't resolve the arrangement
of bodies that must exist in time, mortal, inviolate

sharing one space, then another, a paralleling
like speech itself *I came so far to find you*

Where did you go? to which one might respond
You replaced me, I never left, it was you that got rid of

myself.

5.

A coming into
language

the book's effects and enticements
forging a perimeter of feeling that held us near others

and at the same time created border states
nearly shameful

as if we held nothing
private or self-worthy could not

enter the world
to which we were brought

"a world we wanted to go out into
to come to ourselves into"

like mourning the man who'd set us "free"
once set us free there in another

landscape, not this one
its private and spectacled other

to find a way back through one world
back to another.

6.

Who or what brought us?

A cycle of despair a ritual of pain.

Antigone at the borderline between self-
seeking and self-abnegation. An occlusion where her death

mythopoeticizes something we can't yet grasp—

Where was her duty?
To whom and for what?

The body she mourned dies offstage. Her own
death cannot be rendered

except in the language of the messenger: "Your
wife—dead from knife wounds self-inflicted."

And Creon's inability to measure
that death or sustain it in speech as he cried out.

      So that in two—mother and son—
there is this sacrifice again

newly made, newly seen. *I sat there without*
moving I couldn't say a word. You were right to leave
when you did, the doors had been locked, I waited for you to
be gone, then sure of that I let my own life
run its course without you.

What lives on lives on.

Our exile has led us day by day
away from you.

7.

And to say who.
We are allowed to say it

who killed
who murdered

We are allowed no less
than to say who is dead

beside us who is dying
in words again in death words

like no others she said
no others to us she is saying

in that exchange between us
she is no less than we saying we cannot

undo it
we cannot un-

do death.

"Here we are no less than we are and you cannot undo it."

No less than we were
than we are

able to say *something
started to happen*

"the that fact"
"the it was"

"the after rains"
we paused to see them overcoming us

the very possibility of rains
overcoming us

as we drowned with others (this first
sense memory of death shared)

were left with others (adopted
landscape of black Aegean)

not for dead
but for not dead (waking in this body

Andrew Mossin
no other'
s capsized black letters)

I have prayed for everything I have longed for.

8.

One must continue even as others

remain behind

     "this cannot be"

One must continue even as others do not

     "this must not be"

There is a line isolated blackening sulfuric

in shadows a line

blackening where fathers' and mothers'

pronounced words do not come back to us

Those who take care of things must be given back

Those who took from us must be given

what they took back

In the name of taking they must be enclosed

again in a landscape of black trees they must rest under black trees

they must fall near the river coursing past black trees

What is the name for what we gave them?

When we have loss who will tell it?

Who will?

    We have no name for it.

       9.

When each is illiterate, crying
out to be heard, wordless

in an April night
scenes authorized by memory

not memory but written down
to justify to authorize

the one saying it. . . .

Outside it's April, it's nighttime
two fierce shadows in a fight in nighttime

One hears them in a fight over who will live
who will die, in a night of childbirth one is

fighting to live, one is dying, the sound of names
being said, not said, there is a night

fight going on inside a woman's womb
inside there are two being called

forward, there is one nearly light
one nearly dark, they are fighting

inside the woman, her April night
the news that cannot yet be told

One is fighting to keep them alive
One is fighting to let them die.

Andrew Mossin

10.

Astride alight awash . . .

Not nature of light

Not elements of discontinuity

Not dying early

Not terror when it wanes

Not disappear

But spare things left undone . . .

11.

I travel with the book in hand

I read what it wrote of our names

on a wall of new days each new day

a wall of words

torn from another's book

until we speak in unison of our loss

until we feel pain for another without shame

and attend to him in the dark

and hear him where the book has fled from us

in the pillaged and desolate close of day

passing with him through a vault of   .

incense a shepherded hand passed toward mine

in pale smoke with this stranger passing

a stranger eating beside me

eating beside me in his hunger

sharing with me this hunger this purest

half of my death.

> *When I rise in the morning I see*
>
> *roses on a trellis roses that sprout from essential speech*
>
> *roses blackening on a forehead of rock.*

—For Thomas Bartscherer

Annandale-on-Hudson, NY–Doylestown, PA
August 10–September 10, 2012–May 10, 2014

Andrew Mossin

RED MOON

In the world through which I travel I am endlessly creating myself.

—Frantz Fanon

1.

In the body where the red moon lives
in sulfuric shards broken from the city

in the red book waiting to be written
on hands of black meal herbs calf's snout

on virgin earth in the calumny
of sheared laurel where the text grows

inside a wheel of wormwood and wheat meal
clothed in hieratic papyrus

our barren root sprung holy in the white
April dusk as one might offer lamella and iron ring

forming a ring on papyrus painted red
as the moon is a black penned surface

uttering amorous spells inside and outside
a frame of marked and discrepant writing

for which the name is outlined in charcoal
red writing around a charcoal heart

inside the formalism of canvas
inside the rudiments of a snare drum

blackened by moon water
rising from the inside of a waning spirit

this vocabulary of molecular change
this boundary of epideictic loss.

278

2.

As if in a chain of dusk
portending new night new white

elements of eyesight
shorn of their tropic urge

spun from elliptical navigations
words wrung from holy destiny

in the ghost dance of the goddess
Klotho who will spin out her threads

and bear us new life. In the white
waning moonlight to hear

light adjunct to the potent
precincts of shadow—

Let the bar of Tartaros open
in which forth rages Kerberos

armed with a thunderbolt. Bestir
yourself, Mene, who needs the solar nurse

guard of the dead
let your beams draw us back

let us come back into your ghost-white
silence of one who knows

where we were self-gendered
self-taught on an isle left alone

decades upon the dark wheel
and saw you rise like the morning dove

black miraculous bird of flight
glossy and locked in bloom.

3.

I wake star lion
deprived moon gut

song wrung from the hieratic gleam
locust flowers in your bright hair

morning water blackening
each movement aroused by your appearance.

Night goes into night
another spectacle of my ghost-ridden self

merged with my Beloved—

> *Plunged in darkness, I whirl the wheel for you*
> *The cymbals I don't touch*

Nile's birth cloth

wrapped around you
until you cast dark light from your eyes

enclose my body in traces of jasmine and honey.

4.

In the eidetic glow
these signs from heaven

A colander black water jug silver plate
utensils of home that serve as symbols

I carry the weight of them
in the indexical night storm

without futurity I leap from one
cross to the next

as if the falcon's arc were a meeting place
beyond my left hand

and the promontory deepened
and one morsel of flesh

offered itself again to me
beneath a sky split open

letting loose its mesh of wet ash.

5.

To forge memory again
black tonic of spirit's blackness

where the book of sorrows ends
and the catholic drumming inside a text

whitens until there is only
this transparency left

words inscribed inside a helical
space without guide or guerdon

beneath the pantomimed shards
of early red moon

when we rose to find you inside the paratactic
legend born of another's

cautionary tale
and heard it say, "Lift a single block

of hollowed-out juniper
have an asp covering the top as a capital.

Fashion him during the new moon
and consecrate it in celebration."

For which a coiled snake
makes its way through the silent

partitions between thought and action
as though one had broken his staff

on a circle of red dust
and the snake were a legend

held before us still waiting to be told.

6.

Here in the tangent
formed in a crystal block

Here in the Book of Spells
written in cloud musk daylight

broken from a winged serpent
hand over hand the digital display

that lies like a cataract of vision's
despoiling artifice.

This bent instrument unbraiding itself
to teach us wandering again—

notes of the diaspora
bleak new song of the eidetic son

his image reflected back in the low light of
waning tropic.

*These islands with all their minium and lampblack
islands with the vertebra of Zeus*

In the reimagined reenactment
of ancestry

wandering in the spell-blasted spring
tide of island waters

islands with their drinkable blue volcanoes
shifting steadily westward

Star-coursing heavenly
born register

untiring flame caught
blackening on an iron wick

as if one were planted here
for the duration of a life

inscribing on a surface of blue-gray sand
its desolate cry.

7.

This magical material
stripped of its essentials

carried across the miles
to rest here

in mineral light
in alchemical dark

Born of blood
Shedding blood

putting out roots
androgynous

Born with blood
saffron dyed with golden arrows

A red spell bred from stalwart bone.

283

8.

And what is sea when I know it.
And what is wind from the east when I taste it.

Black cormorants rising
blue shreds of teal

The magical material that was this book
in its first imprint on flesh

Dark bay barley and crab
Sage rose fruit pits

Who will set these where they belong?
Come from the black courtyard

sit and hear the spell recited
like a sleeper daydreaming death

hear the quadrant slip
from her hands and pass back

into night's moon red sway
cylinders jogged from memory

capitalized in blood
sweet arc of penultimate sea hawk

slivered flute of horizon
risen like a metallic horn

A shell of handsome bark passed between us.

9.

And who will survive
the end of the Book of Spells?

Cavern silence
moonlit

crows black winged
in flight away from earth.

Heaven is down there
where the sea divides earth

and we revolve in the light drum
of serene monadic spaces.

A weary cut blazes its way through
canals lit by incense and boatman's candles

far-off inside the systemic barge
the lifted lean-to of cypress and willow

merges with holy waters
drowned bartered pieces of white

writing lifted to the stars
placed on an altar of parchment.

And one is waiting at your bedside
for what she has come to receive

blood of a sea falcon
embryo of a water pigeon

risen to the heavens
dashed on the rocks below

in water and blood.

10.

As She is the Goddess of Three Roads
and claims my heart inside the vessel

Andrew Mossin

spread over these pages
black spirit red moonlit forest

I would rise to meet you here
in the book we are starting to read

like a lantern poised above
our heads

beam-lit bat's cove
written out of saving

To take its body alive
and release it to the heavens

Seize its body and release it
cut from its eyes a portion of one eye

Watch it go blind
cave-bat blind in the blink of an eye

in the fiery tonic of its release
given back to a form

without resistance—
pure alchemical release

of the bat shape inside
the right fist

And the needle threaded
and given back its blood

pages of spells
darkened patches of lettering

ciphers deposited at the crossroads
blackening the bronze point of a stylus

stored among seeds of barley and wheat.

11.

And the choric urgency lifted on high ground

And the sea dark moving past our sight

in time in time the sea moving past our sight

And the moon inside the book swollen from disuse

And the hand laboring past sundown darkened by sun

So labor begins here and forms a ring inside the circuit of one's arm

And the surface is black caked with mud and barley seeds on one's palm

As if prayer were a form of residence on land from which the sea has gone

And flowers are the eyes of Horus and seed is Pan's gift

Washed in resin as the body becomes what it was when it first came to you

placed on pure linen cloth and onto cloth placed on its surface

seven seeds of wheat and an equal number of barley mixed with honey

poured onto the ground from which they grew and mixed their beings

digging up with their hands in black soil what they could find.

April 17–May 5, 2014

NOTES.

"The Language": The work of a number of writers contributed to this poem: including Maurice Merleau-Ponty's *The Prose of the World* (translated by John O'Neill); Charles Darwin's *On Natural Selection*; Hannah Arendt's "What Is Freedom?"; Sophocles's *Antigone* (translated by Reginald Gibbons and Charles Segal); Robert Duncan's "Dante Études"; Rosario Castellanos's "The Other" (translated by Maureen Ahern and Magda Bogin); Mahmoud Darwish's "The Rose and the Dictionary" and *Memory for Forgetfulness: August, Beirut, 1982*; Joan Retallack's "Afterimages"; M. NourbeSe Philip's *Zong!*; and Anne Carson's *Economy of the Unlost*.

"Red Moon": The source text for this poem is *The Greek Magical Papyri in Translation Including the Demotic Spells* (edited by Hans Dieter Betz).

The Childhood of the Reader
Joyce Carol Oates

AT THE ROADSIDE FRUIT and vegetable stand on Transit Road, in Millersport, New York, I would sit reading. Head lowered, scarcely aware of my surroundings, which is the consolation of reading.

Comic books—*Tales from the Crypt, Superman, Classics Illustrated (Ivanhoe, The Last of the Mohicans, Moby-Dick, Robin Hood, Sherlock Holmes, The Call of the Wild, Frankenstein)*—*Mad Magazine.*

Or books from the Lockport Public Library in their crisp plastic covers—Ellery Queen, H. P. Lovecraft, Isaac Asimov. Bram Stoker's *Dracula.* Jonathan Swift's *Gulliver's Travels.* Illustrated editions of the *Iliad,* the *Odyssey, Metamorphoses, Oliver Twist,* and *David Copperfield. Great Dialogues of Plato.*

(Yes, it is bizarre: I was reading, trying to read, Plato as a young girl. More bizarre yet, I was writing my own "Platonic dialogues" on tablet paper—though perhaps Socratic irony was lost on me.)

(Often the librarians at the Lockport library would look at me doubtfully. Who is this girl? Is she really reading these books? *Trying* to read these books? Who is giving her such outsized ideas? But I'd been brought to the library by my grandmother Blanche Morgenstern, whom the librarians knew as a loyal patron with an impassioned love of books; since my grandmother had arranged for me to have my first library card there, the librarians may have felt kindly disposed toward me.)

Difficult to concentrate on any kind of reading in such circumstances! At a roadside farm stand you are distracted by vehicles approaching on the highway, and passing; for the majority of the vehicles pass by without slowing. There is an air of derision, mockery, repudiation in such circumstances that will linger in the memory for years.

Only now and then a vehicle will slow, and park at the roadside, and a *customer* will emerge, usually a woman.

"Hello!"

"Hello . . ."

"Is it—Joyce?"

A hopeful smile. Or is it a craven smile. When you are *selling*, you are *smiling*.

Quart baskets, bushel baskets of pears. How much did my parents charge for a bushel basket of pears? I have no idea; surely not much. Their prices had to be competitive with those of commercial vendors, if not lower. If you were a small-time farmer you could pitch your goods so low that you made virtually no profit and worked for nothing. (All of the farms in our vicinity employed "child labor"—the farm owners' children. Hours of such employment are not negotiable.) Yet I remember the sting of embarrassment when a potential customer, frowning over our pears, or strawberries, or tomatoes, deftly turning back the tight leaves of our sweet corn to examine the kernels, decided that our produce wasn't priced low enough, or wasn't good enough in some way, returned to her car, and drove off.

Sitting at a roadside, vulnerable as an exposed heart, you are liable to such rejections. As if, as a writer, you were obliged to sell your books in a nightmare of a public place, smiling until your face ached, until there were no more smiles remaining.

Years later, as an undergraduate at Syracuse University, I was grateful to work as a "page" in the university library for as many hours a week as I could manage—for one dollar an hour. This was my first authentic job; I could consider myself now an adult. Alone, stationed on one of the upper floors of the library (which seemed immense to me, for whom a "library" was the Lockport Public Library), as I pushed a cart to reshelve books like an enthralled Alice in Wonderland, I could explore the stacks—rows upon rows of stacks—*English Literature, American Literature, Philosophy*; there was an open reading area with a long wooden table that was usually deserted and here I could sit and read with fascination what are called "learned journals" and "literary magazines"—an entire category of magazine utterly unknown to me before college. Discovering these journals was the equivalent of my discovery at age nine of the wonderful *Alice* books.

For here was *Poetry*—in which I read Hayden Carruth's harrowing autobiographical poem "The Asylum"—*Epoch* (the first literary magazine in which a story of mine would appear, under the name "J. C. Oates," in 1960)—*Journal of Metaphysics* (which I read avidly, or tried to read, as if "metaphysics" was as firm and respectable a discipline as physics)—*Modern Fiction Studies* (the first academic literary journal of my life). Equally intriguing were *Philological Quarterly, PMLA, Romanticism, American Literature, American Scholar.* A treasure trove of original fiction, poetry, essays, and reviews—*Kenyon Review, Virginia Quarterly Review, Southern Review, Southwest Review, Kenyon Review, Paris Review, Hudson Review, Partisan Review, Dalhousie Review, Prairie Schooner, Shenandoah, Georgia Review, The Literary Review, Transatlantic Review, Quarterly Review of Literature*—the very "little magazines" in which, over the next several decades of my life, my own work would appear.

(My first published story in a national magazine wasn't in one of these, but in *Mademoiselle,* in 1959. Like Sylvia Plath in a previous year's competition, I'd received an award from this chic fashion magazine in which, in those days, writing by such distinguished contributors as Tennessee Williams, William Faulkner, Paul Bowles, Katherine Anne Porter, Flannery O'Connor, Jean Stafford, and Truman Capote routinely appeared. How improbable this seems to us, by contemporary standards! Yet high-quality fiction appeared in many glossy magazines of the era—*Vogue, Harper's Bazaar, Cosmopolitan,* intermittently even in *Saturday Evening Post* and *Playboy,* as well as in the more likely *Atlantic, Harper's, Esquire,* and *New Yorker.* It did feel to me, at the age of nineteen, that my life had been magically touched, if not profoundly altered, by the *Mademoiselle* citation.)

One of the great reading moments in my lifetime—if it isn't more accurately described as a life-altering moment—occurred in the second semester of my freshman year when I entered a classroom in the Hall of Languages, and idly opened a book that had been left behind—a philosophy anthology in which there was an excerpt from the work of Friedrich Nietzsche. A sentence or two of this German philosopher of the nineteenth century, of whom I'd never heard, and immediately I felt excitement, and a kind of rapport; after class I ran to the campus bookstore, where, with reckless abandonment for one who had virtually no spending money, I bought paperback copies of Nietzsche—*Thus Spake Zarathustra, The Genealogy of Morals, Beyond Good and Evil*—which I have, heavily annotated, to this day.

For here was one who argued as if "with a hammer"—the very weapon to counter those years of enforced passivity as a quasi-Christian conscripted into an adult world of piety in which nothing was clearly explained, nothing was sincere, and all was obscured; my sense that the elders of my world were conspiring to convince me, as a child, and as a young person, of "beliefs" in which none of them believed, even as the pretense was *This is the way, the truth, the light. Only through this way shall you be saved.*

To counter such smug pieties, the devastating voice of the philosopher—*What is done out of love always happens beyond good and evil.*

As a freshman I lived not in a dormitory but in a less costly "cottage" on Walker Avenue with approximately twenty other scholarship girls, all of us from upstate New York. (We were "girls" and not "young women"—in age, experience, appearance. This was an era when "girls" were under a kind of protective custody at universities, subject to curfews that male undergraduates did not have. It is an accurate description of the "scholarship girls" of Walker Cottage that none of us minded in the slightest that we had to be back in our residence by 11:00 p.m. weeknights—we had nowhere else we'd have preferred to be than in our rooms, studying.) My room was a single room, cell-like, sparely furnished, where I could work uninterrupted for long hours; for the first time in my life, I was free of the surveillance of my parents, however benevolent this surveillance might have been. And I could work in the university library, until curfew, at the long oak table that seemed magical to me, surrounded by shelves of "little magazines" I came to revere and even to love; I wrote by hand in a spiral notebook, sketches for fiction, outlines, impressions, which I then brought back to the residence to convert into typed pages. Stories, novels—even poetry, and plays—hundreds of pages of earnest undergraduate work that I would not have known to identify at the time as "apprentice work"—much of it discarded, some of it reworked and refined into the stories that I would submit to the writing workshops I took at Syracuse and that would eventually appear in my first book, a story collection titled *By the North Gate* (1963).

If I open that book, composed and assembled so long ago, it's as if I am catapulted back into that era—I can shut my eyes and see again the oak table in the library, the displayed magazines on both sides; I can see again the room in which I lived at the time, the plain table desk facing a utilitarian blank wall.

As the Lockport Public Library had been a sanctuary for me as a child and young girl, and a hallowed source of happiness, so the Firestone Library at Syracuse University would be its equivalent, if not more, in my undergraduate years. Over all, Syracuse was a young writer's paradise: my professors Donald A. Dike, Walter Sutton, Arthur Hoffman, among esteemed others, were brilliant, sympathetic, and unfailingly supportive. (Disclosure: Not once was I made to feel, by any of my professors, that as a young woman I was in any way "inferior" to my male classmates. However, it did not escape my awareness that there was but a single woman professor in the English Department and no women at all in Philosophy.)

If the university library was a treasure trove to a word-besotted undergraduate like myself, it was also, I suppose, a little too much for me. My memory of my workplace is of a labyrinth so dimly lighted—for stacks not in use were darkened: You had to switch lights on as you entered the aisles—as to inspire hallucination; here was a universe of books, overwhelming and intimidating and seemingly infinite as a library in a Borges fiction. One could never begin to read so many books—it invited madness just to think that each had been cataloged and shelved. Each had been conscientiously *written!*

One day, I would convert some of these experiences into prose fiction—quasi-memoirist fiction, titled *I'll Take You There.* But not for decades.

"Seventy cents? *Seventy cents?*"—it was a shock to me to receive my weekly paycheck for the first time, to discover that I wasn't even earning a dollar an hour but, after taxes, considerably less. My pride in attending Syracuse University and working in the library was undermined by such reminders of how desperate I was, or how naive.

When, after the first check, I expressed my dismay to one of the librarians for whom I worked, the woman said curtly: "It's the same for all of us, Joyce."

Yet I had no choice but to continue at the library. It has been the mantra of my life—I have no choice but to continue.

And years later, as a graduate student in English and American literature at the University of Wisconsin at Madison.

The pressure of graduate school, at least as first-year English graduate students experienced it, was unrelenting: hundreds of pages of reading each week, and these pages densely printed on tissue-thin paper—Old English *Beowulf, The Wanderer, The Dream of the Rood, Anglo-Saxon Chronicle,* works by Bede, Cynewulf, Caedmon; *Liturgical Plays of the Story of Christ, The Castle of Perseverance, Gammer Gurton's Needle, Damon and Pythias, Second Shepherd's*

Play, Everyman, Noah's Flood. Chaucer's *Canterbury Tales* and *Troilus and Criseyde,* Spenser's *Faerie Queene,* witty John Skelton, Jacobean and Elizabethan and Restoration drama and more. Much more. One by one we discovered Sir Thomas Wyatt, and committed to heart the mysterious gem "They Flee from Me" (1557)—

> They flee from me, that sometime did me seek,
> With naked foot stalking in my chamber,
> I have seen them, gentle, tame, and meek,
> That now are wild, and do not remember
> That sometime they put themselves in danger
> To take bread at my hand, and now they range,
> Busily seeking with a continual change . . .

The great works of English literature were monuments to be approached with reverence. Unlike my Syracuse professors, these older, Harvard-trained professors at Wisconsin did not regard literature as an art but rather more as historical artifact, to be discussed in terms of its context; there was little or no discussion of a poem as a composition of carefully chosen words. History, not aesthetics. The thrilling emotional punch of great art—totally beyond the range of these earnest scholarly individuals. One might lecture on Latin influences in pre-Shakespearean drama, or influences in Shakespeare, but the white-hot dynamic of *Macbeth,* for instance, the brilliant and dazzling interplay of "personalities" that is Shakespearean essential drama was unknown to them. If they were explorers, they'd been becalmed in an inlet, while the great river rushed past a few miles away.

Yet, at Madison, I did read, reread, and immerse myself in the work of Herman Melville. For a course at Syracuse I'd read the early, relatively straightforward *White-Jacket,* and the wonderfully enigmatic short stories—"Bartleby, the Scrivener," "The Paradise of Bachelors and the Tartarus of Maids," "The Encantadas." While still in high school I'd read *Moby-Dick*—our greatest American novel, which one might read and reread through a lifetime, as one might read and reread the poetry of Emily Dickinson. At Madison, I became entranced by the very intransigence, one might say the *obstinate opacity* of the near-unreadable *Pierre: or, The Ambiguities*—a pseudo romance written in mockery of its (potential, female) readers, as if by a (male) author who'd come to hate the effort of narrative prose fiction itself. (It isn't surprising that *Pierre* sold poorly, as its great predecessor *Moby-Dick* sold poorly. Tragic Melville—"Dollars damn me!") After a few pages of its curiously stilted, self-regarding prose I fell under the spell of the slightly more accessible allegory *The Confidence-Man*, as well as *Billy Budd*. I wondered what to make of *Benito Cereno*, with its perversely glacial-slow pace: In our racially sensitized era we expect that Melville will surely side with the slave uprising, and not with white oppressors like Captain Cereno, but Melville doesn't comply with our twenty-first-century expectations in this case in which "the shadow of the Negro" falls over everyone—including even the executed rebel Babo.

Writers who are enrolled in graduate programs soon feel the frustration, the ignominy, the pain of being immersed in reading the work of others—illustrious, renowned others—Chaucer, Shakespeare, Donne, Milton—Hawthorne, Poe, Melville, James—when they are themselves unable to write or even to fantasize writing. During these months of intense academic study when my head was crammed with great and not-so-great classic works, of course I had no time for fiction or poetry of my own (as I thought it) except desperate fragments in a journal like cries for help.

Suffocated by books. Crushed by books. Library stacks, tall shelves of books, books, books overturning upon the young writer groping in the dark for the overhead light to switch on.

From *The Lacunae*
Daniel Nadler

अनुवाद

NOTE. THESE TEXTS ARE IMAGINED translations of poems that do not otherwise exist. They are intended to fill invented or actual lacunae in manuscripts of first- to eighth-century CE classical Indian poetry (*Amaruśataka*, originally in Sanskrit; *Kuruntokai*, originally in Old Tamil; and *Gathasaptasati*, originally in Maharastri Prakrit).

43.71

What will you do with these pearls he has given you?
Can you eat them? Can you grind them into honey
and return them to the water, sweeter than they were?
Your neck is not a graveyard for the sea.
So don't become a ghost
that scares away
the fish you must catch for your parents.

(Amaruśataka 8.9, Sanskrit)

51.30

Who are you going to meet tonight
in the tall grass
where even snakes cannot find each other?

Your bare feet
will be the safest part of you.

(Gathasaptasati 10.95, Prakrit)

28.6

I want to boast
around you, like a horse rearing straight up
in the stars.

But I have nothing to say.
Like the night
when the moon is out.

(*Amaruśataka* 1.12, Sanskrit)

22.0

My tigers have left me.
I wake too late in the day,
after a heavy rain
has played its notes on my roof.
I don't even tie them to anything.

(*Gathasaptasati* 18.46, Prakrit)

17.15

Between kisses the air is quiet,
like trees after a snowfall. Talking softly, after,
a branch is shaken loose.

(*Gathasaptasati* 7.38, Prakrit)

15.24

The moon has gone farming at night
in the soil of your dreams. Tall trees
are growing there, for you to climb,
and the flower I gave you during the day
can barely break through the ground.

(*Amaruśataka* 30, Sanskrit)

———————

15.34

You disappear beside me in a forest. Walking, I cannot hear
the moment when fewer leaves are crushed, and I speak to you
as if it made no difference that the forest listened in your place.

For you I learned
that what is near us is never what is near us.

(*Amaruśataka* 30, Sanskrit)

———————

18.0

Do not let the thought of her fill your nights
and the stars
pieces of her.

Come,
we will walk through the streets, and find a table
that doesn't even look like her.

(*Amaruśataka* 32.2, Sanskrit)

———————

15.29

Like wooden planks from a broken ship
dashed against great stones,
my words you made into a spectacle
for the whole village to attend. I only meant to tell you
I love another.

(*Amaruśataka* 30, Sanskrit)

———————

15.32

Your lips are as full as the wound
guarded in battle. Your skin is the color of my eyelids
when the sun passes through.
The sea takes my shape as I float in it,
your hair falls all around you, like the paths of gravity
made visible.

(*Amaruśataka* 30, Sanskrit)

———————

38.90

You hear the sun in the morning
through closed shutters. As you sleep
the early sky is colored
in fish scales, and you open your eyes
like a street
already lined with fruit.

(*Amaruśataka* 3.89, Sanskrit)

———————

15.4

The season is yet unlit
by the glint of the sewing needle.
The thread is stored away, the light
is like an unwoven shirt.

(Gathasaptasati 6.24, Prakrit)

28.12

The sun began eating
the parts of the fruit
exposed to air.

What was lodged in dark soil
would stay whole. Until the leopard
digs it up with its paw
and slices away the poison half
with its nail.

(Amaruśataka 1.12, Sanskrit)

28.13

The animals were slowly digging in the mud, and were frightened.
Laughter was the refuge of the weather, and hunger
sounded like water that had nowhere to drain. More water
was found under the mud, digging.

(Amaruśataka 1.12, Sanskrit)

38.1

The birds aglow in yellow do not carry ashes.
What the river carries their talons cannot trap
and even sand slips through. Where the river narrows
ashes splash together, making the shapes they were.

(*Amaruśataka* 1.11, Sanskrit)

34.15

Cooking under some tress
you must break the salt necklace
and let its white beads
fall into the iron pan.
Rain in the glint of an eclipse.

Your dark breasts grow
darker,
the pan crackles.

(*Gathasaptasati* 6.85, Prakrit)

21.98

You curse the rain outside your window, believing
that it alone prevents your journey.

Your young lover, at the other end of a sea
suspended in the air
would surely understand.

(*Gathasaptasati* 18.46, Prakrit)

28.91

The pigment of crushed petals
was smeared along both sides
of the bird's beak.
But its wings were still limp enough
to drag along the ground.

(*Amaruśataka* 1.13, Sanskrit)

15.33

The soil guards the sleep
of plant roots. When we pull them
they taste soft like night.

(*Amaruśataka* 30, Sanskrit)

15.6

Even your words will not leave you
now that they know
that to lighten your body
by even so much as themselves
would remove the balance
from what had been measured precisely.

(*Amaruśataka* 30, Sanskrit)

Daniel Nadler

28.09

A glacier glows rose pink
from the sun that it encases
in its ice. This is what is told
about time.

(Amaruśataka 1.12, Sanskrit)

98.14

Approach shadows like shallow water
into which you can reach
and touch indigo reefs.

(Gathasaptasati 16.96, Prakrit)

16.13

Brother, don't look away when she glances at you,
and stop trying to find omens in the syllables of her name.
Go up to her, and say out loud
the name of our father, and if your voice doesn't break
she may even see something of his face
in yours.

(Gathasaptasati 6.85, Prakrit)

28.10

The man who grows flowers in a field
for lovers to give to one another
is not himself lonely.

He left last winter to see his brother,
and now his field is wild.

He is not kept company by the wind,
and dawn alone does not steady his heart.
All the elements in the mountain pass
make their way into the soil,
but he sleeps at night in a bed
beside a woman, and is as dreamless as a goat.

(*Amaruśataka* 1.131, Sanskrit)

27.11

On maps the sea carries color.
But a swarm of shadowed fish,
under the surface,
like moving marble
eats the colored bits, gradually.
One day maps will show this.

(*Amaruśataka* 1.11, Sanskrit)

01.13

To the Nightingale an island is not as bright as a star.
But which can it land on?

Is the earth really bent
so gradually
that we can make a bed anywhere?

Not in the dark-skinned sea, or in night,
which fills the shape of your mouth
until your face is bloated,
like something newly born.

303

So we plant ourselves in some clearing, in a forest,
until our bodies break like seeds at night,
until a white tentacle, as tender as a root,
grows in a glass of water.

(*Amaruśataka* 4.2, Sanskrit)

13.38

Why is the forest canopy strung with rope?
What have the children done with the branches?
Now the sun can only reach us through a maze.
As if it, too, had to pass through their games.

We walk around, all of us now, preparing the morning
with a grid of shadows on our skin.
As if we only escaped sleep
illicitly, the print of its servitude
still on us.

It was a cold morning on the forest floor, and wet.
And now, waking to a canopy of ropes,
as if the tree trunks were a spider's legs at night
needling a web around us in the air,
we, awaking already within its mouth . . .

The old man has gone back to sleep another night.
What have the children done with the branches?

(*Amaruśataka* 7.9, Sanskrit)

28.8

The bird is in the center of the sun.
Its outline is silent,
as its nude, smooth wings extend
across its sphere of light.
They almost block it.

I can never tell
which part of nature is posturing:
To the sun the bird becomes a wall of glass,
its eyes, in the middle of its silhouette,
pass pure light—
the fire of the underworld
seen through a slit between two stones.

(*Amaruśataka* 1.12, Sanskrit)

27.7

The dancing girl has veiled her body
in movement. The drums grunt like voices
calling for water in the sun.
Dripping on the hot skin of a drum
droplets would also dance
until it soaked up their sound.

(*Amaruśataka* 1.12, Sanskrit)

34.17

As the village goes up
in smoke
a dry cloud is rotating overhead,
fed like a whirlpool
in the sky.

Daniel Nadler

We press our hands together.
It is better to be
together in life, willingly,
than by any force.

(*Gathasaptasati* 6.85, Prakrit)

34.19

A sand dune came toward us like a sail ship
made of stone
that was breaking in the wind.

(*Gathasaptasati* 6.85, Prakrit)

28.92

Hair covered a face
like old vines conceal a door.
The iron eyes of an owl
open at me
like ornaments from a mother's home
familiar from youth.

(*Amaruśataka* 1.12, Sanskrit)

22.01

My tigers have left me.
I wake too late in the day,
after a heavy rain
has played its notes on my roof.
I don't even tie them to anything.

(*Gathasaptasati* 18.46, Prakrit)

22.02

Friend, we can no longer ignore it.
The wind reminds us that our house has no windows.
Tell it that it has made its point,
and that it can either stay, or leave.
But that it must stop
with this coming and going.

(*Gathasaptasati* 18.46, Prakrit)

22.03

Daughter, along the rim of what you were knitting
I can see the circumference of your will.
You rarely show it,
and most often you end where you are silent.
But somehow, after the edge of this quilt
there is refusal
where there is nothing.

(*Gathasaptasati* 18.46, Prakrit)

22.04

The tree collapsed on itself
leaving a pile of bark
over its roots.

What, foolish daughter,
did you think?
That it would shrink back into the ground?

(*Gathasaptasati* 18.46, Prakrit)

Daniel Nadler

15.30

A lamb blinking over a patch of earth
does not know what you have done. Feed it,
and it will eat from your hand
as if you wore the skin of a washed grape.

(*Amaruśataka* 30, Sanskrit)

Rubrics
Rebecca Lilly

AT THE READY

EARLY A.M., AT MY DESK, documenting this
as it happens—a book on sociopathy, but let
me explain my intentions: at the center of
my chest, the X, the echo of coordinates, is a
base of quantum cursives, pungent and
bitter, the inky fibs glowing, my heart's
music in drums; a hollow pounding and
ugliness result: eye sores, blue rings from
marrying my heart, then scissoring its
strings in violent divorce—documented in
my book draft on sociopathic "friends," the
definitive text on that, where I acknowledge
real-life personas who lie with impunity,
pledging I will not, in good faith, cover
ennui with distaste, or feverish pitches of
wanting, promising I'll not be a desperate
and explosive protégée who authors a book of
"heart's tales," while the eyes of more
merciful books (shelved in dark cubbyholes
with bent spines and hunchbacked lives of
toil) confirm it's the topic of the day: lies,
blasphemy, nothing on blissful states, the
rightful province of the heart—only the
drumroll of a horrid librarian knocking on
the door (and since my library's *in* there, I
don't want her conversing with schemers
and toadies—ear fleas who say the closer to
truth words are, the greater the danger of
misinterpreting meaning)—that's why the
ageless great books get translated yet again
by contemporary monks, or famous scholars

of mind-body consciousness, later on quoted by wry, twisted politicians, who sell them as viruses to white-collar scammers, as if what matters weren't the character's suit, but the wrangling of his muse. In our advancing digital age, truth will be a look, a voyeur surveying windows of the book (if shut, restricting subtleties of oscillations), but the glass blinks in any case, whether transparent or reflecting, and there's a niggling intuition to open it, to let air in before the phone rings and you lose it momentarily in getting down to business.

HARD CHARGER

Found objects, the words, when gathered up, evolve into pictures, then concepts, where-upon I stop—back to pictures, the encounter with *The Thing*, since it's all about commu-nion with the living word: self-referential, entangling the world with self-mattering, until, electrified, it burns itself up. I don't remember the book I've proffered here as an example: dreamt momentarily, a placeholder for authorial personas, some harboring a vengeful motive toward the hero, that generous rebel whose jokey ways and hard charging stave off tragedy—and yet, a frail tension turns the page, desire and patience perfecting a leverage, so the fatal flaw turns out to be a "minor wounded part," in the lingo of psychologists—clandestine, it's a U-turn behind, swerving by a hair's breadth the formidable sword of your own eyes reading close to your gloveless hands.

KEEP IT NEAT

He's more afraid of life than death, so keep it neat—a snarky attempt at publicity, this blurb that fancies the oddness of people living out their books, calling forth more life in persona, his flat-footed, laurel-crowned sorrows limping in to mint the dust, so readers have to wonder why it wasn't just one trampling another. . . .

It's not as simple as it seems: there are subtle differences in suffering; it's a multi-grained phenomenon, an hourglass of umbers and ochers—so this author's color plates were a nice touch, and his website's enticing: an author who invites us to his *homeroom*, but perhaps not into auras of his characters: the one, a notorious villain.

He jokes in the forward on colluding with us: obviously, we're just cosigners, voyeurs, less serious a crime among the literati. As for his milestone of poison pen, authored by the quintessential villain: it was flagged by his publisher (whom he calls, rather baldly, "the Old World Self") as "highly elliptical and probably fictitious as his strolls in virgin woods, and the foundling myths he tells straight from the mouth of the minstrel"—to say nothing of his hopeless lamentations.

Sneak up in the woods and follow him sometime—but if you do, be prepared not to get in print.

PAID WITNESS

Reminiscing, as I was once the author of this piece, but am no longer (a paid witness is revising), I recall a silence of created stillness different from the silence that wells up from nothing. Who I was is null—the real story is this: the book's spine electrified into a blowtorch, which flamed out, sending me tumbling down a sinkhole. I'm not so naive as to upend the book or back up to where I first found myself, although reversible text *is* in fashion, an immaterial cursive running in bifurcated silty channels, while a writer at the wellhead (a stone cairn marking the forest edge) lowers a rusted bucket: the magnetic pull of self—now if the sun's out and it's hot, I'm suspicious of contaminants; I'm smart enough to know I can't drink dirty water, but I confess my lifelong habit is to stop and wait, while my hand's facepalming off the page, and margins recalibrate until I eye up my way to a launch, a flash point where surface lights confound, for waters travel only one direction in the Book of Hours: *forward.* Where is it then: a sky-compass for an eye navigating Styx? When it's choppy enough so waves crash over the hull, you need a paid witness to be a scribe. Only nothing's inviolate. Fact is, sanity is stopping and waiting to be guided. The river recedes into pines—I spy it from the library portico—bright red leaves skitter, pages picked off in the wind, an omen for the blind.

THE ILK OF THE OLD

My book slouches to where sunlight gets a
foothold on the afterthoughts' long breach of
conscious wants. Nothing can be done about
darkness; pressed upon, it holds in what I've
coined *the ilk of the old* in my dank rental
building.

"It's your *language*," the manager professed
with distaste, throwing my book down (one
I'd given him, hot off the press), "the palette
of painterly touches. Why bother when the
moon will do," he spat, cursorily inspecting
the chimney, "assuming it's full enough to
show through?"

To be honest: it's not *my* house of language,
but a rental, and because I'm dissatisfied
with rundown radiators, bats, and spiders in
the chimney, a furnace that creaks, a work
order has been signed as of yesterday—the
manager assures me. "A fire would do to
drive out bats and swifts from the chimney,
but you'd need to scoop out the ashes."

"Chimney sweeping—my old man did it, and
thought he was God's gift, but let me tell
you it's a venerable profession," the surly
manager said, and I nodded. No comment.
(Forgive the aside, but I'm a dyed-in-the-
wool antiquarian, and book burning hasn't,
through the centuries, been a private thing;
it's a contemptible practice of the Inquisition
of Learning.)

Implausibly perhaps, those birds ousted
from the chimney speak my mind, brooms
of pines sweeping soot and ashes from their
feathers, hazing the night sky, gray granny

313

birds fluttering and pecking in the author's head, waking him—

Here I am, wearing a feathered coat of many colors (my body, a metaphor obscuring the close-ups). There *was* an antiquarian job, I recall that much. When he left, the manager said it's imperative to pull the flue for insulation, and my latest rental payment's past due.

As-ever-is, as-ever-is, chirp the chimney swifts outside my window on the gable roof in this little fiction of ears, my excuse to be an Old World poet to whom no one pays notice, as in a modern fable no one looks for clues—laborious, it is, to create books from the ilk of the old, and doubly so to present them as true.

Pages from Days and Works
Rachel Blau DuPlessis

He died, a young and ambitious artist, of a cocaine OD and the related heart attack.

It was a long flight, strong headwinds.

If you read *Standing in Another Man's Grave* in bed, what kind of dreams *do* you expect?

"What am I doing?"
"You're eating sweet things; you're eating sugar. It always happens after a death."

I understand, as if from every angle, the Dante word that means dazed, dazzled, vertiginous, undone, stunned, and awestruck: *smarrito*. At the beginning. At the end. And punctually in between.

Sing through the scintillate deeps of sky, pulse mists with huffs and beeps, and bounce sweet booms off a sublimity that's packed so tight and wrapped so round, it shimmers, shakes, and sometimes downright laughs with its own vast, unreadable astonishment.

"I can pick up the alphabet!" she said. And, as from an artesian well, the other end of the writing came up.

*

At the moment when the book becomes questionable, possibly obsolete, or at least not alone in the world of inscriptions on something like a page, it appears that I think in nothing but variants of books.

315

The stele, the monument, the clay tablet, the scroll, the codex, the electronic screen. A flattened surface on which there are socially legible marks.

Though hypertext externalizes the cultural brain, it cannot sort this out without interventions of another brain.

At a time when—as is claimed by some university penny pinchers—you don't "need" libraries, at a time when digital archives create a potential web of access across worlds, via languages, territories, nationalisms, and holdings (if also potentially privatized, not open source), I am still considering that discrete entity of intervention—the book. Small, contained intentional arrangements, copies put in circulation.

Who would not worry when the precise college president who eliminated a library as unnecessary and put money down on a total electronic "system" was the very college president so up to her neck in malfeasance and criminality that suicide was the inevitable and accomplished end? This is a true story. It was in the news.

Without the book, we die? And with it, also. That story has no moral for the book. There was no causation, just correlation.

And correlation does not mean causation. But weren't there links? Wasn't that administrator seduced by, even paid by, the profiteers in such "systems"?

On the other hand, people and groups have been put to the sword (the flame, the rack, the flail, the bomb) for not seeing one of those books precisely the way some others saw it.

One moral is: Do not destroy the book. Do not destroy the person. Do not destroy the reader.

Awake, awake
today! sings
the wood thrush with a silvery sobbing
gurgling warble

first day of hidden nesting tones.
Tomes.

*

I see a pink screen laced with mesh capillaries. So this is what
holds the eye together! I've just seen the back of everything.

> What happened next was swift
> and brutal. The soldiers seized the
> man and repeatedly stabbed him.
> "He was dead within two min-
> utes," said Peter Bouckaert of the
> New York–based Human Rights
> Watch, who observed the killing.
> Bouckaert documented the vio-

An old woman fusses for coins in a metal-click change purse.
Fingers twisted cannot pick up dimes. The years move along; she
lives in her webbings of electricity making small sparks. She picks
out a quarter. Eventually she will have nothing in her purse and
lack the fine-tuned touch to take the change. O now dead woman,
did you feel an erotic dream of writing and of books—a kind of
desire identifying the words with the breadth of your rapacious and
incommensurate yearning?

The newest dead land story concerns a drained and ruined ecology.
The other news story details another bombing—people in pieces.
One's frustration, one's resistant disgust with the politics of others
(which are also officially one's own), proves what point? What
would social good really look like? The shadowy was taking shape.
This darkness held the "I" together.

> lence in a series of tweeted photos.
> The victim's leg was severed.
> "A man just walked up with
> the severed leg of the lynching
> victim, just walking around,"
> tweeted a shocked Bouckaert.

And the most suggestive recent typo was *allienation*.

317

*

QUATRAINS

Suddenly I realized that I was set
among the dead. I was a mix of old
and young, sporting a formerly
fashionable jacket. Jackal.

The library (inevitably) is close to closing.
The librarian announces,
"This library is almost closing"
and I answer testily, "I know."

There was no time to find any book.
The right book wasn't there anyway.
Set is an Egyptian god. So sue me.
Then I drive home, but was it home?

*

COMPLAINTS

Along the way were lumps of amber big as figs. Too beautiful for
words. This is a complaint.

What Nothing does Zero mean?

In Notarikon, the letters become a moving target. When you fill
each word's letters up with other words, the topics shift faster than
the alphabet. You can't keep up with them or with yourself.
Language takes over, saying too many things. It is always the
wrong idiom, the unnecessary periphrastic word. Awkwardness
rules. There can be no follow-through of any metaphors. The
arguments cannot be consistent. The text becomes a field of broken
arrows. Excess rules.

For instance, in Notarikoning English, one finds way too many th's. What with *the* and *there* and *them* and *their* and *these* plus *those* and *this* and *then*. It looks like not enough good words begin with *h* to make this all worthwhile. Or they are the wrong words and cannot match the words that start with *t*. It's a thorn in one's side. I cannot make it work.

All the poems in the book tried to stand against the book, and yet they were inside a book—

how then to critique the merely literary. Again—how hard it is to make it work.

Destroyed. And disgusted. And destroyed once more. Ripped, remade. Began in 1979. Began in 1964. Began again in 1983. Began in 1986. Began without. Destroyed all "my paintings." Destroyed all "my objects." Destroyed the work by not doing it. Destroyed the work by overdoing it. Never one thing. No making pretty images. No making reasonable objects. No rhetorics of elaboration, no consolation, few expected conclusions. Discontent and resentment. Poems? No poems. No books. No nothing.

*

Can this be both a book, be several books, be no book? Can it open the pages and unbind them beautifully whilst keeping them together, also beautifully?

Can the book keep open while sometimes closing? Who closes it? The reader might. The writer might. Claims of authority might. The book might also wait silently until its moment is ready. Look how I have given agency to the book! But the temporalities are, anyway, multiple, mutable, and diverse. The book, it seems, can be both open and closed.

Can there be a book at the same time about nothing and everything, only about words, and only about concepts; about rips of feelings and pressures of historical fate?

Rachel Blau DuPlessis

Wouldn't you want to say that this is every book?

Every meaningful book?

"Whilst" is British. I'm not, but I like how it sounds.

Writing goes in one direction only, but seeing—can go out in vectors way beyond the frame. This is another unforeseen challenge, to offer the sense of vectors and pulse inside the book without an overload that cannot be read.

How can a book be polysemous and also thesis bearing? It is an inexplicable mystery of writing. Whenever you feel this double air, just breathe deeply in with openhearted breath. And exhale deeper still.

Our universe may or may not have an edge. Most people can think only to that edge. If at all. But a book clearly has an edge. This fact helps us think beyond the edge to what may not have one, or be beyond the all, in a multiverse (in multiverses) of excessive temporalities and explosive burgeoning.

Books are universes of edges.

Books are edges of the universe.

We still do not understand that particular "the." Probably it is less painful to accept it.

*

Why do the extremities of language occur so frequently—the claim that words should just be things, the claim that words are only words in and for themselves—color without resonance, or letters without etymology, or phonemes without a past, or marks without sociality, or messages without specific decoders, their necessities, and their practices. Remember redundancy? remember nuances of tone? remember the intricacies of syntax and of word placement? And what about the claim that anything can be done with words, the claim that matter can become pure text?

320

Why? Because it all has to be experienced, tried, essayed, experimented. And done once more again. Generally this kind of science will have no inhumane consequences. But every once in a while, the experiment goes awry—and some demonic slogan allows for broadside lust in slaughter; then some shibboleth or little lisp or glottal stop or mispronounce will mark your unfortunate head with battered blood.

Anything can be done with words, but what makes those things worth doing?

There is a kind of traditional Korean pottery known as *buncheong*: freedom of design, unusual shapes, and coarse potting. This is, of course, a poetry of bunching, a kind of text known for freedom of design, unusual shapes, and coarse potting. Which is why I am mentioning it.

Walk the seam
with monitors of dusk.
Words fail. Yet there must be words.
Do not cede that territory.
Despite impossible transitions.
Meaning cannot be rescued from commerce, power, war. It is
not rescue that's needed. These uses must be accepted, enveloped,
and yet unveiled as such. These are no more real than any other
use.

Draw the rope of the poem tighter and tighter around the words. Despite the unfortunate metaphor, such tightness "is the only way to achieve the floating or uncertain nature of things." This is the paradox of strife. Of an open closedness.

Ambiguity and the between—these are what abide. Though they wobble and vibrate continuously, and they might thereby be hard to track. So no sitting in a vaunted mythic hut is possible. In the between, there is no mystique. Only tacking, and a few stops for rest, inside a restlessness that does not cease.

There is nothing terrible about surplus meanings, but there is something odd about too many of them all at once.

"Here" and "there" are words in geography and grammar, not in ethics.

Thereupon a blessing, the metaphor of starry skies pouring down. Poiesis is that blessing.

*

What is encrypted here?

What is the shadow of this word?

These pens are inadequate for the perfect scriptorium—and will always be.

Why is the not-yet disclosed so palpable and yet so evanescent?

Wake up, change clocks, download. Uptick.

These pens will only work in the imperfect scriptorium.

Understand that internal translation will never cease.

*

Electric light blue snow at dusk marks the side shapes of structures. Beauty is true (though is beauty truth?), but what about the support systems for all this heightening? Timelessness only exists partially. If at all. He called me up to say that she had died, "in a way silent, mysterious, difficult to discern." What is this world of such disappearance that I am in it? At least those hairy lichens like tinsel on the tree say the air in this forest is still free of impurity. Or so the docent said. But when we did an Earth Day cleanup in another creek, we dredged out bottles, cans, pill boxes, softballs, and Styrofoam. She had looked so pale and hairless, then well coiffed. "It's a wig," she said. Always ready to dot that *i* with utter honesty. Sign in the ladies' room: "Hurting? God Cares." Can't top that, right? A Dedalean tuft scrolled overall like a finial, a cherubic decor. As for me, I've made no secret of it: want deformed words, want bits of alphabet formed into statements facing a sudden encounter, want to know what is really there, want chakra phonemes hanging over the page as from a void. . . .

if you want these things then work with work upon work.

*

Trying for an ultimate, that point of X crossing intensity with fervor and yet beyond those emotions (of excitement, say, or pleasure, or fear, or even awe)—I realize quietly that the ultimate is a filled silence. A silence of matter and languages so rich (yet not turgid), so clear (but not plain), so poised between all and nothing, between poles positive and negative, that it could be called both enlightenment and endarkenment. It does not pass in any way through the ego. It happens outside and yet suffuses the thing I sit inside of—self. The incipient has precipitated. And yet the world is ever in motion and does not stop. This moment cannot be—not as such, not permanent, but perhaps it can be reconstituted, opened by chance, stumbled upon. It's probable that the only way to indicate it—I mean enlightenment over and under endarkenment— is not through the full but through the progressively more eroded, more erased, more empty—that nonetheless feels adequate. Adequate to what is. Representation (as such, as we know it) might simply be beside the point. The conventions of tuning, the consonances, are simply irrelevant. But one might want to show. To demonstrate. To offer.

> Language pulses
> with all that can be made of it
> along the lines of understanding.
> Vulnerability, said the mite,
> and Yes, said the dot.
> Various tree stuff floats through the air
> on puffs of wind, and lands with little pings.
> The words
> people write, the things they say

are investments in
that oddity.

The froth and pleasures of representations—and they are lavish and
lovely—somewhat confuse what choices of words might indicate
such a filled and silent space. Call this space "and yet." Call it "as
such." The dates and days of the week. The works inside those
days. The books are pebbles, stones, boulders, even mountains. Do
you feel it sometimes?—a fecund emptiness in which there are
works. Yet it is not about following one trail but accumulation into
continuum. The first day's sunset had a purple streak; the second
day it was a bowl of orange pink.

At least imagine cryptic outlines of something
for a variety of materials that forward,
poetry porous entity trying continuance
poetry positing but emptying
poetry spontaneous entryway

sang the nightingale wildly
blurting song out
as it often does
at dawn.

*

His passport photo—with its restless, worried look—had gigantic
crackles of glue that had worked through the old photograph,
making open spots on the page. It looked like two bullet holes had
just missed his head. How not to be haunted?

Setting out, yes, but the journey becomes much more wayward
than the traveler had planned, an experience out of range. Turning
to verbs means into risk. What was the ordinary diagnosis?
Accounts and additions. The sourness of too-warm milk. Unheard
words—that contained directions also unheard. Soldiering on,
somehow there were traces. Even though it was vast. The traveler
had one plan, but the journey had another.

Two days later, Sudler was on a gurney, being wheeled back to her room after a test. "Do you have my oxygen tank?" she asked the aide. He replied, "What tank?"

She began to cry. She realized she was breathing on her own.

Nationally, 1,600 people are waiting for lung transplants. In

The thinnest light of the needle settled at the small pool where the birds alight and raise their little throats to swallow. Two universes meet, page to page. Shapes of delicate and fibrous air pass above us. And the hawk clawed the nightingale as they flew along the edge of sky and out of sight.

The Particulars
Brian Evenson

I.

IN THE SECOND VOLUME of David B.'s *Incidents in the Night*, there's a shoot-out in a used bookstore. It's a fairly straightforward gunfight until the moment when one of the villains cries out and looks down to discover a book clamped around his leg like a pair of jaws. A moment later, another book wraps itself around another villain's face, nearly suffocating him to death. "The books," the villains declare, horrified, "they're marching against us!"

When asked by another character what he thinks his books are doing, David B.'s bookseller replies, "They're not MY books, it's their words that bite."

Books are curious creatures in that in one sense their materiality is of little importance: It's the words that bite, and that has nothing in particular to do with the book itself you hold in your hand. In theory, at least, the words bite whether they're digital or printed on paper, whether they're read aloud or silently—though, of course, as soon as you declare that, you can't help but think of the exceptions: the books that can't be read effectively aloud without limiting their meaning, books that gain or lose something from being in one format rather than another, and so on.

Books exist in that strange space between materiality and immateriality, where on the one hand (if hand's the right word) we feel that their materiality doesn't *really* matter and, on the other hand, the physical qualities of the book are absolutely inseparable from the reading experience. The specificity of the reading experience is based on the particulars of the copy of the book you hold in your hands. On the one hand, the digital, hardback, and paperback copies of a book are all the "same" in the same way that all the chairs in the world supposedly partake of Plato's chairness and point back to an ideal, virtual chair. On the other hand, however, once you've verified that the chair you're sitting on has chairness, the peculiarities and the comforts of the particular chair you're sitting on really come to matter.

*

When my son was born last year, I realized that while I couldn't juggle both him and a book very easily while feeding him a bottle, I could manage to read books on my smartphone. On the screen would appear a page of maybe ten lines, forty words or so, and then I would swipe my thumb across the screen to move to the next page. I could hold my son in the crook of my arm, hold his bottle with one hand, and hold my phone with the other. I could put down the phone, turn it off or on, without losing my place. It was, no question, convenient. In many ways it wasn't just the most comfortable book I could manage, but the *only* book, given the circumstances, that I could manage.

And yet, even knowing this, I missed things. I missed most the act of turning the page, that quite minor physical effort. I missed being able to thumb forward to see where the end of a chapter came. I missed being able to tilt the book and compare the thickness of the pages I'd already read to the thickness of the pages left to read. I missed the weight of the book, its so-called heft. I missed balancing a book on my chest in bed as I read myself toward sleep. In addition, after reading several books on my phone, I began to miss the tactile shift that comes from moving from a book with one sort of cover and heft to another with another sort of cover and heft. There was part of me that thought—and still to some extent thinks—that what I was doing was akin to reading a book but wasn't exactly the same, in the same way that listening to an audiobook both is and isn't a kind of reading.

True, I was "reading"—I could discuss these books with others, in some detail. I was getting all (or nearly all, since there are sometimes formatting shifts that do impact the content) of the content and even of the form that I could get out of reading print versions of these books. What I wasn't getting was the experiences that I associated particularly with reading a print book. Rather than turning a page, I swiped. Rather than putting in a bookmark, I touched a corner of my smartphone's screen and got a virtual bookmark. Rather than standing up and getting a pencil to mark a passage I wanted to refer back to, I pushed my thumb against the screen and moved it until the passage was highlighted.

The materiality of the book is what particularizes the reading process. It has little if anything to do with the content or even the form, but everything to do with what stands between us and the words that our eyes pass over and our minds string together to form the reading experience. It is an excess or a remainder: It's not really needed. At the same time, it's comforting and soothing, habitual, even addictive in the way a regularly repeated habit like smoking cigarettes can be. We know we can take the nicotine in another way, perhaps even in a better way (a patch, liquid, an electronic gizmo) but there's something about the habit itself, about what we've learned to do with our lips and our hands, that we cling to. Which suggests that on an important level reading is not just about receiving the form and content that make up, say, a narrative: Reading is a repeated gesture of comfort brought to bear on the particularity of a copy of a given book, the joining of habit to a slightly and subtly unique experience.

When we think back to books that we read, particularly the books that had the biggest impact on us, we remember not only the words, not only the story, not only the form and the content, but the situation of reading, as if that has become for us part of the book itself. I remember reading Robbe-Grillet's *Les Gommes* while camping alone in the middle of the Utah salt flats—something about the terseness of his objective descriptions seemed relevant to the severity of my situation. I remember the smell of the fire I read it in front of, and the way the book smelled of smoke for years afterward. I remember reading *Ulysses* in the Brown Deer Public Library in Wisconsin when I was supposed to be going door-to-door as a Mormon missionary—I remember among other things the table I read it at, the feel of my elbows propped up against it. I remember reading Peter Straub's *In the Night Room* in a streetlight-free and utterly quiet suburban neighborhood in Indiana and the impact that that had on my reading. I remember reading *The Twenty-One Balloons* as a kid, wrapped in a blanket. I don't remember where in my parents' house I read it, but that feeling of being wrapped up, enveloped, still comes over me every time I look at the cover of that book.

None of those memories have anything really to do with these books, and they're not things I can pass along to others. But all of them particularized those books for me, made the experience of reading them material and specific.

Of course, in a way, reading books on my phone while holding my child has done the same thing. It's not that that's an immaterial reading experience, just that it's differently material, and that since the device I'm reading on is identical from book to book, it's the experience of reading on my phone while holding my child that's material, more so than the relationship to any specific book. The books blur together. My phone, unless I change the case between books, always feels the same.

I have a number of books I bought at the same used bookstore. I assume these books were all owned by the same person, though they may have come from the collections of several similar people. In my mind, though, it is one person, someone whose taste in books I can trust, who is also a heavy smoker, and someone, too, who reads all his (in my mind it's a he) books through slowly, carefully, with a lit cigarette centimeters away from the pages. When I open one of these books to read it, it still smells of smoke, somewhat stale but still strong, on every page. If I'd ever been a smoker, perhaps I'd have an experience like the one with Proust's madeleine, but since I never was, what is evoked in my memory is the other books that I've opened to similar effect, a kind of secret library catalog of excellent books that has been formed for me by someone who didn't even know he was doing it, and who certainly didn't do it for my benefit. It's the particularity of my own reading experience—in this case, a particularity tied to smell—following on the heels of someone else's reading habits, that creates the tentative, shimmering connections between those books. And because I tend to share the taste of this imagined reader, when I open a book and smell cigarette smoke, it now comes with a promise that the book is going to be good.

In other words, some of the satisfactions of my reading certain used books are based on smells that allow me to construct a narrative or a story about whom a book belonged to before, to imagine someone reading something slowly and carefully, a cigarette between the yellowed fingers of one of the hands holding the book open, the book interesting enough to him that he forgets to raise the cigarette to his lips.

II.

From a pile of books bought for a few dollars, I seem to have created an affable imaginary man in the process of smoking himself to death, and my reading continues to be haunted by the person I imagine him to be.

Brian Evenson

Yet within books, beings created from books are rarely so benign. In Fritz Leiber's *Our Lady of Darkness*, the main character, Franz, an alcoholic writer obsessed with the occult, sleeps on a bed covered with piles of books and magazines, which, over time, take on a roughly human shape. He begins to think of the pile as his "Scholar's Mistress." Eventually he begins to talk to the pile as if it is an actual woman, and near the end of the book the Scholar's Mistress comes to life, "her thin, wide-shouldered body . . . apparently formed solely of shredded and tightly compacted paper." Then she attacks. "The dry, rough, hard face pressed against his, blocking his mouth, squeezing his nostrils; the snout dug itself into his neck. He felt a crushing, incalculably great weight upon him."

Michael Cisco's first novel, *The Divinity Student*, opens with its eponymous hero being struck by lightning. Once he's dead, they "dump his contents cooked and steaming on the floor, and bring up stacks of books and manila folders, tearing out pages and shuffling out sheets of paper, all covered with writing, stuffing them inside, tamping them down behind his ribs and crushing them together in his abdomen. What pages they select and what books they tear are of little importance, only that he be completely filled up with writing, to bring him back, to set him to the task." A moment later, after a kind of parodic baptism, he comes back to life, a man of words wrapped in skin.

In our imaginations, even after the reading experience has ended, books begin to take on a life of their own, continuing to evolve and develop, to limp on into some continuing life. I remember, back in my early twenties, describing what I liked about Beckett's *Molloy* to a friend only to have him inform me that what I was describing wasn't actually in the book. Going back to reread it, I realized that what I'd picked up on was a certain vector or directionality, a promise or suggestion of something that was only partially fulfilled. It wasn't exactly that I was misreading *Molloy*; it was that I hadn't stopped reading it after I'd closed the book, that, in some nebulous and even mystic fashion, I'd read far beyond the final page.

I read *Molloy* for the first and second time in an unlovely Grove Press mass-market paperback that contained all three books of Beckett's trilogy, with yellowed pages and crowded gutters. It was a translation from Beckett's original French, done by Patrick Bowles and Beckett himself. The third time I read it, I read the original French

330

version in a copy from Editions de Minuit. The curious thing about the English translation is how rigorous it is, how insistent it is about maintaining the French version's syntax and word order, to the degree that that can be done and still sound like English. As a result, I felt less of a difference between the English and the French versions than I normally do between a translation and an original.

But what I did feel, and can still vividly remember, was the difference in format—the ample gutters of the Editions de Minuit copy, the precision of the stamp of the words, the effect of having a larger font, all of which added to the feel of the text. It was similar to the effect that one gets when one has read issues of a floppy comic book and then reads it later gathered as a graphic novel: Not only is the appearance different, the work seems changed.

Since then, I've read the English version of *Molloy* in the collected Beckett and had a still different experience with it: A mass-market copy of a book positions a reader in one way, a hardback collected works positions you in another. The story is still the same, but the way in which I'm being solicited to take it in is different, and the way that my reading is being facilitated is different as well. It's not exactly like you're reading a different book, but it's not exactly like you're rereading the same book either. All these different formats mostly overlap but don't quite, and each of them has a different feel that I've taken away with me.

You can experience something similar if you start reading a book in one format and shift to another, going from a mass-market paperback to a well-designed first-edition hardback, for instance, or from a print book to an e-book and back. It's strange how disorienting those shifts can be. The words are all the same, but the reading experience is definitely not.

In reading physical books especially, one takes in a sort of residue, some of it intelligible, some not. The reading experience is partly about learning to ignore this residue, to not care overly much about the font or the yellowing of the pages or the size of the print. On one level (there are, of course, exceptions—for instance, William H. Gass's *Willie Masters' Lonesome Wife*), reading is about seeing through such things, pretending the window we're looking through isn't changing the view.

But even if we largely ignore that residue, it still affects us, in the same way that the chair we choose to read in, the quality of the light, and so on remain associated with a given book.

In a used book, this residue suggests another person. The previous owner's name might be signed inside the cover. The corner might be turned down on several pages. There might be passages underlined or notated. There might be marginal notes, or even a bookmark with a few page numbers jotted on it. As we move through our own reading of a used book, that sense of proceeding down someone else's path and either following it or diverging from it—while at the same time paying heed to the story with most of our attention—can be one of the great joys or frustrations. We experience a one-sided engagement with how we imagine another's previous reading to be.

There is marginalia when you read in phone and e-readers as well—it's relatively easy to take notes, leave bookmarks, highlight passages, and so on. Yet that engagement doesn't tend to be solitary or passed anonymously from one reader to another as it is through a used copy. On a Kindle, for instance, you only look at someone else's marginalia under two circumstances that I'm aware of. The first is if I "loan" you the virtual copy of a book I have bought, which means that I don't have to imagine a reader: I know who loaned me the book. The second is stranger: Occasionally when you're reading a digital book through Kindle you'll hit an underlined passage that will say, for example, "Twenty-seven other people highlighted this passage." You don't know who these people are or why they highlighted that passage, but you know there are twenty-seven of them. Which makes you feel like you should probably pay attention to it. Marginalia in this case is less an engagement with one other person's reading and more a kind of pressure to conform.

Fifteen years ago I bought a used copy of Jorge Amado's *Gabriela, Clove and Cinnamon* and took it home to find it had a letter tucked in its pages as a bookmark, a letter that had never been opened. It's still in that copy of that book, though a few years after buying it I opened it and read it. It doesn't matter—or doesn't matter to you in this context at least—what the letter said: It was an ordinary letter, not unlike any number of unremarkable letters, subdued expressions of love, a plea to write. What was extraordinary about it was that it was postmarked the same year as the book appeared in English (1962) and had apparently been in the book since before I was born. I was much less interested in the letter than in why and how it had ended up in that book, and in the person who had either put it there and forgotten to open it, or had made a conscious choice not to open it, or had been unable to open it because they had died.

I have never been able to bring myself to read that copy of the Amado novel, though several times I've taken it on trips with me, intending to read it, and I suspect if I'm ever to read it I'll have to get a different copy. Sometimes the residue is too much for us even before the scanning of words on a page actually begins.

III.

Alessandro Baricco's *Mr. Gwyn* is a book about a writer who deliberately stops publishing books. Instead, he decides to be a "copyist," which, over time, he comes to understand as meaning that he will write "portraits" of people.

What this means is hard for him to explain. He rents a space, gets hold of lightbulbs timed to go out after a relatively precise length of time, and then his subjects come and pose nude in the space for a little over a month. They can do anything they like—walk around the room, sit, sleep, etc.—as he unobtrusively watches them, sometimes jotting notes. Once all the lightbulbs burn out, he writes up a verbal portrait that captures who they are. He makes only two copies. One he gives to the person who sat for the portrait, for his or her eyes only, after the person has signed a declaration pledging "the most absolute discretion, on the pain of heavy pecuniary sanctions." The other he keeps in a drawer for himself.

These portraits are not character sketches, at least not in the way we typically think of them as being. Instead, according to the first person he portrays, Rebecca, he writes "a piece of a story, a scene, as if it were a fragment of a book." *Stories aren't portraits*, suggests another character, to which Rebecca responds, "Jasper Gwyn taught me that we aren't character, we're stories . . . we are the whole story, not just the character. We are the wood where he walks, the bad guy who cheats him, the mess around him, all the people who pass, the color of things, the sounds."

Here it's not that the books are coming to life, but that the close and careful observation of people reveals something about how they can be translated into words, and those words serve in turn as a mirror for what they are. It's not the characters in the story that serve as our mirror, but the story as a whole.

We, as tangible material creatures, read in a way that asserts our sense of being material creatures reading, that reminds us in subtle, repetitive ways of our role in making the book come alive. This

333

seems as if it should stand in the way of the reading process, should keep us always at a distance from the worlds reading creates.

And, yet, books come alive nonetheless, and they bring us alive with them.

The Knowledge Gallery
Joanna Scott

I.

"YOU SAVED NOTHING?" I asked, unable to contain my disappointment. I'd been hoping that a woman of her advanced age would have a diary or two in a drawer, maybe index cards or even notes scrawled on the backs of those old envelopes used for Baronial Cards.

She idly tapped the tassel on the window blind to set it swinging. "My dear, multiply two by zero and it would be nothing. If, rather, you mean anything, then yes, the last of it went into recycling when I moved here."

"You have no manuscripts? No letters?"

She observed me, then lifted her head to direct her gaze downward, through the bottom half of her bifocals. "I see you're writing with a pen. On paper. The old-fashioned way. But surely you haven't forgotten that until quite recently, paper was discouraged as an indulgent, poisonous consumption. The taxes on a single ream . . . who could afford it? And if you could afford it, you didn't want your enemies to know. My generation was particularly suspect—thus the public statute requiring accreditation from EcoGreen before we could receive Social Security. Writers, of course, were notorious. Have you heard of Olivia Gastrell?"

I scribbled the name, adding it to a list that was growing ever longer with each writer I interviewed. "Gastrell—with two *l*'s?"

She reached for a glass of water on her bedside table and took a sip. "You haven't read her? Surprising, given your interests. She came late to fiction, published her first novel, *Fortunate Odyssey*, when she was fifty-two. She would have won a Hermes with *Say What You Mean*, but she skipped the ceremony and thus forfeited the award. Not that she needed honors to buck her up. My dear friend Olivia. She was nearly eighty when she hired movers to transfer her papers to a storage unit. Two hundred and five pounds of cellulose pulp—that was two hundred pounds over the personal legal limit. The movers were obligated to file a report. The authorities seized

335

and destroyed everything. She had to pay a fine . . . I don't remember how much, but it was significant."

"Is she still alive?"

She sucked in her lips as she considered her response, then looked toward the door, seeming to will the interruption that came a moment later, the sharp knock startling me to the point that I bounced up from my seat, then fell back.

"Come in!"

The nurse, a bald little man lithe as a dancer, entered holding a paper cup. "M&M time!" he announced, rattling the pills deposited inside the cup. "You need more water, hon?"

"I have plenty, lovey, thank you." She picked out the pills and tossed them both in her mouth, then made a show of taking a swig of water from her glass. "This young lady has come for a chat. So if you'll excuse us . . ." She nodded in the direction of the door.

The nurse hesitated. "You'll let me know if you need anything. . . ."

"Absolutely, sweetheart. Now go, shoo, shoo." She waited until he had closed the door behind him, then leaned over, opened the drawer of the table, and extracted a box. Cracking the lid, she removed the two pills that she had craftily pretended to swallow and added them to a substantial collection of pills in the box. "Don't tell," she said. Her imperious smile was clearly designed to remind me that I was a minion beholden to her goodwill. "Now where were we?"

"Olivia Gastrell."

"Ah, yes. She once told me that she had an ancestor who chopped down a mulberry tree that was said to have been planted by William Shakespeare. To this day, the name Gastrell is banned in Stratford-upon-Avon."

"And Olivia, is she—"

"Fort Worth. I'll let her know you're coming." Suddenly her gaze was harsh, boring into me, daring me to react. I didn't know what to say. I was embarrassed and resentful at being forced into extending my inquiry yet again. Didn't she realize that I was there to preserve the reputation of Eleanor Feal? But in the evasive manner that I'd come to realize was typical for the writers I'd tracked down so far, Eleanor Feal didn't want to tell me about herself. She wanted to tell me about Olivia Gastrell.

It was the same outcome, interview after interview. I aimed to reconstruct a writer's work from scratch but ended up being directed by each of them to the beginning of someone else's story. After six months and twenty-seven separate interviews, I had failed to recover a single book.

II.

There was a welcome coolness in the breeze that skimmed the river. As I crossed the pedestrian bridge, I saw the sleek back of a beaver swimming toward the shore, pushing a newly felled branch that looked like a rack strung with pieces of green silk. In the shallows, a magnificent heron stood patiently, as if awaiting its delivery. The beaver drew nearer, still pushing the branch, changing its course only at the last moment, swimming upstream to some other destination.

I leaned against the iron rail and watched for several minutes. The heron remained stock-still, the current swirling around its legs, its yellow eye unblinking, the blue plume extending from the back of its head like a pomaded spike of hair. I was hoping the bird would rise into the air—I wanted to see the slow beat of its wings as it flew overhead. But it just stood there, so I walked on. Hearing a splash, I turned just in time to witness the heron lift its dripping head from the water and with a deft movement drop the fish that had been clamped in its beak headfirst into its gullet.

There in the heart of the city, the natural world was thriving. Along the path curving across campus, chipmunks scampered ahead of my footsteps. It was early May, and the air was redolent with the fragrance of lilacs. Petals from the magnolias flitted like butterflies in the breeze. The sun, as if summoned by the carillon chiming in the bell tower of the Knowledge Gallery, peeked shyly out from behind a flat-bottomed cumulus cotton ball.

I was in good spirits that day, contemplating the lovely campus and the equilibrium of a planet that had fully recovered from its long fever. The climate was healthy again, thanks to the ingenuity of our scientists. We were like angels dining on wind and light and water. Life itself seemed infinitely renewable.

I was sorry to have to go inside, but I had research to do, and the Knowledge Gallery was scheduled to close early, as it often did, for a special administrative function. The building, a five-story former library with sloping floors that spiraled around a hollow interior, seemed to be more useful as a party house than a location for scholarly research. Still, the resources were vast, with thousands of databases that could be accessed by anyone with a VPN account. There were technical advisers on hand to resolve any problem with a device. Numerous work spaces were furnished with white boards, televisions, self-service espresso machines, and more Macs than there were students enrolled in the university.

If the gallery had one acknowledged problem, it was the noise. Most of the work spaces opened up to the echo chamber of the central gallery. From the main floor, you could easily overhear the conversation of two people on the fourth floor. On a given day you might hear biology students comparing lab results, research advisers explaining how to modify a search, two young lovers setting up their next date. And always in the background was the tap tap tapping of hundreds of fingers on keyboards.

After a year as a graduate student on campus, I'd found a relatively quiet space at the back of the Rare Books Department, behind the cases used to display simulated manuscripts. Most of the furniture in the building was manufactured with repurposed metal or plastic, but in the Rare Books Department there were four beautiful antique tables made of oak. I loved the earthy smell and the rosy heartwood grain of those tables. And I appreciated the serenity of the department. Few visitors came to see the simulations, since everything in the cases was viewable in more detail in online exhibitions.

On this particular day I was verifying references for the second chapter of my dissertation and hoped to start assembling notes for chapter three. My subject was Avantism—a recent literary movement based in the US. Focusing on six writers who identified themselves as Avantis, I intended to argue that Avantism had its roots in once popular fiction of the early twentieth century and drew especially from the work of a little-known Spanish writer named Vicente Blasco Ibáñez.

In terms of its basic elements, Avantism was as diverse as literature itself. There were mysteries, tragedies, farces, fictional biographies, and biographical fictions. One novel used an encyclopedic structure, with chapters arranged alphabetically by subject. Another built its narrative out of a collage of quotes taken from other Avanti texts. Some authors concentrated on providing rich scenic details; others strove to give their characters an expansive interiority. All of the manuscripts were handwritten. Finished books were produced by expert letterpress printers on wove pearlescent paper, with painted cloth bindings.

What united the Avanti authors, besides the care they took with the printing of their books, was their dystopian imaginations. All the

Avanti novels I'd read, plus those I knew of through hearsay, were set in an apocalyptic future, when civilization had deteriorated either into anarchy or tyranny. The plots involved characters struggling with the most basic hardships—there were famine and flood stories, home-steading stories set in harsh lands, stories about super flus and climate change, and stories about the total devastation of a final world war.

The Avantis prided themselves on scorning publicity. They had no websites, sent no tweets, and were rarely photographed. Their work appeared only in hard copy. Once all publications became electronic, the Avantis refused to publish at all, sharing manuscripts only among themselves. The general public was indifferent. By the time I'd narrowed down the subject of my dissertation, few people had ever heard of the Avantis; fewer still had read any of their books.

As a scholar of Avantism, I had to be a clever detective. I was constantly testing the strength of various search engines against the defenses of the Avanti writers. They'd resolved to hide themselves from scholars. I was determined to write their history. By then I'd spent two years on research and had a fellowship that would support me for two more years. In the end, I hoped to have a notable dissertation that would secure me enough interest from foundations to fund a web appointment as a digital humanities scholar.

I was twenty-five years old and confident that all was going according to plan. I agreed with my peers that we were living in a golden age. Except for the endless skirmish in northern Nigeria, the world was at peace. Every question had an answer . . . until the morning when I was typing the final sentences of chapter two of my dissertation on my laptop, writing the words—

What words? Maybe something close to these words I'm writing now, surely involving dependent clauses, nouns, an article, an adverb, whatever, I'll never know because I can't remember the specific words, only the experience of watching the loop of a *b* break away from its stem, an *o* dissolve, an *a* sink to the bottom of the screen and disappear, replaced by symbols: ⊆∑ϕℜξω, and on and on in a blur where there had once been sentences.

III.

I was the second student in line at the Question & Information desk on the ground floor of the Knowledge Gallery. While I stood there waiting my turn, I noticed that the letters on the digital sign above

339

the desk had been replaced by a video of cascading roses. Naive as I was, I didn't connect the roses to the symbols on my laptop screen.

The first student was an undergraduate woman whose PowerPoint had frozen—a coincidental glitch that the techie, himself an undergraduate, managed to repair simply by turning the student's tablet off and on again.

"Hi," he said to me. He had a scruff of a beard, icy-blue eyes, and a bowl of doughnut holes next to his Mac. "What's up?"

I tried to contain my panic. "It looks like I just crashed. All my files—I can't . . . I mean, I can access them, but everything has been scrambled."

"Let's take a look."

I opened the laptop and touched the screen to activate the light. The symbols were still there, a wallpaper of shapes that reminded me of snorkeling: sea grass waving, jellyfish drifting, minnows darting away from my submerged hand.

"Cool," said the techie.

"Can you fix it?" I implored.

"Mmmm." Still staring at the screen, he reached for the bowl, blindly fumbled for a doughnut hole, and popped it in his mouth. He chewed in concentrated silence, pressing various keys and studying the screen for the results that didn't come. While I waited, I reminded myself that a crash was no more than an inconvenience. With every file automatically saved to the Cloud, everything could be recovered. Still, it would take time to restore the files to my hard drive, and more time if I had to buy a new computer entirely.

The Q & I desk was positioned at the rear of the ground floor. It was early, and workstations still had empty chairs. But among the students scattered throughout the Knowledge Gallery, a new kind of sound emanated, a flurry of murmurs and exclamations competing with the rattling of keyboard taps and the burbling of espresso machines.

"Oh just, what, you gotta be kidding!" said a boy loudly from across the room.

"Shit, shit, shit!" called someone from a cubicle on the second floor.

I heard chairs scrape along the laminated floors. I heard a phone buzz and then a thump that sounded like a small bird flying into plate glass. I looked toward the nearest window. The sun was still shining, the magnolia blossoms still dancing in the breeze. At the Q & I desk, the techie tapped my keyboard with impressive speed, then stopped and studied the screen.

"I don't really understand why they call them holes," he said at last.

"What?"

"If it were up to me, I'd call them centers." I realized he was talking about the doughnut holes only when he offered the bowl to me, inviting me to take one. "I mean, the holes are what they leave behind, not what they are. It's like saying they're an absence. Identifying them with the space they once filled."

I wanted to say something insulting, but the rest of my day depended upon this techie's ability to recover my files. I needed his know-how, as did the students who were lining up behind me.

"A hole is a hollow space in a solid body. " He tapped the escape button on the keyboard several times. FaceTime on his Mac rang. "Hang on, will you?" he said to his screen. "On the other hand, there are black holes, defined by such a strong gravitational pull that no matter can escape. They're interesting, don't you think?"

The phone in his pocket buzzed. He looked at the number and answered briskly: "Yeah, yeah, get Daryl down here, maybe Inez, too. Looks like a busy day ahead of us." He clicked off the phone and rested his chin in his hands, studying his own Mac. He poked at the screen, cocked his head to cast a sideways glance at my laptop, then shut his eyes for a long moment, as if giving up the effort to hide his boredom.

"Frankly, I don't know what's going on," he finally admitted.

"What do you mean? You can't fix it?" I asked.

"You have a Cloud account, right?"

"Yeah, of course."

"Then you're safe," he assured me.

"No, she's not," said the boy behind me. "Siri is saying Cloud files are inaccessible."

"My life is over," said a girl wearing cutoff shorts and a vintage Minnie Mouse T-shirt, marching toward us without bothering to take a place in line, her flip-flops angrily slapping the floor. "I give up."

"You're budging," another girl called from the back of the line.

"Look there—" The boy behind me directed our attention to the television on the wall. The subtitles at the top of the screen were garbled symbols; the bottom banner that usually circulated breaking-news headlines was blank. The sound was on mute, but we could see that the newscaster had stopped talking and was looking frantically in the direction of the teleprompter.

"Must be a malware offensive," said the techie, popping another doughnut hole into his mouth. "We'll have to wait for quarantine mandates and the updated firewall. Everyone got the same problem?" More students were arriving in search of help. The line was long and getting longer, with students groaning, complaining, jostling one another, reminding friends about the dance on Friday in the Field House. "Hey, guys," called the techie to the crowd. "Everyone got a problem with text?" There was agreement, cursing, and laughter in the crowd. The techie interlaced his fingers, cracking his knuckles. "Come back in five," he said to us. What did that mean? Five minutes? Five hours?

It would take a good five hours for most of us to become aware of the vastness of the attack, and five days or more to understand the extent of the loss: Everything written in English, new and old, every book that had been scanned (and, as was protocol back then, discarded), every document in a digital archive, every e-mail and text, everything involving the digital transmission of words, everything that provided our civilization with a record of its vast knowledge was gone, dissolved by a virus that had been lying latent in software from the beginning, programmed fifty years in advance to explode all at once, leaving only shreds of meaningless shapes floating with malicious wantonness on screens of English-speaking users around the world.

Luckily, the important diagrammatic programs that keep the infrastructure running, along with images and videos, were untouched by the attack. I suppose this might explain the current blasé attitude about it all. There's general consensus that the essential documents have been recovered, some located as rare hard copies, most supplied through costly translation. The American public has long since stopped fretting over missing materials. But let's not pretend that we've restored the full inventory. Not even close. We can't begin to know what we've lost. All we can do is keep searching, and advocating for funds for the National Archive Project. Where would we be without the NAP?

I'd be without income, for starters. If I weren't an NAP agent, I'd be unemployed. Truly, I'm thankful for the paycheck, but I also believe in the worth of the mission. This whole project is about memory. By remembering, we can avoid repeating the mistakes we made when we considered ourselves ingenious and invulnerable.

IV.

NAP Recovery Record: Cataloged July 17, 2052

1) *Treatise of How to Perceive from a Letter the Nature and Character of the Person Who Wrote It*, author unknown, 1622: translation.
2) *The Queensberry Rules*, London Amateur Athletic Club, 1867: found document, complete.
3) *Letter to Posterity*, Petrarch, 1351: translation.
4) *With Americans of Past and Present Days*, J. J. Jusserand, no date: found document, incomplete.
5) *A Tutor for the Renaissance Lute*, Diana Poulton, copyright page missing: donated by owner.
6) *Self-Portrait in a Convex Mirror*, John Ashbery, 1975: in summary.
7) *Book of the Prefect*, author unknown, 950: translation.
8) *Songs of Experience*, William Blake, 1794: translation.
9) *Horse-Shoe Robinson*, J. P. Kennedy, 1835: found manuscript.
10) *Gazette*, Rhinebeck, NY, from 1947–1949: donated by municipality.

V.

And lastly, No. 11, which I failed to supply but should have consisted of a summary of Eleanor Feal's first novel, as transcribed from our interview.

"You must talk to Olivia in person," she was saying. "Her work is difficult to describe."

Courtesy kept me from pointing out that I'd come in search of books written by Eleanor Feal, a writer whose existence I'd learned of only in my previous interview with the author Timothy von Patten, himself unknown to me until the prior interview with Leonard Dumaston—and so on.

"She was an Avanti?"

"Of course. Any writer worth the time it took to read was an Avanti."

Six months earlier, I'd set out with six Avanti writers to track down. The list had grown to include twenty-seven other lesser-known writers who, I was told, were not at all of lesser merit. That I had overlooked them when I'd been researching the movement for my dissertation now seemed inevitable. Avantism was an elusive prey, with its cohorts keeping a low profile. Like nocturnal animals, they spooked easily and melted into the nearest burrow when threatened, disappearing before they revealed much of anything about themselves, camouflaging their work with the work of a fellow author, as the centenarian Eleanor Feal was doing with Olivia Gastrell.

As far as I knew, all the Avanti books had been confiscated, scanned, and shredded over the preceding thirty years—there were no extant copies left in the world. I was still hopeful that someone somewhere would reveal a secret library. New recovery laws protected book collectors from the criminal charges they would have faced in the past, but no one had come forward with any valuable inventory. In the absence of an actual book or manuscript, I could at least provide a detailed recounting of the work that had once existed—this was the purpose of my interviews. But Avanti writers didn't appear interested in their own work. They wanted to talk about the books by their friends.

"Take Olivia's *Say What You Mean*—a central text for the rest of us," Eleanor Feal was saying. "It tells the story of a young woman . . ." She studied me, squinting, as if searching my face for a minute blemish. "She had green eyes," she said. "Yes." Her satisfaction suggested that she'd solved a difficult equation. "Like yours, the same shade." How could she be so sure? She was speaking of a fictional character as if she'd met her in person, and comparing her to me. Her scrutiny was making me increasingly uncomfortable. "A literary scholar, as it happens." I was beginning to wonder if she was using me as a model to fabricate the supposed main character in Olivia Gastrell's book. "Her name was Juliana. She finds herself living in a time much like ours, after the entire written record of the English language has been wiped out by a computer virus. In the contest of prescience, Olivia wins, hands down. Our young heroine takes it upon herself to . . . come in!"

I hadn't heard a knock, but there was the nurse again, standing in the doorway with a wheelchair, ready to escort Eleanor Feal to the dining room.

"Yumtime!" he said.

"Already? But we were having such nice conversation. I'm sorry, dear. They don't like it if we're late for meals around here!" She was suddenly cheery. "They aim to keep us in tip-top shape, you know, on schedule and such! The longer we live, the more federal funding they receive, isn't that right, lovey?"

The nurse concurred. "It's a win-win," he declared. "Andiamo!"

I stood aside as she lifted herself into the wheelchair the nurse had slid toward the bed. In her eagerness to be done with our interview and take her place at dinner, she seemed transformed—deceptively so. She struck me as a woman versed at playing the part of a beloved grande dame who enjoyed being tenderly cared for. In reality, she was a woman who clearly preferred to take care of herself.

"What happens to Juliana?" I demanded, following the nurse as he briskly wheeled Eleanor Feal out of the room and up a carpeted corridor.

"You'll have to ask Olivia," she said, lifting her hand above her shoulder, bending her fingers in the shape of a python's flat head to signal a wave goodbye, a gesture that had a strange, chilling finality, as if scripted to bring an end to the whole story—this story, I mean, the one I've begun but will never finish. I could have predicted its incompleteness before I asked my first question.

I gave up trying to keep up with them. As I stood watching the nurse roll Eleanor Feal down the corridor, I thought about the pills she had secreted away in that box in her bedside table. I thought about the stepping-stones of my interviews, from one Avanti writer to the next, that had led me here. I wondered about the cost of a round-trip fare to Fort Worth. I thought about *Say What You Mean* by Olivia Gastrell. How could I be sure that it had ever existed? I wondered about all the other books that I would never read.

NOTES ON CONTRIBUTORS

EMILY ANDERSON's work in this issue is an excerpt from *Little: Novels* (forthcoming from BlazeVOX).

AIMEE BENDER is the author of five books, including *The Particular Sadness of Lemon Cake* and, most recently, *The Color Master* (both Doubleday), a *New York Times* notable book of 2013. She teaches at the University of Southern California.

LAYNIE BROWNE's most recent collection of poems is *Lost Parkour Ps(alms)*, published in two editions, one in English and one in French, from Presses Universitaires de Rouen et du Havre.

MAXINE CHERNOFF is the author of fourteen books of poems, most recently *Here* (Counterpath). The current issue of *Red Mare* is devoted to her work.

EDWIDGE DANTICAT's most recent book is *Claire of the Sea Light* (Vintage).

Science-fiction pioneer SAMUEL R. DELANY's most recent novels are *Phallos* (Wesleyan University Press) and *Through the Valley of the Nest of Spiders* (Magnus). He teaches at Temple University. "From *Eclipse: A Romance*" is © 2014 Samuel R. Delany.

"Brightfellow" is an excerpt from RIKKI DUCORNET's recently completed ninth novel of the same title. Her collection of essays, *The Deep Zoo*, will be published by Coffee House in December 2014.

Since closing her long poem *Drafts* in 2012, RACHEL BLAU DuPLESSIS has written *Interstices* (sections of which were published by Subpress in 2014), *Graphic Novella* (forthcoming from Xexoxial), and *Days and Works*, due from Ahsahta in September 2016.

JULIA ELLIOTT recently published her first fiction collection, *The Wilds*; her first novel, *The New and Improved Romie Futch*, is forthcoming (both Tin House). She has received the Rona Jaffe Foundation Writers' Award, as well as a Pushcart Prize for her story in *Conjunctions:56*.

ELAINE EQUI's books include *Click and Clone* and *Ripple Effect: New & Selected Poems* (both Coffee House). She teaches at New York University and the New School.

BRIAN EVENSON's most recent books are *Immobility* (Tor) and *Windeye* (Coffee House). A new collection of stories, *A Collapse of Horses*, is forthcoming from Coffee House in 2015. He teaches at Brown University.

BRANDON HOBSON is the author of *Deep Ellum* (Calamari), *The Levitationist* (Ravenna), and *Desolation of Avenues Untold* (forthcoming from CCM).

PAUL HOOVER's most recent books of poetry are *Desolation : Souvenir* (Omnidawn) and *En el idioma y en la tierra*, translated by María Baranda (Conaculta). He has also published a collection of essays, *Fables of Representation* (University of Michigan Press).

ROBERT KELLY's most recent publications are *Oedipus after Colonus and Other Plays* (drcicerobooks) and *Winter Music*, texts to the photo work of Susan Quasha (T-space). His collaboration with the painter Nathlie Provosty, *The Color Mill*, will be published in fall of 2014 (Spuyten Duyvil) as will his *Collected Essays* (Contra Mundum). He teaches at Bard College.

Among REBECCA LILLY's (rebeccalilly.com) collections of poetry are *You Want to Sell Me a Small Antique* (Gibbs Smith) and *Shadwell Hills* (Birch Brook). She is also the author of *The Insights of Higher Awareness* and *Ego and the Spiritual Self* (both Humanics).

NATHANIEL MACKEY's most recent book of poetry is *Nod House*; his newest, *Blue Fasa*, is forthcoming (both New Directions). He edits the literary magazine *Hambone* and teaches at Duke University.

CAROLE MASO's most recent book is *Mother & Child* (Counterpoint). "World Book" is an excerpt from her novel in progress, *The Bay of Angels*.

EDIE MEIDAV is the author of the novels *The Far Field: A Novel of Ceylon* (Houghton Mifflin/Mariner); *Crawl Space* (FSG/Picador); *Lola, California* (FSG/Picador); and the forthcoming *Dogs of Cuba*. She teaches at UMass-Amherst.

KERRY MILLER (www.kerrymiller.co.uk) is a British mixed-media artist specializing in sculptures created from vintage books. Her exhibitions include a solo show at San Francisco's White Walls Gallery, as well as work in the prestigious "Birds in Art" exhibition at the Woodson Art Museum in Wausau, Wisconsin, through November 16, 2014.

ANDREW MOSSIN is the author of two full-length poetry collections, *The Epochal Body* and *The Veil* (both Singing Horse), as well as the collection of critical essays *Male Subjectivity and Poetic Form in "New American" Poetry* (Palgrave Macmillan). He is at work on a new manuscript of poetry, *The Book of Spells*.

Other imagined translations from DANIEL NADLER's *The Lacunae* have appeared or are forthcoming in *Web Conjunctions, Lana Turner, Boston Review*, and *Denver Quarterly*.

JOYCE CAROL OATES's many books include the story collection *Lovely, Dark, Deep* and the forthcoming novel *The Sacrifice* (both Ecco).

The author of eight books of fiction, a biography, and a forthcoming collection of essays, *A Solemn Pleasure* (Bellevue), MELISSA PRITCHARD (www.melissapritchard .com) teaches at Arizona State University.

MINNA PROCTOR is the editor of *The Literary Review* and teaches writing at Fairleigh Dickinson University. She is the author of *Do You Hear What I Hear?* (Viking) and is working on a personal-essay collection about conflict, dramatic structure, and resolution.

DONALD REVELL's most recent poetry collection is *Tantivy* (Alice James). A translator from the French, he is also the director of graduate studies at the University of Nevada, Las Vegas.

ELIZABETH ROBINSON's recent books include *On Ghosts* (Solid Objects), *Counterpart* (Ahsahta), and *Blue Heron* (Center for Literary Publishing).

JOANNA SCOTT's most recent novel is *De Potter's Grand Tour* (FSG).

RANBIR SINGH SIDHU is the author of the collection of stories *Good Indian Girls* (HarperCollins India/Soft Skull).

The author of many volumes of poetry, COLE SWENSEN is the founding editor of La Presse Books. She coedited the Norton anthology *American Hybrid* and guest-edited the first annual *Best American Experimental Writing* (Omnidawn). Her new book, *Landscapes on a Train*, is forthcoming from Nightboat.

FREDERIC TUTEN's novels include *Van Gogh's Bad Café* (Black Classic) and *The Green Hour*, as well as the story collection *Self Portraits: Fictions* (both Norton). He received Pushcart Prizes for his stories in *Conjunctions:54* and *Conjunctions:60*.

Poet and playwright CHRIS TYSH's latest publications are *Our Lady of the Flowers, Echoic* (Les Figues); *Molloy: The Flip Side* (BlazeVox); and *Night Scales: A Fable for Klara K* (United Artists). She teaches at Wayne State University, Detroit.

ANNE WALDMAN is the author, most recently, of *Gossamurmur* (Penguin Poets), *Jaguar Harmonics* (Post Apollo), and the *Jaguar Harmonics* CD (Fast Speaking Music); and is coeditor of the anthology *Cross Worlds: Transcultural Poetics* (Coffee House). She is the artistic director of the Summer Writing Program of the Jack Kerouac School at Naropa University.

ELIOT WEINBERGER's books of essays include *Karmic Traces, An Elemental Thing*, and *Oranges & Peanuts for Sale* (all New Directions).

ADAM WEINSTEIN is a PhD candidate in creative writing and a Steffensen Cannon fellow at the University of Utah, and nonfiction editor for *Quarterly West*. The writing of the essays in this issue was supported by the Taft-Nicholson Center for Environmental Humanities.

Award-winning writer PAUL WEST's most recent books are *The Ice Lens* and *The Invisible Riviera* (both Onager).

One Foot Out the Door

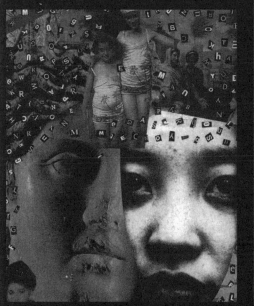

THE COLLECTED STORIES OF LEWIS WARSH

**One Foot Out The Door:
The Collected Stories
of Lewis Warsh**

cover collage: Lewis Warsh
frontispies portrait: Phong Bui
Spuyten Duyvil Publishing
ISBN 978-0-923389-93-2
$20.00   400 pages

Dist. thru SPD
spdbooks.org

spuytenduyvil.net

What a pleasure to have all these stories by Lewis Warsh in one
volume! They tend to be low-key, almost off-hand, but each with
a poetic kernel that infects and defuses throughout, which makes
them (though it is a critical cliché to say it this way) haunting.
But that's what they do. They haunt. That's what the best writing
does, often without excessive flashiness or even letting us know,
as the narrative drifts through the material from which each is
constructed, how it's done. These are extraordinary tales.

SAMUEL R. DELANY

The straight-from-the-shoulder idiom that powers Lewis Warsh's
writing is a marvel of economy. Evoking memory without nostal-
gia, moving the reader without sentimentality, the stories in *One
Foot Out The Door* are lucid, formally adventurous, and emotional-
ly complex. Like Stephen Dixon and Leonard Michaels, two other
masters of plainspoken cosmopolitanism and rueful reflection,
Lewis Warsh uses ordinary language as a means to an extraordinary
inventiveness.

CHRISTOPHER SORRENTINO

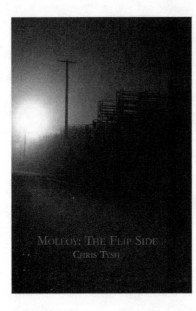

Molloy: The Flip Side transcreates the first half of Beckett's 1951 French novel, narrated by its eponymous anti-hero who is slowly going nowhere. The hobo lyrics of Tysh's book-length poem open up the unendurable abyss of being, yet zing with vernacular and zany humor: "Gotta check out soon/ Be done with dying," Molloy says, but there's a few things he must do first. And so begins the uncanny journey in this poetic B-side of Beckett's masterpiece.

Chris Tysh reads in, around, and through Molloy in this ingenious transformation of Beckett's French prose into compulsively vernacular English tercets. The narrative echoes in *Molloy: The Flip Side* make for an unsettling familiarity, spiked with the verbal equivalent of dark chocolate and homemade rum.

— Charles Bernstein

In *Molloy: The Flip Side*, Chris Tysh transcreates— rather than translates—the Beckett classic into a Matthew O'Connor-cum-Tiresias rant. "Has a leak in his tank/Button missing a hole/In his wig, you feel me?" The indeterminate narrator of Tysh's formal tercets replicates the dialectics of gender, the Oedipal complex ("The thing is Mother and I —/My shitty start — are so old now/ We're like two sere fucks on a rail") and, more generally, the problem of desire and knowledge vis-à-vis the world. That's a heady set of balls to keep up in the air, but Tysh's nimble enjambments and seamless heteroglossia (existential angst dukes it out with post-trip-hop surliness) keep things moving, propelling this mock-epic to its jocular, inconclusive, stop.

—Tyrone Williams

AHSAHTA

POETRY IS ART

"Ahsahta isn't just another press, it's America's avant-garde in poetry. It is consistently publishing work other presses might find ways to blow off." —Djelloul Marbrook, *Galatea Resurrects*

ELIZABETH ROBINSON
COUNTERPART

"The kind of daring found in Robinson's poetry evinces a spiritual courage and moral acuity that recalls Simone Weil and Abraham Joshua Heschel. Her deeply informed suspicion of language has not robbed her of an underlying assurance in the hermeneutical circle of meaning. There's a willingness in her poems to grapple with the aporia of faith and doubt that places her in a line extending from Hadewijch of Brabant and Julian of Norwich to H.D., Robert Duncan and Fanny Howe." —Patrick Pritchett, writing in *Jacket*

CODY-ROSE CLEVIDENCE
BEAST FEAST

"When Elizabeth Sewell proposed in *The Orphic Voice* that grammar is 'an essentially mythological, active field, which still awaits its due inquiry,' could she have been anticipating Cody-Rose Clevidence's startling *Beast Feast*? Here is secret Orphic power, revealed and scrambled, bedecked with joules, singing daggered hymns." —Peter O'Leary

"The total impression is one of a poet who takes nothing for granted, who wants to incorporate every kind of language, every instinct, and every power that positions us—or shoves us out of position—in an all-too-complicated modern world. . . . [the poet] wants to show both how thickly the discourse around us (about bodies, about money and gender, about space and time) holds us in its deadening, deafening grip, and how strongly and strangely and beautifully the body that Clevidence imagines can try to get free." —Stephen Burt

EMILY ABENDROTH
]EXCLOSURES[

"What possibilities can poetics make in a world structured by logics that contain or constrain the human spirit? Abendroth's debut charts some 'improbable' options in a text that manages to sustain its beauty while directly facing this indifference." —*Publishers Weekly*

"Emily Abendroth might say [this book] is about the prison industrial complex. About various sorts of closures. But as she knows, once one starts on something as multidimensional as the prison industrial complex, one has to go wide and deep. And this book is both and more too, more as in meaningful, as in made." —Juliana Spahr

ORDER FROM AHSAHTAPRESS.ORG OR
SPDBOOKS.ORG / 800.869.7553

It was morning and the power was not yet on . . .

BENJAMIN PARZYBOK

"With climate change and ever-increasing consumption, running out of water is a danger we don't readily acknowledge, yet Benjamin Parzybok's *Sherwood Nation* makes that danger vividly real."
—*Library Journal*

"Part political thriller, part social fable, and part manifesto, its every page brimming with gonzo exuberance."
—Jedediah Berry
(*The Manual of Detection*)

SOLID OBJECTS

Miranda Mellis
THE SPOKES

Lisa Jarnot
A PRINCESS MAGIC PRESTO SPELL

Elizabeth Robinson
ON GHOSTS

Lisa Lubasch
SO I BEGAN

Laura Mullen
COMPLICATED GRIEF

Julie Carr
THINK TANK

www.solidobjects.org

HERE COMES KITTY: A COMIC OPERA by RICHARD KRAFT

with interpolations by Danielle Dutton and a conversation with Ann Lauterbach

Monumental incongruities — dazzling composition. Richard Kraft and Danielle Dutton have created a riot of images and words. The exuberance is contagious. A delight. A must. —Rosmarie Waldrop

siglio · uncommon books at the intersection of art & literature · **www.sigliopress.com**

Jena Osman:
Corporate Relations

A work between essay and poem tracks the constitution-
al rights granted to corporations in landmark Supreme
Court cases since the Civil War. It asks, if corporations are
persons, what are persons? machines?

"The poetic gamble with jurisprudence pays off, and in spades.
The book skillfully balances the intellectual demands of its subject matter with unexpected rewards and provocative
insights.—Eric Howerton, *The Volta Blog*

"Osman's a canny operator whose intelligence is that of a literary sharpshooter: She never misses her mark, but the damage
done is often not...the damage you anticipated."—Seth Abramson, *The Huffington Post*

Poetry, 80 pps, offset, smyth-sewn, orig. paperback $14

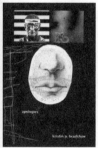

Kristin P. Bradshaw:
Apologies

Apologies. For a new religion? a social=political
discourse? a queer's life? All these plus a reflection on
fragmentation and the tension between immediacy and
emergent understanding. The frame is the author's
"own 'far country,' a quasi historical dream-landscape
in motion from the 'West' of antiquity toward the 'West'
of the U.S." A first book.

Poetry, 104 pages, offset, smyth-sewn, original pbk $14

Claude Royet-Journoud:
Four Elemental Bodies
[translated from the French by Keith Waldrop]

This Tetralogy assembles the central volumes of one of
the most important contemporary French poets. His
one-line manifesto: "Will we escape analogy" signaled
the revolutionary turn away from Surrealism.

"There can be an object so real in a poem...so intensely itself,
that the mystery of it leaves one speechless. Such is the work of
Claude Royet-Journoud."—John Olson, *Tillalala Chronicles*

"This heady book encourages us to think radically about our
relationship to the world and about how it could be 'described.'"—John Taylor, *PN Review*

Poetry, 368 pp., offset, smyth-sewn, original paperback $20

Gérard Macé:
The Last of the Egyptians
[translated from the French by Brian Evenson]

Macé explores Champollion's twin interests: Egypt
and "America's savage nations," his deciphering of
the Rosetta stone and the Indians' deciphering of the
forest. He finally follows Champollion to the Louvre
where he set up the Egyptian galleries, encountered
Indians of the Osage tribe, and felt the sadness of
their slow song.

Novella, 80 pp., offset, smyth-sewn, original paperback $14

Orders: www.spdbooks.org, www.burningdeck.com

Free Minds Book Club & Writing Workshop

Empowering young inmates to write new chapters in their lives

"My Free Mind"
—by William

My mind is now freed
On this pad I let my thoughts bleed
I cried tears cuz I once was in need
I'm still physically locked up
But now my mind is freed
So at 10:45 when my door shuts
I pack my bags, and my mind takes me overseas
I got a gift that we all need
A pencil, lined paper and eraser
So free ya' mind
You'll be surprised where it take ya'

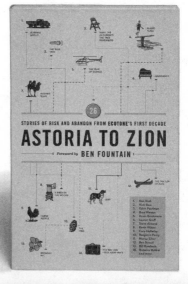

LIBRARY OF KOREAN LITERATURE
VOLUMES 11-15 PUBLISHED ON OCTOBER 27, 2014

dalkeyarchive.com

LTI Korea
Literature Translation Institute of Korea

DALKEY ARCHIVE PRESS
Champaign / London / Dublin